DEADLY LIES

Chris Patchell

ISBN: 1494296527
ISBN 13: 9781494296520

To Gord, my partner in all things, without whose encouragement, cajoling, and occasional goading this story would continue to collect proverbial dust on the server. Thanks for engaging in the endless series of crazy "what if" scenarios. We spent many public lunches plotting the demise of characters who did and didn't make it into the story.

I like a look of Agony,
Because I know it's true—
Men do not sham Convulsion,
Nor simulate, a Throe—

The Eyes glaze once—and that is Death—
Impossible to feign
The Beads upon the Forehead
By homely Anguish strung.

—Emily Dickinson

PROLOGUE

*T*hirteen, fourteen, fifteen.

She ticked the seconds off silently in her head. Her heart hammered painfully, the desperate waves of panic making it impossible to think. *Stay calm. Stay calm,* she repeated as she rifled through the drawers of what once had been her mother's dresser.

Twenty-two, twenty-three, twenty-four.

Shit. It had to be here. This is right where her mother always kept it.

She slammed the drawer closed. The clap of cheap wood echoed in the quiet house. The jarring noise was a dead giveaway.

It didn't matter though. She was out of time.

His boots rang hallow on the stairs. He was coming. She pushed back the waves of panic and tried to focus.

Thirty-three, thirty-four, thirty-five.

It took a total of forty-five seconds for him to climb the stairs and reach her bedroom door. She should know. She'd counted it enough times, lying awake in bed listening to the heavy tread of his footsteps and dreading what would come next.

He passed the top of the landing and headed down the narrow hall. She could feel the reverberation of his boots on the bare hardwood floors as he drew closer. *Maybe five more seconds, if he's drunk.* Maybe. And then he would burst through the door.

Panic overwhelmed her defenses and struck her full force. She knew hiding was futile. She knew he would find her. Unable to stop herself, she ducked into the closet.

1

The dark welcomed her, and she slid through the curtain of her mother's clothes. Her back softly collided with the wall. Inch by inch, she sank down until she sat hunched on the floor. Waiting.

"Ready or not, here I come," her stepfather, Master Sergeant Samuel Morris, called out in that creepy, singsong voice, like this was some kind of sick game.

Her hands shook, and she clasped them in a tight knot under her chin. Her mother's scent—baby powder and cinnamon—filled the small space, enveloping her like a warm cloak, and she wished she could hide here forever. Safe. Untouched.

Tears stung her eyes. God, she missed her mother. It was bad before. His punishments had always been harsh, but since her mother's death, everything had changed.

Hot tears poured down her cheeks. She brushed them roughly away with trembling hands and cursed herself for being weak, for giving into her fear. She had to be strong. She must not cry. If there was one thing Sam liked more than the chase-me game, it was her tears, and she had no wish to give him what he wanted. He could take, but she would not give.

She bit the inside of her cheek until the rusty tang of blood filled her mouth. Sometimes the pain helped her focus. She couldn't win, of course. He was too powerful, too relentless. But she refused to give up. There had to be a way out of the trap. There had to be. She just had to live long enough to find it.

Heavy footsteps stopped outside the door. The light bulb overhead clicked. Harsh yellow light filled the closet. She pulled her knees close, shriveling back into the shadows.

"Time's up, Jill," he said in his rumbling baritone.

Despite her steely resolve, thin tendrils of fear unfurled in the pit of her stomach, and she knew he was right. The game was over. And he had won. Again. Hatred burned in her eyes as she stared at the heavy beige boots encasing his size-twelve feet.

Sam parted the clothes. The hangers squealed against the metal rod, reminding her of fingernails on slate. The sound made her teeth ache.

She could smell his sour mash breath, and a wave of nausea rolled through the pit of her stomach. Tears threatened, and she forced them back behind a frozen wall. Like a caterpillar, she withdrew inside her icy cocoon to a place far beyond, where he couldn't touch her.

"Were you looking for this?" he asked.

Master Sergeant Morris dangled a twenty-two caliber sub-compact pistol from a thick finger. Jill's gaze shifted from the gun to the grotesque smile on his broad face and back again.

The gun. Yes. Every night as he opened her bedroom door, she'd thought about the gun, and pictured a bullet hole centered between his thick black brows. But as usual, he was two steps ahead.

Like Jesse James, he spun the pistol around his finger and tucked it neatly into the back of his fatigues.

"You like games, do you?" he asked.

"Not as much as you," she said, in a voice that sounded steadier than she felt.

His cruel lips flattened into a thin line. Jill remained perfectly still, her face a stony mask. Sam hunkered down. His meaty hands snaked toward her. Hot fingers slithered around her neck. She shuddered and waited for them to constrict, squeezing off her airway. But they didn't tighten. Goosebumps dimpled her icy skin as he caressed the long column of her slender throat. Their eyes locked, and as much as she wanted to, she refused to look away.

Never again, she promised herself. Never again would he touch her like this. He would pay. Somehow this sick game would end.

And no matter what the cost, she would win.

CHAPTER ONE

J ill Shannon stood with her feet planted shoulder width apart and focused intently upon her mark. *Target acquired.* Shoulders relaxed, she squeezed the trigger of the 9 mm Glock. The acrid smell of cordite filled her head.

A cocky smile crossed her face as she stole a quick glance at her husband through the thick lenses of the protective goggles. Pressing the button to retrieve the target, she admired the tight grouping of holes that obliterated the center of the bull's-eye. Dead-on balls accurate, as Master Sergeant Morris used to say.

Alex Shannon kept his eyes trained forward as he completed his round. His grouping was good, a little to the left of Jill's perfect aim. He lowered his gun and cast a crooked, self-deprecating smile in her direction. "You know, you're pretty good at keeping my ego in check," he said as he pulled out his earplugs.

"I'm glad to hear that I serve some purpose," she said, removing her goggles.

"Like that's the only thing."

"A little healthy competition is good for a marriage," Jill said, her smile widening in appreciation of the ironic inflection in his voice. "Besides, you can't be all that bad. They still allow you to carry a badge and a gun."

"Yeah, that helps."

"Girl's got a point, Alex," a deep voice rumbled from behind.

"What are you doing here on a Sunday morning?" she asked.

Jackson Levy was a bear of a man, six foot three, and still built like the linebacker he was back in his college days. Alex was no small guy, but next to Jackson, he looked like an undernourished middle-grader.

"Thought I'd get a little shooting in while the wife is at yoga. My own Zen moment, so to speak."

Jill masked her surprise. Last she heard, Jackson and his wife, Michelle, were separated. If Alex knew about their reconciliation, he hadn't let on. Of course, that was nothing unusual. They didn't talk about work. Truth was, they didn't talk about much at all lately.

"Sometimes I worry about you," Alex said with a grin.

"Me? What about the two of you? If this is your idea of a date, then …" With a cocked eyebrow, Jackson let the words trail off. Stepping forward, he clamped his huge hand onto Jill's shoulder and gave it a friendly squeeze. "How are you doing, girl?"

"Keeping out of trouble."

"Looks like you kicked your man's butt."

"It's not the first time," Alex said, giving Jackson a sidelong glance through narrowed eyes. "Jill's stepfather was Special Forces. She learned to shoot before she could drive. I don't need to hear any shit from you about my marksmanship."

"Well, I've got a lot riding on your shooting ability. I've got to know that you have my back. Maybe I need to take Jill here along with me instead."

"Not a chance," Alex said. The response was fast. Automatic. Jill bristled at the proprietary note in his voice. Before she could respond, he continued.

"There's a big difference between shooting a paper target and a perp. I haven't let you get shot so far, and believe me, that's no small feat given the massive target you present."

Jackson's wide lips parted in a good-natured smile. "Maybe a bigger target is what you need if you plan on hitting anything."

"Don't push your luck, or I might just shoot you myself." Jackson laughed, and Alex cocked an eyebrow. "I'll catch you later. I've got to take Dirty Harriett here to the airport."

Alex clapped a hand on Jackson's shoulder. Jill could still hear his deep, rumbling laugh as she handed in her gear at the desk.

She didn't miss the appreciative glance she got from the clerk behind the counter as she signed out. If Alex noticed, he showed no outward sign. Was he used to the male attention she attracted? Did he still look at her that way? Did he still look at her at all? Over the course of their five-year marriage, they had slid into a routine. Or was it a rut, she wondered.

"What time's your flight?" he asked.

"Noon."

"Why so early?"

Jill followed Alex out of the range and down the long, narrow hallway toward the locker room. Her heart pounded in double time as she considered the question, but she kept her voice light.

"I've got a project review first thing in the morning and I still have to work on my slides."

Alex glanced at her. He still looked like a college student, his short hair cut away from his angular face and a light growth of stubble on his cheeks. Subtle lines carved their way into the corners of his eyes and lent him an air of experience, falling just short of the war-weary look common to most detectives.

The expression in his golden brown eyes gave her pause. Was he growing suspicious of her frequent trips to the Bay Area? The recent expansion of her role at work provided a plausible excuse for all the time spent away from him. But still.

"I guess we should head straight home then. You don't have a lot of time to get ready."

Unaware that she had been holding her breath, she exhaled in a soft sigh. Her long strides kept pace with his as they walked side by side, hands not touching. Jill changed the subject and followed him into the locker room.

"Did you talk to Captain Lewis about the presentation he asked you to do for the conference?"

Once a year, police chiefs from across the country got together to discuss the new strategies and techniques their departments employed. This year, Alex had been asked to present his groundbreaking work on a suite of cybercrime tools. Jill glanced up. Alex's expression was guarded.

"I thought we talked about this already."

"Did we?" Jill asked, eyes wide, feigning ignorance.

"It's a political bullshit assignment. I've got better ways to spend my time."

Jill frowned. It was exactly the type of answer she expected. Tactical. Alex seemed maddeningly oblivious to the types of opportunities that came his way. If only he possessed an ounce or two of ambition.

"Come on, Alex. You're a smart guy. You know there's more to it than that. Think of the doors it could open for you."

"For me? Are you sure it's me we're talking about here, because if it is, you know where I stand. All I want is to get back into homicide. Are you sure we're not talking about what *you* want?"

"That's not fair," she said, controlling her irritation with effort. "The cybercrimes unit has been waiting for a guy with your talent. Think of all of the good you could do."

"Great, so I can put a dent in identity theft instead of tracking down murderers. Hell of a trade-off, don't you think?"

"Forget it," she said, and waved a dismissive hand.

An uncomfortable silence settled between them, and Jill could feel the weight of his stare as they entered the locker room. She deliberately avoided his gaze. There was no point. At times like this, there was no talking to him. The widening gulf between them felt less like a fissure and more like the great divide.

Alex dialed the combination, then handed her a jacket before pulling on his own.

"Listen, Jill, I'm not that guy. Besides, you've got enough ambition for both of us." His voice was soft, and he shot her his best boyish smile in an attempt to take the sting out of his words. "If it helps, Jackson has been pushing me, too."

It didn't help. She brushed past him and left the locker room. Ambitious? Hell yeah, she was ambitious. Spending her high school years dirt-poor and in foster homes was inspiration enough to excel. Alex's Norman Rockwell upbringing didn't instill him with the same needs.

Half way to the exit, Alex's cell phone rang, eliminating the need for further discussion. She pushed open the heavy doors and stepped out into the brisk morning air. Thick, gray clouds choked out the sun, and though it wasn't raining yet, it soon would be. She could feel it.

Jill stayed two strides ahead, carving a path through the parked cars toward the silver Jeep Liberty. The lights flashed as Alex unlocked the door.

"When?" As he spoke into the phone, the change in his tone was instantaneous, sharp, and suddenly all business. Jill turned. The expression on Alex's face was serious. "When was she expected home?"

What now? Here it was, a cool fall Sunday morning, and they couldn't spend an hour alone without a call. She knew what came next. An emergency. An excuse. And she would be finding her own way to the airport while he rushed off.

Shaking her head, she opened the door and climbed inside the Jeep.

"Have you called the police yet?" Alex asked as he settled behind the steering wheel, the cell phone still pressed to his ear. With a quick flick of his wrist, he consulted his watch. "I'll be there in twenty-five minutes."

Hanging up, he glanced over at Jill. Concern was clearly etched into the lines around his mouth.

"That was Abby Watson. I mean Nelson," he corrected with a quick shake of his head. "She got married."

Jill's lips twitched in recognition. An unpleasant stab of surprise shot through her.

"Abby Watson. Your ex-girlfriend?"

"Her sister is missing."

Technically Abby was still in the picture when she and Alex first started seeing each other. There weren't many wives who felt comfortable with an out-of-the-blue call from a long-lost girlfriend. *Fiancée,* Jill amended. And she was definitely not among them.

"And so she called you?" she asked, raising her eyebrows and folding her arms across her chest.

Alex lifted a hand off the steering wheel in a shrug. "I've known the family a long time. I'll drop you off at home before I head over to her parents' place to see what I can find out."

His hand stalled as he reached out to start the engine, and he paused, as if a new thought had suddenly occurred to him. "I won't be able to take you to the airport."

"I'll call a cab."

Jill shifted her gaze out the windshield and felt a cold knot of resignation form in her gut. Duty came first for Alex. Always had. But having him rush off to his ex-girlfriend's rescue was somehow worse. A stab of resentment flared. She pulled in a deep breath and released it slowly.

It didn't matter. Soon she'd be on a plane headed for California. She could forget all about the argument, the phone call, Abby Watson, and everything else. By the time she landed, this would all seem so very far away.

CHAPTER TWO

After dropping Jill off at the house, Alex broke more than one traffic law on his way to the Watson's place. Halfway across the Aurora Bridge, he placed a quick call to Jackson, part of the missing child unit, to get permission to talk to Abby's parents. Hanging up, he glided to a halt beside the curb and stepped off onto the cracked street.

For a moment, he thought about Jill. She'd be away all week on a business trip, and he hadn't really said good-bye. He stuck a hand in the pocket of his favorite jeans and pulled out a cell phone, but before he had a chance to dial her number, the door swung open, and he found himself looking up into Abby's stricken face. Alex's heart skipped a beat.

How many times had he stood in this very spot waiting to see her? Now, here she was. Same petite build, same wavy blond hair, same bright blue eyes. She looked like a young Meg Ryan standing on the wide front porch in faded blue jeans and bare feet. The only thing missing was the playful glint in her eyes.

He pushed aside the conflicting emotions he felt. Too much time had passed. They'd both moved on. They were different people now.

"Hi, Abby," he said at last. He climbed the stairs leading up to the Craftsman-style house. He slid the cell phone back into his pocket.

"Thanks for coming, Alex," she said. Her soft voice sounded strained with worry. "Mom and Dad are waiting."

Alex followed her inside with a growing sense of trepidation. The last time he'd set foot in this house was five years ago, when he'd called off their engagement. Now Abby's little sister was missing, and he was here to help.

Joyce Watson sat hunched over the kitchen table, staring sightlessly at the cup of coffee in her hand. Her silver-blond hair was scraped back into a ponytail, and she looked up at Alex, red-rimmed eyes brimming with worry. This was not the Joyce Watson he remembered, the woman who met them at the door after school with lemonade and a smile. The grim expression on her face told him all he needed to know about her state of mind.

"Would you like some coffee, Alex?" Tom Watson asked. He leaned against the kitchen counter wearing a white T-shirt and a worn pair of jeans. Tom had aged significantly over the past half-decade. His hairline had retreated to a graying wreath that topped his ears, the steely hue matching the rugged stubble that shadowed his ruddy cheeks.

"No thanks," he said.

He wanted to hug Joyce. She looked so small and so scared as she sat hunched in her chair. He wished there was some comfort he could offer. But that was no longer his place. Instead, he seated himself across from Joyce and met her watery gaze directly. She didn't smile. She held his gaze for a moment before looking away. Alex pulled out his notebook and addressed the family.

"Tell me about Natalie. What did she do yesterday?"

Tom cleared his throat, squared his shoulders, and started.

"Nothing out of the ordinary, really. She went for a bike ride and did some studying up in her room. Joyce and I left the house around three. We went shopping at University Village and met friends at Piatti's for dinner. Natalie planned to stay over at a friend's house. When she didn't show up at work this morning, they called here."

Tom paused and rubbed his creased forehead. His anxiety was palpable. "We called her friend. Natalie never made it to their house.

When she didn't arrive, they assumed her plans had changed. We didn't know what to do, where to start looking." Tom glanced at his wife. Joyce continued to stare at her coffee cup, as if an answer might be found in its dark depths.

Alex nodded, jotting a few notes about the timeline and events Tom provided. "What's her friend's name?"

"Emily Jenkins," Joyce looked up as she answered, and her hand fluttered to her bloodless lips.

"Didn't she think it was odd for Natalie not to call?"

Joyce angled her head to one side as she considered the question.

"Emily's what you might call a free spirit. She doesn't have the same rules at home that Natalie does."

She looked like she wanted to say more, but she stopped herself. Alex jotted a few notes, careful to keep his expression neutral. That Natalie typically called, but hadn't, made an impression. As a detective in the Seattle Police Department, he was privy to details about the most brutal child-abuse cases. Although it was not his area of expertise, the stories seemed to infiltrate the department at every level, making it hard for him to tune them out. Making it impossible for him to not worry about Natalie.

Alex looked up to find all eyes trained on him.

"Where does she work?"

"At the coffee shop a few blocks away." Tom's smile was bittersweet. "She's saving up to buy a new bike."

Alex nodded. He'd want to follow up with the people she worked with to learn more about Natalie's habits. Was she reliable? Were there any customers who took a special interest in her?

He could feel Abby's eyes on him. He glanced up quickly, and forced a reassuring smile.

"What did you do after you called Emily?"

Joyce picked up the thread of the story. Her voice, normally soft and soothing, crackled with emotion as she began.

"We called everyone we could think of—friends, work—but no one had seen her. By the time Abby arrived, we were half out of our heads with worry. We called you." Alex could see tears clouding her eyes as she looked away.

"Does she have her cell phone with her?"

"We think so. It's not in her room," Tom said. "We tried calling her, but she's not answering. We've left a dozen messages."

Tom's face had become a mask of stone. His skin had taken on a gray pallor. He watched his wife.

"Does Natalie have a boyfriend?" Alex asked, keeping his voice calm and even. The last thing he wanted to do was add to their worry. Without looking up, he could feel the magnetic pull of Abby's gaze, and he avoided her stare.

"No," Joyce responded quickly. "She's sixteen and doesn't date."

The answer was definitive, typical of an overly protective parent. He wondered if it was accurate. Did Natalie have secrets she didn't want to share? He remembered Abby at sixteen, and he felt pretty sure that there were a few things her parents didn't know.

"Did you have an argument with Natalie last night? Is there any reason you can think of why she may not have come home?"

"No," Tom said, shaking his head. "I wish there was."

"May I see her room?" Alex asked, closing his notebook, his lips set in a grim line. He didn't like where this was going. The hope that there was a simple explanation for Natalie's whereabouts was fading fast. Her family was painting the picture of a responsible girl who did as she was told. So either Natalie was in the midst of a major teenaged rebellion or something significant had happened to her. Or maybe someone.

The room was neat, particularly for a high school kid, he thought as he examined it slowly, his eyes taking careful inventory of each small detail. Books crammed the shelves of the narrow bookcase, and more were stacked on the desk around her computer monitor. He scanned the titles. Natalie was an eclectic reader with a wide range of interests ranging from biographies to vampires to classic adventure stories.

"Is there anything missing? Clothes?" Alex asked, and Tom cleared his throat before answering.

"Not that we've noticed." The members of the Watson family stood close together, clustered in the doorway, seeming to draw strength from each other's nearness.

Alex noted the poster of Lance Armstrong from the Tour de France pinned to the wall above Natalie's headboard.

"Where does she like to bike?"

"The Burke-Gilman Trail is her favorite for long rides," Abby answered.

"Is her bike here?"

Both parents looked at each other in astonishment, as if each had assumed the other had already checked.

"I'll take a look," Abby offered and turned to descend the stairs.

A few photographs were wedged into the edges of the corkboard above the desk, and he stepped closer to get a better look. One picture caught his eye. Natalie's pretty smile beamed out from the snapshot. Her arm was wound around another girl's shoulders. He noted that she was about the same age as Natalie, but that's where the similarity ended. With a round face, heavy eyeliner circling her brown eyes, and dyed black hair, she had the look of a girl who had never seen the inside of a library. A small tattoo of a butterfly peeked out from beneath the neckline of her shirt. He wondered if her parents had authorized that little addition.

"Who's that?" Alex gestured toward the picture of the two girls.

"That's Emily Jenkins," Joyce answered. "Natalie's best friend. They've known each other since kindergarten."

"The same girl she was supposed to visit yesterday?"

They nodded, and Alex continued to study the room.

"You mentioned that Natalie spends a lot of time on the computer. What does she do?" he asked with a growing sense of foreboding. As part of the cybercrimes unit, he had investigated his fair share of child-abduction cases, kids who had been lured by online predators to a dark underworld of sexual fantasy and abuse. Some of them came back to their homes to continue on with their lives, beginning a long journey to overcome their painful experiences. And some did not.

"Schoolwork, mostly. She emails her friends. Watches videos. Normal kid stuff."

A small frown formed between Alex's eyebrows, drawing them closer together. "Do you have any tracking software on your computer?"

"Tracking software?" Tom's brow wrinkled.

"Some parents put it on their computers so they can see what their kids are doing online."

Underneath the bushy moustache, Tom's lips twitched, and he traded worried looks with Joyce.

"We trust Natalie."

Alex nodded. He paused for a long moment, his eyes focused on the computer tower under her desk, mentally listing his next steps. He had tools he could use to track her online activities—email correspondence, websites she'd visited, chat rooms.

"If it's all right with you, I'm going to take her computer with me."

CHAPTER THREE

Jill Shannon sank slowly into the luxurious pile of pillows on the king-sized bed. Candlelight glimmered, reflecting off her long, bare legs. She smoothed down the red silk negligee as she waited.

It seemed like she spent half her life waiting. Waiting for Alex to come home from work. Waiting for the sparks between them to reignite. Once upon a time, their many differences drew them together, like yin and yang. Now it seemed they barely knew each other. Alex was never home. And when he was, they didn't talk. She didn't understand his slavish devotion to duty. He didn't understand her drive, her ambition. They spoke different languages.

Jill took a sip of champagne, savoring the dry, crisp taste.

Well, she was done waiting. She was ready for some action.

A sharp knock on the door interrupted her musings and brought her to her feet in a smooth, fluid motion. Her pulse began to race. With a few graceful strides, she crossed the room. Jill smiled as she swung open the door and found him leaning against the door jamb.

Jamie King was without a doubt one of the sexiest men she had ever met. Salt-and-pepper hair, ice-blue eyes, average height. In his early forties, he was in top condition. Today he was dressed casually in a long-sleeved white linen shirt and dark jeans.

She grabbed his hand and pulled him inside the room without a word, his kiss hot on her lips. With nimble fingers, she unbuttoned his shirt and pushed it off his shoulders.

Jamie looked down, his eyes taking a meticulous inventory from her long glossy hair down to her scarlet-painted toenails.

"My, my, aren't you the little vixen?" he asked in his crisp British accent. His hands ran down her bare shoulders and back, gripping her silk-clad hips.

"I was just thinking about you."

"Good thoughts, I trust?"

"Very bad, actually."

She brushed against him and stretched up on her toes, nuzzling his rough cheek. She breathed in his scent—warm leather and soap—as she trailed hungry kisses down his throat.

"Where did you find this naughty number?" he asked, with a playful smile.

She loved his accent, and how it could make even the corniest lines sound sexy.

"Wouldn't you like to know?" she whispered in his ear, grazing her lips lightly along the length of his throat. He chuckled softly.

"Ah, bought it for your husband. I see."

Jamie grabbed the hem of the negligee. He pulled it up over her head in a smooth, fluid motion, and tossed it carelessly aside. His mouth lowered to hers, smothering her response.

Desire simmered hot through her veins. His hands blazed fiery trails across her skin. Breathing hard, she pulled away and gazed up into his face. His cheeks were flushed, and his eyes glittered in the dim light. A need, sharp and hot, jolted through her.

"I've been waiting. Where were you?"

Jamie backed her up toward the bed, his hand skimming past her waist to cup her breast. Jill groaned as his fingers closed over her nipple, tugging hard before shoving her back. She fell onto the mattress. Her dark hair fanned out across the creamy sheets. She looked up. In the flickering candlelight, she saw his wicked grin.

"You're certainly not the patient kind, are you, Jill? Maybe that's why I like to keep you waiting. I like the pot simmering when I get here."

He shed his clothes and finally bent over to kiss her. She felt the scorching heat of his lips brand her. Cupping his neck with her hand, she pulled him closer. Jamie resisted, though, suspended above her, content to prolong the moment as his fingers and lips played across her body. Slow. Teasing.

She moaned in frustration. She was done waiting. She wanted him.

Jill wound a leg around both of his and heaved against his shoulder. Set off balance, Jamie flipped onto the mattress. He looked up, electric-blue eyes wide in surprise. Jill straddled him, smiling sweetly down into his face. His breath quickened. He gripped her hips and guided her into position.

"I don't like to be kept waiting," she said, sinking slowly along the length of him, savoring each delicious sensation rippling through her.

"I can see that."

Jamie's grip tightened. He arched his hips and thrust deep inside her, and Jill forgot everything else.

* * *

Stretched out face-down on the sheets, Jill opened her eyes slowly as she surveyed the hotel room. Clothes were strewn across the Berber carpet in a trail that began just past the doorway with Jamie's shirt and ended a foot from the bed, where the silky negligee lay, discarded in a pool of red satin. She turned her head to one side, a lazy smile slanted across her lips.

"Well, that was as good as advertised," she sighed.

"Right. Customer service is our number-one priority, ma'am," Jamie said as he reclined against the pillows, the sheet folded at his waist. She rolled over on her side facing him, legs stretched out, with only her feet tucked under the covers. The bare curves of her body were exposed to the air, allowing her velvety skin to cool. If she were a cat, she'd be purring right now.

Jill felt the warmth of his gaze on her as she met his blue eyes with a sated smile. He ran a finger across the jagged, two-inch line on the side of her neck, scar tissue raised against the soft skin surrounding it.

"Remind me again how you got that," he said, retracting his hands and folding them behind his head.

Jill swung her hair around her shoulders, hiding the scar from view. "Missed the jugular by inches," she remembered the doctor telling her stepfather, whose stony expression revealed no hint of emotion. No relief. No hatred. Just a yawning blank emptiness that stretched between them. A few inches to the right and her name would have been added to the headstone, alongside those of her mother and brother.

Feeling a chill, she rolled onto her flat belly, breaking eye contact.

Over the years, she had concocted a number of stories about how she had gotten the scar. All plausible. All entertaining. All a safe distance from the truth. After so many years, she almost believed them. But for some reason she didn't care to define, she told Jamie the truth. The short version of it, anyway. Free from the crunching of metal and her mother's scream, followed by the profound silence of falling snow.

"Car accident when I was a kid."

"How old were you?" he asked.

Jill averted her gaze. She didn't want to think about the accident, or the years that followed. Some things were best forgotten. She had spent those years learning how to forget. That's the problem with telling the truth. One question led to another and then …

Reaching out, she pulled the leather-bound menu off the nightstand and opened it.

"Are you hungry?" she asked, chin propped on her fist, abruptly changing the subject. Jamie let it drop.

"Not really. You?"

Relieved he didn't press, she said, "Starving. I'm ordering room service. Would you like anything?"

"Not me." He shifted to the side of the bed and pulled on his boxer shorts. She glanced up when she heard the jingle of his belt buckle just in time to see Jamie slide his dark jeans over his lean hips.

"And just where do you think you're going?" she asked, a seductive smile drifting across her face. "I'm not finished with you yet."

"I'm afraid I can't stay." He picked the linen shirt up off of the floor and buttoned it.

"What do you mean?" she asked, dropping the menu and pulling her knees up to her chest. "It's still early. Why don't you stay and finish the champagne at least?"

"Not tonight. I need to prepare for a meeting with the executive team. It's been a mad week, so I've not been able to get to it." Jamie sat back down on the edge of the bed and pulled on his socks.

"You know what they say, 'All work and no play makes Jamie a dull boy,'" she said, grinning playfully and tugging gently at the back of his shirt. The banter was part of their routine, one of the best things about being with Jamie. He was smart and witty. But tonight he was not engaging with her in quite the same way. She could feel it, as if there had been some subtle shift in the landscape between them. His lively edge was sorely lacking.

"Are you finding me dull?" Jamie asked, not glancing back as he continued to dress. "I'm sorry. Perhaps your expectations are a tad too high."

He sounded anything but sorry, she thought. Jill's features hardened, and she felt her cheeks flush. She tried to keep anger from seeping into her tone, but her voice turned icy.

"If you told me you were busy, I wouldn't have bothered flying in so early."

"Right, Jillian. Do I need to email you my bloody itinerary?" he asked, his frigid tone matching hers.

"It wouldn't hurt," she snapped, and cocked her chin defiantly.

"You, of all people, know what's going on at the office," he said. He finally turned to look at her, and his voice thawed a bit. "I would stay if I could, but I do need to get going. You understand, don't you?"

She didn't answer. She held his gaze for a moment before turning her attention back to the menu.

"You have a presentation of your own to work on tonight, don't you? You'll want to make sure that everything is letter perfect for tomorrow's review and still have time for your beauty sleep."

She bristled at the chauvinistic comment and looked up in time to catch his wink.

"Sure thing, boss," she said, and flipped him a sardonic salute.

The fact that she reported to him gave him the upper hand in all work-related issues and made the affair a little more exciting—if not a little dangerous—for both of them.

Was that part of the allure, she wondered. Power? Influence? So far, Jamie had done nothing but promote her career and provide her with opportunities. Still, if things didn't go his way, what would he do?

Jill pushed the troubling thought aside. She wasn't the only one who stood to lose if news of their affair leaked out. In any company, sleeping with one of your employees could get you fired.

"That's a good girl," he said with a nod. "I'll see you in the morning."

"Good night," she replied.

With a quick glance over his shoulder, he let the heavy door of the hotel room click shut behind him.

Reclining against the pillows, Jill released an exasperated sigh and pulled the covers up over her chest. The encounter had not gone as expected. Perhaps the novelty of the affair was wearing off. One thing was for certain, though: this type of drop-in service was definitely not what she had in mind.

CHAPTER FOUR

Alex stood by the desk in Natalie Watson's room. Tension knotted his shoulders. The situation felt wrong. Alex made a note in his spiral notebook to run an online check for Natalie Watson. A general search would help him find listings for any social-networking sites that she might be posting to and let him see what other information was available on her. Pictures, personal information—it was all out there for anybody to read. Anybody.

"Her bike isn't in the garage," Abby said breathlessly when she reached the top step of the staircase. Her blue eyes locked on Alex, transmitting her fear. Silent tears pooled in Joyce's eyes, and she turned quickly, leaving the room. Tom's face was granite, his mouth a grim line.

"I'll need to get a description of the bike. A serial number would be great, if you have it. I can run a check to see if it has been turned in at a lost-and-found facility."

Tom nodded, hands deep in his pockets. His gaze dropped to the floor. "I'll see if I can find the receipt from the bike shop."

"Hopefully I'll find something helpful on the computer."

Okay, he wasn't doing everything by the book. There was protocol for this sort of thing. But with each passing hour, the chances of Natalie walking through the front door diminished. He was anxious to jump-start the investigation.

"Whatever you need, Alex," Tom offered in a voice that sounded near to breaking. "We really appreciate ... we really need your help."

Alex nodded. He wished he could do more. He wished there were some obvious clue to help him zero in Natalie's whereabouts. He wished in some way he could help make up for the pain he'd caused Abby and her family. Turning toward Abby, he met her eyes.

"How about taking a drive over to Emily's with me?"

***

Alone in the car with Abby, Alex felt as if he had stepped into a time warp. He couldn't begin to count the miles they had logged driving side by side, hands linked. Now everything had changed. They sat as stiff and awkward as strangers.

"Tell me about Natalie's relationship with your parents," Alex said, breaking the silence, as they rounded the corner to the Jenkinses' house.

Abby's sigh was soft.

"Not much to tell, really. She's a good kid. Genuine. I think the most trouble she's ever been in was last year when she got caught skipping school so she could catch Lance Armstrong's personal appearance at Key Arena."

"Big fan? Even after the scandal?"

"He's still a sport's icon, and the Livestrong Foundation does great work. A few years back, one of her friends lost a battle with leukemia. Now Natalie volunteers for the foundation. I think it makes her feel like she's doing something for her friend. She never takes her bracelet off."

Alex stared out at the road ahead, hoping that the Livestrong mantra was not something that Natalie would need to cling to.

"Does she have a lot of rules at home?"

Abby's eyes met his in an ironic stare.

"Come on, Alex. Has it really been that long?" She shifted and looked out the passenger window. "You know my parents. They expect a lot from her. She doesn't seem to resent it."

"She never snuck out of the house to go to a party, get drunk, and have the cops deliver her home?"

Alex cast Abby a wry smile. He could still remember the police driving the two of them home after one such incident and the punishment that followed. His father prescribed two backbreaking weeks of building and painting the Watson's garage, during one of the hottest summers in Puget Sound history. They had both been grounded for weeks.

"Let's just say that she doesn't have the type of friends that would lure her into trouble." The lopsided grin on Abby's face was good to see. The faintest touch of pink stained her cheeks, and Alex looked away.

"Ah, right. It was your friends who got you into trouble. I seem to remember you had something to do with it."

"It's not fair," she said, still looking out the window, eyes focused on the road. "You know all of my secrets."

"Not all of them." A beat of silence rested between them before he added, "Besides, everyone has secrets."

"Not you. You have always been a straight shooter."

"I'm too dumb to lie." Abby shot him a skeptical look, and he shrugged. "At any rate, let's see if Natalie's friend knows hers."

Pulling up next to the curb outside Emily's house, they both stepped out of the Jeep.

Nora Jenkins's expression was wary as she opened the door to admit Alex and Abby. Her watery eyes and gin blossoms gave Alex the impression of someone who had seen the bottom of a bottle or two.

"What's this about?" she asked. There was nothing friendly about her tone.

"Natalie's missing," Abby said, wasting no time in getting to the point. She had always been very direct. It was one of the things Alex liked best about her. "We're here to talk to Emily, to see if there is anything she knows that might help."

Nora's face blanched, and she stood rooted to the spot.

"She's in the kitchen." Nora gestured toward the back of the house, and with a nod they walked down the hall. Alex followed Abby, who seemed to glide down the narrow passage with natural grace.

Emily was standing at the cluttered counter pouring juice as they entered. Alex noticed the dishes piled high in the sink, the food scraps encrusted on the Formica surface, and the half-empty bottle of vodka by the stove. For a second, he wondered if it was just juice in her glass.

Barely a hair over five feet tall, Emily's muffin top poured over the band of her too-tight jeans. Her thick, black hair pulled away from her face in a hasty ponytail. Residue from her heavy makeup still smudged the outline of her brown eyes.

There was nothing welcoming about Emily's gaze, and she glared at them as if they were alien intruders.

"We wanted to talk to you about Natalie," Abby began. "This is Detective Alex Shannon, from the Seattle Police Department."

Emily turned to pick up the glass and drank some juice as she stared over at them as if trying to mask a flicker of surprise.

"What about Natalie?" Her voice was deep, unexpectedly gravelly, and dripping with teenage attitude.

"Mind if we sit?" Alex asked. Her shrug was noncommittal, and he took a chair at the kitchen table. Abby perched on the bench opposite him. But Emily stayed where she was, arms crossed. Alex fixed her with a long stare. Her guarded eyes never wavered from his.

"When was the last time you saw Natalie?"

Not answering right away, she transferred her gaze from Alex to Abby and then back again. Chubby fingers gripped the juice glass as she finally spoke.

"Friday after school. We came here to listen to music."

"Did Natalie spend a lot of time over here?" Alex asked. Emily shrugged, trying to mask a small smirk.

"Sometimes. Her parents don't allow loud music."

"And your parents?"

"They're not around much. Dad's long gone and Mom ... Well, Mom doesn't mind." Her eyes moved across the counter to the bottle of vodka, expression guarded.

"Natalie was supposed to come here yesterday afternoon, right?"

"Yeah, I guess that was the plan."

"You guess, or you know?" Abby pressed, her temper flaring quickly to the surface. Alex glanced sharply at her before looking back at Emily.

"It's not my day to watch her," she said placing her glass on the counter and propping her fists on her hips.

"So you're saying that you didn't have plans with her?"

A hiss escaped Emily in the form of an exasperated sigh, and she rolled her eyes.

"She was planning to come over. But when she didn't show I figured, whatever."

"Did she call?"

"Like I said, I don't keep tabs on her." She angled her gaze away from him to make a thorough examination of the black polish flaking off her fingernails.

Alex continued to study her while he considered tactics. Given his unofficial status, badgering her was not going to help. The harder she was pushed, the more she would withdraw. But her lack of concern for Natalie disturbed him.

"Does Natalie have a boyfriend?"

A shadow rippled across Emily's face, and he saw the answer in her eyes.

"No," she lied.

"You're sure? Is there someone she liked to hang out with? Someone that maybe her parents didn't approve of?"

"God, didn't I just answer that? No." After another oh-my-God three-sixty, she gnawed at the corner of a fingernail. Her eyes flashed to Abby before angling away. Another direct hit, he sensed.

"Christ, Emily, you're supposed to be her friend. Natalie's missing. Aren't you the least bit concerned?" Abby asked. Her face was beet red as she glared across the table at the teenage girl. Small hands were clenched in tight fists, as if she were fighting the urge to wrap her fingers around the girl's neck.

Emily's head snapped up, and her fingers dropped away from her lips. Her eyes rested on Abby before taking in the countertop and the bottle of vodka again. She licked her lips absently.

"Listen," he began softly, "Natalie's family is worried about her. Is there anything you can tell us that might help? We just want to find her. Make sure she's safe."

Emily nibbled on her lower lip, looking uncertain. Alex allowed himself to hope she might open up and start telling the truth. Then her expression closed, and hope evaporated.

"Look, I don't know where she is."

The conversation was going nowhere. There was a guy. He knew it the same way he knew pressing Emily now was a waste of time. With any luck he would find out more by combing through Natalie's hard drive.

"Okay, thanks for your time," Alex said. He pulled a business card from his pocket and handed it to her. She made a show of studying it. "If you think of anything, please call me. Anytime."

Emily inclined her head in a sulky nod, and stubbornly refused to look up as they passed. Nora hovered in the doorway, concern reflected in the downcast turn of her lips. Alex thanked her for their time as he stepped out onto the creaky porch. The warm sunlight did little to penetrate the deepening chill he felt.

"We can't just leave," Abby said, her voice low and terse as they heard the front door close. "She's lying, Alex. We both know it."

Abby trudged back toward the front door with a look of grim determination on her face. Alex stopped her, his hands gripping her shoulders. He felt the hum of an electric current race between them. Abby looked up, as if she felt it, too. All at once, Alex released her and stepped away, breaking contact.

"Emily knows something, but she's not going to say it in front of you, her mother, or anyone else. I know this isn't easy, but you've got to let me handle it. You've got to trust me. Can you do that?" Their eyes met, and after a long moment, her expression softened. She gave a grudging, but compliant, nod.

Alex fished the cell phone from his pocket. His every instinct told him Natalie was in trouble and needed help. Turning toward the Jeep, he hit a number on speed dial. Too much about the situation bothered him. The sooner he got the official investigation under way, the better.

"Jackson, it's Alex. I'm on my way to the office. Meet me there."

CHAPTER FIVE

"**W**ow, I think I need a drink after that review. What did you do to piss off Dana Evans?" Rachel Meyers asked. She set her lunch tray down on the table opposite Jill and squinted against the bright sunlight that streamed into the busy ZyraNet cafeteria.

Jill stared down at the salad in front of her and grimaced, still fuming. "Believe me, I have no idea. It's the first time I've actually met her."

Not only had Evans interrupted Jill's project status report, but she'd drilled in on the problem areas with all the delicacy of a pit bull gnawing on a pug. Once her jaws locked, Dana refused to let go.

"Why didn't Jamie shut her up? I thought he would at least jump in to stop her, but he said nothing, which is unusual for him. I've never seen him at a loss for words before."

Jill forced a casual shrug. "I know he's concerned about the performance issues we're tracking, but yeah, I expected him to step in, too."

His lack of support bothered her more than she was willing to let on. Up to now, he was her biggest advocate. But this morning she felt a definite shift in his demeanor, like something had changed, and she didn't know what.

"I thought he was your biggest fan," Rachel said, her eyebrows arched above her dark eyes.

"Apparently not." Jill leaned forward, picking at her Cobb salad.

"How bad are the performance problems?"

"Well, tests show a significant slowdown in the software," Jill admitted, and she slowly sighed. "The team is working day and night to try and uncover the source of the problem, but so far, no luck."

Rachel nodded. Her look was sympathetic.

"With the WebNOW demo in a few weeks, we've got to get it fixed. It won't look good for Jamie to be onstage in front of thousands of people and have latency issues. The world is watching."

"Did he offer any suggestions after the meeting?" Rachel asked, nibbling on her sandwich, eyes not wavering from Jill's face.

"Are you kidding? That's why we're managers, right? It's our job to fix the problems. Not his. Mind if we talk about something else?" The problem weighed heavily on Jill. Her lips were twisted into a bitter frown as she picked up her fork to shuffle around some bacon.

"Hey, speak of the devil." Rachel's sharp, dark eyes met hers across the lunch table. Her Botoxed lips twisted into a conspiratorial grin. Rachel inclined her head toward a table near the windows.

Jill's gaze shot across the room, following the trajectory of Rachel's nod. Her eyes widened as they focused on the table where a curvy blond woman perched on a chair opposite Jamie. Dana Evans was smiling, and Jamie laughed at something she said. With a rising sense of dread, Jill watched as Dana reached across the table, her hand resting a full five seconds casually on Jamie's forearm before pulling away. The gesture seemed comfortable. Familiar. Inappropriate.

"You know they used to work together?" Rachel asked, taking a dainty bite of her sandwich.

Jill swallowed hard, bile tasting bitter at the back of her throat.

"They did?"

"Yeah. Rumor has it they did more than work, if you know what I mean."

A jolt shot through Jill, followed by a terrible sinking, spiraling sensation. Was Dana the reason for the shift in Jamie's demeanor last night? Did he have someplace better to be? He seemed a little brusque. Maybe it wasn't just work.

Through a sheer effort of will, she rearranged her features into a neutral mask before looking back at Rachel.

Her fork clanged against the bowl as she reached for her water. Despite the delicious smells of forbidden foods like fresh bread and burgers that filled the cafeteria, Jill was losing her appetite. She took a long pull from her bottle, struggling to contain her emotions.

Turns out Rachael was right. She *could* use a drink about now. What she wouldn't give for a martini. Water wasn't going to cut it.

"You don't think there's something going on there, do you?" Jill said, keeping her tone light. "Surely, Jamie is smarter than that."

"You're kidding, right?" Rachel snorted. "Jamie has a reputation. You can't tell me you haven't noticed his preference for young, attractive women. And as for the delightful Ms. Evans, they've been joined at the hip since she stepped out of orientation. I wouldn't be surprised if he recruited her for the position." Tossing her graying mane over her shoulder, Rachael continued to observe the pair.

"Can't really blame her, though. He's not exactly hard on the eyes. I sure wouldn't kick him out of bed for eating crackers. You can't tell me you haven't noticed that he has a certain … appeal." Rachel's gaze was shrewd as she peered across the table, trying to read Jill's thoughts. Digging for more gossip perhaps?

Jill didn't flinch. She forced a careless shrug and dodged the question.

"Well, she's new. Maybe he's taking her under his wing until she gets settled." Her insides felt like they were being squeezed in a vice so hard it was difficult to breathe. Rachel was the closest thing to a friend she had in the San Jose office, but there were things Jill didn't share with her. With anyone. Jamie was one of them.

"Like a mentor? Ha. I don't think it's the kind of mentorship Human Resources has in mind." Rachel's words dripped with innuendo as she arched an expressive eyebrow at Jill, leaving little doubt as to her opinion.

Jill's lips twitched.

"Whatever. You think everyone is getting some." She fought the magnetic pull of her gaze toward Jamie's table.

Rachel's throaty laugh was bitter. She ran her fingers absently over the place her wedding ring used to occupy. "You may have a point there. God knows, I'm not."

"Is the divorce final yet?" Jill asked, taking full advantage of the chance to change the subject.

Rachel grimaced and shook her head.

"No, the bastard wants me to sign over the cabin in Big Sur. No doubt to take his teenage, Barbie-doll girlfriend there to commune with nature."

"He's still seeing her?"

Jill looked across the table and instantly regretted the question. Rachel's lips pressed together in a tight line. Her eyes were liquid pools of acid.

"They've moved in together."

"I'm sorry. How are you doing?"

Jill was tempted to stretch her hand out to touch Rachel's arm. She knew it was a good-friend thing to do. But instead, she let her fingers to fall back to the table. Rachel's twisted grin was bitter.

"I'm a tough old bird. I just wish I had extracted my own pound of flesh, if you know what I mean."

Jill didn't, but that was okay. She knew Rachel was working her way through the stages of grief and might be stuck in anger for a while. Who could blame her? She tried not to picture Alex's face as she looked across the table. After all, their situation was different. She wasn't planning on leaving Alex or anything. She was just …

"Fucking online dating sites," Rachel muttered.

"Excuse me?" Jill snapped back to the conversation.

"That son of a bitch had posted his profile on three online dating sites and was actively nailing anything in a skirt while we were still together. That's how he met Barbie."

Across the table, Rachel's moist eyes met Jill's.

"It's so cliché. Married man goes in search of a little something on the side. Lying about himself to get what he wants. Really, what kind of bastard does something like that?"

Jill shook her head and glanced over toward the windows in time to see Jamie follow Dana Evans out of the cafeteria. Her eyes bore a hole into the back of his striped Hugo Boss shirt.

What kind of bastard, indeed?

CHAPTER SIX

No smoking gun lurked in Natalie Watson's email account. Alex ran a hand across his tired eyes. He'd spent hours late into the previous night sifting through information on Natalie's computer, searching for some clue, some inkling into where she might have gone. To no avail.

Disappointment tasted as bitter as cold coffee. He was sure he'd find something on her hard drive. His instincts, typically dead-on, were telling him the secret to Natalie's disappearance lay somewhere in the online world. But so far, no dice. And no Natalie, either. It was as if she'd just vanished.

Although this was now officially a missing-persons case, with Jackson in charge, Alex couldn't leave it alone. He spent part of his morning talking to the principal of Ballard High School, lining up interviews with Natalie's teachers and some of the students.

Alex glanced at his watch and waited for the bell to ring as he stood outside the main entrance to the high school. He wanted to meet Emily Jenkins, Natalie's best friend, on neutral territory. After her adamant refusal to open up to him yesterday, he had decided to come alone. One on one, he might have more luck.

Pale November sunshine warmed his face. The smell of fried onions and bacon reminded him it was time to eat. With all respect to Jill's healthy-eating, no-skin-on-the-chicken mantra, a burger and a shake would taste mighty fine right about now, he decided.

A few minutes later the doors opened, and hordes of hungry students poured from the building, a torrent of under clad teenage girls and scruffy teenage boys. The mob streamed passed, and Alex searched for a familiar face. As the last few trickled out, he wondered if he'd missed her somehow. But then Emily trailed out of the building, walking apart from the crowd.

Emily wore a micro–denim skirt. Her chubby legs were clad in black tights that slid into a pair of low, combat-looking boots. The plunging neckline of her shirt revealed more than just her butterfly tattoo as she strode down the stairs, hands dangling loosely at her sides.

She spotted him and, angling her body away, stopped, waiting for the last of the students to filter past. Finally she looked up through the unruly fringe of her dark hair, lips twisted into a slight pout, and heaved a long, inevitable sigh.

"I don't suppose it's a coincidence that you're here," she said hopefully. A note of dark irony touched her voice. Alex smiled.

"I'm afraid not, Emily. Listen, I'm starving, so what do you say I buy you a burger and we talk?" He inclined his head toward the diner across the street and waited.

"I don't suppose you'll take no for an answer?"

"Well, we could talk before or after I eat. Your choice."

Emily did not say a word but turned instead in the direction of the crosswalk. Alex fell in step beside her. Her makeup was lighter today. Yesterday, her style bordered on Goth. But today, it seemed she was in the mood for something lighter. Her puffy eyes hinted at a restless night, and he wondered if Natalie's disappearance was wearing on her. He hoped it was and that it would provide him with an opening. At this point, it was obvious to him that Natalie's disappearance was not just a fit of teenage rebellion.

"How are you, Emily?"

They stepped over the thinning grass and onto the sidewalk. She shrugged without looking at him.

"Okay, I guess."

They found a booth at the back of the restaurant. The noisy chatter from the tables surrounding them provided an odd sense of privacy. A waitress stopped by to give their table a cursory wipe with a grimy cloth before taking their order.

Alex crossed his arms casually on the table and leaned forward, his eyes meeting Emily's. She looked away.

"So, Emily," he started in a quiet voice. "What can you tell me?"

A flurry of emotions crossed her face as she struggled to decide what to say, or perhaps what to feel. Finally, she sighed and shook her head.

"You know, Emily, secrets are funny things. I'm sure you don't want to betray your friend's trust. But I've got to tell you, some lies are deadly. And when it comes to finding Natalie, the sooner we know where she was going, the better."

Emily propped an elbow up on the table and rested her lips against her clenched fist for a long moment before she spoke.

"I don't know where she is," she finally blurted out in her gravelly voice. "But I do know where she was going. Well, sort of."

Alex nodded, a prickly sensation burning across the back of his neck. He remained perfectly, deliberately silent. A stream of questions queued up in his mind, but he stopped them before they escaped his lips, determined to listen.

It was a long time before she spoke again. When she did, her voice faltered, as if she didn't know quite where or how to begin.

"Natalie wasn't allowed to date. Her parents are kind of strict, and really, there wasn't anyone in school she had a thing for anyway. Boys."

Emily rolled her eyes in disgust.

"But there was someone," he prodded gently. Slowly, he cautioned himself. Too much pressure and she might shut down.

Emily turned to look out the window, and nodded.

"There was someone." Then she added quickly, "But I don't know who. I mean, I don't know his name."

"Do you know anything about him?"

She slouched back in the booth. A mist of tears clouded her eyes, and she stared hard at the empty table.

"Not much. I know she met him online. They chatted a few times, and she said that he was older. Liked motorcycles, you know?"

Alex's heart jolted as he got the first real lead in the case. He pulled out his notebook and started taking notes.

"Do you know how they met online?"

"Um, I'm not sure. A chat room maybe? She mentioned something about him a few weeks ago."

"Did they email?"

"I think so."

Alex frowned and considered this new information. He hadn't found anything unusual in her email correspondence. Surely he wouldn't have missed emails like this in his search. He'd need to look for secondary accounts. She might have accessed other accounts on another computer, at the school or library perhaps.

"Do you know his email handle?"

"Not really." Emily shrugged. "God. Natalie mentioned it once. It was stupid. Something to do with motorcycles, but I don't remember what it was."

"Did she chat a lot?" His pencil started to scratch on the paper as he focused on what she was saying.

"Sure, we all do. She used her email account."

Emily paused to take a sip from her Coke and then continued. "I could tell she was excited about him. She said something about meeting him for coffee on Saturday. Asked me to cover for her."

Alex stopped writing, fixing his piercing stare on Emily.

"Her email account?" Bingo. There it was. The missing piece.

"Sure. Free sign-up."

"How does she access it?"

"God, what do you mean?" she shook her head. "She logged onto it through her Me page." Emily rolled her eyes.

"But I looked and didn't find her on a Me site." The search Alex had made of all the social-networking sites had turned up nothing on Natalie.

"She didn't use her real name. She wasn't dumb. Her parents were just the type to go snooping around in her stuff. They're like that, you know? My mom wouldn't have a clue. But Natalie's parents ..." She trailed off and looked back at Alex. "God, she's smart with computers."

"What is the address she used?"

"Slipstream115@xmail.com." Emily shrugged, and a faint smile touched her lips. Alex's brows creased together in a frown, and he scribbled some notes. "Slipstream ... cycling jargon. That's pure Natalie—nothing flashy." Emily's voice trailed off.

Her fingers pressed against her lips, and Alex noticed the brutally short fingernails coated in a fresh layer of black nail polish, the evidence of her nail-biting habit effectively camouflaged.

The waitress stopped by the table to deposit their food and then skittered away. Emily reached for the ketchup and spent a long time creating a red pool beside the large order of fries heaped on her plate. The black-tipped fingers pinched together to capture a fry, then hesitated and fell back to the table.

"When she didn't call on Saturday night—" Her voice suddenly choked off. She stopped, cleared her throat with a wet, noisy sound, and continued. "I figured maybe things had gone well. She made me promise not to tell anyone. I thought maybe she had spent the night with him, and I didn't want to blow her cover."

Alex nodded as if in agreement. Misguided loyalty was something he understood. The fact that she was talking to him now, spilling Natalie's secret, was proof enough that her indifference yesterday had been a well-crafted act. She played the part so well, in fact, that he had to wonder what things in her life had caused her to shut down. He recalled the dirty kitchen, the half-empty vodka bottle, and her mother's watery expression. Compassion for the girl flooded through him.

As he silently reviewed the information Emily had provided, he found himself doodling on the page where he had written his notes. The face of a teenage girl quickly took shape, her features mostly hidden by an unruly fringe of bangs. Dark eyes downcast. Expression pensive.

Alex looked up and saw Emily studying the page, too, and his pencil stilled. He loved to draw, had ever since he was a kid. Even though the sketch was rough there was no mistaking Emily's face. He turned the page.

"Weren't you worried when you found out she didn't show up on Sunday?"

"Sure, but I thought she'd come home."

"Anything else you can tell me?"

"No," she said. "That's all I know." Her eyes met his. Fear glimmered in their depths. "Please find her."

Alex nodded and closed the notebook. He took a sip of his milkshake, then quietly thanked Emily. Hope fluttered within him for the first time all day. A secret meeting. An email account. It was a damned good place to start.

CHAPTER SEVEN

Jill Shannon's fingernails clicked against the hard shell of her computer's mouse. Jamie had been maddeningly unavailable. During the long week she spent in San Jose trying to corral the burgeoning number of project issues, he was holed up in meetings and otherwise occupied. Or so his administrative assistant claimed.

Lost in thought, she started at the sound of a knock on her door. Dana Evans glanced down at her through eyelashes so ridiculously thick, they had to be fake. She wore a knee-length black skirt, a sleeveless olive-green scoop-neck blouse, and high-heeled black boots. The look suited her, Jill grudgingly admitted to herself.

"Got a minute?" Evans asked.

Jill made no attempt to hide the scowl on her face.

"Sure."

Dana strode in and closed the door behind her. A nauseating cloud of floral perfume filled the office, almost choking Jill. A closed-door meeting? Her eyebrows rose in surprise. Jill swiveled in her chair, facing her unwelcome guest.

"I came to apologize. My feedback the other day was rather blunt."

Jill nodded. Blunt was one way to put it. She had other words for it.

"It's fine."

"So, that's it. We're square?" Dana asked.

"Sure," Jill said, hitching her shoulders in a casual shrug. Whatever. She had no interest in airing her opinion on Evans's unprofessional behavior. That was Jamie's job.

Still, the way Dana stared at her caused her hackles to rise. There was more to Dana's visit. She could feel it. Whatever it was, she wished Dana would just cut to the chase and get the hell out of her office. The woman gave her the willies.

"Is that it?" Jill prompted, keeping her gaze locked on Dana.

Dana smiled then, a rather unpleasant smile. Though at first glance she'd thought Dana attractive, on closer inspection Jill found the woman's features coarse, her hazel eyes a little too far apart. Dana spent hours at the gym, no doubt about it. The thick muscles of her arms testified to the number of pull-ups she could do. It was all a little mannish for Jill, who preferred her own sleek runner's build.

"Jamie thought I'd upset you."

Jamie. The hairs on Jill's arms prickled. She forced a smile of her own.

"So Jamie told you to apologize? Do you always do what he tells you to?"

Dana's expression hardened. Jill could see the cracks in her makeup as her mouth flattened into an angry line.

"I'm not his lap dog."

"What are you then?"

Dana cocked her head. Wry amusement lit the woman's hazel eyes. A smile curved her thick lips.

"A colleague."

"Nothing more?"

"Why do you care?"

"I don't," Jill lied. "I just want to understand the political landscape."

"Hmmm," Dana said, skeptically.

With slow, deliberate strides, she sauntered toward the door. Her hand gripped the knob, and then, turning back toward Jill, she paused.

"Just a little word to the wise about Jamie," she said, her voice dipping low, into a conspiratorial purr.

"What's that?" Jill asked, feigning boredom.

"Jamie's fickle," she answered, and turned on her heel.

Jill stood up and watched Dana's retreating form slither down the hall. Was that a warning? Was Dana trying to mark her territory? The idea rankled Jill, and she decided there was only one way to find out.

Her heels clicking on the tile floor, Jill stopped outside Jamie's door. He looked up at her soft knock and cast a subtle glance over her shoulder, as if checking the hallway to see if they were alone.

"Jill."

"Mind if I interrupt?" Her smile was disarming.

"I've got ten minutes," he said, letting her know that it was not an open-ended invitation.

With a nod, she entered, closing the door softly behind her. He swung his chair around to face her, and her heart jolted in response to the intensity of his blue eyes. There was something electric about his presence that set her on edge.

"Apologies. I haven't had much time for you this week. My schedule has been a bloody mess."

Her lips twisted as she stared at him. His attempt to disarm her was not going to work.

"You've been busy," she said,

"It's been a right mad week." He glanced past her toward the door, as if worried that they might be interrupted, before returning to her face. "So what can I do for you?"

"I just had a visit from Ms. Evans."

"Oh, good. Did the two of you patch things up?"

Jill frowned. Patch things up? He made it sound like they were two girls having a catfight on a playground, not grown women. Professionals. Colleagues. Would he have phrased it this way if they had been men? She thought not. An awkward silence stretched between them, and a bitter smile crossed Jill's face.

"Well, she apologized for being blunt, if that's what you mean."

"Good. Dana is very results driven. She's a little too aggressive at times."

"Aggressive." Jill cocked an eyebrow. "She's that, all right, but I don't think she came to my office to apologize."

"Oh?"

"Time for a little truth now, Jamie. Is there something going on between the two of you?"

Jamie's gaze shot past her. His eyes narrowed, and she saw a flicker of irritation flare in his blue eyes.

"I'm sure I don't know what you mean," he said, the last vestige of warmth stripped from his voice.

Jill inclined her head slightly, her eyebrows arched, her expression knowing.

"Don't play dumb. You're a smart guy, it should be easy to figure out." Sarcasm spilled easily from her lips, and she felt a bitter pool of acid bubble at the pit of her stomach.

Jamie cocked his head as he regarded her with a sour look. She raised her chin, refusing to let him intimidate her.

"I'm not engaging in this conversation, Jillian."

Jillian. He was pissed. He only used her full name when he was angry. If she had any remaining doubts about how he felt, all she had to do was look at his face. Anger glittered in his hard eyes. Although part of her knew she should stop pushing, she couldn't. He was going to tell her the truth. He owed her that much.

"Why not? Too personal?"

Jamie's face flushed scarlet as he stared at her, the thin veneer of tolerance stripped away. She knew at once that she had pushed him too far.

"Personal. Inappropriate. Take your pick." His words were clipped and icy.

"Is it?" She crossed her legs, eyes defiant. She knew she shouldn't push any further, but she couldn't stop the flood of resentment she felt from spilling over. She already played second fiddle to Alex's career. She wasn't going to stand in line for him behind another woman, especially not a bitch like Dana Evans.

Jamie leaned so close she could smell his cologne. Leather and soap. Unbidden images sprang to mind—nights in her hotel room, the taste of his mouth on hers. His voice grew dangerously quiet.

"This isn't the place."

"Then when? I haven't seen you all week." Her voice bumped up a notch in volume, and she cringed inwardly, hearing the whiny tone of a disgruntled teenager. He shot a meaningful glance over her shoulder, and she said, more softly, "You've canceled our one-on-one. You've avoided me all week. Just when are we supposed to talk?"

"I have a video conference with the team in India this evening, but why don't we meet for dinner afterward? Say around eight-thirty at A. P. Stumps? We'll get a booth, have some wine, and talk things through. Sound good?"

His smile was disarming, and despite herself she felt the frigid wall between them shift. This was more like it. Maybe she was overreacting. Maybe Rachel's paranoia about cheating men was rubbing off on her. Maybe Dana Evans wanted Jamie back and was trying to scare off the competition.

"I'll wear something nice," she added with a wicked twinkle in her eye.

Jamie nodded and gave her a tight smile.

"Lovely," he said.

CHAPTER EIGHT

The five-degree drop in temperature was welcome, Alex noted as he opened the door to the lab. The sophisticated cooling system hummed, pumping out cold air to compensate for the cluster of computer servers and workstations running on overdrive.

Alex strode purposefully to the back, anxious to get an update on Natalie's secret email account. She had been missing almost two days now, and every hour was critical. He went in search of Kris Thompson, the unit's top technical guy—*girl*, he corrected himself. Too young to officially bear the title of Guru, Kris was a recent MIT graduate and the most gifted hacker Alex had ever met, although her technical prowess was overshadowed by her innate shyness.

Kris was as straight-laced as they came. Raised Mormon, she had broken with the church and her family when she left for college, but the deep-rooted, conservative morals remained. Her sharp mind was masked behind a shy smile and an assortment of shapeless sweaters. Alex sometimes wondered if her dedication to her job was at the expense of her social life. Or in place of one.

Kris looked up as Alex approached.

"What did we get from Natalie's hard drive?"

"I found two email accounts. The default one you've already seen. Nothing of interest, just friends, school assignments, the usual. The second was linked to her Me account." This news confirmed what Emily had told him.

Kris's mouth was set in a grim line. "There's a handful of emails from a guy who goes by the handle '47Knucklehead.'"

"Doesn't exactly roll off the tongue." Alex rubbed his chin. "What does it mean?"

Kris stared at her screen as she shrugged. "I'm guessing that it's not a nickname from an overly critical parent. I've done a lookup on the term, and aside from the obvious, there are a few other references. A kids' clothing line, brand name for acoustic-guitar strings ..."

"You're kidding, right?" asked another technician whose workstation bordered Kris's. Terry Parrish raked his long hair out of his face and smirked at Alex.

"Don't you two *knuckleheads* know anything about motorcycles?

"Okay, *Motor-head*, enlighten us."

Alex sighed. Terry delighted in needling Kris. Mostly, she ignored him, but now her eyes filled with a look of pure irritation. With a cocky half smile, he angled his chair toward hers.

"What's it worth to you?" Terry's suggestive smile met Kris's dark frown.

"Come on, Terry. Out with it," Alex said, the warning evident in his tone. This wasn't the time for grandstanding. Terry sighed, looking over at Alex.

"The knucklehead was an engine designed for a Harley-Davidson motorcycle."

"No shit?"

"No shit. It was named the knucklehead because of the distinctive shape of the rocker covers. You know what rocker covers are, right?" Terry flashed a condescending grin. "They stopped making the knucklehead in 1947 and replaced it with the panhead engine in '48," Terry added, continuing to recite the history of Harley-Davidson engines. "Followed by the ever-popular shovelhead in '66."

Alex tuned out the running commentary on the history of Harley-Davidson engine types and verbalized his train of thought.

"So, if Knucklehead has one of these motorcycles ..."

"Hogs," Terry corrected. "You've got to respect the classics, man. There was the '65 Mustang, the '62 Corvette, and the '47 Knucklehead. It was the best of its class."

"Right. Hogs," Alex said, barely skipping a beat. "Can we use this to narrow the search?"

"'Fraid not," Terry said, eyes darting back to his computer screen in a reflexive motion before settling back on Alex. "There are enough of them floating around that it wouldn't pinpoint him. But we could use it as a cross-check once we have a little more to go on."

"What do you say? Want to go for a ride?" Terry winked at Kris and patted the motorcycle helmet beside his monitor.

"Shut up," she snapped, and turned away.

"Good God, woman, you have a mouth like a sailor."

"Are you still talking?" Kris asked, stubbornly staring at her computer screen.

"Terry," Alex suppressed a smile and shook his head.

"What about the IP trace?" he asked Kris

"Sadly for us, the guy's no dumbass. He's using a software program to spoof the IP address so we can't pinpoint the location of where the email was sent. At least not yet. I'm still working on it. We'll need a warrant to trace his identity through his ISP. I'll start the paperwork." She adjusted her glasses with a quick, unconscious movement and peered back at Alex.

"Son of a bitch," Alex grumbled. He knew there were lots of ways someone could change the email header information to substitute the IP address of the originating computer for a phony one. The email programs capable of manipulating a user's IP address ran the gamut from simple to very sophisticated. Alex hoped that their suspect wasn't too smart.

If the guy took the time to spoof his IP address, he would bet money that this was no innocent encounter. He was trying to cover his tracks. Pedophiles were notoriously paranoid—with reason. There were ways to penetrate this type of online smoke screen, but they took time. And Natalie didn't have time.

"Here's a copy of their email exchanges." Kris handed Alex a file folder.

"Does the pattern match any of our known operators?"

"This guy's new. I haven't found anything using OPPS."

Kris inclined her head slightly as she met Alex's grim stare. The Online Predator Profiling System database was one of the department's best tools for identifying and apprehending online predators, and as he pondered this development, Kris continued.

"I do have some good news, though. They were planning to meet for coffee in Fremont on Saturday afternoon."

"That's something. Fremont. A Harley-Davidson would stick out like a nun in a brothel there."

"You sure about that?"

Terry peeked around his monitor as he continued. "Harleys are pretty common, I'm just saying. There are a lot of doctors and lawyers who drive them, not just the outlaw biker types you see in movies."

"Hippies don't drive hogs, and the IT crowd along the canal drive Ducatis," Alex sighed.

"Maybe." Terry's shrugged, sounding unconvinced.

"I'll keep following the IP trail," Kris said.

"Call me as soon as you get something."

"Sure thing, Boss."

Alex thumbed through the email printouts on his way back to his desk. Tossing the file on top of the already cluttered surface, he ignored the thick stack of pink while-you-were-out messages. He knew what they were—a long list of updates he needed to provide on other cases. But they could wait. Instead, he dialed Jackson's extension. After four rings, he was transferred through to voicemail.

"I've got an update on the Watson case. Call me when you get this."

He hung up, leaned back in his chair, and studied the emails more closely. The first few were "get to know you" types. Innocent enough on the surface. Natalie sounded older than sixteen. Good vocabulary, prose free from the typical slang. No *dudes* or *likes* to be found. No telltale IM colloquialisms. The emails to Natalie were simply signed "J." No name.

After the initial flurry, the tone between them changed and became more familiar. Knucklehead asked questions about where she went to school and what she liked to do. So he knew that she was a high school student, but he made no specific age inquiries.

Alex rubbed his chin as he continued to read. Knucklehead requested a picture, which she sent, and although he was definitely older, he did not come across as menacing. He wanted to win Natalie's trust before he tried to set up a meeting.

Smart. Not too fast, not taking a chance in scaring her off. He'd probably done this before, and it was also quite likely, given the standard pattern of pedophiles, that Natalie was not the only girl he was stalking.

This thought chilled Alex. With each passing hour that Natalie was missing, the possibility of her not making it home safely to her parents became more real. Natalie sounded like a shy teenage girl who wanted to get noticed, not a girl trying to escape her life.

The last email was dated the day of her disappearance and fixed the location of the meeting at a coffee shop in Fremont. His telephone rang, and the display showed Jackson's extension. He picked up the phone without identifying himself.

"Meet me downstairs in five. Coffee's on me."

CHAPTER NINE

This was not the type of place he would expect to find an online sexual predator stalking a teenage girl, Alex thought as he stepped through the doorway of the Fremont Coffee House. The converted craftsman was cut up into small rooms crammed full of retro-hippie types bent over their laptop screens. The crowd seemed a little old for Natalie. He doubted that she was a regular, but that might work in his favor. With any luck, someone would remember seeing her here on Saturday. Each passing hour since he had taken the case made the clock in Alex's head tick louder. They needed a break. And soon.

Jackson Levy followed, angling his bulky frame though the narrow front door. With his close-cropped hair and mahogany complexion, Jackson tended to cut a wide swath through crowds, and this was no exception. Alex didn't know whether it was his size or his get-the-hell-out-of-my-way attitude, but there were times when it sure came in handy.

"I should have worn my goddamned Apple T-shirt." Jackson's thick voice was a low growl.

"I didn't think they came in your size."

"What can I get for you?" the guy behind the counter asked. Alex flashed his badge.

"Detective Shannon, Seattle PD. This is Detective Levy. We're looking for someone."

The girl working the cash register looked over sharply now, and Alex showed them Natalie's picture.

"Have you seen her? We think she was in here on Saturday afternoon."

The guy shook his head, bored brown eyes taking a cursory glance at the photograph.

"She's not a regular, and I didn't work on Saturday."

The girl studied the photograph a few seconds longer. Her face twisted into a thoughtful expression.

"Is she in trouble?" Her eyes met Alex's.

"Did you work on Saturday?"

"Yeah, I opened." Her words were clipped, guarded.

"Any chance you saw her?"

Jackson flashed a brilliant white smile, rolling out his best "charming guy" routine. He loomed over the young woman, and Alex saw the tight line of her mouth soften. She glanced back at the picture, her eyes narrowing.

"Maybe. It was a busy afternoon, lots of people, but I think I waited on someone who looked like her. Hard to say for sure, though."

The bell sounded as the door opened again. A cluster of caffeine-deprived customers pushed through the door, adding to the line behind them.

"Around what time?" Alex persisted. The guy behind the counter shot them a meaningful look.

"Come on, man. There are people waiting." The guy leaned against the espresso machine.

"And this is official police business. Got a problem with that?" Alex leaned further over the counter. Needing to get as much information as quickly as possible overrode the need to satisfy the geeks jonesing for caffeine.

The girl shot her coworker a sharp glance.

"Let's take it over there." She pointed to a stand-up bar near the side door.

"She came in around three, I think." The girl looked back at the line of customers.

"Was she alone?"

"Yeah, that's it." She snapped her bony fingers and took the picture from Alex for a closer look. "She came in alone. But when I looked up a little later, I'm pretty sure she was sitting over there with some guy." She gestured toward a small table by the window in the next room. "That's what got my attention."

Alex's heart began to beat faster, and he traded a quick look with Jackson. Could she describe Knucklehead?

"Why?" Alex held her gaze as she considered his question.

"He looked a little rough around the edges. Not the type we usually get in here."

"What can you tell us about him?" Alex prompted.

"It's not like he asked me out," she said, rolling her eyes. "I didn't get a really good look at him. He was sitting with his back to the counter. He was older than she was, with shoulder-length blond hair. Not as light as hers, more of a dirty blond. I remember a leather jacket. Black. I think it was black."

"Any patches or insignias on the jacket?" Possible gang affiliation Alex wondered. She shrugged.

"Don't think so."

"Anything else you remember about him?"

She placed her folded hands on her hips and shot Alex a give-me-a-break kind of look.

"Do you know how many people come in here every day?"

Alex sighed.

"Did he drive a motorcycle?"

"Not in here, he didn't," she quipped, her expression part playful, part exasperated. "Look, the door was closed, and there's a lot of street noise. I didn't see a helmet, but I wasn't really looking either."

"Did they seem friendly?"

"I guess so. I didn't watch them or anything. Like I said, it was busy."

"Anything else you can tell me?"

"When I took my break at four, they were gone."

"Any chance you've got video?"

"Does this look like the kind of place that has video?"

"Right," Alex said. "Just a few more questions, then I'll let you get back to work. Did anyone see a bike outside?"

"I told you, the door was closed." She folded her arms across her chest and cast a not-so-subtle look at the clock behind the counter.

"No, I mean a bicycle. A black Trek," Alex said.

The girl shot a look over at her shoulder toward her coworker, and Alex saw something unspoken pass between them. Her coworker blushed before looking away. "Uh …"

Bingo, Alex thought.

"Did you see a bicycle like that outside? Maybe when you left?" he asked, his pulse picking up as he focused back on her.

"No, but …" she trailed off, and shot a meaningful glance at her coworker.

"How about you?" Alex asked turning back toward the counter.

"No," he said quickly, staring hard at the girl. She placed her hands on her hips and fixed him with her best maternal "Don't lie" look. Alex noted that the barista, no longer bored, was standing at full alert.

"Sunday morning when I went to the dumpster to throw out some trash, I saw a bike propped up against the trees. Figured someone was trying to get rid of it. Rode it home after my shift was over. I wasn't trying to steal it or anything." His white face lost even more color, making his skin appear almost translucent as he grimaced.

"Is it here?" Alex asked, equal measures of anticipation and dread mingled in his gut. Reluctantly, the kid nodded. Alex caught Jackson's eye as the barista led them out of the shop, through the side door, and to the alley. If indeed it was Natalie's bike, this wasn't good news.

Sunlight filtered through the trees at the back. The canopy of leaves created a pool of shade for the dumpster. Jackson squatted down beside the bike and read the serial number. Alex cross-referenced it against the one Natalie's father had provided.

"It's a match. Looks like you're going to have to walk home tonight," Alex said. After a philosophical shrug that seemed to say "Easy come, easy go," the kid wandered back inside.

Alex dipped his head a fraction, taking in this new piece of information. There was no doubt left in his mind as to whether Natalie had been abducted. There was no way she would leave her bike back here. According to Tom, it was too important.

With grim expressions, they searched the small wooded area behind the coffee shop for any additional sign of Natalie and found nothing. Staring at the green Dumpster, Jackson flipped open the lid and watched the flies take flight, a look of disgust crossing his broad face. Alex wrinkled his nose. The smell of rotting garbage filled the alley.

"I wonder when it was last emptied," Alex said, contemplating the garbage bags piled up above the Dumpster's two-thirds marker. "I think it's your turn." His eyes locked with Jackson's.

"Didn't I do the one over in Pioneer Square?"

"You're forgetting Belltown," Alex pointed out.

With a resigned look, Jackson scaled the side and jumped in as Alex pulled on a pair of latex gloves with a telltale snap.

"Jesus Christ," Jackson muttered from within the Dumpster, knee-deep in garbage. "They sure don't show this in any of the recruitment brochures." He lobbed another slick garbage bag over the lip of the dumpster, and it landed beside Alex with a wet thud. "I'll never get this shit off my shoes, and the smell …"

Alex probed through the contents of the bag with his gloved hands. Coffee grounds, food scraps, stir sticks, paper napkins. No additional signs of Natalie so far.

"You want to trade out?"

The stench of rotten banana peels and mildew turned his stomach. He counted his blessings that the Dumpster was in the shade. If it were basking in the full glory of the sun, the bugs and stench would be worse.

"I wouldn't want you cybercrime geeks to get your hands dirty."

The good natured barb rumbled from within the Dumpster, and Alex couldn't suppress a grin.

"Aw, is Princess getting dirty?"

"Fuck off, Shannon."

A little more rustling from within the Dumpster before Jackson's head popped up. His jaw was set in a grim line as he held up a black backpack. Alex felt as if he had been kneed in the guts as he dropped the sack of garbage and held his hands out.

Jackson tossed him the bag and climbed out of the Dumpster. Alex pulled on fresh gloves and was already checking the contents by the time Jackson reached him. Novel, notebook, pens, and a small purse were in the main compartment. The wallet contained some cash and a student ID. Natalie Watson's face smiled up at them.

"Damn it," Alex swore softly as he handed the ID to Jackson and searched the other compartments of the backpack.

Alex stopped, and he sat back on his heels as he rooted through the bag. "No cell phone," he said. Jackson crouched down beside him.

"Do you think she still has it on her?"

"Phone records show no outgoing calls since Saturday afternoon. We couldn't ping it."

Standing up, he took another look around, his eyes slowly combing the area. Reflected sunlight winked at him from between the stairs. Stepping closer, Alex saw a discarded pop can.

"Shit," he said and was about to turn when he saw something else. Pushing the can aside, he pulled out a cell phone. The outside casing was cracked, and it was dead.

"Damn," Jackson muttered.

Turning it over, Alex checked to see if the battery was intact. It was missing. Had Knucklehead removed it? It was a Samsung Galaxy. Same model as his. With any luck, it would still run. He popped the battery out of his phone and placed it in the one he'd found. A quick push of the power button and the splintered screen display came to life. The two detectives smiled. "Let's hear it for hardware."

There was no access code on the phone, and Alex quickly scanned the list of recent numbers that had been called. He recognized Natalie's home number right away, alongside a few that he did not. He would cross-reference them against the phone records once he got back to the station.

On a hunch, he took a look through the directory of photographs. The most recent photo was taken on Saturday, a partial shot of a man's face framed by shoulder-length dirty-blond hair. Well, well, who did we have here?

"Hello, Knucklehead," Alex said.

CHAPTER TEN

Jill perched on a stool in the restaurant bar and glanced at her watch. She was right on time, and Jamie, as usual, was running late.

The bartender deposited a vodka martini, straight up with two olives, on the napkin in front of her. She nodded her thanks with a practiced smile that, while playful, was not too inviting. Looking down at the drink, she could feel his eyes linger on her bare shoulders. The black halter-style dress she was wearing exposed her back to the cool evening air.

Scanning the crowded restaurant, she noted that it was busy for a Thursday night. The place oozed with the kind of old-boys'-club charm that appealed to the clusters of businessmen who lined the booths. The supercharged atmosphere may have explained why it was one of Jamie's favorite places. The scent of power and affluence blended perfectly with the smell of prime steaks on the grill, awakening Jill's appetite. She picked at the bowl of nuts on the bar to tide herself over as she waited.

Two businessmen entered, settling onto stools beside her. Their conversation centered on Monday night's 49ers game and the team's chances of securing a spot in the playoffs. Alex was a big football fan, and sports talk was the spit that greased the wheels of the business world. She could play that game, too.

"Their chances would be better if they had a broader offensive strategy than giving the ball to their running back. What's his name? Frank Gore?" Jill said, snapping her fingers as his name rolled off her lips.

The two businessmen looked over at her, obvious surprise written clearly on their faces. The younger of the two men's lips twitched into a smile. Mr. Tall-Dark-and-Handsome, with an athletic build and dark eyes. Engaging. Nice suit. *He's trouble,* she thought.

"You may have a point there, but we've got a killer defense this year."

"A great defense doesn't win championships. But hey, what do I know?" she asked, taking a sip of her martini.

"And you are ...?" the older man asked. A smile creased the corners of his brown eyes.

"A Seahawks fan."

"Oh man, I should have guessed," the younger man groaned with a good-natured roll of his eyes.

His cell phone went off, and as he reached to answer it, Jill glanced back over her shoulder toward the door. Still no sign of Jamie, she surmised as she drained the last of her drink. She looked around for the bartender, hoping to catch his eye, but he was busy serving patrons at the other end of the bar. Her fingernails drummed the empty glass.

"Someone is in trouble," the younger man beside her said, cell phone now resting on the bar. His friend had vacated his stool, leaving him alone with Jill, and he glanced over at her with a smile.

"Just running late," she shrugged. Her fingers tightened on the coaster.

"Right," he said as if he didn't quite believe her. He nodded toward the empty glass in front of her. "Can I buy you another while you wait?"

Jill hesitated for a moment before tilting her head with a smile. What was the harm? He might turn out to be a fun distraction, and besides, it might needle Jamie to have another man buy her a drink. After all, he was making her wait.

"Why not? Dirty martini—"

"Straight up with two olives. Got it." He winked and signaled the bartender.

"You don't miss much."

"I'm into details." His shrug was casual, and despite herself she had to admire his easy confidence.

With fresh drinks in front of them, Jill sat back in her barstool and tried to relax, but she was keenly aware of each second that ticked by. Jamie's meeting must have gone late. Damn Rachel for planting the seeds of doubt. Dana's pretty face stayed rooted in her brain.

"Thanks." She tipped the glass toward the man beside her in a salute.

"My pleasure." He sipped his bourbon and water. "I'm Brent."

She shook his outstretched hand and felt hers engulfed in his firm grip. "Jill."

"Nice to meet you, Jill." His warm smile enlivened his dark eyes, and his low, velvety-smooth voice pleased her ear.

Jill swirled the olives around in her drink, deliberately breaking eye contact. Oh, yes, he had charm all right. Brent looked like the kind of guy who was used to winning. Confident, but not cocky. It was a charismatic combination.

"Whoever he is, he should know better than to keep you waiting."

Jill chuckled. "Yes, he certainly should. I'm not known for my patience."

"Who needs patience when you have so many other lovely attributes?" His look was suddenly intimate, and her defenses shot off a warning flare. He had just crossed the line. Too bad, really. Playful banter aside, this situation could turn problematic in a heartbeat. It was time to shut him down.

Jill's smile deepened as she leaned dangerously close to him. She concocted a look that was part conspiratorial, and part naughty. Taking her bait with a knowing grin, Brent leaned toward her, their arms almost touching on the bar. She could feel the heat from his body and the crisp, sweet scent of his cologne. Again she detected his total confidence. She looked up, and her eyes met his in an unflinching stare.

"You're an inventive guy, Brent. Smart, creative, observant. Right?"

"So I'm told."

"The kind of guy who doesn't miss much?"

"True."

"If that's the case, I have to wonder ... Is that the best line you could come up with? Really?"

She reached her hand across to rest casually on his arm for a moment, showing off her wedding ring to its best advantage.

"And I have to believe that a smart guy like you would not consciously hit on a married woman. What would your mother say?"

Brent's laugh was good-natured. He sat back in his stool, angling his gaze to the television screen perched high at the corner of the bar. *Message received.* A few moments passed in silence before he turned back toward her.

"You caught me." He smiled, cheeks slightly pink. "Sure, I noticed the ring, but you can't blame a guy for trying."

Jill straightened, swirling her olives. If she had a dime for every guy that had tried to pick her up, she'd be a rich woman. As if she wanted the attention. What was it about a woman alone in a bar that drew men like flies to honey? And a married woman ... She glanced down at her ring and stilled her fingers.

A married woman. She was married to Alex, and Alex was married to his job. While Jamie ... well, he certainly hadn't picked her up in a bar. Their long-standing flirtation had bubbled over into something more a few months ago, bringing some spark back into her life. But maybe for Jamie, it was all about the conquest. Now that he had her ...

Brent's cell phone rang again, interrupting her thoughts. Jill watched him pick it up, check the call display, and push a button to make the ringing stop. Reaching into his pocket, he deposited some cash on the bar before glancing back at Jill. His look was keen, his voice velvety smooth as he leaned in.

"If you don't mind my saying so, Jill, I don't think it's your husband that you're here to meet."

Jill arched her eyebrows, feigning surprise. "Really?"

"Really. See, it's a Thursday night, not exactly a date night for a married couple, and dressed like that, I'm willing to bet that you're not waiting for your husband."

"Whatever." She waved a dismissive hand, not missing his triumphant smile.

"My friend says that women are like parking stalls. Some are taken, some are empty, and some are handicapped. Which one are you?"

With a quick nod to the bartender, he let his gaze linger on Jill for another moment before leaving. Jill glanced back at her empty glass, her mouth feeling suddenly dry.

After ordering her third martini, she checked the time. Jamie was now a full forty-five minutes late. Her cheeks flushed, and she spun her watch face around her slender wrist so it could no longer mock her. Sipping her drink, she studiously avoided making eye contact with any of the bar's patrons and worked out her next move.

She fished the cell phone from her pocket and hit speed dial.

One. Two. Three rings. She waited. On the sixth ring, Jamie's voicemail picked up. The familiar voice cut through her as she was encouraged to leave a message. *A message. As if.* She slapped the phone down on the cardboard coaster beside her drink.

Draining the contents of the martini glass slowly, she left the two olives for last. Had he made the date intentionally planning not to show? Or had something else come up? Something better? Or someone. Jill's simmering anger bubbled over.

The bartender paused in front of her. "Would you like another?"

"No thanks," she said hastily and climbed off the bar stool. Pulling some cash out of her wallet, she tossed it onto the bar. "But if a British guy comes in looking for me, tell him he's too fucking late. I'll deal with him tomorrow."

"Yes, Ma'am," the bartender said, with a slanted smile and a mock salute.

***

Jill stepped out into the cool night air. Glancing around at the busy street, she saw cars speed by in both directions. Pedestrians passed her as she stood on the sidewalk. She felt light-headed from downing three martinis on an empty stomach. The air felt good on her bare skin as she turned on her heel and walked the six blocks back to the hotel. Screw the taxi, screw the blisters from the stiletto heels. The walk would do her good, help blow off some steam.

Covering the blocks quickly with her long strides, she ignored the blatant stares as she passed. The question of what to do about Jamie circled around in her head. Should she forget about him and go to bed, or should she confront him for standing her up?

She wasn't the type to run away, and waiting for him had gotten her nowhere this week. As she neared the hotel, she made up her mind. She was going to go find him.

***

Jill drove the sleek Lexus sedan the short distance to the ZyraNet office, barely aware of the traffic or stoplights she passed along the way. A quick tour of the parking lot showed no sign of the familiar black BMW. After circling the lot twice, she gave up.

Had there actually been a meeting, or had he lied to placate her? It was time to find out. Tires squealed as she pulled out into traffic, heading toward the freeway.

Jamie lived in Palo Alto in an upscale condo building across from Johnson Park.

Jill took a left onto Waverly, parking down the street from the attractive four-story building. Jamie occupied the large corner unit on the top floor, facing the park. She turned the car off and settled into her seat, determined to wait it out.

Time ticked by slowly and she consulted the clock, peering out the car window at the darkened windows above. No lights on at ten o'clock.

Twenty minutes passed. Just as her resolve was about to crumble, she saw Jamie's black BMW swoop gracefully past and enter the building's underground parking garage.

Jill's heart thudded painfully in her chest as she watched the taillights of the car disappear from view. She steeled herself for the inevitable confrontation.

Light spilled from the condo's windows, and she reached for the door handle. Looking up, Jill froze. Jamie stood by the couch, face angled away, toward someone else. A woman approached, winding her arms around his neck, pushing up onto her toes for a kiss. Jill stared up though the car window, instantly recognizing the woman. Dana Evans. Jill squeezed her eyes shut.

Anger flooded through her like the tide. Her stomached roiled, and she felt nauseated. Jamie had used her. He had lied to her. Whatever game he was playing had to come to an end. She wouldn't allow him to treat her like garbage. She deserved better.

Looking up, Jill saw the lights in Jamie's bedroom flick on. Unwelcome images flooded Jill's head, a tangle of memories and projections of intertwined limbs and heat. She pressed the palms of her hands against her closed eyelids in a vain attempt to blot them out, but they refused to leave.

She hated herself for trusting him. A bitter cold bloomed in her heart as she slammed the gearshift into drive and sped back to the freeway.

Nobody made a fool of her and got away with it. The affair may be over, but Jamie wasn't going to get away with ending it so easily.

She'd go after the one thing that he cared about most.

CHAPTER ELEVEN

Jill crossed the main entrance of the ZyraNet building with long, purposeful strides, a coffee cup clutched in her hand. Sunglasses muted the glare of the morning sun through the glass panes. The warm marble tile floor gave off the subtle scent of lemon polish as she wedged her way through the crowd and moved to the rear of the elevator, studiously avoiding eye contact. The image of Jamie embracing Dana was still etched into her brain, and she took a sip of the strong black brew in a vain attempt to clear her head. Sleep would help more than caffeine, but there was no time for that.

Pushing through the door to her office and tossing her laptop bag into a chair, Jill paused to stare sightlessly out the window. Dana Evans. Surely Jamie would at least have the balls to tell her in person it was over. Maybe that was what he was planning to do last night before he lost his nerve. Or got busy, so to speak. She slammed the cup down on her desk and contemplated her next move.

Jamie valued his career above all else—savoring the position and power it offered him. Given his broad sphere of influence within the company, there really was only one sure way to bring him down. A harassment claim would bring his grandiose plans screeching to a halt and quite possibly end his career at ZyraNet. But how safe was it to make those types of allegations? What was her exposure?

Jill sat contemplating the question when a brief knock sounded on her office door. She glanced up and her heart took a painful stutter step. Jamie's appearance was as unexpected as it was unwelcome.

"Got a minute?"

Jill forced a smile.

"For you? Of course."

Jamie closed the office door. Strolling to the window, he propped casually against the desk, hands stuffed casually in his pockets. Tension coiled in Jill like a spring as she waited for him to speak.

"I'm sorry about last night."

"Meeting ran late?"

"Right, you know how those meetings go. Once you start digging into the squishy details, they drag on and on." His smile was meant to be disarming, but the intended effect was lost on her.

"Really? Where was the meeting?"

"Here of course. Why?" Jamie widened his stance. His leg brushed Jill's knee, and she rolled back, breaking contact between them.

"Funny, I was working late, too, and I didn't see your car."

Jill cocked her head as she watched him, wondering if he was planning to lie his way out of the situation or simply stretch the truth, whatever *that* was.

"You must have missed it. I parked on the other side of the building."

"Really?" She stared at him. Anger burned through her patience, and she decided to cut to the chase. "Look, why don't you save me the bullshit story about how the dog ate your homework and just tell me what is going on."

Jamie's eyes widened in surprise, and then his expression turned cold.

"Oh, poor Jill," he said, in a mocking tone. "Did you wait long at the restaurant all by your lonesome?"

"Fuck you." The words were out before she could stop them, and for a second, she saw a chilly smile touch his lips. In a flash it was gone, and his expression grew stern.

"Lower your voice," Jamie commanded. "You would do well to remember that you still report to me, and that there's more at stake here than a half-rate affair."

"Are you threatening me?" His words stung, and her anger turned colder, darker. She eyed him with the deadly focus of a cobra.

"Do I need to?" he asked.

She sensed a power shift between them as he regained the upper hand. He leaned back, a smug smile on his face. He let the words settle between them, pregnant with meaning. Their eyes clashed as he shrugged his shoulders.

"You're a smart girl, Jillian. Smart enough to know that this is not a game you want to play. Make no mistake about it, you will lose."

Jill crossed her legs. She struggled to control her anger. He'd used her. He'd lied to her. If he was just honest about things, well ... she might still hate him, but she could respect him a whole lot more. But lying and stringing her along was a cowardly thing to do.

She had to think. Her next move had to be smart.

"I wouldn't be so sure you hold all the cards."

"Really? What do you think you have?"

His expression was a perfect blend of amusement and contempt. It made Jill's blood boil. It took all of her self-control not to lash out at him but rather to play it cool.

"How do you think HR would respond to a story about a senior manager using his position to pressure a female reporting to him into a compromising position?"

Jill remembered her conversation with Rachael and Rachael's insinuations about Jamie's reputation. Jamie's stoic expression faltered, and anger burned in his blue eyes.

"That's a load of bullocks, and we both know it."

A slow, satisfied smile spread across Jill's face. Her blow had landed a direct hit where he was most vulnerable. If all Jamie cared about was his fucking job, he wouldn't want to risk it over an office affair.

"Prove it," she said. "Who do you think most people would believe? Me, or you?"

"I'd be careful about what you say and to whom. Your career may depend on it."

His voice was dangerously quiet, and he paused, choosing his next words carefully.

"You may think that you control this situation, Jillian, but trust me when I say that your hand isn't nearly as good as you think it is. Besides, you've got more to lose than just your job. I wonder what your husband would think if he knew the truth."

A stab of fear pierced Jill's cool composure, and she stiffened.

"You wouldn't dare tell Alex. Admitting the affair will damage your career more than mine," Jill said. "Forcing me into a sexual relationship would not only get you fired, but would also destroy any prospects you have for climbing the corporate ladder. For me, it would be an unfortunate situation that I need to put behind me. The company might be worried I'd sue for sexual harassment. Thanks to you, I've got a pretty good reputation here. I'm a married woman. No one has any cause to question my integrity. Can you say the same?"

She gave a light shrug of her shoulders. "I'm willing to take my chances and see what happens. Are you?"

"Right. We'll see who has the stronger hand."

He pushed away from the desk and walked toward her, stopping mere inches away. His back was to the door, shielding them from view.

Jamie's fingers reached up and touched her face. Slowly he traced the line of her jaw, down her throat, lingering on the jagged scar, his expression softening. She could feel his warm breath fan her cheek. The hairs on the back of her neck prickled at the contact.

"It doesn't have to be like this, Jill."

His face inclined toward her ever so slowly. The scent of his cologne filled her head—leather and spice. She tried to hold steady, breathe evenly, maintain eye contact despite the revulsion she now felt at his touch.

As the seconds clicked by, her instincts overcame her control, and she flinched away. His hand dropped to his side, and a knowing smile twisted Jamie's lips as he pulled away from her. Without another word, he left the office.

She could feel her skin burn with a deep flush as he closed the door behind him. Releasing a ragged breath, she stared at the open office door, struggling to regain her composure.

This was no longer about Dana Evans. This wasn't about the review meeting or their affair. This was something more. He had threatened her job and her marriage. She had the weekend at home to plan what to do next. Perhaps the distance would provide the perspective she currently lacked. There was one thing she was certain of: playing the harassment card was risky, for both of them. But in the end, it might be her only way to get the upper hand.

CHAPTER TWELVE

"**W**ow, that looks good."

Alex crossed the kitchen and stood behind Jill, who was stirring the bubbling sauce on the stove. The scent of the apples and raisins cooking in a spiced brown-sugar-and-butter sauce filled the room. His hands rested lightly on her waist, cheek ruffling her hair.

"I hope it is good. First time with a new recipe."

She stepped away and crossed the kitchen to open the refrigerator. The last thing she wanted tonight was a dinner party. But it was Alex's family, so she had to play the part of the hostess. The best she could hope for was to tune out and enjoy the wine. Man, she could use a drink.

Jill fished an armful of vegetables out of the fridge and deposited them on the island's granite countertop. Deftly peeling an onion, she started to chop. Alex poured her a glass of wine, and she glanced up to catch him watching her.

"We haven't had much chance to talk since you got home. How was your trip?"

The knife stilled as Jill paused long enough to look up at him.

"It could have been better."

"Why, what happened?"

"Jamie wasn't very happy with the state of the project, and voiced his displeasure with me in particular in front of the team."

"Why would he do that? Why wouldn't he save his criticism for a private conversation?"

"Who knows?" The knife resumed its steady rhythm. "There's a lot riding on the success of the project."

"Still, why would he single you out publicly? I can think of many ways he could get his point across without undermining your leadership in front of the team."

Jill released an exasperated sigh.

"Damn it, Alex, I don't know—because he's an asshole. Can you stop playing the detective for one night?" The knife slipped and sliced easily through the pad of her index finger. "Shit."

She dropped the knife and raised her hand to examine the cut. Alex's glass clinked on the countertop, and in no time he led her across the kitchen to the sink. A hiss escaped her lips as he held her hand under some cold water, the sting of the water burning.

Alex handed her a paper towel, and she applied some pressure to the cut as the doorbell rang. A quick glance at the clock confirmed her suspicion.

"They're early."

"I'll get it."

Molly, their yellow Labrador, followed Alex out of the kitchen, her gait fast, toenails clicking on the floor. Voices filled the breezeway, and she could hear the footsteps approaching down the hallway. Jill had time to bandage the cut before they stepped through the doorway.

"Something smells great," Mike said. He stopped and sniffed his shirt. "Oh, it's me." He stooped to kiss Jill's cheek. "Hey, hey, Good-Looking, what you got cooking?"

Jill straightened, her smile tight as she met her brother-in law's gaze. His big frame fit his bigger-than-life personality. Dark hair and hazel eyes. His ruddy complexion spoke of long hours spent outside. His wife, Emma, seemed to float like a fairy at his elbow, his bulk making her seem all the more petite. Blond curls framed her heart-shaped face.

"Pork chops and corn pudding."

"Corn pudding. Sounds southern."

"It's kind of a soufflé," she shrugged, taking a sip of her wine.

"Getting all fancy-fancy on us." Mike turned toward Alex. "Well, I'm going to get all blue-collar on you and start with a beer."

"Coming right up." Alex handed Mike a bottle and Emma a glass of wine.

"Anything I can do to help, Jill?" Emma asked, smiling a gracious thank you at Alex. She took a tiny sip from her wine glass and then placed it on the island.

"Got it all under control. Maybe you and Mike could help Alex pick out some music. Otherwise we'll be listening to '80s metal all night long."

Alone in the kitchen once more, Jill turned toward the window and sipped her wine. Her ghosted image reflected in the dark pane. Despite her cleverly applied makeup, she could see how drawn her face looked. The long week in San Jose had taken its toll. Even the punishing morning run along Alki Beach hadn't done much to get Jamie out of her head. The threat he posed to her career felt all too real.

There had to be a way to neutralize him, but she didn't know what it was. Not yet. The latest update from her team did not offer any hope of resolving the performance issues. Despite the thorough review of all new code in the project, the team hadn't pinpointed the source of the problem.

"How was your trip to California?" Emma asked from the doorway. Jill jumped at the sound of her voice, so deep in her own thoughts that she had not heard her sister-in-law enter the room. "Sorry, didn't mean to startle you."

"I need to switch to decaf," Jill said, forcing a crooked smile. "Would you mind putting this on the table?" She handed Emma the salad bowl.

"Looks great. You're such a good cook. Did your mom teach you?"

Jill tried not to cringe at the question. Her mom had died in the car accident that also claimed her brother's life. No time for cooking lessons. Not that she had shared that information with Alex's family. As much as she had once yearned to be part of their family circle, familial comfort didn't come naturally to her, and sharing wasn't exactly her forte.

"I waited tables in college. Learned a thing or two working in the kitchen."

"I'm a whiz with pasta—everything else …" Emma trailed off, her blue eyes twinkling in her pixie face. Jill knew she should like Emma. Everyone did. Her open, friendly manner made her easy to talk to, but Jill didn't find it easy to connect. The shell she'd built around herself was formed early, and few were able to penetrate her defenses.

"I don't know how you find time to cook at all with your crazy schedule," Jill said as she served the plates. Emma was a crime reporter with the *Seattle Times*. There seemed to be no shortage of stories to cover. Bad news abounds.

As they settled around the table, conversation steered toward current events.

"Any news on the Watson case?" Emma asked Alex. "Strictly off the record."

"No," he said, staring at his glass. Jill frowned, realizing that she hadn't asked him a single thing about the case since she got back from San Jose.

"How are the Watsons holding up?" Mike asked.

"It's been tough." Alex took a sip of his wine, and his gaze shifted to Emma.

"You're sure she didn't just take off? Kids do that sometimes. It's scary, really. They have no idea what they're getting themselves into."

"It doesn't look that way."

"Is Jackson on the case?" Mike asked, his eyes settling on his brother.

"He's the lead investigator. I'm helping out."

"And why is that, Alex?" Jill asked, unable to stop herself. All eyes turned toward her. Alex was the first to look away. He studied his wine glass for a second before answering.

"Because there is an online angle to the case. That falls directly within my purview."

"She met someone, and you think that maybe this person was responsible for her disappearance?" Emma asked, then held up a hand. "Sorry. Occupational hazard."

Alex didn't answer, and Jill couldn't let it go.

"Oh, an internet connection, is that it?" Jill nodded slowly, her voice betraying her skepticism. While there may well have been an online angle to the case, she would be willing to bet money that Alex wouldn't step away from the investigation and let Jackson do his job. He would find a way to stay involved.

"And what do you mean by that, Jill?" Mike asked, his tone cutting through the tension like a whip.

"Nothing."

"Right," her brother-in-law scoffed under his breath.

"Mike," Emma said, quietly placing a hand on his arm. Mike jerked it away.

"I suppose, like everyone else, you think that Alex needs to rush to Abby's rescue?" Jill fixed her gaze on Mike.

"Jill."

She recognized the warning in Alex's tone but barreled ahead.

"Seriously, Mike, there's a whole missing person's unit available to look into Natalie Watson's disappearance. Jackson is a very capable investigator. Why do you think Alex needs to be involved?"

"Jill," Alex repeated, louder this time.

Second warning.

She turned toward Alex.

"Seriously, why don't we all just admit that if this wasn't Abby's sister, you would have passed the case on already? In fact, you wouldn't have been involved in the first place. You're still looking into it because of your relationship with Abby."

"Of course he is," Mike said, his face reddening. "Alex has known the Watson family since we were teenagers. Something awful like this happens, and you expect him not to care, not to want to help?"

"Is that what this is about?" Jill asked quietly, a cynical smile stretching across her lips.

She stood quickly and set her plate on the kitchen counter, her gaze shifting to each of them in turn. Emma looked embarrassed. Mike looked angry. And Alex refused to meet her stare.

No one said anything for a long, tense moment. To Jill, the answer was obvious.

"Coffee?" Alex asked at last.

***

Long after their guests had departed, Jill stood at the sink, her hands in the hot, soapy dishwater. She could see Alex reflected in the window as he finished clearing the dinner table. He had not said a word to her since Mike and Emma left. Jill scrubbed the large skillet in silence. Molly's long nails clicked on the kitchen floor as she circled the island, tail wagging. Jill felt the dog brush up against her leg.

"Damn it, Molly, go lie down." Jill snapped her fingers and pointed toward the doorway. "Go."

Jill watched as Molly slunk out of the room, her head hung low. Turning back toward the sink, she couldn't avoid Alex's disapproving stare.

"What?"

"What is wrong with you?"

"What? I'm tired of her begging. You'd think we never feed her."

"That's not what I'm talking about, Jill."

"This really isn't the right time." She held her hand up, like a traffic cop.

"Unfortunately there is never a right time with you."

"What's that supposed to mean?"

She dropped the skillet back into the soapy water and spun toward him. Her eyebrows were drawn close together in a deep frown.

"You want to talk? Let's talk."

"Forget it. We've been drinking. You know the rules. We should wait until tomorrow."

"Those are your rules, not mine."

Alex had turned away from Jill and started to walk out of the room, but her words stopped him cold.

"Get back here. You don't get to start something and then not finish it."

"Why, have you cornered the market on that move?"

Jill stared at him in silence, and his glare softened. "I'm sorry, that was uncalled for," he said.

"Yes, that was a cheap shot. You got any more that you want to get in?"

Feet planted in a wide stance, Jill crossed her arms and waited for him to continue. She knew it was an unfair question. He had apologized, after all, but sometimes sorry didn't cut it.

Alex sighed, closing his eyes for a moment before focusing back on her.

"Listen, Jill, I honestly don't know what's up with you lately, but you've been in a foul mood since you got back from California."

"Poor Alex." Her tone was condescending and perfectly calculated to needle him.

"Okay, if you don't want to listen, there is no point in continuing this conversation."

Without another word, he left the room. Jill stood drying her hands on a dish towel and considered the exchange. They were both angry. She had started the fight. Maybe she should finish it. After taking a few deep, calming breaths, she followed him into the living room.

Alex was seated in the large black leather chair across from the fireplace. Molly was stretched out on the floor at his feet. His brown eyes fixed on Jill as she entered the room. She perched on the edge of the coffee table, facing him.

"I'm listening," she said at last when Alex didn't give her an opening.

"You've been on edge for weeks, maybe months. You blow in and out of the house like a storm. You're distant, you pick fights, and you squirm away from me whenever I touch you."

"That's not true." Jill shook her head in automatic denial.

"It is true. Are you really worried about Abby? Or is something else bothering you?"

Alex's voice was firm and unwavering. Jill sighed, her fingers laced tightly together as she watched him.

"Look, Alex, I can't say I'm happy about you running to her rescue. But it's more than that. You're never here. You've always got some case you're working on that seems more important than us."

"You knew you were marrying a cop. It's not exactly a nine-to-five job."

"So I should just suck it up? I should be grateful that you're out saving the world?" Sarcasm wasn't helpful. She knew that, but she was too angry to stop herself.   "We both know this isn't all about me and my job. You're never home, either. When you are, you're thinking about work."

"What do you want me to do? Quit my job? Stay at home? Have babies? Is that what you're looking for in a wife? Maybe you should have married Abby."

Alex's jaw clenched, and she saw anger flash in his eyes.

"That's not what I'm saying, Jill."

"Of course it is. Did you find time to call me last week when I was in San Jose, Alex, or did you forget? Too busy tracking down leads to be bothered?"

"The phone works both ways."

"Sure it does, but when you're the one accusing me of being absent, you should look in the mirror once in a while. You might see your own face staring back at you. I know you're busy saving the world and all, but you might want to save something for me, too."

He cringed, and she could tell her words had hit their mark.

"That's enough for tonight." Alex held up his hands.

"Actually, I haven't even gotten started."

"Well, I'm done," he said as he got to his feet. "Good night."

From her living-room chair, Jill could hear the sound of his footsteps pound up the stairs as he made his way to the bedroom. The chill in the night air deepening, she shivered and inched closer to the fire.

CHAPTER THIRTEEN

Ensnared in the grip of a dream and unable to awake, Jill found herself in eerily familiar surroundings. The living room of her stepfather's house came into sharp focus. She could see the worn fabric on the brown corduroy couch, the scarred veneer surface of the coffee table, and the cabinet-style television console that flashed light from its curved screen.

The smell was also familiar. Stale whiskey steeped the air. Her gut clenched hard as she paused in the doorway. Her stepfather coming home drunk was nothing new. Master Sergeant Samuel Morris had been known to tie one on now and then. He was a mean drunk. Many a bar fight outside the officers' club had either started or ended with vicious blows from his meaty fists, but the after show was always the part of the night that Jill dreaded most.

Some nights he would roll through the kitchen door, bottle in hand, spoiling for a fight. Other nights, the ones that Jill learned to fear, she would turn to see him standing in the dark. Master Sergeant Sam's silence was unpredictable. The yelling, the hitting—that she could deal with. She had strategies for that. His calm was far more menacing, like being caught in the eye of the hurricane.

After her mother's death, Sam had withdrawn further into his brooding silence. Drinking binges became more frequent. Without her mother to help blunt the edge of his violent outbursts, Jill found herself fully exposed to the gale force of his anger. But Jill had devised a strategy for dealing with Sam's drunken outbursts—something she dubbed "Operation Pass Out." She had ground up some pain pills from the car accident and dissolved them in the bottle of Wild Turkey that Sam used to help him sleep. She was hoping that, with a swig or two under his belt, he would go straight from the arrive-home-drunk stage to passing out on the couch without stopping long enough to howl at the moon.

On this particular night, Sam arrived home in a rage, and Jill barricaded herself inside her bedroom, waiting for the sounds of his anger to dissipate. After watching several hours tick by on the clock, she crept down the stairs to gauge the success of her experiment.

Blue light from the blaring television cast an eerie glow on the walls as Jill eased into the room. It took her eyes a few seconds to adjust to the dim light. But within moments she could see the open bottle of Wild Turkey on the table next to a half-empty tumbler.

A smile touched her lips as she saw Sam's face, slack in a calm mask of slumber. Edging closer now, she moved toward the couch so she could remove the bottle and the glass, and put them away so he wasn't tempted to pick up where he'd left off once he awoke. Maybe she'd even start a pot of coffee.

She eased around him as she would a junkyard dog, careful to make as little noise as possible. She picked up the tumbler. Then her hand tensed as she saw a small vial beside the glass. With a quick glance over her shoulder, she confirmed that Sam was still unconscious. Keeping a safe physical distance from him was always at the forefront of her mind. Sometimes he struck without warning.

In her free hand, she picked up the vial. The label read "Vicodin." Looking back at Sam, she noticed a waxy sheen to his skin. Was it from the heat? God knew that in midsummer, the temperature in the living room could skyrocket well past simmer. But that wasn't it. Sam wasn't snoring. In fact, Sam was oddly still.

Jill's pulse thudded in her ears as she stared down into his supine face, trying to detect any sign of movement. She had ground up at least a dozen sleeping pills and dissolved them in the bottle of Wild Turkey. Between them, the alcohol, and the painkillers, was it all too much?

The glass fell from Jill's fingers and shattered on the coffee table, spraying her bare legs with shards of glass and sticky liquid. Just then, Sam's eyes—Sam's dead, green eyes—snapped open. A large, meaty fist shot out toward her, clenching her arm in an iron grip.

"You bitch. You little bitch," he ground out, spittle escaping between clenched teeth and spattering her cheeks in stinking spray. "What did you do? What the fuck did you do?"

Jill's eyes snapped open. Heart still at full gallop, she found herself hugging the side of the bed, crowded to the edge by Molly's sleeping form, Alex and the dog snoring in unison. Careful not to wake either of them, she rose, took a deep breath, and eased out from between the damp sheets. She paused in the bathroom long enough to splash some water on her pale face.

Trembling fingers gripped the sides of the sink as she met her gaze in the mirror. She could see naked fear reflected back at her. It had been years since Sam had made a special guest appearance in one of her dark dreams. Stress could sometimes induce these episodes, and between the fight with Alex and the threat posed by Jamie, there was plenty enough stress to conjure up the specter of her long-dead step-father. Jill drew a shaky breath, forcing his image from her mind. That was one nightmare she had no desire to relive.

Downstairs, Jill started a pot of coffee and climbed onto a stool at the island. She rubbed her face with her hands and raked her hair back behind her ears. The bass drum in her head boomed in time with her throbbing hangover. Too much wine, not enough Advil makes Jill a dull girl. She winced and closed her eyes.

Alex had been fast asleep by the time she climbed into bed. How could he have been able to sleep when she'd spent the whole night tossing and turning, replaying their argument in her head? Maybe it was her conscience getting to her. She had picked the fight. She had pushed Alex hard—maybe too hard.

This morning she would try to put things right. Extend the olive branch. The pressure Jamie was exerting gave her no right to jump all over Alex. It wasn't his fault she had made lousy choices. She had only herself to thank. Blame.

From above, she heard the telltale thump-thump of Molly jumping off the bed, and then the jingle of her dog tags as she walked into the kitchen.

"Good morning," Jill said as Molly trotted over to brush against her leg. She scratched Molly's head. "Do you need to go out?" The dog swung her tail in wide, happy arcs, bat-wing ears angled back.

Jill crossed the kitchen and opened the back door to let Molly out. The overcast day mirrored her glum mood. With any luck the rain would hold off long enough to get in a run. Both she and Molly could use the exercise.

Pausing by the counter, Jill took a few moments to flip through the stack of mail waiting there, automatically sorting it into piles—junk mail, bills, catalogs—when her hands froze.

Alex had used the back of a crisp, white envelope as a sketchpad. Jill was used to finding little etchings of his on newspapers, cocktail napkins—whatever Alex found lying around. He had done this for as long as she had known him. It was a habit that she found endearing. For her, it provided little insights into how he saw life. But this morning, what she saw made the blood chill in her veins, and an unfamiliar stab of doubt pierced her heart.

Staring up from the back of the envelope containing their mortgage statement was the unmistakable face of Abigail Watson. The serious set of her lips did little to detract from her fragile beauty.

Jill flipped the envelope over. Maybe she wasn't the only one having doubts about their marriage.

Within minutes, Alex descended the stairs. His bare feet slapped against the hardwood floor as he walked down the hall. Reaching into the kitchen cupboard, Jill pulled out a mug.

"Would you like some coffee?"

"Yes, thanks," Alex said quietly as he sat down at the island.

Silence hung heavy between them, and Alex directed his gaze toward the newspaper, quickly skimming yesterday's headlines. Avoiding eye contact, Jill surmised. He wasn't going to make this easy. Then again, why should he?

Turning, she opened the door for Molly. The big yellow Lab came in and trotted across the kitchen to Alex, tail swinging behind her.

"Good morning, girl," Alex said, stroking her head, and was rewarded with a lick on the hand.

"I'm sorry we argued last night," Jill said, breaking the silence at last.

"Me, too." Alex did not glance up.

"I said some things I shouldn't have."

"It's nothing that you haven't said before."

"You're right. I'm awful. Why do you stay with me?"

Her tone was venomous, an outpouring of bitterness and guilt. As soon as the words were out of her mouth, she wished she could take them back, but as usual, it was too late. Her reflex to strike back seemed to win out every time. When would she learn to control her impulses?

Alex looked up, his brown eyes meeting hers.

"Come on, Jill. Let's just talk, okay?"

"Okay." She let out a long, shaky breath.

"What's going on with you?" Alex said, leaning back in his stool, studying her intently.

"I told you, work has been stressful." She fought to keep her voice even. His gentle but steady probing was unnerving, bringing last night's argument back into sharp focus.

But what could she say? There were so many parts of herself that she didn't want to share. Couldn't share. Especially not with him.

He stared at her as if waiting for her to say something more. When she didn't, he shook his head.

"Work pressure is nothing new. I think there's more to it."

"You're reading too much into things."

His head cocked to one side as he watched her. The urge to squirm was squelched under the intensity of his gaze. Despite his soft tone, she couldn't escape the sense of being interrogated

"Maybe, but I don't think so. I've noticed a change in you ever since you got your promotion."

"Like what?" she asked, an edge creeping into her voice. Did he know about Jamie? Was he waiting for her to tell him about Jamie? No, Alex wouldn't be the type of guy to sit around on the sidelines and wait for her to confess. But still, she couldn't shake the uncomfortable feeling that he knew more than he was letting on.

"Small things. You're edgy. Distant. You don't seem to enjoy being at home. You're dressing differently."

"Different how?"

Alex paused, his head tilting to one side, as if choosing his words carefully.

"More skirts, fitted blouses, high heels. Sexier."

"Yeah, I got a raise so I bought myself some new clothes. Are you complaining about me spending money?" Her heart raced. Maybe he did know and was baiting her.

"Of course not. You know I don't care about that stuff." He angled his head as he watched her. "It's just different."

Alex reached across the table to rest his hand on hers. The warmth of his fingers radiated up her arm. Her automatic impulse was to withdraw her hand, but she left it in place. They needed to work through their problems, and pulling away from him now was not going to help matters.

"Listen, I just want to know what's going on with you. You can tell me anything, you know?"

Jill felt her eyes moisten, defenses wavering ever so slightly. Maybe she could open up. Maybe she should tell him how scared she was feeling, about work, about their marriage, about so many things. Alex was gentle in a way that still caught her off guard, and with the morning light filtering through the kitchen windows, she caught a glimpse of the man she had fallen in love with. For a moment she wished everything could go back to the way it used to be. Simple.

Her lips parted as she searched for a way to begin.

Then Alex's cell phone went off, interrupting her thoughts. The opening strains of his ringtone played the distinctive slow tolling of AC/DC's "Hells Bells." Their eyes met across the island. Jill turned away in resignation. They both knew that he was going to answer. It was what made him such a good cop. And made her such an angry wife.

Jill shifted in her chair, breaking eye contact, and took a sip of coffee, for once grateful for the interruption.

Alex glanced at the call display and closed his eyes for a split second, a wince of regret.

"I've got to take this," he said as he held the phone to his ear. "Alex here."

His eyebrows furrowed as he listened intently.

CHAPTER FOURTEEN

"I've got good news and bad news. Which do you want first?" Kris Thompson asked, her voice all business.

"Start with the good news," Alex said. He looked past Jill to stare sightlessly out the kitchen window.

"I finally got the report from the ISP linking a suspect to the emails in the Watson case. Scumbag's name is Jerry Honeywell. He's a certified mechanic for—get this—Harley-Davidson in Renton. He's the registered owner of a big old '47 hog." Kris drew out the last part with a fake southern drawl. "He also owns a Chevy S10 truck. Driver's license photo is a match for the one we found on Natalie's phone."

"Is he working today?"

"The dealership's showroom is open, but the garage is closed." Kris paused, giving Alex time to process the new information. "Now for the bad news: he has prior arrests for sexual assault. He likes his girls young. There wasn't enough evidence to make the charges stick. The girls refused to testify."

Electricity crackled along his nerve endings as he gripped the phone harder. Given the prior arrests, there was a high likelihood that Honeywell would escalate his behavior. Escalate to what though? Abduction? Murder? Was he capable of such things? Maybe he didn't want to leave any witnesses behind this time. Alex hoped to Christ that he was wrong, but given that Natalie had been missing for almost a week, optimism was hard to come by.

"I'll call Jackson. I'm on my way in." Alex said, his eyes flicking back to Jill, who was staring at her folded hands. "I want everything you have on this guy on my desk. Phone records. Bank accounts. Does he own any firearms? Let's get to know this asshole."

"You got it."

"Listen ...," he said, turning back toward Jill.

"Go." Jill brushed her hand across her lips. "It's okay." She forced a smile that didn't quite reach her eyes.

"I'm sorry. We'll talk later." Alex bent to plant a soft kiss on her hair before jogging upstairs.

***

Search warrant secured, strategy set, SWAT on alert, and the green light to bring Honeywell in for questioning given. Yet the case they had developed to this point, though compelling, was purely circumstantial. They needed physical evidence linking Jerry Honeywell to Natalie's abduction to make the charges stick. Alex wanted to leave no loopholes for the bastard to slip through. If more care had been taken building the previous sexual-assault cases, maybe Natalie would be safe at home this very moment.

Alex and Jackson spearheaded the small team that was positioned outside Honeywell's home in the Skyway neighborhood. The place just felt right. This was the guy. The truck was in the detached garage, but the motorcycle was nowhere in sight.

Alex directed several members of the precinct's anticrime squad around the back of the house, praying that Honeywell was home. The officers moved swiftly and silently into position. Natalie might be inside, so every precaution had to be taken to keep her safe. The house was quiet. No outward signs of activity.

Standing to the side of the doorframe, Alex looked over at Jackson. His partner was ready, tense lines etched deep into his face, gun pulled. A Kevlar vest tightly encased his barrel chest. He tipped Alex a terse nod. The go signal. An SPD squad car pulled up, announcing their presence. Stretching out his hand, he rapped on the wooden surface of the door. Flecks of white paint stuck to his knuckles. They waited.

Inclining his head, Alex held his breath. No sound came from inside the house as he raised his hand once more. The second knock echoed in the still morning air. No one moved. No one even breathed.

No answer. Alex nodded, then glanced back at the other officers standing at the ready before lifting his foot and kicking the flimsy front door. Rotting wood gave way easily. The sound of splintering timber shattered the heavy silence.

"Seattle Police," he called in the darkened interior. There was no response. Was Natalie in here? No pounding of feet or answering voices. Dead quiet.

Cautiously, Alex swept his way through the living room. More officers followed. The air was stagnant, smelling of cat litter and rotting garbage. Dusty drapes covered dirty windows, and in the dim light he could make out the bulky outline of a battered sofa and chair. A computer desk sat in the corner of the room, the flat-screen monitor dominating its cluttered surface, pizza box balanced on its top, while a bulky CPU tower hulked beneath.

A sudden crash to their right trained all guns toward the kitchen amid a dry cacophony of chambering rounds. A gray cat landed with a soft thud on the countertop, its yellow eyes wary.

Alex let out a rush of breath. Drops of sweat slid down his neck as he turned away, continuing to search the house, leading with his Glock. Natalie could still be here, he thought as he moved down the hall with smooth, athletic grace. In one of the back bedrooms?

The creak of the floorboards seemed to echo all the way up the walls as he made his way slowly down the narrow hall. Bathroom clear. First bedroom on the right. Twin bed. Stacked boxes. Motorcycle parts. Clear. One more door on the left. Jackson followed Alex down the hall toward the bedroom.

The door was closed, and Alex moved to the far side. His eyes locked with Jackson's for a heartbeat before he threw the door open. Double bed unmade. Light filtering in through the cracked window.

Empty.

Fuck.

The smell was different in here. Stale sweat soaked into bed sheets. An image sprung unbidden into Alex's mind. A girl tied up on the bed, mouth gagged, fear glittering in her pleading eyes. He blinked hard, dismissing it.

A search of the bedroom turned up no obvious signs of Natalie. Despite the unmade bed, there was no indication that the occupant had spent the night. Apparently, cleanliness was not next to godliness for Jerry Honeywell.

"Where the hell *is* she?" Alex said, lowering his gun and glancing over his shoulder at Jackson. "Let's get forensics in here and do a thorough search. Maybe they'll find something."

Alex led the way back to the living area while Jackson checked out the kitchen.

"Not much in the fridge except leftover takeout containers and some sour milk. The boy doesn't like to cook for himself, that's for damn sure. No cat food in the dish," Jackson said.

"No cleaning lady, either. Lucky for us." If there was some trace of Natalie here, they would find it.

The small team conducted a slow crawl through the house. Bed sheets were bagged, surfaces examined, furniture moved, kitty litter sifted in a search for any DNA evidence that might tie Natalie to this location. As the team made their way through from room to room, Alex shuffled through the papers on the desk, finding the usual bills, flyers, and credit-card offers. The magazines were a little less run-of-the-mill. Porn. Bondage. Nasty stuff. He pressed his lips together, trying to stem the images of Natalie that sprung unbidden to his mind as he squatted next to the desk. With any luck, they would be able to trace Honeywell through his online activities.

The computer tower sat under the cheap IKEA desk. Alex took great care in meticulously detailing, labeling, and diagramming the hardware configuration before detaching it from the computer's peripherals. Everything had to be recorded just so before they took it into the lab to do brain surgery on the hard drive. If there was one mantra that the cybercrime team lived by, it was preserving the sanctity of the evidence chain.

Alex ensured that the computer was nestled safe like an egg in its carton, bagged keyboard balanced on top, before he handed off the box to one of the uniformed officers, with explicit instructions to deliver it directly into the capable hands of Kris Thompson. Together they would create a mirror image of the hard drive and would run their diagnostic tools on the image. They'd find out just what Jerry Honeywell was doing online without risking the integrity of the original data.

The overcast day had finally given way to rain. A few tentative drops fell at first, and more followed in a steady, driving rhythm. Alex stepped out onto the front porch, surveying the neighborhood. The street was quiet. The post–World War II construction and spotty upkeep of the surrounding houses spoke of hard times. From this vantage point, Alex could see Jackson and the other officers fan out to canvas the neighborhood. Maybe somebody had seen something that could help. He could hope anyway. Reaching for his cell phone, he called Kris Thompson.

"Bastard's not here. Flood the media with his picture, stating that he is a person of interest in Natalie's disappearance. Put out an APB out on his motorcycle. Keep digging into his background. Look for a secondary residence. Where does his family live? Does he have close relatives or links outside of Seattle in Washington State? Out of state? He's a mechanic. Where did he get his certification? Let's see if 'Knucklehead' pops up online—chat rooms, email accounts. I want to nail this son of a bitch quickly."

"We're on it."

"Good. Has anyone spoken to Natalie's parents?"

"No. We were hoping to have some good news to share before we contacted them."

Alex sighed, and he closed his eyes for a fraction of a second. He dreaded breaking the news to the Watsons. He could already picture Abby's stricken face.

"I'll take care of it. Hold off on contacting the media until I give the word. Don't leak any info out into the wild until I've brought them up to speed."

"Sure thing, Boss."

"I'm sending you a present. Don't unwrap it until I get there."

Alex hit the End button and shoved the phone back into his pocket. With Jackson in charge of the troops on the ground, he rounded the corner to his parked Jeep. Lips pressed into a grim line, he took the keys from his coat pocket and climbed inside.

This news he had to deliver to the Watsons in person.

CHAPTER FIFTEEN

Medford, Oregon, was a dead town on a sleepy Sunday night. The truck's engine rumbled and huffed to a halt in the crowded parking lot of the Best Western. Warm light spilled from the window of the Brown Bear Café down the street, and he needed a pit stop—long enough to grab a quick bite to eat and some coffee before hitting the road once again.

Jerry Honeywell drove on to the Brown Bear parking lot and stepped out of the truck. The cold wind blasted the tangled blond hair away from his face, and he blew warm breath into his cupped hands. The night drive over Mount Shasta would be hairy. And while part of him wanted to stop for the night, he knew he had to keep going.

The door to the café squealed open, and he held it, allowing an elderly couple to shuffle past. Theirs was the last car in the café parking lot. The diner was empty, save for the two waitresses starting the nightly cleanup.

Jerry took a seat in a corner booth, not far from the counter.

"Coffee?" the older waitress asked. Jerry nodded. She dropped a menu on the countertop in front of him. It landed on the Formica with a thwack. "You'd better order quick. We're closing up."

"Cheeseburger and fries."

She nodded and waddled away, scribbling his order on her notepad. He glanced around the diner. The other waitress glanced up from her work. She was young. Cute. Tendrils of blond hair escaped her ponytail, twisting in gentle waves around her face. Dark eyeliner encircled her bright blue eyes. She smiled at him.

"Here ya go."

The waitress placed a ceramic coffee mug down on the table. Bitter steam rose from the dark brown sludge. It was definitely not fresh. Not surprising. With the clock counting down the minutes until closing time, why bother?

"Cream?" she asked.

Honeywell shook his head. The waitress grunted and disappeared into the back. The girl circled behind the counter to where a line of sugar jars waited to be filled. She glanced back at Jerry, and he grinned.

A pretty thing, she looked about seventeen, maybe a little older. Her ripening curves strained at the confines of her cotton polyester uniform in all the right spots. Head bent over the sugar jars, she filled them one by one.

Jerry watched her, cupping the ceramic coffee mug in his cold hands. At least the shit was hot. He took another swallow, wincing at the bitter aftertaste.

Speaking of shit, the truck he was driving was a card-carrying, certified piece of shit. He'd picked it up off a buddy for eight hundred, cash. Though mechanically sound enough, the rusting body flaked off bits of metal like a shedding tattoo. The goddamned heater wasn't working, and it smelled like something had either shit or died behind the driver's seat. He was a little nervous about taking it over the mountain passes. The tires were mostly bald, and he didn't want to spend the night stranded in a ditch. Or worse.

He should cruise the hotel parking lot and steal a new set of plates before he crossed the border.

"Sugar?"

Jerry looked up. The girl placed a full sugar jar beside his coffee cup. Her nametag read "Kayla."

"I take it black," Jerry said.

Kayla shrugged. A small smile played at the corner of her lips.

"You need anything else?" she asked.

Before he could answer, the older waitress set a platter heaped with fries and a burger down in front of Jerry. She gave Kayla a stern look.

"The bathrooms need to be wiped down."

Kayla flipped her a mock salute the moment her back was turned, and Jerry chuckled under his breath. He watched the exaggerated sway of Kayla's slender hips as she disappeared into the back. She knew she had an audience. She liked it. He could tell by the way she moved.

Jerry ate in silence. He waited for another glimpse of Kayla, but she didn't reappear. Apparently the conditions inside the commode required more than a cursory wipe down to pass morning inspection. He hit the head before he dropped enough cash on the counter to cover his bill and then sauntered out of the diner into the cold night.

The diner closed five minutes late, and the fat waitress left first. Like its owner, her Chevy F-10 looked as though its best years were in its rearview mirror. It dipped under the old gal's hefty weight as she climbed behind the wheel. He watched her leave the parking lot, red taillights winking in the dark.

He waited.

Minutes later, Kayla swung out the door. Her blond ponytail swayed in the wind. He checked the parking lot for prying eyes. Not finding any, Jerry put his truck into drive. Kayla glanced up sharply, startled by the sound of the motor heaving close beside her.

"You need a ride?" Jerry asked through the open window.

"My car's right over there," she said, nodding toward a beat-up piece-of-shit blue Plymouth Sundance.

"Well, maybe you could show me around town. I'm new around here."

He smiled his most charming smile. It must have worked, because Kayla hesitated, thinking over his offer. Her parents probably told her not to talk to strangers, but she wasn't a good girl. He could tell by the way she looked at him, the mischief sparkling in her bright blue eyes.

"Come on. I don't bite," he said. It wasn't exactly true.

Kayla's white teeth closed around her plump pink bottom lip.

"Okay, but I have to be home by ten. I work the morning shift tomorrow."

"No problem," he said.

CHAPTER SIXTEEN

The Seattle office was eerily quiet this early in the morning. Jill pushed back in her chair and stretched her arms toward the ceiling in a lazy cat stretch. It had been a long night of reviewing code and looking for answers. Picking up her coffee mug, she spit the cold brew back into the cup. She hadn't pulled an all-nighter since college, but these were desperate times.

Rising from her chair, she glanced out the window. Framed in the elegant curves of the Aurora Bridge, the first rays of dawn streaked the morning sky. She checked her cell phone. No messages. Disappointment mixed with resolve, and she couldn't help but take a mental inventory of her current state of affairs.

The argument with Alex was indicative of the widening gulf between them. The confrontation with Jamie on Friday left little doubt that their affair was at an end, and her career was in jeopardy.

Maybe the best thing to do was to swallow her pride and bury the hatchet with Jamie. If he had moved on, fine. The affair was a mistake. No need to compound things further by escalating the conflict between them.

She sent him a meeting request for later that morning, leaving the subject line vague.

No sooner had she hit the send button than a new email landed in her in-box with a decided thud. The announcement hit her like a ton of bricks. She had to read it twice to absorb the content. Jamie had been promoted to vice president—title and all.

The stakes had just risen. Jamie's new position gave him even more political clout.

Jill sat back in her chair and stared out the window at Lake Union. Stray golden leaves clung stubbornly to tree branches in the gusting wind. She pressed her fingers to her lips as she considered the situation.

Now more than ever, making peace with Jamie seemed like the smart thing to do. The next email in her box resulted in a sinking sensation at the pit of her stomach. Her meeting request had been automatically declined. Looks like Jamie was out of the office for the week.

Jill stared at the message for a long moment. She blinked. Where the hell was he? One thing was for sure: she didn't want to let a week go by without addressing the issues between them. While she didn't know where Jamie had gone, she knew one person who would.

She dialed Rachel's extension.

"Jill. What's up?" Rachel asked in a friendly voice.

"I'm looking for Jamie. Do you know where he is?"

"You're kidding, right?" Rachel didn't try to disguise her surprise at Jill's question. "It's his planning week. He holes up at his cabin in Tahoe and puts together his annual goals for the organization. Didn't he mention it to you?"

"No."

"Well, that's Jamie for you," Rachel said. "We joked last year that it was a little like Moses going to the mountain and coming back with the stone tablets. In a few weeks he'll arrange a meeting with his reports to discuss the goals before they get rolled out to everyone else."

"Do we have any say in his roadmap for the organization?"

"What do you think?" Jill could picture Rachel's ironic shrug. "You know Jamie. He's always in control and likes it that way. He's good about promoting others, but when it comes right down to it, he's a one-man show."

"Any talk about what he's planning to do to backfill his position?" Jill asked, trying her best to sound casual. Rachel hesitated.

"Not much. I expect he'll talk about that at the next staff meeting."

Jill felt her jaw tighten as she looked straight ahead. She had the distinct impression that Rachel knew more than she was letting on.

"If you don't mind me saying so, Jill, I'm surprised he hasn't talked to you about any of this. You must have done something to really piss him off."

Jill stared down at her keyboard. If Rachel only knew.

After bringing the conversation to a quick close, Jill rested her chin on her fist. She had two choices. She could sit idly by and let Jamie write her out of his plans, or she could go to Tahoe and plead her case in person. Their conversation was certainly one better held in private.

Maybe a trip to Tahoe would help smooth everything over. She made the travel arrangements before she had a chance to change her mind.

CHAPTER SEVENTEEN

Just past the turnoff from Interstate 80 onto California 89, heading south to Lake Tahoe, the snow began to fall steadily, heavy flakes driving into the windshield. Jill tried to stay focused on burying the hatchet with Jamie, but as the miles fell away, her apprehension grew.

Oblivious to the scenic beauty of Emerald Bay Road, she tried not to dwell on the danger of the worsening road conditions. Heavy snows this early in the season were rare, but the weather report out of Reno convinced her to avoid the passes and take a longer route to her destination. Her throat was tight as the mountains seemed to close in on the vehicle, their sheer cliffs looming high above her, while the other side of the road fell away in a steep decline toward the lake.

The intensity of the storm made it seem much later than it was. Through the gloom, she took the turn off to Fallen Leaf Lake Road. She was driving a little too fast, and her tires slid on the compacted snow. Easing her foot off the accelerator, she slowed down even more. It hurt to breathe. The smell of snow filled her nostrils, and she tried to shake the sense of foreboding that had settled in as she skirted the edge of the lake. The force of memory was too strong, stubbornly pulling her back to the day her life had changed.

Like it was yesterday, she could hear the car radio blasting Creedence Clearwater Revival's "Green River" as she sat in the backseat of the Volvo station wagon. Her stepfather, Master Sergeant Sam

Morris, was taking the family on a ski vacation at a resort deep in the Cascade Mountains. Her brother, Derek, was four years her junior. And at eight years of age, he was so excited about his first ski trip that he had barely stopped talking since they climbed into the car. It was hard to ignore Derek, and she had to admit that his enthusiasm was infectious.

Sam was on a mission to teach his only son how to ski, and Jill felt grateful to be included. The initial plan was to have a father-and-son getaway, but at the last minute Jill's mother convinced him that they all should go. How she wished her mother had failed. How different everything would have been.

Her stepfather seemed in an unusually good mood that day, despite the heavy snow and slick driving conditions. Jill looked on as his big paw left the steering wheel to cover her mother's hand in a rare gesture of affection. He turned to say something to her, his head angling toward hers with a smile. Jill could remember the sound of the windshield wipers swishing back and forth on the wet glass as the song ended. The pause between songs was filled with the soft chuckle of her mother's laugh.

The shrill, terrifying blast from a horn came next. Jill started, and dropped her Nancy Drew book. She saw the tractor trailer jackknife on the snow-encrusted road. Time slowed into single frozen frames in her memory as her stepfather stomped hard on the brakes. Both hands closed around the steering wheel in a death grip that turned his knuckles white. The car spiraled into a deadly spin. Snow everywhere. Utter darkness.

Jill blinked hard, clearing the memory. She forced herself to focus on the narrowing road ahead of her. She muttered a soft but emphatic curse as the road reduced to single-lane traffic. This was why Jamie kept an old four-by-four at the cabin, she thought as she passed a sign notifying drivers that the road was not plowed in the winter. She swore again. There were fewer cabins on this end of the road. Large boulders jutted out of the snow as she passed.

The swish of the windshield wipers across the glass filled her head, and as if by reflex, her hands tightened on the steering wheel. *Almost there*, she assured herself. There was no turning back. Seeing Jamie was the only way she could think of to regain control and neutralize the threat he posed to her career and her marriage.

***

Jill pulled the rented SUV up to Jamie's A-frame cabin. The glow from her headlights barely penetrated the curtain of falling snow. Switching off the engine, she leaned back in the leather seat, drinking in the silence. Jill tried to think of the best way to begin what would no doubt be a difficult conversation. Jamie didn't like surprises, but as the seconds ticked by, nothing came to mind. His recent promotion made it too risky to try to outmaneuver him. Her only chance was to extend the olive branch and make peace, at all costs.

Her boots crunched on the snow as she walked toward the cabin, which was nestled among a thick stand of evergreen trees pressed up against a hillside. The nearest neighbor was easily a quarter of a mile down the road. It was the perfect place for a getaway if you wanted to get away from everything. She shuddered to think what it must have cost. But then for Jamie, there wasn't much that was out of reach.

Smoke rose from the chimney, twisting like a gray gnarled finger reaching into the overcast sky. She climbed the wooden stairs and stopped in front of the cabin's door. Her throat felt tight, and she swallowed hard as she looked skyward with a sense of apprehension. The last thing she wanted was to get stranded out here in the storm. Without giving herself a chance to turn around, she knocked.

After what seemed like an eternity, Jamie answered the door. The shock registering on his face turned quickly to disdain. His gaze was even colder than the frigid wind blasting through her flimsy jacket.

"Christ, Jill. What in the bloody hell are you doing here?"

The snowflakes stung her hot cheeks as she looked up at him, her mouth suddenly dry. "We have to talk."

"Talk? What could we possibly have to talk about? Didn't we say everything necessary last week?"

Jill did her best to ignore the indignant expression on his face. She brushed past him into the warm interior of the cabin. Vaulted ceilings gave the impression that the room was much larger than it was. The kitchen was off to one side. The back of the house was a wall of glass, opening up onto a large deck surrounded by trees. In the center of the room, an open laptop sat on the coffee table across from a rustic leather couch. He had been working.

"I need to talk to you." Stripping off her gloves, she placed them on the kitchen table.

"I have two words for you: business hours. It's completely inappropriate for you to interrupt me here." He crossed his arms and glared at her. She unflinchingly met his gaze, holding his icy stare.

"Maybe so, but there's a lot left to be said, some of which it would be better to say in private."

His jaw clenched for a moment as she saw him struggle to control his rising temper.

"Don't you get it? Are you really that dense? Do you need me to say it?" He shook his head in mock wonder. "Whatever we had between us is over, Jillian. Over. Do you get it now? How much more plain do I need to be?"

Turning away, he stalked toward the fireplace and placed his hands on the mantel, staring down into the flames.

"That's not why I'm here," Jill said, stepping forward. Her hands clenched into fists as she continued. "I think it's shitty how you ended things, but that's how it goes. I'm here because I wanted to see if we could find a way to put the past behind us. Move on."

His stare was flat, and she pushed the creeping doubts aside as she continued. "Getting involved was a crazy thing to do. We both showed poor judgment."

"So?" Jamie blinked at her, as if not grasping her meaning.

"So, can't we forget about the affair and just focus on business?"

The stern look on Jamie's face shifted to reflect pure incredulity.

"You threaten me with a sexual-harassment lawsuit, and you think that you can make it all go away? How bloody delusional are you? I take it that my promotion has been announced and has finally clued you in to the desperate circumstances in which you find yourself."

"I saw the announcement, but—"

"But what? You were hoping that I would somehow forget?"

Jill shifted, placing her hands on her hips as she stared at him. The face she once thought of as handsome now contorted into a cruel smile. She could feel her cheeks burn as the enormity of his words sunk in.

"Come on, Jamie. It doesn't have to end like this. We're both adults. Be reasonable."

"Reasonable?" He jabbed a finger toward her. "You're a pretty serious liability. No one threatens me and gets away with it, Jillian. You should have known the stakes in the game you were playing."

Placing his hands on his hips, he regarded her for a long moment. "I was in the middle of cooking lunch when you came by. You'll understand if I don't invite you to join me."

Without another word, he elbowed his way past her and exited through the open French doors to the deck. Jill stood rooted to the spot. Her head swam. She felt like she was under water and fighting her way to the surface. Nothing she could say would make any difference. He was done with her and was going to find a way to get rid of her, the sooner the better.

At length, she followed him out to the snow-covered deck and stood watching as he placed a salmon filet on a plate and turned off the grill. The smell should have awakened her appetite. She had not eaten all day. Instead, her stomach turned.

Tears burned her eyes, and she bit her lip hard, struggling to regain her composure. Was this really how he was going to end things?

By dumping her? Ruining her? Destroying her marriage? How could it be this easy for him? She would not, could not, give him the satisfaction of seeing her cry.

"Isn't there some way to make this better?" she asked, fighting to keep her voice steady.

"Poor little Jillian, you really don't like to lose, do you?" The words hung between them in the frigid afternoon air. "Still trying to squeeze out some pitifully small victory from this pathetic situation?"

She stood tall, squaring her shoulders as she drew in a deep breath. Round three.

"Actually, Jamie, I won't lose this time." Her voice projected a confidence she didn't quite feel.

"Really? How do you figure?" He set the plate down beside the barbecue and leaned back against the railing of the deck, his venomous gaze fixed on her.

"Okay, let's look at this objectively. You took on a high-profile project and put it at risk. How am I supposed to feel good about your leadership capabilities?" He tilted his head as he looked at her, a crooked smile twisting his lips. "I'm afraid you're falling short of expectations."

Jill clenched her fists hard, struggling to keep her voice even. "That's it? My career at ZyraNet is finished?"

He nodded, his smile thin.

"If you're smart, you'll resign and quietly fuck off."

Jill's mouth worked, but no sounds came out. Several moments passed before she found her voice.

"I've worked my ass off, and this is how you repay me?"

"Did you really think I would allow you to continue after what you've done? Are you daft? If you had just let it go, you might have stood a chance. Instead, you've threatened me with sexual harassment, followed me out here. How could I possibly trust you? Really, Jill, you had to know this is how it would end."

Jill drew in a shaky breath, trying to absorb the import of his words. In a tremulous voice, she continued.

"Didn't I mean anything to you?"

A smirk twisted his lips as he studied her.

"Sure. Just another *perk* of the position."

Jill gasped, like she'd been punched in the stomach. A swell of rage broke over her, and despite the cold air, a furious heat pulsed through her veins.

"A perk? I'm a fucking perk? Like the lovely Ms. Evans?"

Surprise rippled across his face before he masked it with an arid smile.

"Something like that. In fact, I consider her an upgrade."

"You egomaniacal bastard. Who the hell do you think you are?"

His smile hardened. The snowflakes landed on the barbeque cover with a hiss.

"Lovely. I'm glad we had this chat, but now it's time for you to leave. Off now. Go back to your husband while you still have him."

"This is between you and me. Leave Alex out of this."

Jamie placed a hand on the snow-covered railing. He touched his lips as his mocking expression turned thoughtful.

"You know, I can't help but wonder what kind of detective your husband is. Can't be very good if he doesn't see through your pathetic little act."

"He trusts me."

"Ah, a good judge of character, then," he said with a grin. "I wonder how he'll react when he finds out what you've been up to. Do you think he'll forgive you?" Jamie raised his eyebrows, his expression speculative.

"He won't find out about you," Jill said with more confidence than she felt.

"I wouldn't be so sure about that." He faced her again with his arms crossed, voice deliberately slow, as if speaking to a child. "Listen carefully to me. Jillian. I'm only going to say this once. It would be better for both of us if what went on between us stays a secret, but I do promise that if you cause any more trouble, I will tell him every tawdry detail of our little affair."

He paused, letting his words sink in.

"Do you get it now, Jillian? I have nothing to lose, but you will lose everything—your husband, your career. That much I promise you."

Jill felt the blood drain from her face as she fought to suck in a breath of the cold mountain air. Time seemed to slow to a halt as she stared at him. The snow was falling steadily. The sound of her heart hammering in her chest was almost audible. What *would* Alex do if he learned about the affair? One thing was for certain: she did not want to find out.

"You wouldn't do that." She could barely breathe now. The murderous look on his face told her that he was dead serious.

"Just fucking try me, bitch," he hissed, turning toward the French doors.

A wave of intense heat coursed through Jill's body. Her vision narrowed and blurred around the edges. She screamed. She felt the rage inside her bursting from her chest. Surging forward, she slammed her palms hard against his shoulders. He lurched sideways.

There was barely time to breathe as she saw him stumble, sliding on the icy deck. Jamie grasped for the railing and missed. Jill stared in horror as he went careening wildly down the steep staircase.

There was no time to reach out for him. He was gone in the blink of an eye. She heard the crash of wood as the railing splintered underneath his weight. Jamie screamed. And then there was nothing. Jill stood alone on the deck, scarcely able to believe what had just happened.

The terrible silence that followed was suffocating. She was not sure how much time passed before the world around her began to move once more. She could hear the rustling of the swaying trees. Her hot breath escaped her lungs in a cloud of steam as she waited.

"Jamie," Jill called out, easing her way cautiously forward to the top of the stairs. She choked on a gasp as she looked down into the snow below.

Jamie had landed on the frozen ground at the foot of the stairs. His head had struck a boulder near the base of the staircase and was propped up at an odd angle. Bright-red blood stained the snow.

Jill wanted to look away, but she was transfixed by the sight below. His glasses were askew, and she could see his lifeless eyes staring up at her. She recognized the mask of death, had seen it on her little brother's blood-streaked face through the twisted metal of the car wreck.

Jamie was dead. And she had killed him. Her hand covered her mouth as she drew in a ragged breath.

Oh, my God.

Eventually the cold brought her out of her daze. She struggled to make sense of her own thoughts. Should she call 911? What would she say? Would they believe it was an accident? Alex would find out everything. If they linked her with this scene, everyone would find out what had happened between them and that she was responsible for his death. Her life, as she knew it, would be over.

No. Too risky, she decided. They had a history between them, and involving the police might expose the nature of their relationship. If the truth was revealed, she might lose everything. Could she cover her tracks? Jill stood in the snow and stole a fleeting glance inside.

Maybe. There were few connections between her and this place. She'd taken the day off and hadn't told anyone where she was going. After her all-nighter, work would assume she'd gone home to sleep. Alex assumed she was in San Jose. Jamie didn't expect her. No one knew the truth. No one knew she was here.

Jill's racing heart slowed, and an eerie calm descended upon her. She felt like she was watching herself from a great distance. The snow fell from the gray sky in fat, chunky flakes. If this kept up, there would be no evidence of her footprints or the tire tracks outside.

With one last look at Jamie, she turned and walked back toward the cabin. Stopping long enough to strip off her snowy boots, she stepped through the French doors and quickly scanned the interior of the living room. What had she touched? What clues had she left behind?

Think like Alex, she told herself.

She had spent precious little time inside the house. The only thing she had taken off was her gloves. She paused, looking back at the door. He had opened it. She had not touched the door. She would leave it open, she decided. The deck was icy. It was plausible that he had slipped and fallen on his own.

Jill eyed the room with a clinical detachment, confident that if she kept her cool, she could make all of this go away.

She used the towel to swab away any tracks her boots had made on the floor. She wiped down anything she might have touched, then balled up the towel and shoved it into her coat pocket. Standing at the front door, she spun around for one last look. *That should be it.*

Pulling her gloves and boots back on, she let herself out, twisting the lock behind her.

Back in the SUV, she slid the gearshift into drive. The urge to pin the accelerator to the mat, to get as far away from the cabin as fast as she could, was palpable. Exercising the limits of her self-control, she pulled away from the cabin slowly. Her eyes searched the rearview mirror and focused on the cabin disappearing in the distance. Snow caked on the steepled roof. Gray smoke billowed into the cold air. The passing trees marked her progress, and the windshield wipers swished as she drove down the winding road. She checked the mirror again and again until at last the cabin behind her disappeared from view.

Jill forced herself to relax her hands on the steering wheel and drew in a deep, cleansing breath. She had to be careful now. She couldn't afford to skid off into the ditch or get into an accident. She couldn't be noticed by anyone she might pass on the road. It had to appear like she had never been here.

The gloom of the afternoon closed in around her. The white beam of the headlights reflected off of the snow drilling into the windshield. The sooner she could get back to Interstate 80, the better. There was no telling when conditions would deteriorate to the point that the road might close, leaving her stranded. Her heart skipped a beat as she saw flashing lights approach.

The police? She went rigid with fear. Could someone have heard Jamie's scream? No. Yellow lights. A snow plow passed, going in the opposite direction. Reflexively, she checked the rearview mirror again as she drove by.

The spray from the plow covered the rented Escalade's tracks in a white flurry of powder. If the forecast was right, heavy snow would continue to fall for the next several days. The road would likely close. If her luck held out, it would be days before anyone missed Jamie. She would be home in Seattle by midnight, tucked safely in bed beside her husband, the cop.

Jill tried to block the images from her mind, but as hard as she tried, all she could think about was Jamie growing cold in his open grave. His red blood sinking into the pristine snow blooming scarlet, like a winter rose.

CHAPTER EIGHTEEN

The rain hammered relentlessly on the roof of the cab. The hiss of the blasting heater seemed too loud, the oppressive heat adding to her queasy desire to escape. It felt too close in here.

She handed him thirty bucks and told him to keep the change.

"You wan' receipt?" the taxi driver asked in passable English.

"No," Jill replied and stepped into the rainy night. The less evidence of her trip, the better. She had already left more of a paper trail than she wanted. The damp chill of the air cut her straight to the core. She pulled her coat closer.

The door squeaked on its hinges as she opened it. Entering the house, Jill could detect the lingering scent of embers smoldering in the fireplace. *Cedar.* A small nest of warmth on this miserable Seattle night.

Home. Safe. Relief flooded through her, the feeling so strong that her knees threatened to give way. *Home,* she thought again, *far from the horrors of Lake Tahoe.* Jamie's broken body laid to rest under a frigid blanket of snow.

Jill pulled off her coat and hung it on the wall rack by the door. Leaving her bag on the landing, she climbed the stairs, fatigue having long since set in.

The house was quiet. The ticking of the mantel clock faded in the distance as she traversed the hall on the second floor. Molly emerged from the bedroom door, wagging her tail as she approached Jill. The dog stopped a few feet away and took a long sniff in the air. Her tail stalled midswing.

"Come here, girl," Jill said softly, reaching out a hand toward Molly's muzzle. The dog did not respond. After a long moment, the Lab returned to the bedroom, leaving Jill alone in the hallway.

Jill stared after her. Could Molly sense death? No, that was crazy. She needed to forget about Jamie. She needed sleep.

With tired hands, Jill stripped off her clothes, letting the garments fall heedlessly to the floor. Pulling back the sheets, she paused, looking down at Alex's sleeping form.

His face was barely visible in the dull light of the room. He looked so young lying there. Tranquil. Innocent. For the longest time she sat on the bed, aching to touch him. She reached out toward him, fingertips suspended inches above his face before she let them drop to the cool sheets. *Best not to wake him,* she thought.

His chest rose and fell with his deep, even breaths. At last Jill slipped in between the sheets, giving in to her exhaustion. Lying here beside Alex made everything all right. Feeling at peace, she started to drift away.

Teetering on the soft edge of sleep, she suddenly opened her eyes. Had she forgotten anything at the cabin? What if someone found out about the affair, or her visit to Tahoe? In the darkened room, underneath the warm covers, she could picture Jamie's body slowly disappearing under a blanket of snow.

✳✳✳

Jill felt a hand gently shaking her shoulder. Reluctantly she pushed through the warm layers of sleep that enveloped her and allowed herself to surface. Her eyes squinted against the dull morning light seeping through the bedroom windows.

Alex perched on the edge of the bed, his hand still resting lightly on her shoulder.

"I brought you some coffee," he said, inclining his head toward the night table.

"Thanks. What time is it?"

"Well past eight."

"Damn," she said, rubbing her eyes and propping herself up against her pillows.

"You got in late last night. I'm surprised you didn't stay over in San Jose."

Averting her eyes, she reached over to pick up her coffee.

"I've been away long enough. I just wanted to get home." She took a sip from the steaming mug, wrapping her fingers around it for maximum transfer of heat.

"I'm sorry we were interrupted on Sunday." Alex said with a serious look on his face.

"A break in the case?"

"Yes and no. We have a suspect, but we haven't found him, or Natalie."

"I'm sorry. I know how hard you've been pushing on this one."

"So about Sunday ..."

Jill did not flinch, but met his gaze directly. She had created the distance between them, with work, with Jamie, with the secrets she'd been keeping. Fear hovered beneath the surface of her emotions. Fear of losing Alex. Fear of her role in Jamie's death being discovered. The world felt fragile to Jill, as if the smallest of shifts could bring everything crashing down around her.

How could she share any of it with Alex? She couldn't. There was no way she could make him understand. Duty came first for him. He'd call the authorities in California, and everything would be exposed. Everything. No. She would involve him only if she had no other choice. Some secrets were meant to be kept.

Jill swallowed hard, and forced a crooked smile.

"Yeah, well, I knew I was marrying a cop."

"Still, I'm not very good at balancing work and home. You were right about that and—"

Leaning forward, she silenced him with a kiss. His hand reached around to cup the back of her head, and the kiss deepened before Alex finally pulled away.

"Shit," he said, looking at the bedside clock. "I've got to get going."

"I think I'm going to work from home today," Jill said as she eased back against the pillows.

Surprise flashed across Alex's face.

"Are you feeling okay?"

"Just tired." She rested her hand on his, hungry for physical contact. "Any chance you'll be home for dinner tonight?"

"I'll see what I can do," he said with a smile.

"I'll make it worth your while," she promised.

"I like the sound of that."

And with a squeeze of her fingers, he was gone.

CHAPTER NINETEEN

"**T**he bastard didn't just evaporate," Alex growled, head tilted back as he stared at the stained, pockmarked ceiling tiles. "We must have missed something. Let's go over it again."

Jackson sighed, rubbing his hand across the stubble on his cheeks.

"Honeywell's long gone. He hasn't been to work in days. We have people watching the house, but so far, nothing. Did you get much from his computer?"

Alex laced his fingers behind his neck and shook his head.

"Like Kris said, the guy's no dumbass. He kept his data files on a thumb drive, the kind you plug into a USB port. Probably took it with him."

"Or maybe he threw it down a storm drain." Jackson's expression was grim as Alex continued.

"Either way, it's a dead end. We found a steganography program, along with some more traditional photo-editing software."

"Steg-a-what? What the hell is that?"

"Steganography," Alex explained, "is a technique used to embed one message inside another. In ancient times, it was used by the Romans and the Greeks. Terrorists sometimes use this technique to exchange information. Pedophiles also use it to send pictures of their latest conquests to their network of like-minded souls."

"Sick fucks."

"But I'm guessing that Honeywell didn't plan this all the way through."

"True. It took time to empty his bank accounts," Jackson said, inspecting Honeywell's bank records. "He needed traveling money. But where's he going?" Jackson's look was pensive.

Kris Thompson burst through the door looking wide-eyed and pale. Dressed in a baggy sweater and jeans, she looked like she had spent the last two weeks cramming for exams. The dark circles under her eyes underscored the solemn expression on her face, making the hair prickle at the back of Alex's neck.

"There's a girl missing in Medford, Oregon."

She handed Alex a copy of a police report. He skimmed the details, giving Jackson the highlights.

"Kayla Miller. Eighteen. She's a waitress at the Brown Bear Café. She disappeared two days ago after her shift."

"Any suspects?" Jackson asked, holding his hand out for the report. Alex handed it to him.

"Not so far. They're looking into her ex-boyfriend. Her friends say he was an asshole. Threatened her."

Jackson rubbed his chin, staring at the report.

"She fits the profile," Kris said, looking grim.

Alex nodded and rubbed his eyes.

"If Honeywell was headed to California, Medford's along the way." Alex straightened in his chair. He plucked a sheet of paper out from amid the stack piled on the conference table. Tapping it with his index finger, he continued. "That's where he did his certification for his mechanic's license. We need to find out more about his life there. Who did he hang out with? What did he do in his spare time?"

"You think he'd be dumb enough to go back there?"

Alex shrugged.

"It's a logical choice. His money will run out soon. He's got to find work. Only he's going to have to do it under the table. He needs connections. The farther away, the better."

"Do you think he'd be dumb enough to pick up another girl?"

"He already got away with it once. Why wouldn't he do it again?"

Jackson studied the police report on Kayla's disappearance with narrowed eyes and pursed his lips.

"Let's call Medford, find out if they have any more leads on Kayla." Jackson nodded.

"There's more," Kris said. "I did a property-records search. Honeywell's uncle owned a hunting cabin in Winthrop."

Alex and Jackson traded sharp looks.

"Let's call the locals."

Jackson visibly winced at the suggestion. He met Alex's stare with a hard one of his own.

"We handle this ourselves. If he's there, we can't risk scaring him off."

"I hear you, man," Alex said, slapping Jackson's shoulder. "But Natalie may still be alive. We've got to act fast."

***

After coordinating with the Winthrop sheriff's department, Alex and Jackson assembled a small team to head over the mountains. In addition to Alex and Jackson, there were two forensics technicians and their gear packed into an SUV.

"All set?" Alex asked as Jackson fell into step beside him.

"Ready as we're going to be." Jackson nodded and turned toward the lead forensics tech. "Got everything we need?"

"If there's anything in that cabin, we'll find it."

Alex's stomach clenched. A memory of Natalie flashed through his head. She was three years old and wedged into the stands beside Abby at a high school basketball game. Her voice could not be heard over the roaring of the crowd, but Alex caught a glimpse of her face, speckled with sticky cotton candy as she cheered him on.

Stealing a glance over at his partner, Alex could read resignation in the set of Jackson's jaw. The news of the Winthrop cabin had fixed a scenario in his own head of a remote place where Honeywell could do what he wanted, with no one around to stop him. Climbing into the vehicle, he hoped that they were both dead wrong.

***

The roads were dry as they started to climb into the foothills of the Cascades. Jackson's cell phone went off, and the opening strains of the *William Tell* overture blasted through the tinny speakers. Alex cast an irritated glance over at Jackson, wondering what would possess someone to choose that particular piece of music for a ringtone. The phone fell mercifully silent as Jackson pushed the Talk button.

"Yeah, what did you find?" Jackson's voice was tense and his eyebrows furrowed as he listened intently to what was being said on the other end. "Shit. What color and type?" He glanced over at Alex, angling the cell phone away from his mouth. "What kind of shoes was Natalie wearing the day she disappeared?"

"Camouflage Converse sneakers with pink laces, size seven," Alex replied without missing a beat. He had been through the file so many times that the details of her appearance, including what she was wearing the last day she was seen, were burned into his memory.

Jackson relayed the information, and his expression darkened. His lips formed into a tight line as he instructed the local cops not to touch anything until they arrived. Dread pooled at the pit of Alex's stomach, and he ran a hand across his eyes.

"What have they got?"

Jackson hesitated, glancing out the car window before he answered.

"They found a shoe matching the description of Natalie's underneath the couch in the cabin."

"Fuck. I'm guessing no sign of either of them at the cabin?"

Jackson shook his head

"They had an early dump of snow. Given the undisturbed conditions outside of the cabin, it doesn't look like anyone has been in or out in the past few days."

Alex stared out the window at the bleak afternoon sky. The first clumps of snow clung to the evergreen trees as they passed. The engine growled as the SUV switched into four-wheel drive. They were still several hours away. Alex's mind churned as he wondered what else they would find at the cabin.

"She may still be alive," Jackson said, trying to inject optimism into his voice.

"Why the fuck would he bring her all the way to Winthrop if he had no intention of hurting her?" Alex asked.

Jackson fell silent, leaving Alex to dwell on his own morbid thoughts. What would he say to Natalie's parents, to Abby, if he confirmed his current suspicions? He promised them he would find their daughter. What if she was dead? The painful thoughts clouded his mind. Pushing them firmly aside, he focused instead on Honeywell and how goddamned satisfying it would be to bring the bastard in.

Speeding through downtown Winthrop in a blur, Alex caught sight of the old western-style storefronts capped in snow. They traveled north east of the village until they reached Old Cabin Road. The eight miles of road between the Winthrop and the cabin didn't look remote on the map, but as the valley fell away in the truck's rearview mirror, Alex sensed the isolation as the trees closed in around them.

Red and blue lights flashed up ahead, their glare reflecting off of the glistening snow. The SUV slowed. The local police had bottlenecked the road leading into the cabin. Presenting their badges, they pulled around the barricade, making the final turn onto Bear Fight Road.

The chunky wheels of the SUV fought to grip the icy path. Rocks jutted up through the crusty snow. The last nerve-racking mile of the journey cemented Alex's conviction that Jerry Honeywell chose this isolated location for one reason only: so that no one would hear Natalie's screams. He prayed he was wrong, but his every instinct told him otherwise.

Alex stepped out of the car and into snow that came up to his knees. Introductions were made between the local police officers and the Seattle contingent quickly. In their snow parkas and brown hats, the Winthrop officers looked like carbon copies of each other. Finally one of the officers led them inside.

The cabin was small and dark, with a main room that dominated the open space. One corner contained an ancient stove and refrigerator that showed no signs of having been used in years. A threadbare couch was shoved against the back wall of the living space. The bare floorboards squeaked with every step the officers took toward it. Alex crouched down to examine the faded orange fabric, frayed and dusty. His eyes watered, reacting to the musty smell in the air. Dust, mold—whatever it was—triggered his allergies. He blinked a few times and fought back a sneeze.

"Where exactly did you find the shoe?" he asked the police officer.

"Right there under the couch, shoved back about six inches. Probably didn't see it before he left."

Careful not to touch the surface of the couch, he looked underneath to see if there was any small piece of evidence that may have been moved when they fished out Natalie's shoe. Aside from the deep trail the shoe had carved in the generous coating of dust, the area was clear. The forensics technician set his case on the floor and opened it, preparing to look for evidence.

"Did you find anything else?" Alex asked, glancing up.

"No, but we didn't look really hard, either," the Winthrop officer explained. "Didn't want to disturb the scene. You know, just in case," he finished awkwardly, glancing away.

Alex nodded, moving his eyes around the cabin slowly, searching for all the places evidence might be hiding. He squatted by an area near the couch. Small, dark spots looked like they had seeped their way into the exposed wooden planks of the floor. Could be blood. Gesturing toward the area, Alex caught the forensics tech's eyes, his meaning acknowledged with a terse nod.

"Check the warrant. Let's make sure we do everything right."

Dropping his head low between his shoulders for a moment, Alex stood slowly. With a deep sigh he looked at the Winthrop officer. The man was older, a gold wedding band adorning his left hand. Underneath a dark, bushy mustache, his mouth was set in a grim line. Alex wondered if he had children of his own. Judging the man to be in his late forties, Alex figured that if he had kids, they might be around Natalie's age.

"Do you have dogs?" he asked at last.

All eyes turned to focus on Alex, and the silence that followed the question was leaden with the words that no one wanted to speak. Finally the officer nodded.

"There are a lot of hunters in the area. I'll make some calls."

"We need to search the woods," Alex said. With heavy steps, he crossed the room to stand in front of the water-stained kitchen sink. His jaw tightened as he glanced at the worn couch before turning toward the dirt-streaked window. His gaze drifted up the hill, settling on the dense line of trees that curved around the back of the cabin and climbed high toward the ridge.

* * *

The dogs went out first, and Alex could hear barking as he walked around the small cabin. A thorough search of the interior had turned up no other visible signs of Natalie. The forensics technician was busy lifting DNA samples from the couch. Hairs were bagged, stains were being sampled and cataloged, photographs were being taken, and there was growing certainty in Alex's mind that they would find more evidence to link Honeywell to Natalie's disappearance.

The crisp air stung his cheeks as he stepped out of the cabin with Jackson. Together they followed the path the dogs had carved up the hill. Neither man spoke as Alex felt his shoes soak through, and the cold began to numb his toes. The air was fresh, infused with the subtle scent of snow and pine trees. On any other occasion, Alex would relish being out in the woods. But now he burrowed his hands deep into the pockets of his coat and mentally plotted the dimensions of the ten acres of land belonging to Honeywell's uncle.

How many times had Honeywell and his uncle hunted in these woods? How far could he drag a body up the hill?

Alex continued to follow the trail cut by the dogs. The paw prints drew them deeper into the dense line of trees. He was not sure how far they had walked when the sound of the barking grew frantic. The local police officers had come to a stop and stood pooled around a stand of trees, talking softly as they looked down into the snow. Their words were drowned out by the furious barking of the dogs.

Alex's stomach clenched. He hunched his shoulders against the raw wind as he continued forward. The officers glanced toward the Seattle detectives, careful to avoid eye contact. The cluster parted as the two approached.

Jackson stopped first and looked down at the frozen ground, his bowed head dipping a fraction lower. Alex approached slowly, his eyes magnetically drawn to the spot where the dogs had concluded their search.

A surge of electricity raced along his nerve endings, and he fought to control the emotions on his face.

There, at the base of a tree, he could see blue fingertips poking up from beneath the thick blanket of snow, like the petals of a periwinkle crocus. The edge of a yellow "Livestrong" bracelet barely crested the crusty surface. His pulse pounded in his ears.

Natalie.

CHAPTER TWENTY

Tucked up against the foothills of the Cascade Mountains, the snowcapped finials of Liberty High School looked picture-perfect on this frosty November afternoon. With the help of the Winthrop Police Department, Alex and Jackson had made the rounds, interviewing some of the people who had known Honeywell back in the day, and this was their last stop.

The antiseptically clean smell of the school brought back distant memories of textbooks, backpacks, and basketball as Alex sat wedged into a student desk. Jackson stood leaning against the wall, arms folded across his massive chest, forgoing the opportunity to either destroy a desk while trying to fit his considerable frame inside its improbable dimensions or dismantling it on his way out. Alex stared down at a copy of Honeywell's school records: mediocre grades, spotty attendance. Given what he already knew about Jerry, it was the type of account he had expected to see.

The principal had passed them along to Mrs. Nelson, a middle-aged teacher with a freckled nose and thick glasses. She set an open yearbook on the desk in front of him. The shinning faces of high school seniors peered out from the neat rows of photos. He picked Honeywell's out in an instant. Middle of the page. Jerry's face was partially obscured by a thatch of long blond hair. He did not smile for the camera; his face was devoid of expression.

"What can you tell me about Jerry Honeywell?" Alex asked.

The woman shrugged her soft shoulders, eyes looking past Alex, as if envisioning a teenage Honeywell. Her smile was distant as she spoke in a pleasant voice, subtly infused with a midwestern twang.

"There was more to him than what you'd find written in this file. He was a smart kid. You might not get that by looking at his grades, but he had an aptitude for language and arts."

"How well did you know him?"

Mrs. Nelson shrugged, and Alex could see curiosity magnified through the thick lenses of her glasses. Even in a town this small, it would take a few hours for news of Natalie's dead body to spread. Instead of satisfying her own interest, she answered the question.

"About as well as any of his teachers."

"Did he have family?" Jackson asked.

"Mr. Gibson took him in after his father was imprisoned. Talk around here was that his father had killed his wife's lover after catching them together. Crime of passion." Her eyes flashed scandalously at the two detectives. This information dovetailed with what Alex already knew. Honeywell's father had died in prison."

"And the mother?"

"She abandoned Jerry a few months later. No one quite knew where she took off to. There was some talk about her shacking up with a new man. There was also talk about her mending fences with her family in Baton Rouge. They were wealthy, you know. They disapproved of Jerry's father—maybe Jerry, too. Lots of talk, though no one knows for sure."

"Did Jerry ever see her again?"

"Not that I'm aware. She never came to Winthrop, that's for certain. Something like that would have surely caused a stir." She chuckled softly to herself. "No wonder the boy was quiet. He had a lot of family history to live down."

"What classes of yours was Jerry in?"

"I taught him English in his junior year."

"What was he like?"

"Like I said, he was a smart kid, but he didn't work to his potential. He only showed up for half of his tests, so his grades were low. He sure could write, though. I had the students spend the first ten minutes of each class journaling, and I always enjoyed reading Jerry's entries."

"Why? What did he write about?"

"What does any teenage boy write about? Wanting to be somewhere else, mostly. Unlike most small-town kids, it wasn't the bright lights of the city that Jerry craved. He dreamed about cruising the open road on his motorcycle and traveling to remote places. He drew some pretty sophisticated sketches of his motorcycle in the pages of his journal, as I recall."

"Do you still have a copy?" Getting to know Jerry through his writing might be insightful. The artistic inclination could fit in with the photo-editing and steganography software they found on his computer. But any hopes he had were dashed with the wagging of the teacher's head. Her faded red curls brushed the collar of her starched white shirt.

"Long gone, I'm afraid."

"Anything else you remember about him?"

"Well, there was one person he was close to." Mrs. Nelson leaned in closer, angling the book toward her for a better look as her eyes skimmed the rows of smiling faces. Her finger landed on a photograph at the bottom of the previous page.

"Lisa Cullen."

Jackson left his perch on the wall to hover over the book for a closer look. Alex stiffened as he looked at the photograph. The hairs on his neck stood on end. The girl in the photograph looked sixteen or seventeen years old. With her long blond hair and blue eyes, she was the spitting image of Natalie Watson, minus the glasses.

"Did they date?"

"Yes, through most of their final two years. I swear that if it hadn't been for Lisa, Jerry would not have finished high school. The only time I ever saw him smile was when he was looking at her."

Alex stared at Jackson. You would have to be blind to miss the uncanny resemblance between the two girls. Maybe if they could find Lisa, they could learn more about Honeywell.

"Is she still in the area? We'd love to talk to her."

Mrs. Nelson shook her head, using her index finger to poke her Coke-bottle glasses farther up the narrow bridge of her nose.

"I'm afraid not. Her parents moved when Lisa was halfway through her senior year. Jerry closed down after that."

"Where did they go?"

"California. Santa Rosa, I think. Can't be sure though. It was a long time ago."

Alex traded another look with Jackson. Was Lisa part of the reason Jerry had gone to California?

"And Jerry stayed here?"

"For a few years, anyway. The garage fell on hard times, and when his uncle died, Jerry left town."

"Thanks for your time," Alex said. "Can I get a copy of their pictures? I'd also like whatever information you have on Lisa Cullen."

CHAPTER TWENTY ONE

Abby's wide, frightened eyes stared up at Alex as she answered the door. Without thinking, he reached out and grazed his fingers along the soft curve of her cheek. It was meant to be a gesture of comfort, but the twist in his gut as their eyes locked served as a warning that he was crossing into dangerous territory. He dropped his hand away and followed her inside.

Joyce sat hunched on the living-room couch, Tom close at her side, a supportive arm circling her narrow shoulders. Abby perched beside him, anxiety etched into the lines of her face. Alex searched for the right words, but they wouldn't come. With a heavy heart, he cleared his throat.

"Honeywell's uncle owned a hunting cabin in Winthrop. We found …" Seeing the tears in Abby's eyes, he faltered. "We found Natalie."

"Is she?" Tom asked, in a ragged, breathless voice.

Alex nodded. Joyce wailed. Her shaking hands covered her face. Her shoulders shook with the force of her sobs. Tom clutched her, burying his face in the curve of her back. Abby sat still as a stone, rigid with shock.

"I'm so sorry," Alex said.

Abby blinked, her eyes huge in her pale face filled with anguish. She raised her shaking hands to cover her face. Alex rose and took a halting step toward her. He wanted to comfort her, to find some way of making this nightmare fade. But he could do nothing but stand stupidly by.

At last, Abby spoke. Her voice trembled with the force of her emotions.

"Find him, Alex," she said. "Promise me you'll find him and make him pay."

All the way home, Abby's words rang in his hears. He'd promised. It was the one thing he could do for the Watsons now.

***

The remnants of a fire burned low in the grate as he stepped through the front door of his house. All was quiet. Jill must have gone to bed. Draping his coat over the back of a chair, he crossed through to the kitchen and poured himself a tumbler of scotch. Neat. No need for ice or other niceties. Not tonight.

Glass in hand, he turned toward the door to the living room but then pivoted back to grasp the bottle and take it with him. Slumping into the leather chair across from the fire, Alex poured himself another three fingers of Scotch. Orange flames licked the charred logs as he heard the jingle of dog tags.

Molly approached, head down, tail wagging gently behind her. She stopped by Alex's feet, and he scratched her ears. As if sensing his mood, she circled twice before settling at his feet.

"Hey."

"Jesus," he said, almost jumping out of his skin at the unexpected sound of Jill's voice.

"Sorry, maybe I need to start wearing dog tags, too." Her smile was wry as she settled on the coffee table. Her skin glowed in the soft light from the fireplace. She studied him with a thoughtful gaze.

"Rough day?"

"Sorry I woke you."

He took a sip of his drink and glanced back toward the smoldering fire.

"You didn't. How are you doing?" she asked, perching on the arm of his chair. Alex set his glass down on the end table.

Reaching around him, she rubbed his knotted shoulders. He rolled his head back, feeling the tensions in his shoulders ease.

"You know?" he asked her.

"Jackson called."

Alex sighed. Picking up his glass, he took another long pull of whiskey.

"We found Natalie's body buried in the snow."

"Snow?" Jill's fingers stilled but remained on his shoulders.

"Outside a cabin in Winthrop. That's where we found her."

Jill was silent for a long moment before she resumed the massage.

"How's the family?"

"About how you'd expect."

She leaned back. He could feel her eyes on him, and when it was clear that she wasn't going to move away, he looked at her.

"And how are you?" she asked again.

"Just another day, right?" He shrugged, taking a drink. The words sounded hollow. False bravado at its finest.

"Yeah," she said, taking the drink from his hand and depositing it on the coffee table. She moved off the arm of the chair and onto his lap. Her arms wound their way around his neck, and her warm body pressed against his. Her hair smelled like jasmine, and the hard, icy shell that had formed around his heart started to crack. His hand slid across her back, feeling her sharp shoulder blades jut underneath the smooth cotton tank top.

Jill pulled back far enough to tilt her face up, her lips brushing his in a gentle kiss. His body's response was instantaneous. He cupped back of her neck, and he kissed her hard. The horror of the day faded as he pulled her close. He felt his need, his hunger, rise. All thoughts of Abby were pushed aside as he pulled Jill close.

Tonight he just needed her.

CHAPTER TWENTY TWO

"**O**MG Jill, call me," the instant message read on Jill's computer monitor. It was from Rachel, in the San Jose office, pinging her with what she could only assume would be news about Jamie. Jill's heart lurched in her chest, its rhythm accelerating to double time.

Directing her gaze out the office window, she stared down at the gray waters of the ship canal below, waves crested in white peaks. The barren trees outside her window swayed, brittle branches flailing in the furious wind.

Three days had passed since she left Jamie in his icy grave. Each passing hour was agonizing as she waited for news. Surely someone had found his frozen body in the snow. Dana Evans? A neighbor? Her fingers trembled slightly as she dialed.

Rachel picked up quickly, her voice a little breathless.

"Is your door closed?"

"Yeah," Jill said. In fact, she had spent most of the past few days canceling meetings and burying herself in work within the quiet sanctuary of her office, claiming to be under the weather.

"What's up?" Jill asked, doing her best to adopt a light, casual tone. There was a momentary pause on the other end of the phone.

"I'm not even sure how to say this. Jamie is dead."

Jill pressed shaky fingers to her lips, and she struggled to find words.

"What? How?"

"You know he was at his cabin in Tahoe, right? Well, he apparently slipped on the ice on the back deck and fell down the stairs. They found his body last night."

"Was he alone when he died?" she asked. Her back was rigid, and her hands clenched convulsively around the receiver as she waited for Rachel's response.

"Apparently so. Get this—Dana Evans found him. I told you something was going on between them." Rachel clicked her tongue before pulling in a long breath. "Talk about freak accidents. Anyway, I thought I should let you know. The announcement is due to go out any minute, and I didn't want you to get blindsided."

"Thanks."

Jill swallowed hard and closed her eyes. Her head swam for a moment, and she could see Jamie's sightless eyes glaring up at her from his snowy grave. Her throat ached, and she struggled to draw in a shaky breath.

"You still there?" Rachel asked at length.

"Yeah," Jill stammered. "Just shocked, you know. Never expected…" Her voice trailed off. "How does something like this happen?" She had to ask the question. The extra time she had taken to clean up after herself should have paid off, but there were no guarantees. The cold fingers of fear closed around her heart, choking out whatever guilt she might have felt.

"From what I understand, it was a freak accident. The investigation was pretty clear-cut."

Jill could feel the pounding of her pulse slow perceptibly at the revelation. She straightened in the chair and directed her gaze out the window, watching the boats bob on the choppy water.

"Life has crappy timing, you know?" Rachel's voice trailed off.

"How so?" Jill's senses snapped back to high alert.

"Well, so close to his promotion and all. I mean, he had accomplished so much. Strange how life works out sometimes."

Jill managed to say something she hoped passed for agreement. "I'd better go," she said at last. "I'll want to be available once the announcement goes out." She barely heard Rachel's response before she hung up.

***

Scarcely an hour later, the email announcing Jamie's death landed in her in-box. Few details were provided. The message focused on the unexpected tragedy and expressed sympathy for Jamie's friends and family. From an organizational perspective, the executive team would need some time to figure out the necessary changes. Jamie's boss promised to forward the details for the memorial service as soon as he could.

Jill's fingers rested lightly on the keyboard. She read the announcement for the third time, thinking about how ritualized the ending of a life was. All those decisions about the funeral, the coffin, the service, and the graveyard.

She closed her eyes. Unwelcome memories flooded back in a rush. Two polished coffins, one long and one short, flanked by a kaleidoscope of flowers at the front of the church. Her stepfather's drawn face. The sidelong glances of friends and strangers cast her way. The feeling that she might suffocate in the oppressive silence of the house, left alone with her stepfather.

***

In the days that followed, the office was quieter than usual. Team members went on with their work, bugs were fixed, and Jill uncovered the source of the software slowdown. The project was back on track.

Early Monday morning, Jill flew to San Jose for the memorial service. Not to do so would have raised questions. The mood in the chapel was somber, and the procession of prayers and speeches passed in a blur as a deep numbness settled over Jill. Only the sight of Jamie's younger brother gave her a jolt. He looked like a smaller, younger carbon copy of Jamie.

Staring at the front of the sanctuary, Jill didn't think about Jamie. She didn't think about her mother. She didn't think about anything at all. Even Dana Evans's wailing exit from the church barely registered.

On the way out of the church after the service, Rachel cast a sly, sidelong glance at Jill. "Don't be surprised when Barry comes looking for you." There was a knowing glint in her eyes, a clear sign that she knew more than she was letting on. She'd met Barry Reynolds, Jamie's boss, a few times during project reviews but had not anticipated an audience so soon after Jamie's death.

"About what?" she stammered.

"You'll see." Rachel's enigmatic smile made Jill's pulse skyrocket. Pressing her lips into a thin line, she stepped out of the chapel and into the California sun.

Safely ensconced back in the guest office at ZyraNet's headquarters, Jill closed the door and tried to bury herself in work

Staring blankly at the computer screen, her eyes strayed down the hallway to Jamie's corner office. The door was open, and she could see the empty desk. She didn't want to think about Jamie, but she couldn't stop the memories from flooding in. It was the beginning and not the end of their relationship that filled her head: Jamie as she remembered him best—sharp, witty, and engaging. If only he hadn't backed her into a corner. If only he'd been honest.

The gentle rap on the door took her by surprise. She started at the interruption. Glancing up, she half expected to see Jamie's face. Instead, she saw Barry.

Jill forced a shaky smile. Mentally, she collected herself. *Get it together, girl.*

"Sorry, I didn't mean to startle you," Barry said as he eased the office door open.

"I think everyone's on edge." Jill angled her eyes down toward the carpet, struggling to maintain her composure.

"Rightfully so. How are you doing?" Barry leaned against the doorjamb, voice warming with compassion. She wondered how many of these conversations he'd had over the past few days. Of course, none quite like this, she acknowledged. She had a *special* relationship with Jamie.

"I'm hanging in."

"Good. When do you head back to Seattle?"

"Tomorrow afternoon."

"Are you free for dinner? I know it's short notice …"

Jill glanced up in surprise. What could he possibly want to talk about? Had Jamie shared some of his doubts about her? Did Barry know something about their relationship?

"Sure. Of course."

"How about A.P. Stumps—say, seven o'clock?"

"See you there," she said with a tight smile as Barry turned to go. A.P. Stumps. Of all of the places to pick, he had to choose that one. She had spent an hour waiting there for Jamie only a few short weeks ago. She wondered if the bartender would remember the scathing message she had asked him to pass on to Jamie as part of her grand exit. She sincerely hoped not.

***

The hostess seated them at a table for two by the window. Jill looked over the menu, pausing as she felt Barry's eyes on her. Her smile was subdued as she met his gaze over the top of the menu.

"How is the Seattle team taking the news?" Barry asked.

"They're okay." She set the menu down on the table, pausing to take a long sip of water. "It was a shock for them. For all of us," she amended.

Barry nodded slowly. He studied her face, and she stilled herself, quelling her impulse to squirm. She kept her features arranged in a cool mask.

Fortunately, the waitress arrived just then, and they ordered dinner. She sipped the Pinot Noir slowly and waited for him to say what was really on his mind. At last, Barry spoke.

"You've done a good job getting the project back on track."

"Thanks. The team has really stepped up. Feedback on the public beta has been positive, and the bug count is starting to ramp down. We're on track."

"Rachel said that after weeks of the team frantically reviewing code, you were the one to actually identify and fix the issue. Pretty impressive."

"We were taking a narrow view of the problem. The code itself was fine. It wasn't until I took a look at it from a more holistic perspective that the conflict with the antivirus software became apparent. Working around it was the easy part."

"You've got good instincts." Barry tipped his glass at her in a silent salute.

The first course arrived, and Jill picked up her fork to start working on her salad. Barry hesitated, looking at her over the rim of her wine glass. His expression was inscrutable.

"I've been thinking about your role."

Jill tensed. About what, exactly? About firing her? About stripping her of her management title and making her an individual contributor on the team? Her resolution of the code issues at least showed that she still had her engineering chops. Setting her fork down, Jill met his gaze directly.

"What were you thinking?" Her voice sounded strained. Thin. Dry. Fragile.

"For starters, how would you like to present the demo at the WebNOW conference?"

A rush of air escaped her lungs in surprise.

"That's the week after next."

"True, but you know the technology inside and out." Barry took a sip of his wine as he waited for her to process the request. "I could do it, if you'd rather."

"No. I'll do it." She knew that she'd be a fool to pass up this type of opportunity for visibility.

"Excellent." His smile underscored his approval.

They both picked at their salads as the color trickled slowly back into Jill's cheeks. Her appetite suddenly improved as the second course arrived.

Barry swirled the red wine around in his glass, Jill's eyes fixed on the dark, velvety teardrops sliding down the bowl, settling in a pool at the bottom. Dark red. Almost black. Almost like blood. Jill shook her head and shifted her eyes away from Barry's glass. She looked up to find him watching her.

"Jamie and I had a few conversations about you," he said at last. Jill shifted in her chair, searching for the right thing to say.

"You know what they say: 'Only believe half of what you read and less of what you hear.' Or something like that." She gave a self-deprecating shrug.

Barry's laugh was a deep rumble that started in his chest.

"Well, you know Jamie. He wasn't generous with praise."

Jill forced a smile as she dropped her gaze to her wineglass. *Boy, you don't know the half of it. Some perks come with a hefty price tag.*

"But he did have good things to say about you. He trusted you with the biggest project on the team. That's no small thing. It speaks to the level of confidence he placed in you."

Jill straightened and grew still as she wondered where this was going. A prickling sensation traveled along her spine as fear started to dissipate and was replaced by curiosity. Anticipation. Barry bent forward.

"So I asked you here to see if you were interested in taking on a larger role within the organization."

"What kind of role?" she asked, though she could hardly breathe.

"A director position. You'd keep responsibility for your current team, of course. But I would also want you to take on some direct reports in San Jose."

"You're kidding, right?"

"No, not kidding, actually." Barry chuckled. "I've seen how you perform under pressure." His head angled to one side, as if he was weighing his words. "Normally, we'd do a search, interviews—you know the process. But given the circumstances, it didn't seem appropriate. The job is yours if you want it." He took a sip of his wine while he waited for her to respond.

"How about it?" he prompted at length.

Jill's pulse raced, and for the first time in what felt like forever, she smiled—a genuine smile, the kind that came from the heart. All the weeks of stress, all the feelings of anger and betrayal fell away. Her hard work over the past weeks and months had paid off. And all despite Jamie.

She picked up her wineglass and held it aloft.

"I'd love to," she said without further hesitation.

CHAPTER TWENTY THREE

Alex stood waiting outside the front door of a small house in the Greenwood neighborhood. Hands shoved in his pockets, he hunched his shoulders against the steady drizzle. Days had passed since he had delivered the shocking news of Natalie's death, and he couldn't get Abby out of his head. Hearing the footsteps in the hallway, he straightened.

As the door swung open, Abby's blue eyes rounded in surprise. An emotion he couldn't name rippled across her face.

"Alex. Come in," she said quickly, moving back so he could enter.

He followed her down the cluttered hallway. A small mountain of shoes was piled near the door, and Abby followed the trail of toys into the living room.

"Sorry about the mess," she said over her shoulder. "We weren't expecting guests."

Clearing space off the couch, she gestured for Alex to sit. As he eased into the soft cushions, he saw a little girl playing with a doll-house in the corner of the room. From the toddler's round cheeks and sturdy hands, he gauged her to be around three years of age. He smiled at her, and she went back to arranging her dolls.

Abby sat at the other end of the couch.

"What brings you here this morning?" She sat very straight. The tension in her body was like a coiled spring ready to burst, and she looked as if she was bracing herself for more bad news.

Standing on the front porch, he had asked himself the same question.

"I just wanted to stop in to see how you were doing."

She sighed, her shoulders sagging ever so slightly. Red-rimmed eyes glistened in the pale morning light.

"Oh, I'm managing." She flashed a half smile as she looked away, directing her gaze toward her daughter.

"How about your parents?" Alex's fingers fiddled with the edge of a pillow, and he realized coming here was a mistake.

Only the news of Honeywell's arrest would bring Abby and her family comfort. Anything short of that was useless. So why was he here? Because he wanted to see her. The truth was as simple, and as unsettling, as that.

"Mom's a mess. Dad's a rock. You know how they are. Any news on the case?"

Alex paused, considering the question.

When he finally tracked down Lisa Cullen's family, her mother had been surprisingly tight-lipped. Eventually he learned that Lisa had died seven years ago, the victim of a hit-and-run. Mrs. Cullen claimed Lisa hadn't heard from Jerry Honeywell after the family left Winthrop. While her tone was emphatic, Alex couldn't shake the feeling that there was more to the story than she was letting on.

Telling Abby about Lisa Cullen wouldn't help. Abby needed something concrete, something actionable, something that he could not give her.

"Unfortunately not. We're looking for any sign of Honeywell to surface, but so far he's flying under the radar."

She took in the status with a slow bobbing of her head.

"I know you're doing everything you can to find him. I know you probably have a mountain of other work on your plate. I can't tell you how much it means to me that you've been working the case, Alex."

Her blue eyes were bright with tears. As she blinked them away, he was reminded of her gentleness. Abby was good. She didn't deserve this kind of pain. Alex stretched his hand out toward her when he felt a tap on his knee.

"Tea?" the little girl asked, holding out a plastic princess cup on a pink saucer. She had the voice of a baby bird, sweet and clear.

"Hannah, not now," Abby said softly to her daughter.

"I'd love some tea," Alex said, taking the cup away from the girl and making loud, slurping sounds as he pretended to drink the liquid.

"Hot?" she asked, eyes solemn as she looked at him.

"Very, but I'm being careful so I don't spill. What's your name?"

"Mamma said no talk to strangers." Her tone was so serious he had to smile.

"Well, that's good advice, but you see, I'm a policeman. I'm here to help." Setting the teacup down on the corner of the coffee table, he pulled out his badge to show her. "See?"

Her mouth formed a silent, reverent 'Oh' as she looked at it. "Police."

"My name is Alex. What's yours?"

"Hannah," she said and looked over at her mother. Slipping his badge back in his coat, he handed her the cup.

"Could I have some more tea please, Hannah?"

With a bright smile, she gripped the teacup in her chubby fingers and hurried across the room to where her dolls sat encircled around a small table. Empty teacups were placed in front of each.

"She's lovely," Alex said, glancing over at Abby, who was staring at the floor.

"Yes, she's a real comfort."

"When do you go back to work?"

"In a few days. Routine is probably good right now."

"How's Darren?" Alex was pleased that he recalled her husband's name. They had only met in passing a few times. He had the vague recollection of a big guy, short blond hair, and stern face.

Abby grimaced, and Alex instantly regretted the question.

"Well, we've hit a rough patch. He's moved out for a while." She tucked her hair behind her ear. The line slid from her lips with the ease of a memorized verse. Alex cringed and wondered how many well-meaning relatives had asked the same question.

Then Hannah was back, bearing more tea. Grateful for the distraction, he took the cup and started to sip. Looking over at Abby, he caught her eyes.

"Sorry."

Abby's dry laugh came out as a short bark.

"How could you know? I barely told my mother before this whole nightmare began. I didn't want to hear the I-told-you-so. She never liked Darren much. I think she always hoped I'd marry someone more like—"

She stopped short, as if realizing how the revelation would sound. An awkward silence fell between them. A deep pink flush stained Abby's cheeks.

"Want more?" the girl asked, offering the princess cup to Alex.

"No thanks, Hannah. It's very good tea, but I have to get going."

"Mommy sad," the little girl said, her small, star-shaped hand resting on his knee.

"Yes, but I know you're taking good care of her." Alex brushed his hand lightly over the child's soft hair. He admired her perfect beauty. Pixie face. Blond hair in wispy curls. Hannah looked a lot like Natalie had at her age. A lump formed in his throat, and he swallowed hard.

"I help."

"I'm sure you do." The smile he gave Hannah was soft, but his eyes fixed on Abby. Her head was lowered, and he couldn't see her face through her soft curtain of blond hair. But he didn't need to see her expression to know that she was crying. Her hands balled into tight fists as she tried to pull herself together.

Hannah caught sight of the cat walking across the room and took after it at a run. Alex stood up.

"I need to get going," he said softly.

"Sorry. I just don't seem to be able to stop crying." Abby nodded and rose to her feet, roughly wiping the tears from her eyes.

He wanted to say something, but the endless platitudes that came to mind sounded trivial. Instead, he held out an arm. She closed the distance between them, burying her face in the front of his coat. Alex could feel her shudder with silent sobs, and he flattened his palm against her back, wishing there was something he could do to ease her pain.

The smell of her hair filled his senses. Warm peaches. The welcome feel of Abby in his arms felt achingly familiar. She was the first girl he'd kissed, and a flurry of memories flooded back in a rush. He could remember the first time he'd kissed her, at a friend's house. His hand buried in her hair, he realized he didn't want to let her go. He also realized that was probably reason enough to get the hell out of here.

The appropriate length of time to hug a friend had long since passed, and he tried to step back, but her arms remained closed tightly around him. She tipped her head back, and he stared into her blue eyes. She looked so lost. So vulnerable.

His hand cupped her cheek. Stroking a thumb across her soft skin, he brushed away her tears. He wanted to kiss her, like he'd done a thousand times before. He could almost taste the salty sweetness of her lips.

He knew it wasn't right.

"I've got to go," he said quietly as he gently disentangled himself from the circle of her arms. Abby stepped back. Her lips formed a pursed white line.

"If you hear anything ..." Her voice trailed off.

"I'll call."

He waved good-bye to Hannah before turning to leave.

The feel of Abby in his arms stayed with Alex long after the door to the small house in Greenwood closed.

CHAPTER TWENTY FOUR

Thanksgiving feast at the Shannon household was something Alex always looked forward to. Football on the television, beer in the fridge, great food. What could be better? Today, though, as he stood outside his parents' brick Tudor house, Alex tried to get into the spirit of the holiday. *Family. There was one family who had little to be thankful for.* He tried to push the image of Natalie Watson's dead body out of his head. The desire to find Jerry Honeywell consumed his every waking thought.

Squaring his shoulders, he took the concrete steps two at a time. The house smelled like turkey and sage, and his stomach rumbled in appreciation. An afternoon with his family promised a welcome distraction from the case.

"Alex," his mother said, a smile on her lined face as she greeted him. Crossing the room quickly, she enveloped him in a warm hug. After spending thirty years as a nurse, his mother had turned her passion for caring for people into a love of everything green. She took pride in tending her garden, which was now the showpiece of the block.

"Hi, Mom."

Rebecca Shannon looked behind him.

"Where's Jill?"

"She'll be along in a little while." He ignored the frown on his mother's face and stepped through the curved entry into the living room. Bending over to kiss Emma's cheek, he held out a hand to Mike, who shook it warmly.

"Where's Dad?" Alex asked.

"In the kitchen pretending not to watch football," his mother said, casting a sly look over her shoulder.

Alex followed the delicious scents down the hall and into the kitchen. Michael Shannon Sr.'s large frame was bent over the oven door, one hand gloved with an oven mitt while the other held the turkey baster, poised over the perfectly browned bird.

"Another fifteen minutes and this baby will be ready to come out." Michael eased the turkey back into the oven and swung the door closed.

"Good news. I'm starving."

"Can I get you a beer, son?" His father's ensuing smile was wide.

"Absolutely."

Michael grabbed a bottle from the fridge. Then he froze in mid-stride, staring at the television as the Detroit Lions completed a long pass downfield. The crowd cheered silently, the volume turned all of the way down in a vain attempt to avoid detection. His fingers still gripped the bottle cap he had not yet twisted off.

"Need help with that?" Alex asked, gesturing toward the beer.

"Huh? Oh, this?" He grinned at his son. With a quick twist of his hand, he removed the cap and handed the bottle to Alex. "You know your mother doesn't like it when I watch football before dinner on Thanksgiving."

"Hate to burst your bubble, Dad, but I think she already knows." Alex's smile was wry.

"Haven't seen you in a while. How are you doing?"

"Busy. You know how it is."

Michael nodded slowly as his eyes studied Alex's face. He took a sip of his beer. "I heard about the Watson girl. Tough break. How is Abby?"

Alex averted his gaze, directing his stare out the window toward the garden. His hand gripped the bottle as he took a long sip. The last thing he wanted to do was to talk about the case. As hard as he tried, he hadn't been able to get Abby out of his head.

"Sometimes things don't work out the way you plan."

"How are you holding up?"

Alex inclined his head to one side and shrugged. The concern in his father's voice was apparent.

"We're still looking for the son of a bitch that killed her."

"Any leads?"

"Hunches. Nothing solid yet." Alex took a long pull from his beer bottle.

"Hell of a thing." Michael shook his head slowly and paused, measuring his words. "You know, sometimes I wish you'd gone to art school, taught school—done anything but join the force."

His father's look was serious, and Alex knew if anyone understood the indelible images that you carried around in your head, it was his father. Alex was certain that, after spending a career as a firefighter, his father had memories he wished he could erase.

"Art school?" Alex's smile was wan. "And do what? Paint houses, maybe business signs? Seems kind of trivial."

"Sometimes that's not such a bad thing. One thing's for damn sure: you wouldn't be digging dead girls out of the snow."

Alex did not respond. What was there to say? There was no arguing with his father, particularly when faced with such a crushing blow. The Watson family would never be the same, and the sadistic bastard who had killed their youngest daughter remained at large. But this certainly wasn't a conversation he wanted to have right now. There would be plenty of time to obsess about Jerry Honeywell's whereabouts in the days to come.

"So what have you been up to?" he asked his father at length. Michael's grin was lopsided.

"Your mother has me busy digging up the backyard." He gestured over his shoulder with a shrug.

"Again? What's she doing now?" Alex peered out the window toward the garden.

"She's decided she wants a fountain over in the corner near the cherry tree."

"Of course she does." Alex smiled, and Michael rolled his eyes.

"It's always something."

"What are you complaining about?" Becky asked as she breezed into the kitchen.

"Nothing, dear." Michael tipped Alex a furtive wink.

"What's the score?"

Alex grinned at the sheepish expression on his father's face.

"The Lions are up by seven."

"Hope they can hold on. They've been dying in the fourth quarter," Becky said as she opened the refrigerator. Michael's face looked stricken.

"Why do you have to go and say things like that? They could go all the way this year."

"Uh-huh." she met Alex's warm gaze, her eyes twinkling. "Honey, Jill's here. She looks like she could use a glass of wine." Pouring some Chardonnay into a glass, she handed it to Alex.

Jill stood in the living room by the fireplace. A smile parted her lips as he entered the room. Her eyes broadcast silent thanks as she took the glass from his hands.

"How was your run? How far did you go?"

"Eight miles. Molly was full of beans."

Alex nodded, thinking he would have some catching up to do. Jill was a fantastic runner, and he didn't like to fall too far behind in his training. Otherwise, he wouldn't be able to keep up, and there would be no end to the gloating.

"Your timing is perfect. Dad's about ready to pull the turkey out of the oven."

"I wonder if they need any help in the kitchen," Jill said.

Emma stood to her feet.

"You stay, I'll check in with Becky."

"Thanks," Jill said in a flat tone and sipped her wine.

An awkward silence fell over the trio. Jill shifted uncomfortably. Her gaze looking everywhere but at Mike.

"I'd ask how the case is going, but I've read the updates in the papers. Anything new?" Mike asked.

"Not much."

"Shit."

Finally Alex asked about the new subdivision that Mike's company was building out in Redmond. The tension between his brother and his wife was palpable, and again, Alex found himself in the middle. *Life would be so much easier if Mike and Jill just got along.* But wishful thinking didn't make it so, and when the conversation petered out, he decided that a change of scenery might help. Alex led the way to the kitchen.

Becky and Emma were working side by side, smiling and chatting amicably as they got the vegetables ready for the serving dishes. Alex saw a dark look cloud Jill's expression as she watched the two. Wondering if Jill was feeling left out, he placed his hand on the small of her back and felt her tense at the contact.

"Anything I can do to help?" Jill asked again.

"Sure, dear. Could you fill the water glasses on the table?" Becky asked.

The foursome worked together quickly, and within minutes the dining-room table was ready for the feast to begin. Michael and Becky sat at the ends, with a couple on each side.

"Everything looks wonderful," Jill commented as they sat.

"Happy Thanksgiving," said Michael, raising his glass in a simple toast.

Everyone raised their glasses, and the passing of the food began. Chatter was flowing smoothly around the table when Alex tapped his glass with a spoon.

"I have an announcement to make." All heads turned toward him. "Jill has been promoted to Director of Engineering."

"Hey, that's great," Mike said, and the other voices around the table agreed. Jill's cheeks flushed with appreciation as she received their congratulations. Her eyes met Alex's in a warm smile.

After a few moments, Mike picked up his glass.

"Well, we have a little news of our own. Emma is expecting."

"Expecting what?" Alex asked.

"A raise. What do you think, you ass?"

"Oh, Mike, what wonderful news," Becky stood and rounded the table to kiss Mike on the cheek and hug Emma around her shoulders.

"Congratulations," Alex said warmly. "When is the baby due?"

"June," Emma answered.

"How are you feeling?" Becky asked, her cheeks glowing with pleasure.

"Good. Tired."

They spent the next half hour eating and talking about babies. Alex studied Jill over the rim of his glass. She remained quiet throughout the meal, her smile politely detached. He wondered what she was thinking. Was she disappointed that Emma's news upstaged hers? Was all the talk about babies boring her? Something had certainly caused her to draw inward, but he wasn't sure what.

After hugs and kisses all around, they left. Returning home, Alex followed Jill inside the house, helping her with her jacket. He hung it on a hook inside the door.

"You look lovely tonight," he said, admiring her in the soft glow from the lamp.

"Thanks," she said, turning away.

"Are you okay?"

"Yeah," she answered, but he wasn't convinced.

"You sure? You've been pretty quiet all evening." Alex placed his hands on her shoulders and stepped close to her, planting a soft kiss on her fragrant hair.

"Not much to say, I guess."

Drilling straight into the heart of the matter, he looked down into Jill's face. "Great news about Emma and Mike."

"Yeah." Jill stepped back, breaking contact.

"That was heartfelt."

"What do you want me to say? Emma and Mike have managed to procreate. Good for them. What an accomplishment."

Alex's mouth sagged into a slight frown.

"I get it. You feel upstaged. But their pregnancy is great news, and from my parents' point of view—well, they've been waiting for ages for one of their kids to reproduce. I think Mom has been ready to be a grandma much longer than she'd admit.

"They'll be waiting a whole hell of a lot longer for us to be making that announcement." Jill's answering smile was sardonic, her razor-sharp tone slicing into him.

Alex's expression was guarded as he tried to gauge Jill's hard expression. Was she just angry? He took a deep breath.

"Wouldn't you like to have kids?"

"Are you kidding?" she asked. "Maybe someday, but I've just gotten a very big promotion. The timing couldn't be worse, not to mention the weight gain, the stretch marks, the breast feeding ..." Jill rolled her eyes.

They'd never talked seriously about having kids. He assumed they both wanted kids, and when the time was right, well, they'd throw birth control away and get started. Maybe it was Thanksgiving. Maybe it was Emma and Mike's news. Whatever it was, he didn't want to hit the snooze button on the biological clock.

"When do you think the timing might be right?" he asked.

"Why do you ask?"

"Well, I was thinking that maybe we shouldn't wait too long." He flashed a boyish smile at her, in hopes of lightening the mood. "You know I've heard that trying is half of the fun."

Her expression soured, and she turned, stalking past him.

"Maybe you should have married perfect Abby. She's got a kid, right?"

"Jill," he called to her.

She stood framed in the doorway to the kitchen as she looked back at him.

"I need a drink," she said.

CHAPTER TWENTY FIVE

Alex bent forward, both elbows planted on the cluttered surface of the desk. He reviewed the autopsy and forensics reports on Natalie Watson for the third time. His eyebrows pinched together as he focused in on the words, building a clear mental picture of the last few moments of the teenage girl's life. The results of the autopsy held no big surprises. Death by strangulation. Sexual contact. No semen. Skin under her fingernails showed that she had put up a fight.

The toxicology screen was clean, but that was inconclusive. Many of the typical date-rape drugs were flushed out of the victim's system quickly, and that's what Alex thought had happened to Natalie. It would have been easy for Honeywell to slip something into her coffee, knocking her out cold for at least six hours. The drug would have worn off in time for her to be conscious for her struggle. The state of the body marked the time of death within eighteen hours of her disappearance. At least she hadn't suffered long.

Forensics showed that the blood samples lifted from the floor of the Winthrop cabin did indeed match Natalie's. They had a few hair samples from the couch; some matched Natalie's, and some that proved a DNA match to the skin sample they had taken from the corpse.

After Winthrop, the trail grew cold, and Alex was certain that Honeywell had left town soon after burying Natalie on the hillside. Curling his hand into a tight fist, Alex pressed his fingers against his lips and continued to think about Honeywell. Kayla Miller was still missing. He was convinced Honeywell had fled to California, and he wondered if Kayla was another of his victims.

The Medford police said the waitress working with Kayla the night she disappeared saw a guy who looked like Honeywell in the café but couldn't be sure it was him. She swore he left before the café closed. Without more to go on, finding Honeywell was like trying to find a needle in a haystack. How long could the bastard hide?

"Alex?"

Swinging around in his chair, Alex saw the smiling face of Kris Thompson, with Jackson lumbering in behind. He noticed that Kris and Jackson carried matching cups of coffee. Leaning back, Alex allowed himself to hope for some good news. "What have you got?"

"A ping on Honeywell's bank account."

"Tell me," Alex said, glancing past Kris to a sober-faced Jackson.

"The hit comes from an ATM machine in San Jose, California."

"Son of a bitch must be hurting for cash."

"Let's get the tape from the ATM camera and see if we've got a clear picture of Honeywell mugging for the camera," Alex said.

"Already under way, Boss. I'm having them upload the footage to our secure server. I'll let you know when it's ready." Kris's smile was radiant, and Alex nodded in approval.

"Great work." After the long dry spell since finding Natalie's body, the welcome lead had him smiling for the first time in days.

Less than two hours later, the trio was huddled around Kris's computer, examining the black-and-white video stream. Instead of seeing the face of Jerry Honeywell captured by the video from the ATM's security camera, they saw a skinny guy, early twenties, wearing a white T-shirt and a leather vest bearing what looked to be gang insignia.

"Get some hard copies. Face. Vest. Let's nail down the gang affiliation."

Jackson nodded at Alex.

"I've got a buddy in the SFPD. Luka Petrovich. We used to work Vice together back in the day. Bet he knows how to track down this son of a bitch. He's got some pretty persuasive interrogation tactics."

The two locked eyes. The timing was perfect. At Jill's goading, Alex had agreed to present at the Major City Chiefs' Conference in San Francisco. Maybe he could do a little legwork on the case while he was there.

"Let's give him a call."

CHAPTER TWENTY SIX

After giving his address to the crème de la crème of the American law-enforcement community, Alex left the Major City Chiefs' Conference and made a beeline for the Hall of Justice, home of San Francisco's homicide squad. He found himself escorted back through the winding maze of industrial-mint hallways, which opened up to the homicide's bull pen.

"He's over there." The sergeant pointed a gnarled finger toward the back corner of the room.

"Thanks," Alex said.

Detective Luka Petrovich was slumped in a chair behind his desk, facing away from Alex as he approached. A thin woman was perched on the edge of the detective's desk, arms folded, face stern, looking like a librarian scolding a student. Her thick red hair was pulled severely back from her face, further emphasizing her disapproving glare. Slowing, Alex hung back, still within earshot.

"So how did the suspect end up breaking his nose?" she asked, eyes narrowed as she focused on the detective. Her thick orange eyebrows formed a straight line over her hazel eyes, and she impatiently awaited the answer.

"He tripped and hit the table." Broad shoulders shrugged beneath a wrinkled white shirt, and Alex discerned a thick Russian accent.

"That's not what he said." Eyebrows lowering further, the woman glowered.

"You could check camera," Petrovich suggested in a helpful tone, as if she hadn't thought of that already.

Her lips pressed into a thin line, and her eyes cast fiery arrows at the detective. "Why yes, I could have, if the video hadn't failed."

"Really?" Head tilted to one side, the detective continued. "Well, station in Vallejo is not well maintained. Budget shortages." He shook his head in what appeared to be mock wonder. "What can you do?" His accent made his *w*'s sound more like *v*'s. Based on the look on the woman's face, she remained unconvinced.

"This isn't the first time we've had this discussion, Detective Petrovich. If I get one more complaint about you, I'm going to recommend a thorough investigation into your conduct." Her voice trailed off then as she glanced at Alex.

"Detective Petrovich? I'm Alex Shannon, Seattle PD. We spoke on the phone."

Luka rolled back in his chair and stood, extending a hand, an easy smile crossing his face—one that was strictly at odds with the scowl sported by the woman facing him.

"This is Detective Shelia Holmes. Internal Affairs."

Alex tried not to let the surprise he felt register on his face when he shook her hand. Ignoring Alex, she cast a disapproving glance toward Petrovich before stalking away, her thick heels clacked on the floor.

"Hope I didn't interrupt." They both watched her leave.

"Redheads hate me," he said, with an impish smile. "She'll be back. Coffee?"

"Sure."

"Good, let's go." Luka stood and grabbed his jacket. The Russian accent was now more subtle, and Alex suppressed a grin. Was playing the rube a tactic Petrovich used often to deflect uncomfortable questions? If so, it was a good one.

As Luka headed toward the exit, Alex shot him a quizzical look and glanced over toward the break room in an unspoken question.

"We could stay here, I guess," Luka said in his accented English, "but I wouldn't want to kill you on your first day in San Francisco."

Luka sped through the roller-coaster city streets. Winding their way through the Tenderloin district, Alex briefed Luka on the case. The car came to an abrupt halt outside a little bakery on Russian Hill. Alex could hear the bells from Saints Peter and Paul Church tolling the hour, its twin towers reaching up into the blue sky. Several tables lined the sidewalk in front of the large plate-glass windows. Coffee-drinking patrons huddled around their steaming cups, cigarette smoke swirling into the brisk morning air.

An old man occupied the seat closest to the door, squinting against the stream of acrid smoke. He traded nods with Luka. The detective clapped him on the shoulder as he walked past. "Hey, Pops."

Just as Luka opened the door, a pretty woman, dressed in business attire, strode past. Alex caught the look that passed between the two. Mutual admiration. He couldn't help but notice that the San Francisco detective turned his share of female heads with his Slavic good looks and movie-star smile.

"So what will you have?" Luka asked as they reached the counter.

"Coffee, nothing fancy," Alex said, and he glanced around the bakery. The smell of bread and pastries filled the air, and his stomach rumbled in response. A woman emerged from the back. She called out in Russian over her shoulder and finished tying the apron around her narrow waist. Her thick auburn hair was pulled back into a loose bun. Dark, almond-shaped eyes dominated her face. The smile on her lips froze as she gaze shifted from Alex to Luka. Her expression hardened, and she placed her hands on her hips.

"Good morning, Sasha," Luka said with a lopsided smile. "Two coffees and two chocolate-almond croissants, and some Liru compote."

The woman stood staring at him for a long moment, as if she hadn't quite heard what he had said. Her eyes bore into the detective before she gave a quick nod. Without a word she deposited the coffee mugs and the pastries on the counter. Elegant fingers poked the cash-register keys as she rang up the sale.

Luka handed a coffee to Alex and gestured toward a small table in the corner. He fished a wad of cash out of his pocket, flattened out a couple of rumpled bills, and gave them to the cashier. "Thank you." '

Balancing the plates of pastries and the coffee mug in his large hands, Luka took the stool across from Alex.

"Best pastries in San Francisco," Luka said as he pushed a plate across the table.

"She likes you." Alex nodded toward the counter. The cashier still stood glaring at Luka's broad shoulders.

"We have some history," the San Francisco detective shrugged.

"You don't say?" Alex took a sip of his coffee and glanced back at the woman.

"She's my ex-wife."

Alex tried not to spit the hot coffee out of his mouth. Luka's full lips twitched at the corners, and he glanced past Alex and out the window. Alex cleared his throat as he set the cup down in its saucer. "You're right about the coffee. It's great."

"This is my father's bakery."

"And your ex-wife works here?"

"They still consider her family." Luka's shrug was slow.

Alex dipped a corner of the pastry in the compote as he watched Sasha stalk into the kitchen. The door swung closed behind her.

Wadding the croissant into his mouth, Alex closed his eyes for a fraction of a second, appreciating the contrast between the light buttery texture of the pastry and the rich, bright berry compliment.

"What's the jam? I've never heard of Liru compote. Is it a Russian native dish?"

"It's just a mix of regular berries. 'Liru' is the name of the person who invented the recipe," Luka explained.

"A Russian pastry chef?"

"An ex-girlfriend," Luka said with a smirk. "Pop liked the recipe."

Alex laughed. Clearly this guy had a girl story for everything and was quick on his feet.

"You got a wife?" Luka asked.

"Her name's Jill."

"What's she like?" Luka asked as he sat back in his chair, blue eyes curious.

Alex inclined his head and considered the question. "We met in college. Gorgeous, brainy, top of her class."

"How did she end up with a loser like you?"

"Just her good fortune, I guess."

Luka smiled across the table, and Alex continued. "Jill was used to being the smartest person in her class, always getting the answers right, always getting top marks. She wasn't ready to take second place, particularly to a career detective with no formal computer training."

"How'd she take it?"

"Not too well, actually. We had a class project where you had to secure your network, and the other students tried to hack in. Most of the networks were easy to crack, but I have to admit that Jill didn't make it easy. She'd constructed a pretty elaborate defense system. It took me a while to get in."

"I sent her a pop-up message during class that asked her out for coffee. Looking back, it was a pretty cocky way to let her know I'd circumvented her security." Alex smiled as he sipped his coffee.

"Did she accept?"

"Hell no. She shot me an icy look over her shoulder and sent a message in response, a text graphic of an extended middle finger. It took a while, but I eventually wore her down."

"Ah, persistence pays off."

"She was dating a jock at the time, and he helped matters along."

"Really? How thoughtful of him."

"Not exactly." Alex chuckled. "They were out dinking one night. The guy she was with got a little physical. She came to class with a shiner, so I paid the asshole a little visit. Jill had already dumped him, but the follow-up visit made an impression and helped soften her shell. I wasn't exactly her type, but she came around. Eventually."

"Assholes like that deserve to have their bells rung." Luka took a bite of his croissant. Powdered sugar clung to his lips, and he wiped it off with the back of his hand.

"He deserved a little more than he got, but after that he stayed away from Jill." Alex paused, sitting back in his seat, and glanced out the window. "You been divorced long?"

"Five years. Cops don't always make the best husbands."

"Jill is just as absorbed by her career as I am by mine. Ever think of trying again?"

Luka flashed Alex a quick, enigmatic smile.

"I don't think I'm the marrying kind. Ask Sasha. She makes good pastry, though." Luka's gaze settled on the kitchen door for a moment. Alex laughed as Luka slurped his coffee.

"So your guy, Honeywell, he's been hanging out with the Bay Area chapter of the Gunns. They're a nasty offshoot of a Southern California motorcycle gang. Apparently his cousin is the Gunns' chief badass. The cousin's been questioned in several homicides, but nothing's stuck so far."

"Is Honeywell there now?"

"I've got some buddies in vice who suggested we talk to the ATF. They have the clubhouse under constant surveillance. Drugs. Guns. I figured we'd take a drive down there to see if your boy's still around."

"I appreciate your help."

"Any friend of Jackson's is a friend of mine." He waved his hand in a dismissive gesture. "We worked together back in the day. Good guy. How is he?"

"He's a foul-mouthed hardass."

Luka's smile broadened. "So, the same? Good to know that some things don't change."

They finished the pastries and coffee and left the bakery. Alex brushed the powdered sugar off his jacket and climbed into the car.

"Ever do surveillance on a motorcycle gang?" Luka asked.

"Never had the pleasure."

"You're in for a treat."

CHAPTER TWENTY SEVEN

Luka flashed his badge as they walked through the door to a non-descript three-story office building at the edge of the San Jose business district, just off of San Carlos Street. The noise from the cars passing by on the Guadalupe Parkway was muted by the closing of the thick glass doors.

"Good morning," Luka said, smiling at the receptionist. "Luka Petrovich, SFPD. We're here to see Agent Russell Stone."

"I'll tell him you're here," the receptionist said. It was hard to tell if Luka's good looks garnered any favor with her as she pointed to a row of chairs lining the back wall. She didn't smile. Alex took a seat in the narrow chairs. The place had all of the charm of a DOL office. Luka sat next to him and spoke quietly so that only Alex could hear.

"Stone's the head of the San Jose investigation. You wouldn't want to sneeze on a Gunns gang member without letting him know first."

"Sounds big." Alex glanced at the receptionist, who murmured into her headset as she eyed them through her heavy horn-rimmed glasses.

"It is. The investigation spans three states. The main focus is down in So Cal, outside of LA, but there's a fair bit going on in the Bay Area, too."

"Detective Petrovich?"

Russell Stone was a thin man in his late forties. His face had a delicate, birdlike quality, with sharp eyes and pinched features. Behind a set of rimless glasses, his gaze shifted from Alex to Luka, then back again. After a brusque greeting, he led them down a hall to a small corner office.

Stone motioned for them to take a seat as he settled into the plush leather chair behind a glass and chrome desk. The ultramodern office furniture seemed at violent odds with the early 1970s industrial décor.

Dressed in an immaculate navy-blue pinstriped suit, the ATF agent carried the bureaucratic air of a ladder climber, someone who played by the book and was eager to get his share of the spotlight. The photographs on his desk featured the smiling faces of a plump wife flanked by two teenage girls posing in front of the stone structure of a church. Agent Stone was a God-fearing family man.

"So what's your interest in the Gunns?" Stone got right to the point.

"We're actually interested in a man we think is hanging out with them. Jerry Honeywell." Alex said as he handed Stone the case file. "His cousin is a member of the gang. We're hoping to flush him out so we can extradite him to Washington for the murder of a sixteen-year-old girl, Natalie Watson."

Pushing back in his chair, Stone flipped through the case file. His eyes skimmed the pages. After the obligatory amount of time, he handed it back. Alex discerned no hint of expression on his narrow face.

"So he crossed state lines? Isn't this case now a matter for the Bureau?" Stone's sharp gaze bore into Alex.

"No kidnapping charge since the victim is dead, and as far as I'm aware, Honeywell hasn't committed any crimes here in California," Alex was quick to state his counterargument.

"Would you really want the Bureau sniffing around the Gunns?" Luka asked matter-of-factly. Alex watched Stone's expression harden as he considered the possibilities. After a fraction of a second, he stared back at Alex.

"No. I don't want anyone involved who could potentially screw up our case. That includes the two of you. No offense, Detective

Shannon, but your guy is small potatoes considering the case we're building against the club. This is a huge operation—murder, gang rape, drugs, and firearms. Your one murder, albeit tragic, is a drop in the bucket."

Alex let the statement hang between them, waiting for Stone to continue. His first impression of the agent—that he was an ambitious guy who liked to be in control—proved true.

"Trust me—you have no idea what you're stumbling into. And if you don't want to take my word for it, you can hear it straight from the horse's mouth." He held up a finger with one hand, and with the other he pressed the button on his speakerphone.

"Send in Agent Wilde." He sat back in his chair, pressing steepled fingers to his pointed chin. "Jacob Wilde has been working on the Gunns' surveillance detail for over a year now."

Without the precursor of a knock, the door swung open, and in strutted Jacob Wilde. With his shaggy hair and intense gray eyes, he had the look of a hard-core geek, right down to the "Think Different" T-shirt.

"Agent Wilde, meet Detectives Alex Shannon and Luka Petrovich." Russell made the introduction, looking like a proud papa introducing his son, the Yale graduate.

Wilde acknowledged them with a wide smile, and he shook both detectives' hands with a strong grip. Leaning back in his chair, Wilde propped his Converse sneakers on top of Stone's desk. Flecks of dirt flaked off onto the pristine glass surface. Alex saw Stone's jaw tighten a fraction. The look that passed between the two had Wilde lowering his feet to the ground. Alex saw the ghost of a smile cross the agent's lips.

"So what can I do for you?" Wilde's eyes were bright with curiosity.

"Detective Shannon is from the Seattle PD. He's looking for a murder suspect named Jerry Honeywell, who may be holing up with the Gunns."

Wilde nodded and shifted his keen gaze to Alex, who wasted no time getting to the point.

"He killed a sixteen-year-old girl."

"I was telling Shannon his case is a drop in the bucket compared to the one we're building against the Gunns." Stone leaned forward, and Alex saw his gaze focus on the flecks of dirt on his desk before shifting to Wilde's face.

"They're into some pretty fucked-up shit, that's for sure." Wilde nodded. Alex saw Stone flinch at Wilde's colorful characterization. His lips flattened into a tight line, and he shot the agent a sour look. Wilde ignored him.

"Have you seen Honeywell?" Alex pulled a photograph from the case file and handed it to Wilde. The agent took a second to process it.

"He's there all right. The prick's cousin, Henry Dugan—a.k.a. Duke—is part of the club's muscle. Honeywell is one fucked-up dude. Quiet. He's working under the table, fixing the gang's shit. Mostly bikes. Nothing relating to the case," he said, catching Stone's eye. "The girls seem to steer clear of him, though. I hear he likes it rough."

That last comment earned Wilde another dark look from his superior before Stone turned, jabbing his outstretched finger toward Alex.

"Whether he's there or not, I want you to stay away from him and the other members of the gang. All I need is for the two of you to go in guns blazing and blow this thing wide open. You are way out of your jurisdiction, Detective Shannon. He's off-limits. Got it?"

Before Alex could respond, Stone's cell phone rang. Irritation flared as he checked the call display.

"I've got to take this," he said and rose to leave the office. Stone wedged his way past Wilde's loose-limbed frame. The door snapped shut with an audible click.

With Stone out of the way, Wilde leaned forward, his high voice almost conspiratorial.

"Look, Duke's heading to a bar outside of town called Axel's to do a little business tonight. Rough place, but if you want to ID the guy yourself, that's where he'll be. The two of them stick pretty close to each other. Watch out for his cousin. You don't want Duke to catch sight of you. He won't care if you're cops. He'll happily toss your ass in the middle of a landfill without thinking twice."

Wilde paused to let his warning sink in.

"We've got a guy in with them. Undercover. Tough son of a bitch. He'll be tagging along with Duke tonight. He can't save you if you step in it without blowing his cover. But hey, Axel's is a public place. There's nothing to stop you from having a look yourself," Wilde said, shrugging his shoulders. Muscles rippled beneath the tight T-shirt. Luka grinned first at Alex, then at Wilde.

"Your boss wouldn't like that."

Wilde's smile broadened in response, showing a line of crooked teeth.

"Probably not, but let's be clear." The smile faded and the expression on his lean face turned serious. "You'd be on your own, with no back up. And if Stone catches you sniffing around his case, there'll be hell to pay."

"Thanks."

Wilde eased back in his chair and swung his feet back up onto the desk, and Stone entered. The bureaucrat's piercing gaze settled on each of them in turn before he spoke.

"Gentlemen, I have a meeting to prepare for. Unless you have anything else …"

"Thanks for your time," Alex said and extended his hand toward Stone. The Agent's grip was buttery soft, and he eyed the trio with a sharp look.

"Stay away from the Gunns," Stone warned.

"Yes sir," Alex said as he passed by Wilde. Shielded from Stone's view, Wilde's left eye twitched in the quickest of winks.

CHAPTER TWENTY EIGHT

Music flooded through the open door of the bar, and Allen Collins wailed out another triumphant rendition of "Free Bird" from the jukebox. Alex and Luka brushed past the row of motorcycles that lined the font of the rundown clapboard building. The neon signs crowding the window were the only light source capable of penetrating the thick layers of cigarette smoke coating the glass surface.

Casting a dubious glance over his shoulder, Alex hoped Stone and his battery of ATF agents weren't watching as the door swung closed behind them. Disobeying a direct order when you were way out of your jurisdiction was risky business. Besides, they were just here to identify Honeywell, not haul him in. Luka and the SFPD would take charge of the arrest and extradition when the logistics were set. Tonight, he just wanted to get a long look at Jerry Honeywell with his own eyes.

Alex followed Luka inside. The bar teemed with activity: blue-collar workers blowing off steam at the end of a hard day over beer and a game of pool. They took the two empty stools at the end of the bar. From this vantage point they could see everything from the restroom to the pool tables.

"What can I get ya?" the bartender asked as he eyed the two men suspiciously.

"Beer," Alex said. "Whatever's on tap."

"Same." Luka inclined his head toward the pool tables.

A small cluster of men wearing leather jackets milled around the back, pool cues in hand. Pitchers of beer adorned the small tables in the middle.

Alex sat back, eyes scanning the crowd. The hairs at the back of his neck prickled. He saw a man with shoulder-length dirty-blond hair make his way through the crowd toward the back of the bar.

Hello, Knucklehead, Alex thought as the bartender set the pint glass down on the bar, foam head spilling over the rim. Picking it up, Alex took a sip. Clad in hip-hugging jeans and a tight fitting T-shirt, Honeywell caught the attention of more than one female as he walked by. Some flashed enticing smiles that went ignored, Alex noted as he continued his covert study.

What's the matter, Knucklehead? Do grown-up women not turn your crank? Are you only into teenage girls? The image of Natalie's smiling driver's license photo filled his head, and he looked away.

Alex glanced toward the television behind the bar. Taking little note of what was playing, he tried to slow his racing pulse.

"You see your boy?" Luka asked, his eyes glancing up into the mirror behind the bar.

"He's over at the pool table closest to the door."

Luka's nod was slow as he checked out the group.

"Looks like he fits right in."

"It's probably not the first time he's worked alongside them," Alex said. "I'll bet his cousin's the tall guy."

"Maybe we should ask them to join us for more dirty, warm beers." Luka smirked. Pursed lips conveyed his disdain toward the quality of beverage served in this fine establishment. Alex grinned, too, as he swallowed a mouthful of the watered-down swill.

A figure, big and burly, emerged from the crowd and made his way toward the restrooms. Looking up, Alex wondered if this was the undercover agent that Wilde had spoken about. If so, he looked every bit the part of a card-carrying, badass member of a motorcycle gang. His bloodshot eyes strayed toward them for a moment, and he spat on the floor as he passed. The bartender glanced over just then, and Luka grinned at Alex.

"Friend of yours?" he asked, for the bartender's benefit.

"No, but he looks a little like your girlfriend."

"More like her mother," Luka said with a laugh.

The two talked sports while the minutes crawled by. Typical guy talk. Nothing that would raise suspicion. Luka got up to go to the restroom, leaving Alex by himself at the bar. One of the girls with the Gunns was making a show of dancing at the table, her slender form moving seductively to the beat of the music. A few men crowded around to watch. Honeywell peeled away from the group and walked up to the crowded bar, coming to a stop a few stools down from Alex.

"Hey, man, those your bikes outside?"

Honeywell's flat eyes fastened on Alex's face.

"Fuck off."

Alex raised his eyebrows, curving his lips in a disarming smile.

"Sweet rides, that's all."

Honeywell nodded to the bartender, who poured another pitcher of beer. Alex studied him. On the surface, he was a good-enough-looking guy with a scruffy goatee. No obvious tattoos. The tips of his fingers were stained black—probably engine grease—but there was something hollow about his flat, blue eyes. Or was that just the cop in him talking? Surely it's nothing a girl like Natalie would have noticed.

"Know anything about bikes?" Honeywell asked. His voice had a lilt to it, a hangover from his formative years in Louisiana perhaps?

"A little," Alex said. "My buddy has a Ducati." Alex cocked a thumb toward Luka's pint of beer.

"That makes him the fucking expert." Honeywell's attitude was dismissive, but Alex thought it seemed a little forced this time.

"Yeah, that's what I told him. You want a real bike, get a Shovelhead."

Honeywell paused, his eyes fixed on Alex, who held his gaze without flinching. This was the moment of truth. Would Honeywell engage? Alex's pulse picked up as he waited for a response.

"Look, Asshole, you don't know shit about bikes." Honeywell rolled his eyes. "If you did, you'd know that every dickhead and his pup owns a fucking Shovel and thinks they're Easy Rider." Honeywell leaned in, resting his elbow on the bar. "If you want a ride, get a Knucklehead. It's ten times the bike of a fucking Shovel, and you won't look like every other swinging-dick-weekend-warrior-fucknut on the road."

"Well okay," Alex said, looking like he'd just been schooled by Honeywell's response. "Not sure that I've ever seen one," he said, taking a pull from his beer. "What's so great about a Knucklehead?"

"Oh, man. If you have to ask …" Honeywell shook his head slowly from side to side in mock incredulity.

"Yeah, I know." Alex grinned. He waved his hand at Honeywell in a self-deprecating gesture. "The wife is dead set against it."

"Fucking poser."

"Aren't we all?" Alex asked. "We're all so busy trying to look different that we all end up looking the same."

That won him a soft chuckle. He was getting somewhere.

"Tell you what," Honeywell said. "I'm going to bust out of here soon. Follow me outside, and I'll show you the difference between a Shovelhead and a Knucklehead."

"Cool."

Honeywell wound his way through the crowd carrying the pitcher of beer. Alex watched as he exchanged a few words with a guy that Alex could only assume was none other than the infamous Henry "Duke" Dugan, Honeywell's big, badass cousin.

Duke's dark hair was short, clean cut, and Alex could see small silver hoops winking from his earlobes. He was in his early thirties with a deep scar on his chin, and the same dead, blue eyes as his cousin.

Alex saw Duke glance toward the bar and give a quick nod. Then Honeywell turned and headed toward the door in no particular hurry. Alex knew this was the moment of truth, his one chance to get Honeywell on his own. The smart thing to do would be to let him go. But the urge to get to know the guy who'd killed Natalie was too strong.

Luka hadn't returned by the time Alex stepped outside. The night air was cool on his hot skin. The parking lot was set back from the road, and he could hear the hum of cars passing by. Honeywell stood beside one of the motorcycles. As Alex watched, he slid his key in the ignition, and he motioned for Alex to come closer.

Alex's gut clenched as he closed the distance between them. Hyperaware of his surroundings, he focused on Honeywell's eyes, which glittered darkly in the bright glow from the neon signs. Honeywell pointed down the line of motorcycles.

"Shovelhead, Panhead, Knucklehead. Three different eras, three different motors. The V-Twin Pan came after the Knuckle. Shovel came after Pan. This one here," he curved a long finger at the bike beside him, "has a Shovelhead engine. See how the rocker covers look like old coal shovels? Panheads have rocker covers that look like upside-down cake pans. Knuckleheads look like the knuckles on your hand." Honeywell's fingers clenched into a fist.

"Now, if you lean in here and check this out," he gestured, indicating something behind the rocker cover that Alex was certain he would find fascinating if he could bring himself to give a damn. "Seriously, check it out. This is the shit right here."

Alex leaned in, aware of the danger. Following Honeywell out here into the darkened parking lot hadn't been smart. Drawing in a slow breath, he lowered his hand to his ankle. Luka had lent him a gun from his private collection.

"You know my daddy used to tell me that it's not until you've lost everything that you're free to do anything. Now, do you mind telling me, boy, what the fuck you want?"

"Not sure what you mean," Alex stalled, raising his eyebrows in what he hoped passed for surprise, fighting the urge to pull the gun.

"Don't play games with me, cop," Honeywell said through clenched teeth. "I could sniff you out clear across the room. You think I'm some kind of hayseed? You think I'm stupid?"

"Hey, buddy, it's time to go," Luka called over his shoulder. The music from the bar escaped in a burst of sound, silenced once again by the closing of the door.

Alex didn't tear his gaze from Honeywell. He knew they were outnumbered. He knew he couldn't risk moving on Honeywell. Not without backup. Still, Alex found it damned near impossible to disengage.

"Alex," Luca said.

"Right," Alex shot back over his shoulder. "Hey, thanks for the Harley tutorial," he said, rising to his feet. A thin smile crossed his face as he read the naked hatred in Honeywell's eyes.

CHAPTER TWENTY NINE

"That went well," Alex said bitterly, taking the beer from Luka. "At least we know where to find him. Now we just need to get the logistics in place."

"If he doesn't bolt first. He had me made as a cop."

"Maybe not." Luka flopped in the leather chair across from him. "Hey, look on the bright side—Axel's is a pretty nice place. I have a new favorite hangout."

Despite the gravity of the situation, they both laughed.

"I should have just let him go so your guys could handle him." Alex rolled his head back against the couch and stared up at the ceiling.

"Shit happens," Luka said with a philosophical shrug. "We'll get him later."

"Guess it could have been worse. We could have had the ATF all over our asses."

"For what? We're just a couple of guys out for a beer." Luka took a long swallow from the chilled bottle. With one foot he pushed an empty pizza box off the coffee table onto a pile of newspapers stacked on the floor.

"Hell of a place you've got here." Alex scanned the room full of IKEA furniture, empty beer bottles, and dirty dishes.

"Bachelor pad. The maid comes on Thursdays."

Despite his grim mood, Alex managed a smile. After a long pause, he sat up, staring at his beer bottle.

"What now?" Luka asked.

"Now we go to work," Alex said. Luka's eyes flashed at him.

"What do you have in mind?"

"Honeywell had a high school sweetheart who moved to California. Lisa Cullen. Blond hair. Blue eyes. Looked a lot like Natalie Watson. She was killed by a hit-and-run driver about seven years ago, when she was in college, right around the time that Honeywell was here."

Luka's eyelids dropped to half mast as he considered the implications.

"I'm not big on coincidences."

"Me neither," Alex admitted, draining the last mouthful of beer from the bottle. "I was thinking that maybe tomorrow morning we could take a drive. I'd sure love to meet Lisa's parents in person."

***

Albert and Mary Cullen lived in Windsor, a quiet town in the heart of the Sonoma Valley. Luka pulled up to the curb of a well-maintained bungalow in a picturesque neighborhood bordering on a park. Perfectly pruned trees studded the immaculate lawn. The neatly trimmed rosebushes flanked the short walkway leading to the front door.

Alex emerged from the passenger seat slowly. The painful drumming in his head from last night's beer picked up in tempo as he pressed the doorbell. Some nights, beer was like potato chips. Why stop at just one?

A melodic tinkle of chimes unleashed the skittering of toenails on the floor followed by the slow clicking of high heels.

There was nothing welcoming in the frosty expression on Mary Cullen's face. Her eyes were the flinty color of Puget Sound before a storm. She looked from Alex to Luka, then back again. The unsmiling lips tightened a fraction more.

A flurry of furious barking erupted from the fluffy dog at Mary's heels. Not the deep belly barks Molly uttered, but high-pitched yipping that made Alex wince—the cringe-worthy high-pitched tone of finger-nails squealing down a slate chalkboard.

"Rocky, shush." The dog flinched as if struck, but fell mercifully silent. She turned back toward Alex. "What can I do for you?"

"I'm Detective Alex Shannon. This is Detective Luka Petrovich. We'd like to speak to you about your daughter, Lisa." Alex held out his police identification.

Mary shifted subtly, placing her weight on a back foot, like a fighter poised to meet an opponent. The flawless coat of makeup she wore looked on the verge of cracking as her eyes narrowed. Alex thought about Joyce Watson. While the similarity between Natalie and Lisa was unmistakable, their mothers could not have been more different. Mary's cold, ice-queen beauty could not hold a candle to the natural warmth that radiated from Joyce Watson's smile.

"Detective Shannon, didn't we already speak?" Mary asked, in a sharp, clipped voice. "Aren't you a long way from home?"

"Yes, but—"

Mary was already closing the door before he finished his sentence, red-tipped fingers of her knobby hand pressing against it firmly. Alex stopped the door with his shoe. The meaning behind Mary's glare was clear. They were not welcome. But Alex had come too far to leave empty-handed. One way or another, she would talk to him.

"Mrs. Cullen, please. We'll only take a few minutes of your time. It's in regards to the death of a young girl in Seattle. Your daughter knew the suspect, Jerry Honeywell."

A trace of indecision flashed in her eyes, and Alex smelled victory. With an exasperated sigh, Mary stepped back and opened the door.

"You have ten minutes," she said, retreating down the tiled hall, the small Pomeranian skittering at her feet. Trading a wary look with Luka, they fell into step.

Mary led them back through the immaculate house. The color scheme was a sterile white on white. Alex checked the walls for family photographs and found none. The house looked as if it were being staged for sale, well decorated, but with no personal touches. Like the rest of the house, the kitchen was a study in white, accented with a few splashes of color—red apples in a ceramic bowl, a vase of golden sunflowers placed dead center on the kitchen table.

The smell of coffee filled the room. Alex stole a wistful glance at the coffee maker, wedged into the corner of a cupboard. He had little doubt that Mary was not inclined to share. Coffee would only extend their visit.

With a quick wave of her hand, Mary motioned for them to sit at the kitchen table. They complied. Rocky stood guard at her master's feet, growling softly and showing the tips of his sharp fangs.

"I understand that Lisa and Jerry were a couple in high school. What do you remember about him?" Alex asked, forcing his taut body to relax, adopting a comfortable air.

Mary's face tightened another notch. Her eyes flinty eyes met his.

"Jerry came from a troubled home. He lived with his uncle in a cabin north of town. He met Lisa in art class during their junior year." Mary averted her gaze. "I don't know what else I can tell you. It was a long time ago."

"They were close?" Luka asked, and Mary's lips pursed in response.

"It was a high school crush. Of course, everyone thinks that their first love is their last. There's nothing new there."

He knew what she meant about first love. There was a time when he thought Abby was the only woman in the world for him. And then there was Jill.

"Why did you leave Winthrop?" Alex asked.

"It's simple. My husband got a new job in California."

"How did Jerry take the news?"

"I don't know what you mean."

The resolute line of her mouth assured Alex his instincts were right. There was more to this story. Prying it out of Mary wouldn't be easy.

"I think you do. Was Jerry angry when Lisa left? Did he follow her?"

"As far as I know, they never saw each other again after we left Winthrop."

"Really? I find it hard to believe that a boy who has no one else in the world would let Lisa go so easy." Alex kept his eyes glued on Mary's face as he let the silence stretch out between them. Her gaze was razor sharp as an exasperated sigh escaped her parted lips.

"Why are you here, Detective? Lisa's dead. No good can come of this. Why are you so anxious to dig up the past?"

Rocky's low growl bumped up a notch.

"Hush, Rocky," Mary commanded in a voice that was no longer detached.

Rocky flinched and grudgingly obeyed. If a dog was capable of looking pissed, Rocky pulled it off. Alex watched Mary struggle to maintain her icy exterior, a battle she was losing. Her cheeks flushed red, and she fidgeted with the frayed edge of a placemat. Leaning forward, he spoke softly and hoped that by opening up about Natalie, he could tip the tide in his favor.

"Natalie Watson was sixteen years old when she met Jerry Honeywell online. I found her body near a cabin in Winthrop two weeks ago. Here's a picture of your daughter in high school." Alex placed a photocopy of the yearbook photo on the table. "This is a picture of Natalie Watson." With their photos side by side, there was no denying the similarity between the two girls.

Mary's lips trembled as she studied the photographs. She covered her mouth with a shaky hand.

"I still don't see what any of this has to do with Lisa." Her words were blunt, but her tone was less emphatic now.

"I think that learning more about Lisa will help me figure out what makes Jerry tick. I know this is painful. I know you want to leave what happened to Lisa in the past, but I don't think Natalie will be the last girl he hurts. I think he's only getting started. I need your help, Mary."

The sound of the telephone cut the tension in the room. Ignoring it, Mary stared out the kitchen window. She sat so perfectly straight and still, Alex wondered if she heard it at all. He stole a quick glance at Luka. Luka gave an encouraging nod. Mary's hand left her lips and traveled to her throat. She swallowed hard.

"Can I get you coffee?"

"Sure," Alex said.

"Please," Luka agreed.

Rising from the table, Mary crossed the room and poured three cups of coffee. Playing the part of the gracious hostess, she brought out the crystal cream and sugar containers, placing them in the center of the table between the two detectives. She settled back into her chair. Alex resisted the urge to prompt her. At last, she began.

"Lisa and Jerry were joined at the hip. At first, Albert and I thought that it was puppy love and it would pass. We thought about trying to put a stop to their relationship, but knowing Lisa, that would only have made her more determined."

"What was it about Jerry that you didn't like?"

Mary inclined her head, considering the questions.

"We didn't object to him. Not really. Not at first anyway. It was how serious the relationship seemed. Lisa was so young. They both were. We didn't want her to get off track, you know?"

"But there was something about Jerry," Luka pressed.

She nodded wearily. Her eyes shifted from Alex to Luka.

"He was possessive. She started to shut out her other friends. Pretty soon, he was the only one she spent time with. We didn't think it was healthy. After we aired our concerns to Lisa, Jerry refused to come to our house. It made things worse."

"How did Lisa take the news of moving?"

"Like any teenager in love would. But we didn't give her a choice." Mary's wistful expression told Alex just how painful talking about Lisa was.

"And Jerry?"

"Jerry became—what's the word for it?—unhinged." Mary shifted forward in her chair, her back ramrod straight. She brushed the rim of the coffee cup against her lips before setting it back on the table. "You see, Lisa was pregnant."

Luka set his coffee cup down with an audible thump. Alex's gut constricted.

"Jerry knew about the baby?"

Mary's lips parted in a dry smile, almost a grimace, as she continued.

"He wanted Lisa to run away with him. They cooked up some crazy scheme about getting married and raising the baby together. They were just kids. It wouldn't have worked, and Lisa would have been ruined, with no college education, no hope for a better life."

"So you moved?

Mary hesitated. Drawing in a deep breath, she expelled it from her lungs in a slow hiss. Finally she nodded.

"Yes. And then Lisa had an abortion."

Silence pooled in the kitchen.

"And after that?"

Mary sipped her coffee. Her voice was thick with emotion when she finally spoke. Her shoulders hitched in the smallest of shrugs.

"Well, Lisa was never the same. Oh, she went to college, she studied hard, got good grades. But it was like there was something missing. Lisa lost her spark. Albert thought she just needed time, but she never got it. In her senior year of college, she was riding back to her apartment after work on her bike and was hit by a car. The car didn't stop. She was left bleeding by the side of the road. We didn't make it to the hospital in time to say good-bye. Lisa died on the operating table, alone."

Tears pooled in Mary's blue eyes, but she refused to let them fall. Clearing her throat, she took another sip of coffee.

"I'm sorry," Alex said.

The pain reflected in Mary's blue eyes reminded him of the grief on Joyce Watson's face. He waited until Mary composed herself before asking his final question. "Was there anything different about Lisa before she died?"

"Different? How?"

Alex held her steady gaze, and kept his tone deliberately soft. This next part was going to be hard for Mary to hear. After many years, she had finally come to grips with the loss of her daughter. He didn't want to rip open old wounds. But he had no choice. He had to know.

"Jerry Honeywell got his mechanic's license in California. He was living in the Bay Area at the time of your daughter's death."

Alex could hear a sharp intake of breath as she processed his words. She cast a stony stare into her coffee cup, her fingers clutching it tightly. He could only imagine what thoughts were running through her head.

"You think …"

"It may mean nothing," Alex offered.

"It may mean everything," she answered, meeting his eyes at last.

As Alex and Luka made their way back to the car, Alex pondered the similarities between the story of Honeywell's parents and his painful past with Lisa. For a moment, he put himself in Jerry's shoes: a pregnant girlfriend with disapproving parents, and an aborted child. In the intervening years between Lisa leaving Winthrop and his move to California, how much had Honeywell learned to hate? Had he come here looking for Lisa? If so, what had he hoped for? Reconciliation? Or revenge?

* * *

"There are no eyewitnesses," Alex said, looking up from the report and over at Luka. "The police didn't have much to go on. There were no traffic cameras in the area back then. Another motorist saw Lisa on the side of the road and called it in."

Alex pulled up a chair at the end of Luka's desk and was reviewing the report on Lisa's accident. He reached for the bag of pastries as his cell phone rang. The call display showed a local California number. Alex stiffened and then hit the Talk button.

"Dude, I told you not to talk to the guy."

Alex's eyes fluttered shut for a second as he recognized the voice of Agent Jacob Wilde from the ATF on the other end of the phone.

"It didn't go exactly as planned."

"That's the fucking understatement of the year. Your boy's hit the highway."

"What?"

Bitter disappointment descended on Alex like a lead weight. He rubbed a hand across his eyes.

"Yeah, that's right. After they left the bar, Honeywell packed up his shit and struck out for parts unknown. I thought you'd want to know."

"And you just let him go?"

"You heard Stone. He's not a target."

"Fuck," Alex growled, his headache reasserting itself. Exhaustion set in.

"No shit, Batman. Anyway, if I were you, I would hightail it out of town before your little stunt gets reported to Stone. He's going to go ballistic when he hears you disobeyed his direct orders."

"I'm not worried about him."

"You should be. He may be a douche bag, but don't underestimate his political clout."

Alex slammed the phone down on Luka's desk.

"Son of a bitch."

"What is it?" Luka asked.

"Honeywell's taken off. He left last night after the scene at the bar."

Luka pushed back his chair and swore.

"Perfect. He's got a twelve-hour head start."

"We don't even know where he's going."

"I wonder if we could get some information on the vehicle he left in."

"That was Wilde. The ATF isn't going to help us."

Alex sighed as he considered the disastrous turn of events. He'd fucked up. It was his fault Honeywell had slipped through their fingers. What would he tell Abby?

How long could Honeywell hide?

"What's done is done." Luka's shrug was philosophical. "I think we should continue to dig into the hit-and-run. Maybe we can find evidence linking him to Lisa's death and Kayla Miller's disappearance."

"What good does it do us if we can't find Honeywell?"

Alex released a long, slow sigh.

At three in the afternoon, his cell phone rang again. This time he did recognize the number.

It was his boss, Captain Lewis. And Alex definitely did not want to take the call.

CHAPTER THIRTY

J ill missed Alex. In the aftermath of Jamie's death and the dissolution of the affair, it was as if the scales had fallen from her eyes. If any anger remained, it was hers alone, she realized as she considered what she had risked for Jamie and what she would have lost in Alex. Vanity. The affair had been borne of vanity, and she vowed not to risk what she had so unwisely again.

Their planes could have crossed in the air as Alex flew back to Seattle and hers landed in San Francisco. It seemed unfair that they couldn't overlap by at least a night. With Jamie out of the way, their relationship was back on track. Clean. Simple. Just the way she liked it.

Now as she stood center stage in front of hundreds of people, basking in their thunderous applause, she decided life didn't get much better than this. As one of the featured speakers for the WebNOW conference, she had just given her third demo. The first two were standing room only, and the conference organizers had quickly added a third. She would bet anything that ZyraNet's stock had risen over the past few hours.

With a gracious nod, Jill surrendered the floor to the moderator of the panel. She threaded her way through the crowded conference center to the bar. She'd been guzzling water all day to help keep her voice in prime condition, and now she was ready to celebrate with something a little stronger.

"Dirty martini with three olives, please," she said as she caught the bartender's eye.

With a quick nod, he set to work on her drink, and Jill smoothed her long hair away from her face. Public speaking was a rush. Engineering was a solitary job that typically attracted introverts. Unlike most of her counterparts, she reveled in the opportunity to show off her work. The response to her demo was beyond gratifying. This kind of public recognition was like a drug, and she wanted more.

"Here you go," the bartender said, bringing her back to earth.

Angling her body toward the bar, she slowly stirred the olives around the glass and savored the high. Glancing up into the mirror behind the bar, she took a sip of her martini.

"Jill Shannon?" a voice sounded beside her. It was more of a statement than a question, and she swung her gaze to the man facing her. He extended his hand. "I'm Peter Young, columnist for *Tech Savvy* magazine. I caught your demo. Pretty impressive stuff."

"Thanks," she said, shaking his hand, voice raised to be heard above the din.

"Can I buy you a drink?"

"Got one already, and by the way, they're free." She inclined her head toward him, as if imparting a secret.

"Guess that makes you a cheap date," he said, with a mischievous glint in his eye.

"Cheap, but not easy." She found his slightly rumpled, boyish appearance appealing. His hair was medium length, angling in toward his face in a shaggy cut that mimicked the hip crowd of the day. The style was a little young for him, but he managed to pull it off. His hazel eyes sparkled with humor. With a leather satchel slung across his body, and a rumpled button-down shirt, he looked every bit the part of the reporter.

Signaling the bartender, he ordered a beer before looking back at Jill.

"I do profile pieces for the magazine, and I'm thinking that you would make a terrific piece."

The provocative phrase dripped with innuendo. But instead of being offended, Jill smiled, enjoying the banter.

"What would be involved?"

"I'd like to interview you. A stunning, intelligent woman would be a nice change of pace from the balding, geeky types I usually get stuck with." He paused, taking a sip from his beer bottle. His intense gaze was locked on her face, and she felt her cheeks warm under his careful examination. "What do you say?"

His smile was contagious, and she considered his offer for roughly two seconds. Just enough time to make up her mind.

"It's a deal."

"Cool." He clinked his beer bottle against her glass and tipped a salute. "Let's finish our drinks and get out of here."

Jill stiffened, placing her glass back on the bar, as she eyed him warily.

"Go where?"

"Somewhere quieter. It's too loud in here," he explained, his smile almost apologetic. "Besides, I'll want to take some pictures of you for the piece."

He had a point. The crowd noise buzzing around them was overwhelming. The high ceilings of the cavernous room made the situation worse, and they were on the verge of yelling to be heard. The strain from all of the talking she'd done over the past few days had left her voice hoarse.

"Look, I know how this sounds, but the magazine set me up with a suite. It's at the Hilton, just a hop, skip, and a jump through the skywalk. No funny business. I promise."

"Scout's honor?" Jill managed to suppress her grin but couldn't keep the playful edge from her voice.

"Scout's honor," Young said, flashing the three-fingered boy scout salute.

Jill took a long moment to consider the offer. Being featured in *Tech Savvy* would be quite a boon for her career. The publicity wouldn't hurt the company, either. Draining the martini from the glass, she ate the olives one at a time.

"You're on."

"You ready?" Peter asked, not quite meeting her eyes.

"Sure, let's go."

The crowd thinned as they left the main conference area and traversed the skyway to the Hilton hotel. Even though she was in high heels, her long strides kept pace easily with his. They traded small talk about themselves. How long had he been at the magazine? What had he done before that? How long had she been at ZyraNet? The friendly chatter put her at ease as she followed him to his suite.

Peter swiped his access card, and Jill heard the weighty click of the door mechanism unlocking. She half smiled as she followed him inside.

The suite was open and airy. The furnishings were tasteful, and the coffee-cream-colored walls made the room seem larger than it was. The faint smell of lemon furniture polish hung in the air—compliments of the cleaning crew, no doubt. Peter removed his satchel and tossed it on the couch as he crossed the room, heading toward the minibar.

"Can I get you something to drink?" he asked.

"Got any wine in there?"

Opening the door to the small refrigerator, he rummaged around. She could hear the clinking of bottles as he took inventory. "Bubbles or no?"

"No bubbles."

Peter pulled out a small bottle and twisted the cap off. With his back turned toward her, she couldn't see his face, but she could hear the smile in his voice as he poured the wine into the glass.

"I can't vouch for the vintage …"

"Thanks," she said, taking it from him. She settled into a white armchair at the end of the long coffee table and waited. He fixed himself a drink and sat on the couch. Pulling his laptop out of his bag, he placed it on the coffee table and waited for it to boot up.

"Have you ever been interviewed before?" There was a warm curiosity in his eyes as he smiled at her. She tried to guess his age. Early thirties maybe?

"Once in college. I was on the track team and broke some state records."

"Impressive. Still run?"

"As often as I can."

"I'm more of a team-sports guy myself," he said, his eyes remaining riveted on the monitor. "Would you mind if I captured the interview on the webcam? I may want to upload parts of it to the magazine's website as a teaser when the piece is in print."

Again with the disarming smile, Jill thought as Peter's lips parted, revealing a row of even white teeth. Somewhere an orthodontist had built a swimming pool in exchange for that perfect smile. Jill shifted in her chair, taking a sip from her wineglass. Liquid courage to settle her nerves? The wine burned its way down her throat, and she set her glass on the table, out of the range of the webcam.

"Okay," she said.

"Great, let's get started."

Peter asked background questions at first, about her education, her career path. Jill felt herself relax as she answered. She rested her back against the pillow, hands smoothing her skirt over her bare knees.

The next round of questions centered on the new technology that Jill had demoed. How long had it been under development? When was it due to release? What was Jill's role on the team? Jill found herself smiling and leaning in toward him as she answered. A gentle warmth spread through her. Was it the wine or being in the spotlight that contributed to the glow?

Peter wrapped up the interview with a barrage of questions about what it was like to be a female at the top of her game in a male-dominated industry. She laughed as she answered, revealing that she had never found her gender to be a drawback. Her work spoke for itself, and she was considered one of the sharpest engineers on the team, earning her respect the old-fashioned way. Sure, it sounded a little like bragging, but what the hell. She was damned good.

"You know, I interviewed a colleague of yours."

"Oh yeah? Who?" she asked, meeting his glance.

"Jamie King, last year. He won the Millennium Technology Award, right?"

"He did." Jill's lips twisted into a frown as her thoughts turned to Jamie and his broken body in the snow.

"Kind of full of himself. Still, it's a shame what happened to him." Peter paused, and she could feel his eyes on her. "What was that?"

"What?" she asked, pressing her lips together and focusing on his face. He studied her intently.

"That look?"

"Nothing. Really." She forced a laugh and averted her gaze. "Is that it? Are we finished?" she asked, feeling suddenly uncomfortable. She raised a hand to the collar of her blouse and tugged it away from her skin. Was the air conditioner on the fritz? The room felt too warm, and her cheeks burned. Picking up her wineglass, she took another sip. The cool liquid felt silky on her tongue.

"Almost. All I need is a few stills and we're done," Peter said as he rose from the couch. Jill set the glass down on the table and pressed her hands to her cheeks. Her mind felt a little fuzzy around the edges. Perhaps she had drained the martini at the bar too quickly. The wine definitely wasn't helping, and she hadn't eaten since lunch. Given that the sky was now dark, city lights twinkling through the window, it must be getting late. Too much to drink on an empty stomach was unwise, she mused.

Moments later Peter returned with Nikon in hand. She sat straighter and peered into the camera lens, forcing a smile. The flutter of the lens sounded as he cranked off some shots.

"Come on. You can do better than that," he said. One eye peeked out from above the camera, and she could hear his smile.

Jill tried to relax and smiled again, this time wider. But there was something wrong. She felt dizzy. Peter moved closer, his fingers working the lens, bringing her into focus as he squeezed off a few close-ups.

"That's better," he said. His voice was quiet as he stepped near, his leg brushing hers as he squatted in front of her. She jerked her legs to the side. If he noticed her recoil, he showed no sign. "Nice. Just a few more." His voice was softer still, almost soothing, as he pointed the lens at her. Again she heard the whisper of the shutter. Her head swam.

Snapping her eyes wide open took an effort, and she focused on his face, which seemed abnormally large. He loomed only inches from her. Peter was staring at her in the strangest way, and her skin began to prickle at the back of her neck. He let the camera dangle from its strap. His fingers gripped her bare thighs, just above the hemline of her skirt.

His touch seared her on contact, and Jill shrank back.

"Are you feeling okay?"

Peter's voice sounded concerned, but she sensed something else, something almost predatory, about the look in his eyes. Then he smiled. Those perfect teeth looked less perfect now. His narrow lips pulled back, revealing sharp canines that looked more like a wolf's than a human's.

She shook her head. This was crazy. Her imagination was getting out of hand. Was she seeing things?

"I think I need to go."

His smile widened, and in a quick, jarring movement, he rose.

CHAPTER THIRTY ONE

Jill stood too fast, swaying precariously on her high heels. Peter had his back turned and was fiddling with the laptop as she took a sideways step. The movement was disorienting, and she blinked hard to clear her vision. What was wrong with her?

"You might want to lie down," Peter said without glancing up.

Jill's confusion deepened. He seemed disturbed by none of this. Anyone sane would be bringing her water, calling a doctor, offering some helpful advice. He seemed to expect …

What the hell was this? Her eyes strayed to the coffee table, zeroing in on the wineglass. Had he put something in her drink? Whatever was going on, she was sure of one thing: it was time to leave.

A few more fumbling steps got her closer to the door. Her heart was fluttering wildly in her chest, and her breathing felt ragged. The door seemed a million miles away, but she stayed focused on it as she ordered her legs to move.

"Hold on, now. Where do you think you're going?" Peter caught up to her in a few quick strides.

"Gotta go," she said, trying to push past him.

"I don't think so, sweetheart. Maybe you should sit for a while. You don't look so good."

Something really wasn't right. She fought the fuzziness that nibbled at the edges of her mind. Pulling in a few deep breaths through her nose, she tried to clear her head. If she stayed any longer, she might not be able to leave. Finally, the room started to shimmer, and she felt a weakness in her knees.

"How are you feeling?"

"I'm okay," she managed. "Sleepy. I think the wine—"

"Why don't you sit down, and I'll get you a cool cloth for your head?" He gripped her elbow, and she followed him toward the center of the room. Her eyes tracked his every movement. To the casual observer, it might seem that he was guiding her. But as his fingers dug into her flesh, there was no mistaking his intent.

There wasn't an escape route in sight as she stumbled toward the couch. Her head spinning, she tried to stay focused on the objective. But with each passing second her limbs grew heavier. She sank into the cushions of the couch like a lead balloon.

"Can I get you something to drink?" Peter asked.

*** *** ***

Those were the last words that Jill remembered as she opened her eyes. Had she passed out? Her head still felt fuzzy as she took in her surroundings. There was a buzzing noise in the background that seemed to come into focus as it drew closer. Talking. She looked up to see Peter talking on his cell phone.

Pushing herself up into a sitting position was not easy, but she managed it. Peter was standing behind the couch, watching her as he ended his call.

"Sleeping beauty awakes," he said with a slight smile.

"What happened?" Jill raised a hand to her forehead, massaging the skin in wide circles.

"I'm not sure. You said you weren't feeling well, so I got you to the couch, and you passed out."

Jill tried to process her thoughts. Is that what had happened? Why couldn't she remember? Nothing like this had ever happened to her before. She'd only had two drinks—the martini at the bar and the glass of wine here in Peter's hotel room. Even rip-roaring drunk, she'd never blacked out. Something akin to panic stirred in her chest.

"Can I get you some water?" he asked. The incongruity between the implied concern of words and the flaccid expression on his face puzzled her still further. She'd passed out. Why wasn't he worried? As she watched his retreating back, she noticed he was wearing different clothes. He had changed into jeans and a T-shirt. His bare feet made no sound on the thick carpet as he ducked into the bathroom.

She was a mess. Her skirt was wrinkled and twisted, exposing a fair expanse of bare thigh. The top two buttons of her blouse were undone. With trembling fingers, she tugged her skirt down and straightened her top. She ran a hand through her long hair.

Peter handed her a glass, the ghost of a smile playing at the corners of his lips.

"How long was I out?"

"Not sure. A while. How are you feeling?"

"Groggy," she said before taking a gulp of water to wet her parched throat. As she set the tumbler on the table, she noticed that the wineglass was gone. How odd was that?

"Do you need me to call you a cab?"

Jill stared blankly up into Peter's face for a long second as she processed his words. The need to get back to a safe place was pressing in on her, and she rose awkwardly to her feet.

"No, I'll be okay."

"Cool. I'm going to take a shower. You can let yourself out."

Shocked, she watched him disappear into the bathroom. The sound of the shower's spray blended with the buzzing in her head. She bent to slip on her shoes. It took longer to find her purse.

Her mind still stuck in slow motion, she groped for the name of her hotel. She had to get back to her room and sleep. From the corner of her eye, she spied the card key, and crammed it into her purse. The door clicked loudly behind her as she maneuvered her way down the hall.

***

What's wrong with this damned door? For the third time, Jill inserted the card key into the lock of her hotel-room door. The light blinked red. Feeling hot and exasperated, she tried again. To no avail. The door remained locked. Caught up in the mechanics of trying to get in her room, she did not hear the man approach until he was at her elbow.

"Excuse me," he said.

Jill visibly started at the interruption.

"Sorry, didn't mean to scare you. It looks like you're having problems with your door. Can I help?"

His smile was disarming, and the soft, lined features of his face gave him a paternal look that reminded her of Santa Claus with twinkling blue eyes. Without a word, she handed him the card and stepped out of his way.

"I think I see your problem."

"What?"

"This card is for the Hilton. We're at the Fairmont, dear."

Jill's mind raced as she took the card from him. Depositing it in her purse, she fished around for another card key and found it tucked into the folds of her wallet.

"Oh," she said, her cheeks flushing red. "I'm so sorry."

"No problem." The Good Samaritan took the new card from her and slid it into the lock. With a dull clicking noise, the lock disengaged. He twisted the door handle and propped the heavy door open for her to pass through. She took the card key from his hand and put it back into her purse.

"Thank you."

"Are you sure you're okay?" His wrinkled brow echoed the concern in his voice, and she forced a smile.

"Yes, I'm fine." She let the door close behind her. But the truth was, she felt anything but fine.

CHAPTER THIRTY TWO

Jill awoke, disoriented. Shifting her eyes around the dark room, she tried to get a fix on what time of day it was. The heavy drapes pulled across the bank of hotel windows made it difficult for any light to penetrate. Glancing over at the clock, she saw it was late. Ten in the morning. How long had she been out? Why hadn't she heard the alarm?

Head pounding like a bass drum, she shoved herself off the bed and headed toward the bathroom. She needed some water, and, grabbing a glass off the countertop, she filled it twice before setting it down beside the sink.

The cold marble tile felt good on her feet as she crossed the bathroom to start the shower. Steam coated the glass stall with a thick film, and Jill shed her bra and panties before stepping inside.

The hot spray from the shower streamed over her, and she tried to clear her head. What the hell had happened last night? She remembered going to Peter's hotel room. She remembered the interview. She remembered drinking half a glass of wine and feeling a little woozy. But beyond a vague recollection of the cab ride home and fighting with the door, she remembered little else.

The bath towel felt like sandpaper against her sensitive skin. As the steam cleared from the mirror, she caught sight of her naked form. Leaning in, she saw what looked like small bruises on her breasts. What the hell?

Had something happened while she was passed out on Peter's couch? Random snatches of memory flashed through her head. Peter's unconcerned face hovering above hers. Her heavy limbs as she sank into the sofa. Waking up in her disheveled state. Peter heading toward the shower in different clothes than what he'd been wearing before.

Had Peter put something in her drink? Had he done something worse than that? Certainly that might explain some of what she was feeling this morning. Her head throbbed like the worst kind of migraine. She was sore in places she shouldn't be. A lightning strike of realization flashed through her.

Jill gagged, and, swaying back on her heels, she leaned over the sink. Dry heaves rocked her body. There was nothing in her stomach to bring up. After a moment or two, the nausea passed. She splashed some cold water on her face.

Was Peter capable of rape? If he had spiked the wine, it would explain the wooziness, the memory loss. And... And...

Oh, God.

Sinking to the bathroom floor, Jill covered her face with both hands. Memories rushed back in like a tidal flood. She remembered the stifling dark of her tiny bedroom, the sound of his feet on the bare hardwood floors, and the boozy stench of her stepfather's breath. His calloused hands digging painfully into her shoulders as he held her down. The fear. And the pain. Oh, the pain.

All of the things she worked so hard to forget surfaced in a terrible moment of understanding, and a deep, burning hatred swelled in Jill's frozen heart. Silent tears streaked indelible tracks down her face.

Slowly, one by one, Jill opened her eyes.

She was a defenseless kid when her stepfather preyed on her. But she wasn't a kid anymore. Jill gripped the counter and pulled herself up off the cold tile floor. Drawing in a series of deep breaths, she regained her equilibrium. Compartmentalize. Pushing the fear, the shock, the shame back, she focused on the one emotion that still remained. The hatred.

Whomever Peter thought he was dealing with, he was wrong. She was no victim. She wasn't going to shrivel up in a little ball and let him win. But what could she do?

Perched on the edge of the bed, she planned her next move. She could go to the cops, but the cops would launch an investigation. Date-rape drugs were in and out of the system so fast, they were virtually undetectable. There might be physical evidence of . . . what? Rape? Or intercourse? It would be her word against his. And she was a married woman. A married woman who had had an affair, and whose lover had careened down a flight of icy stairs to his death.

Peter would hire his own investigator, and what would he find? No. She couldn't risk it. There were too many secrets in her past. Too many lies.

Jill's hands shook as she raked her wet hair out of her face. He wouldn't get away with it. She wouldn't let him.

She would make Peter pay.

With steadier strides, Jill crossed the room, snatching her purse off the night table. Unceremoniously, she dumped the contents onto the bed and rifled through it until she found what she was looking for. She remembered having trouble with her door last night, and the kind stranger who had helped her. Between her clenched fingers, she clutched a white card key bearing the Hilton's logo, and she realized she must have inadvertently taken the key to Peter's room in her haste to get back to her hotel last night.

The conference was scheduled to start later this morning and would end well into the evening with the closing night banquet.

Jill pressed the plastic access card to her lips as a plan began to form in her mind. Tonight Peter Young was going to get more than he bargained for.

*** * ***

Jill dressed to blend in with the tourist crowd at San Francisco's Pier 39. The peak of her baseball cap sat low on her forehead, her long hair pulled starkly away from her naked face. The cold wind blowing off the choppy water of San Francisco Bay carried the smell of salted fish.

Hands buried deep in the pockets of her jacket, Jill veered away from the pier in search of a pawnshop. She was looking for the kind of place willing to break the rules. Instead, she met the gaze of a homeless man who was standing on the corner. Coarse gray hair spilled from the confines of a grimy woolen hat. The frayed collar of his green canvas jacket was pulled up in a vain attempt to shield his neck from the biting wind. His hands held a sign: "Vet down on his luck. Anything will help."

Watery eyes met hers, and Jill was about to pass as she noticed something else that stopped her dead in her tracks. While this wasn't exactly part of the plan, sometimes fate had a way of intervening. Without further hesitation, Jill pulled a hundred dollar bill from her pocket and ripped it in half. Catching the man's eye, she dropped it into his bucket and ducked around the corner. The last thing she needed was for a video-happy tourist to capture this transaction on tape. Some business dealings were meant for dark corners, and this was definitely one of them.

"Hey," he called after her as Jill ducked into the alley, her heart beating like bat's wings in her chest.

The alley was deserted, and Jill kept her back to the chipped brick wall as the bum rounded the corner. He held the ripped bill up for her examination. Before he could say anything, she stepped forward.

"You've got something I need."

She grabbed the waistline of his pants to pull him closer. The gap-toothed smile he gave her was that of a man down on his luck who suddenly finds himself in possession of a winning lottery ticket, one with a big payoff.

"Hey, little lady. Not sure what you had in mind, but—"

In one quick movement, she reached around him to touch the bulge at the side of his waist. His lips parted, and his eyes hardened as he grasped her meaning.

"Now what would you be needing with something like that?" he asked, his tone part curious, part scolding. Jill had no intention of making idle conversation. Instead, she brushed past him on her way out of the alley.

"Come on now, don't be so hasty," he called after her, and she stopped.

Jill turned with a knowing smile. Pulling the other half of the bill from her pocket, she handed it over in exchange for what she wanted.

The revolver was old but looked in perfect working condition as she stuffed it in her coat pocket and headed back toward the pier. As she crossed the street, her body shook with adrenaline. Whether from triumph or fear, she couldn't say. But there were two words that formed in her head, causing the slightest of smiles.

Mission accomplished.

CHAPTER THIRTY THREE

The card key disengaged the lock, and Jill let herself into Peter Young's room. The maid had already been there, and the suite was in immaculate shape, from the high polish on the desk to the comforter pulled so tight across the bed, it would have passed her stepfather's stringent coin-toss inspection. Peter wouldn't be back soon, probably not for a few hours. The closing speeches would drag on and on, and then there would be drinking. Lots of drinking. One thing you could count on at an event like this was an open bar, and Jill was willing to bet Peter would take full advantage of that fringe benefit.

She took her time searching the suite. The bathroom held all of the usual toiletries—deodorant, shaving cream, toothpaste. Stashed away in his shaving kit, she found something that made the rhythm of her heartbeat accelerate to a full gallop. There were three little white pills in the clear baggie. She would bet money that a fourth little white pill had made it into her glass of wine. On one side the word "ROCHE" was etched into the surface. On the other, a number one appeared stamped within a circle. Roofies.

Peter Young wasn't just a rapist. He was a fucking coward. He took what he wanted without a struggle. Jill closed her eyes. She could almost smell the bitter stench of her stepfather's breath. Master Sergeant Sam Morris preyed on the defenseless, too. A picture of his cruel face filled her mind, and she pushed it away. She refused to let the memories surface. She held everything back behind the thick wall of her resolve.

Everything except the hate. Hate seared through Jill's veins. And she thought about Peter and the one thing he hadn't counted on. Her. She had come here ready to fight. The comforting weight of the gun in her pocket guaranteed it.

Jill turned off the bedroom light and disappeared into the large closet, pulling the sliding door most of the way closed. The bag of roofies was clenched tightly in her fist. All senses were on full alert, waiting for Peter's grand entrance.

***

There was nothing stealthy about Peter's arrival. The door banged shut, and she heard him stumble through the living room. He stayed there awhile. How long, she couldn't tell. Antsy, she thought about leaving the safety of the closet, but no sooner had she thought it than Peter shuffled into the bedroom.

Peter bumped and crashed his way through the room in the dark. Jill glimpsed his shadowy figure as he passed by the closet door. He let out an earsplitting fart, and Jill grimaced. *Pig.* Next, the bathroom light flipped on and she was serenaded by the sound of a long, gratifying piss in the toilet. The lights clicked off, and Peter's discarded clothes hit the floor in a heap.

Not long after that, the buzz-saw sound of his snoring filled the suite. Jill waited as she went through the plan again and again in her head. Peter would pay for what he'd done. Anger uncoiled at the pit of her stomach. Jill slid the closet door open and stepped out into the darkened room.

Her gloved hand sweating, she gripped the butt of the revolver. The barrel of the gun trembled slightly as she pointed it at Peter's sleeping form. It was evident from the boozy cloud of breath he dispelled with each bed-rattling snore that Peter had made the most of the open bar. She hoped he was still lucid enough to understand what was happening to him. And why.

Leaning forward, Jill shook his shoulder, still keeping the weapon aimed directly at him. Maybe it was the smell of Wild Turkey on his breath. Maybe it was the adrenaline coursing through her veins. Whatever it was, for a moment Jill was transported back to the small bedroom in her stepfather's house. She could see Sam's sweaty face poised inches above hers in the darkened room as his gravelly voice called to her.

"Jill."

Her pulse pounded in her ears. She gritted her teeth and focused on the man in front of her. He was not Sam. He was a small, pathetic coward. And she was not a scared teenaged girl. Not anymore.

"Peter, wake up."

Snoring.

"Wake up," she demanded, shaking him even harder this time.

"What? What?" He asked, waking with a start. His eyes, at first squinting in the dark to get a look at who dared disturb his peaceful slumber, popped wide as he caught sight of Jill, and the gun.

"What the fuck?"

"Bet you didn't expect to see me again so soon." Jill's tone was dangerously soft in the quiet room.

"Goddamn it, Jill, what the hell are you doing? Have you lost your mind?"

Even in the dark, she could see the hard glitter of fear in his eyes. Adrenaline spiked through her veins. She was gratified by the terrified look on his face.

"You know, I can't believe I fell for all of that 'Scout's honor' bullshit. What did you do to me last night?"

The expression on Peter's face turned from fear to dread, and a cold certainty stole through Jill. Her hands steadied. She knew she was right to come here. With each passing second, she felt less like a victim and more like an avenging angel.

"I don't know what you're talking about," Peter lied in a shaky voice. His hand darted toward the night table, and she cocked the gun.

"What do you think you're doing?" she said. He froze.

"Reaching for my glasses, that's all. We should talk this through."

"Unless you want some extra ventilation for your brain, I'd keep your hands where I can see them."

"All right. All right," he repeated, holding his hands up in surrender. "Let's talk."

"Talk? Well, sure. Let's talk about these." Jill dropped the baggie with the pills she had found in the bathroom onto his heaving chest. "I think you slipped one of these pills into my drink last night so you could do whatever you wanted to me. Which was what, exactly?"

Peter's eyes fluttered closed, and his Adam's apple bobbed. Jill's gut twisted—a mixture of disgust and certainty. This is what she'd come here for. It was as close to a confession as she expected to get. Hate blossomed within her, and her hand tightened on the gun.

"Listen, Jill, I'm sorry. Okay?"

"You're sorry," she cocked her head in disbelief. "You raped me, and now you're sorry?"

A humorless bark of laughter escaped her lips. She plucked the baggie off the bed and stuffed it into her pocket.

"Rape is a strong word," he stammered as his eyes shifted away from hers and toward the phone. But it was too late to call for help.

"Rape *is* a strong word. But having sex with someone against their will is the very definition of the act, is it not? Did you think you could get away with it? Did you think I wouldn't tell? Did you think that your little white pills would put you in control?"

"I'm sorry, Jill. I didn't mean—" Peter's warbling voice was barely a whisper.

"You didn't mean what? Please!"

Jill glared down at him with a look filled with pure loathing as he shrank back. Pity was the furthest thing from her mind. She thumbed off the safety.

"You're the worst kind of coward. Give me one good reason why I should let you get away with what you did to me."

Peter sniffed. Tears formed in his eyes. Jill grimaced in disgust. "Please, Jill. Please, forgive me."

"Forgive you?" she cooed in a soft, sweet, mocking voice. "Sorry, Baby, I'm just not that kind of girl."

A soft, whimpering sound escaped Peter's lips. Without hesitation, without time for a second thought, she pressed the gun to Peter's temple and pulled the trigger. The tight seal of his skin to the muzzle of the gun muffled the sound of the single shot.

Staring down into Peter's lifeless eyes, Jill felt a dizzying surge of heat shimmer through her, followed by a high far more powerful, more complete than anything she had experienced before. She felt alive, every nerve ending on fire, every sense heightened.

Whatever Peter had stolen from her, Jill had taken back. And she felt justified in the knowledge he would never hurt anyone again.

Leaning forward, she grasped Peter's limp arm and placed the gun in his hand, Gently she coiled his fingers around the grip, making sure to position his index finger on the trigger, hoping the powder from her gloves would transfer over onto Peter's skin.

With one last look around the room, Jill stripped off her gloves, shoved them in her pocket, and left the room. She paused by the sofa, staring down at Peter's open laptop. All she wanted to do was put as much distance between her and the dead body cooling in the next room as possible, but she couldn't. Not yet.

After changing into a fresh pair of latex gloves, she switched the system clock on Peter's computer turning back the time so it didn't coincide with the time of death. Finding the notes from the interview, the video, and the still shots from the Nikon was easy. Getting rid of them, really getting rid of them, would be much harder. Instead, she modified the document, deleting most of its contents, and used the search-and-replace feature to change her name. Jill Shannon became Anne Willis. She renamed the image files. The last thing she did was reset the system clock. If the computer forensics guys went looking for evidence, a modified file was less suspicious than a deleted file.

Then Jill had another thought. What was a suicide without a good-bye note? Squatting down by the keyboard, she opened the word processor and typed a few lines. Some drivel about not being good enough, not being able to take the pressure anymore, needing to find a way out. Whatever. Even if the police didn't buy the suicide angle, she had covered her tracks well.

With the memory card from the Nikon tucked safely in her pocket, Jill let herself out of the suite. She expected to feel panic. She expected the aftermath of the adrenaline rush to leave her jittery. Instead she was filled with a calm, steady sense of relief. The bastard had gotten exactly what he deserved.

CHAPTER THIRTY FOUR

Alex slammed the door to Captain Lewis's office on his way down the hallway. Still steaming from the reprimand, he looked up in time to see the stunned expressions on the upturned faces as he passed. Most recovered quickly, averting their eyes as they tried to look busy.

"Get back to work," he muttered to himself. "The floor show's over." He was sure that, as soon as he ducked back into his own cramped office, the whispering would begin as they rehashed the whole stormy scene.

This time Alex did resist the urge to slam his door as he dropped into his chair and spun to look out the window. He'd barely had time to release a muted stream of obscenities when a timid knock sounded at the door.

"What?" he yelled, his eyes shooting death rays as he turned.

Kris Thompson hovered in the doorway, her face white as she peeked in. Everything about her, from the wary look in her eye to the tentative hand on the knob, told him that if she had any other choice, she wouldn't be here.

"Never mind, it can wait." She spun on her heel and was about to leave when he stopped her.

"It's fine. What do you need?"

"I need you to sign off on a request for a warrant."

"What case?"

"The Gillespie case." Kris pointed at the mound of unread files on his desk. The blank look on his face conveyed his total and complete ignorance. Reluctantly, Kris stepped through the doorway and flipped through the neatly piled stack of plain manila folders on his desk. Selecting one from the pile, she opened it and handed it to him, exposing the relevant information. Chagrined, he admired her ruthless organization.

Alex quickly reviewed the paperwork. Everything looked in order, and he signed the request. Handing it back to her, she met his eyes, and he managed a tight smile. Conflict management was not exactly her forte, and he could see that she was anxious to escape as she muttered her thanks.

"Thompson," he said as she skittered toward the door. His voice stopped her cold in her tracks, and she faced him.

"Yes?"

Alex pushed back in his chair and eyed her, rubbing his fingers against the grain of stubble on his chin. There was something different about her, but he couldn't quite put his finger on it. Something about her face …

"Did you change your hair?"

It was shorter, swinging above her shoulders. Free of all that weight, the layers curled around her face. Kris's cheeks flushed pink, and she hugged the file tight against her chest. Her lips parted, as if suspended between surprise and pleasure.

"Last week."

"It looks … nice."

"Thanks," she stammered, and she spun and scurried back toward her desk.

Alex stared after her for a long moment. It wasn't just her hair. Jill taught him to notice women's fashions. Today she wore a fitted white blouse instead of one of the oversized sweaters she usually draped herself in. Skinny jeans were tucked into a pair of high leather boots. It was as if she'd been kidnapped by one of those television makeover shows. She looked … great.

He swung his chair around to face his computer screen. Jackson didn't wait to be invited inside. Closing the door behind him, he wedged himself into the narrow guest chair. Normally Alex would have offered him the more comfortable leather chair, but he didn't feel like being courteous. If Jackson was here to smooth things over, that was his choice. He could suffer.

"What the fuck do you think you're doing?" Jackson's big voice boomed.

Clenching his teeth, Alex bristled at the question. He hadn't expected Jackson to soft-pedal his approach. That just wasn't his style. But still, who the hell did he think he was?

"Working. What about you?"

Jackson folded his arms across his chest. Alex could feel the weight of his glare but refused to look up. As if that would be enough to discourage his partner. *Yeah. Right.* It would take more than that for the big man to butt out.

"I'm trying to stop you from committing career suicide, you dumb shit. You're one stupid son of a bitch, aren't you?"

"Is that a rhetorical question?" The ironic inflection was not lost on Jackson.

"Guess so, since we both know the answer."

"Then why don't you get on with it? Say what you need to say. I've got work to do."

If the venomous edge to Alex's voice caught Jackson by surprise, it didn't show on his face. The wide lips were firm, and he looked like a lecturing principal.

"Me? Oh, I don't need to do anything to beat you down. You're doing a damn fine job of that all by yourself."

Jackson pressed his hand to his chest, fingers splayed.

"Me?" Alex mimicked. "What the fuck is that supposed to mean? I'm busting my ass to find a killer, and Lewis has the gall to penalize me for it."

Like venting steam from a simmering pot, his words came out in a rush.

"Jesus Christ. I've got important cases waiting. Like credit-card fraud compares to the murder of a teenager. Like I'm a fucking rookie or something."

Alex shook his head, glaring at Jackson through narrowed eyes. The stack of new case files on his desk had grown. He didn't need Kris to point out the obvious—that he hadn't spent much time on them. He already knew.

"Then stop acting like a damned rookie. We all have that one case that we can't let go of. Honeywell's yours. We all get it, Alex, but maybe it's time to pull your head out of your ass and move on."

Alex let out a sigh and cast his eyes toward the ceiling. His cell phone rang, cutting through the heavy silence. He pulled it out of his pocket and stared at the call display. He closed his eyes for a split second before pressing it to his ear.

"Hi, Abby." He evaded Jackson's knowing look as he angled his gaze out the window. "No, nothing yet. How are you doing?"

He listened for a minute or two longer as Abby talked before he said good-bye. He set the phone down on the desk beside his keyboard. The sympathetic look on Jackson's face spoke volumes, and Alex knew Jackson had his best interests at heart.

"Not so easy to do when it's personal," Jackson said, his tone uncharacteristically gentle. "And since I'm all up in your business, you'd better get control of that. History can be a dangerous thing when it comes to relationships."

Jackson shot a meaningful look at Alex's phone. A stab of guilt pierced Alex's heart. He gritted his teeth.

"You think I don't know that?"

"Do you think I'm too dumb to see where this is heading? You'd better think long and hard before you act. I'm living proof that there are some lines you shouldn't cross."

"Michelle?"

The last vestiges of Alex's anger fizzled, and Jackson shook his head.

"Moved out. It's over, man. Has been for a long time."

"You never said anything."

"No point." Jackson's stare was sober as he held Alex's gaze. "Listen, just do as Lewis says. Hunker down and get through your caseload. Let Homicide do their job."

"I can't let Honeywell go. Not yet."

"I know, but not at the risk of sacrificing everything else. I want this bastard, too, but you've got to listen to what Lewis is saying. Whether you want to admit it or not, he's right."

"He ordered me to take a couple of days off."

"Then get the hell out of here. Why don't you and Jill plan a weekend away? It may help you get perspective on things."

The inclusion of Jill in Jackson's statement was not lost on Alex. They weren't just talking about work anymore. They were talking about his marriage.

"Pull your head out of your ass before it's too late."

"You know, if this cop thing doesn't work out, you've got a real future as a therapist."

Jackson's deep, rumbling laugh filled Alex's office.

"What do you say we get out of here? First round's on me."

Alex glanced at the stack of case files on his desk. Maybe Jackson was right. Maybe a weekend away would help. Jill had been working long hours, too. They'd hardly seen each other since she'd returned from the conference in California.

Rising from his chair, Alex thumbed the power switch on his monitor and grabbed his coat.

"Let's get out of here," he said.

Halfway down the hall, Jackson let out a wolf whistle that nearly deafened Alex. Kris Thompson walked past.

"Whoa. Look out. We've got a hottie coming through. Looking damn good, girl," he called out loud enough for the whole floor to have heard. A furious blush stained her cheeks, and she averted her gaze, but not before Alex saw her smile.

"Very subtle. If you're not careful, you're going to earn yourself a crash course in sexual harassment," Alex said as he strode down the hallway.

"No need. I already know how to harass."

"She does look good," Alex admitted.

"You know why, don't you?" Jackson's look was sly as Alex shook his head "She's got herself a man."

The deep rumble of Jackson's laughter filled the hall.

CHAPTER THIRTY FIVE

"**E**njoy your stay in Vancouver," the desk clerk said with a friendly smile.

Alex gripped the access card and followed Jill through the ornate lobby of the Fairmont Hotel toward the elevator. Convincing Jill to spend a weekend in Vancouver had been much easier than he had anticipated. They had a full itinerary planned. Christmas shopping on Robson, dinner in Gastown, catch a Canucks hockey game. It was the perfect balance between he and she activities.

Unwillingly, he acknowledged to himself that the tension in his shoulders eased once they'd crossed the Canadian border. He was loath to admit that Captain Lewis was right about the therapeutic value of taking some time off.

Traffic in Vancouver was always a nightmare, but as they crawled along the Cambie Street Bridge, he saw the construction cranes draped in Christmas lights. That, coupled with the softly falling snow, helped set a holiday mood.

Normally, a weekend at the Fairmont would be well beyond Alex's pay grade. But with Jill's frequent trips to California, the accumulated hotel points made a three-night stay affordable. Traveling had its perks, and as he pushed open the door to the luxuriously appointed room, he vowed to make the most of it.

"So what did you want to do first?" Jill asked as she collapsed on the bed, arms folded behind her head.

"A little shopping, then dinner?"

Robson Street was the Mecca of high-end shopping for the Vancouver elite. Alex followed Jill from store to store. Carrying bags from Salvatore Ferragamo, Louis Vuitton, and La Senza, Alex felt his credit card smoking. But then, so was his wife. With each step, he felt his mood lighten.

After depositing Jill's booty at the hotel, they took a stroll to Gastown. The melting snow made the cobblestone streets slick, and Jill wound her arm through his as they walked by the tourist shops. Native art figured prominently in the windows of the high-end art galleries. The iconic steam clock struck seven as Alex led the way into the Water Street Café.

The smell of simmering tomatoes and garlic filled the dining room. Sipping wine and nibbling on fresh pasta and bruschetta, Alex sat back in his chair and enjoyed the comfortable silence that stretched out between them. Jill looked tired. She'd been working hard, establishing herself in her new role.

"How did the demo go?" he asked.

Jill's look was sharp, and she took a sip of wine before answering.

"It went well. Standing room only. In fact, the demand was so high that they added a third session."

"Well, that's great, isn't it?" He was puzzled by the change in her demeanor. She seemed on edge. "How is everything going at work?"

"What do you mean?" Her tone was sharp, eyes wary. "Everything is fine."

"With Jamie's passing, and your promotion there's been a lot of change. Has it been weird for you?"

Jill sipped her wine, considering his question.

"It's been okay. Most people are supportive."

"Not all?"

Jill cocked an eyebrow.

"Some people like to play politics."

"Meaning?" he asked, curious about the dynamics of Jill's work life. He knew she didn't always play well with others.

"Well, there is this one woman, Dana Evans."

"What's her deal?"

Jill's grin turned conspiratorial.

"She joined the company about a month before Jamie's death. She's aggressive. Ambitious. Apparently she and Jamie worked together at another company. Rumor has it, they were having an affair."

"Really? Do you think there's any truth to the rumor?"

Jill shrugged.

"Jamie was no choirboy."

"Aren't interoffice affairs at the management level kind of risky?"

"Jamie had a reputation as a ladies' man."

Jill's matter-of-fact statement piqued his interest, and Alex wondered what else lay beneath the assertion.

"You never mentioned that before."

Jill's cheeks stained pink, and her eyes met his.

"Really? I guess it didn't seem relevant."

"Did he ever hit on you?"

His senses on full alert, Alex saw the muscles in her neck flex ever so slightly as she swallowed.

"Well, he was tipsy at our last ship party and got a little too friendly."

Alex's gut clenched.

"Did you break his fingers?" Alex asked. He was only half kidding.

"Not exactly, but I made my thoughts on the topic crystal clear. After that, it was never an issue."

Alex considered her answer. Jill was a smart, beautiful woman. If Jamie was a womanizer, of course he would have been attracted to her. In his experience, a wedding ring wasn't even a speed bump for most commitment-phobic men, less a deterrent than a draw.

Jill's fingers brushed her arm.

"I'm sorry I brought Jamie up. Whatever he did is in the past. Let's not let it spoil our night."

"You're right," he said, trying to shake the growing sense of discomfort he felt. Was she lying? He couldn't tell. But before either of them could say more, his cell phone rang. Alex dug it out of his pocket. Checking the call display, he sighed and skipped the call. Glancing up, he caught the look in Jill's eyes.

"Who was that?" she asked. Her legs were crossed, and he saw the tip of her boot swing back and forth impatiently, like a cat twitching its tail.

"It's not important." He hoped she would let it go. She didn't. That wasn't Jill's style.

"Abby?"

Alex nodded and picked his wineglass up off of the table. He swirled the Cabernet around in his glass. Thick tears of wine rolled down into the bowl.

"She's checking in to see if there are any updates on the case."

"Wouldn't you call her if you had news?"

"Sure, but everyone handles this type of situation differently. In Abby's case, she finds it easier to call. Waiting for the phone to ring just makes her anxious."

Jill arched her eyebrows, never shifting her gaze from his face.

"Is that all it is?"

"Yes," he said, careful to mask the twinge of guilt he felt.

From the look on Jill's face, it was clear she didn't fully believe him, but for whatever reason, she let it go.

The wine worked its magic, and on the way back to the hotel, the snow fell harder, blanketing Gastown in a postcard-perfect layer of white. As they strolled back to the hotel, Alex draped his arm around Jill's shoulders and pulled her close. He felt her stiffen, and he wondered if she was still thinking about Abby's call.

They stopped in the hotel bar for a drink before heading back to their room. As the door closed behind them, Alex dropped the card key on the desk. Jill sat on the end of the bed to remove her boots.

Alex hunkered down in front of her. His hands ran up the length of her legs. She shivered at his touch. Slowly, gently, he removed her boots, setting them beside the bed. His lips touched hers. He felt her hand circle around his neck and tangle in his hair, and he deepened his kiss.

Jill pulled back, her breath catching in her throat.

"Are you okay?" he asked.

"Yes," she breathed, and kissed him again.

Placing his hand on the round firmness of her breast, he felt everything fall away. Abby. The case. Everything.

CHAPTER THIRTY SIX

Back at home in West Seattle, long after she'd made herself a quick bite to eat and straightened up the kitchen, Jill logged on to her email account from the comfortable leather armchair in the living room. The rain outside was coming down in a dense drizzle, but the cheerful fire in the hearth was doing its best to ward off the late-night chill. Molly lay on the area rug, her back edged as close to the dancing flames as possible without setting her fur on fire.

Alex was working late. The cases that had accumulated since his return from California were finally getting some much needed attention, and that suited Jill just fine. The long weekend in Vancouver had left her with some extra work on her plate, too, and she set about scanning the new items in her in-box.

Most of it was run-of-the-mill stuff. She deleted junk mail from her favorite online shopping places, notifications of upcoming training courses and conferences, software build notifications. After parsing through a couple of dozen emails, she had pruned the list to less than ten—all things that she needed to read.

The latest project status reports assured her that all major work items were on track. She'd spend some time tomorrow adding a little extra color for her boss before sending it along. Rachel sent her a notification for an internal technical discussion that she should sit in on. She paused before opening the next unread message. She didn't recognize the address. It was from a xmail account. With an email moniker like Casanova3569@xmail.com, she figured it could only be one thing: spam. Typically this was the type of thing that her junk email filter weeded out. It was odd that this one had made it all of the way to her in-box. Her finger hovered over the Delete button for a second before she dropped her hand to her side.

Just spam, she thought again, but an uneasy feeling churned at the pit of her stomach. Unable to ignore it, she clicked on the message.

I know your secret.

An image. A single still frame of her face, eyes closed, made her heart lurch. Below the image, there was a link. In the few seconds it took for the video to load, Jill's heart stopped.

Holy shit. Peter had captured the rape on video. She could see her unconscious face slack behind Peter's naked shoulder. She slammed the laptop screen closed and dropped it on the table as if the metal case had scorched her hands. Jumping to her feet, she started to pace.

Molly let out a soft yelp, her feet twitching as she slept. Jill watched the sleeping dog for a moment before she shifted her gaze back to the laptop. Who sent the video, and just what exactly did he know? That she was Peter's victim, or that he was hers? If there was someone out there who knew the role she played in Peter's untimely death, wouldn't they have come forward by now?

As much as she wanted to, she couldn't ignore the email. A few searches later, she realized that her video was not the only one posted to Peter's illicit website. The videos, ten in all, featured three men who filmed their sexual exploits with a variety of women. The women did not all look like willing participants. Some looked drugged. A few were actually bound and gagged, eyes wide with horror as they were raped. Jill's gut clenched. A wave of nausea washed over her.

Three of the videos starred Peter Young as the male stud. Four starred a man she didn't recognize. With his bleached blond hair and dark tan she guessed he lived somewhere warm. Either that or the bastard owned a tanning salon. His large teeth flashed at the camera, and Jill stopped the video feed.

The remaining three belonged to a lithe, dark-haired man who liked to tie his victims up. Watching his videos, Jill had no doubt he liked the game. The rougher, the more painful—the better.

Who were these women, and what happened to them once they served their purpose? Did they get emails, too? Did they pay money to make their problems go away? Did they keep silent about what happened to them? Were they all like her, married women who had their own reasons for not going to the police?

Jill's hands clenched into fists as she paced the hardwood floor. Was the sender trying to scare her? If so, he was doing a damned good job of it. She felt helpless. Exposed.

Helpless? Jill stopped pacing. No. She wasn't helpless. There were tools she could use, reverse lookups that would provide her with more info—who he was, for starters.

Dropping back into her chair, she picked up her laptop. Choosing from a dozen email lookup tools, she typed in his email address. Seconds later the results came back. Her lips compressed in a flat line. Not surprisingly, the bastard used a fake name. The email address belonged to a Charles U Farley. She scowled, unimpressed by the flaccid attempt at wit.

Fingers drumming the keys, she studied the report. Email accounts generated from this source were largely anonymous, and the ISP was a large hosting company, so no help was to be found there. The IP address would provide more specific information. The police could get a warrant compelling the ISP to release the name of the subscriber. But she was not the police, so, short of reporting the rape to the authorities, that route was closed to her. There was another option, though.

The email lookup program she selected offered the option of providing more information on the subscriber for a small fee. All she needed to do was supply the email name for the reverse lookup. Fifteen bucks seemed like a small price to pay for a little piece of mind, so she authorized payment to her credit card and waited.

Jill's heart jumped in her chest as she viewed the results. She still had no name, but Casanova3569 belonged to several online dating sites. After saving the results to a text file on her hard drive, a few quick searches confirmed that most of the sites were dedicated to married people hooking up online.

Casanova was looking for a woman who was married and lived in the southern US. His ideal woman fit the profile of a twenty-two-year-old yoga instructor. Yeah, well didn't everyone's? Jill clicked on his picture. The smiling face of a man stared up at her from his computer monitor. Her jaw clenched. She recognized him, all right. He was one of the other men featured in the sex videos on Peter's website. Son of a bitch.

Jill drew in a long breath as she considered this information. Somehow he had figured out her identity. But how? Had Peter sent him information about her?

I know your secret.

What game was he playing? Extortion? Would he come looking for money? Was it blackmail? "Keep your mouth shut, or I'll post this for the whole world to see?"

Jill didn't know. Whatever the game, though, she was going to play. Just not by his rules.

Molly groaned and stretched as the fire crackled in the grate. She stole a quick glance at the clock and noted that it was past ten. Alex would be home soon.

Quickly, she listed out her next steps. First, she needed to get rid of the video. She could design a virus—a worm that would destroy the website. Viruses had become more sophisticated since she studied network security at school, but it wouldn't be that hard. Taking down the website would prevent them from sharing the link. If the videos resided on their hard drives—well, that was a problem she couldn't solve. Not yet, anyway.

Second, she needed to uncover Casanova's real identity.

Did she? A new thought dawned, and for the first time since she'd seen the email in her in-box, Jill smiled.

Who he was didn't matter. She knew *how* to find him. After all, Casanova was looking for an attractive married woman. And, staring at his online profile, Jill knew just where to find one.

Unfortunately for him, romance was the last thing on her mind.

CHAPTER THIRTY SEVEN

The next night, Jill left Alex in front of the television watching hockey and walked the few short blocks to the Alki Bakery. She was on a mission, and she couldn't risk Alex looking over her shoulder. Besides, whatever she did on her home network would leave an IP address that could be traced back to her. She had to remain anonymous.

Baiting the hook for Casanova should be as easy as concocting the right online persona. The tinkling of the bell rang over her head as she pushed the door open, the smell of coffee and warm croissants filling her senses.

"Jill, where have you been?" the barista asked from behind the counter. The bakery was a typical stop after her weekend runs with Molly, but with everything that had happened lately, nothing was routine.

"Crazy busy."

"California?"

She nodded, pulling some cash from her wallet.

"I've made a few trips."

"Must hate coming back to the rain. The usual?"

"Thanks, Joey." She waited while he filled a jug with milk and the steam flowed out from the frothy liquid.

"Where's Alex?"

"Home. Glued to the tube."

"His loss. I have you all to myself." He twitched his eye in an exaggerated wink. She grinned.

Joey chuckled as he served her coffee. She dumped the change into the tip jar. Balancing the saucer in her hand, she crossed the room, choosing a table in the back.

The crowd was sparse tonight. What looked to be a couple of college students were huddled in the corner, seeming more interested in each other than the iPads laid flat on the table between them. An older man sat by the window looking out into the dark night, his lined face reflected in the rain-streaked glass. A young woman hunched over a novel, fist pulling her bangs out of her eyes. Dark strands of hair poked between her clenched fingers as she read.

Jill set her cup and saucer down carefully, the creamy liquid touching the edge without sloshing over, and dropped the bag on the chair. She pulled out her laptop and placed it on the table, powering it up.

She sat and sipped her latte. It was bitter and creamy, just the way she liked it. Turning back to the screen, she thought about her profile. She needed to find the right name, the right look, the right everything to attract Casanova. She thought about the disturbing sex videos she'd seen on his website. Casanova's women were blond, fit, with athletic builds and big breasts.

It took only a few minutes to fill out the profile page. Age twenty-nine. Height, five-foot-nine. Weight, one hundred and twenty-five pounds. Eye color, blue. Marital status, definitely married. Name? Her fingernails clicked on the keys. Name, Lilith, she mused with a grin.

According to religious scholars, Lilith was Adam's first wife—before Eve. Legend had it that Adam abandoned Lilith when he found out she was barren, moving on to Eve. But Lilith did not go gentle into that good night. She was said to bed demons.

Jill smiled. The irony of the cheating husband and the scorned wife seemed poetic. She entered an email address that pointed to an email account she'd set up only moments earlier.

Picking up her coffee cup, she curled her fingers around the wide bowl, savoring the heat. She thought about the cyber trail she was creating. The café had free Wi-Fi access. There would be no IP trail to her home network. She was using an assumed name and an anonymous email account. Casanova might be clever. But he'd need more than a passing knowledge of computers and network security to trace her.

Finally, she would need to post a picture. She frowned at the thought. She could pull down a random image from the web, someone whose face fit the profile she had created. That would be one way to handle it. But maybe she could do one better.

Opening another browser window, she entered the address for a popular social-networking site for professionals, the same one she belonged to. Logging in, she did a quick directory search and found just the face she was looking for. Dana Evans. She fit the profile perfectly. Okay, she was a little shorter and a little heavier than the woman described in the profile, but she would do nicely.

With a quick save to her hard drive, Jill placed the image in the profile and hit the Submit button. The wait cursor twirled on the computer screen as Jill waited for the file to be uploaded.

You know my secret, Casanova? Well, I know yours, too. A smile crossed her lips, and she sat back in her chair, glancing up.

Her heart jumped in chest her as she saw a man staring intently at her. His dirty, shoulder-length blond hair framed his pale face, and his blue eyes bore into hers for the briefest of seconds. He sat a few tables away, and a faint smile touched his lips as he watched her. There was something odd about the intensity of his flat blue eyes. The inexplicable metallic tang of fear filled Jill's mouth.

The man looked away quickly, shifting his gaze back at the cell phone he held cradled in his hand. *Jesus.* She was going to have to lay off the caffeine if she couldn't control her jittery nerves. The man dialed a number as he rose from his table, taking his cardboard cup of coffee with him as he strolled out of the bakery. She detected a faint hint of a southern accent as he spoke. *See. Harmless,* she told herself as the jingle of the bell signaled his exit. *Get a grip.*

Just as she was about to shut down the computer, another thought flashed into her head. She had found Casanova's profile on a social-networking site. Did Peter Young belong to any social-networking sites? If so, he would have a friend list. Maybe she'd be able to find the real Casanova after all.

CHAPTER THIRTY EIGHT

Alex was following up on a lead in one of the five fraud cases he'd been assigned. Hanging up the phone, he scribbled notes in his spiral notebook. Each new lead spawned five others. He blew out a long breath, envisioning the tedious day ahead. Picking up his coffee, he took a sip. Cold. Disgusting. But after all of the cold coffee he had consumed in his time at the SPD, he drank it anyway. After all these years, he'd come to like the taste. Swallowing, he set the mug down with a thump, swearing softly as it slopped over the edges.

"Hey, Boss," Kris said from the doorway.

"What's up?"

"The incoming spam filter caught something that was routed to you. I think you should take a look at it. I'm sending it through."

Moments later, the email appeared in Alex's Inbox. The sender, arewehavingfunyet@xmail.com had sent no text in the body of the message, but there was an attached file.

"I've scanned it and didn't find anything funky," Kris assured Alex as she leaned toward the screen to get a closer look.

The attachment was a JPEG image. Alex double-clicked on the file to open it. The resulting picture was something that you might find in the waiting room of a kid's dental clinic. A kitten was seated in a red toy car, with sunglasses resting above his whiskers. The caption read "Have a nice day."

"Any clue what it means or who could have sent it?" Kris asked as she hovered over his shoulder.

Alex shook his head slowly from side to side. "There's something weird about it, though."

"Or maybe you've been a cop too long," a gruff voice said from the doorway. Both turned to see Jackson, his massive hands propped on the edges of the door frame. "What have we got here?"

"Some kind of joke, but I'm not sure I get the punch line." Alex stared at the screen for a long moment. The knuckles of each fist rubbed lightly against each other as he considered the possibilities. Suddenly the movement of his hands stilled, and he sat up ramrod straight in the chair.

"What is it?" Jackson asked, catching the change in Alex's expression.

"Honeywell had image manipulation and steganography software on his computer, right?" He turned to look at Kris, whose face had drained of color.

"I'll run a steganalysis on it now."

✳✳✳

Oblivious to the two detectives clustered around her workstation, Kris scanned the results of the analysis on her screen. Alex's hunch was right: there was another image buried inside the picture of the cat.

Alex's blood chilled as he saw Jill's face staring back at him from the monitor. Kris's hands jerked away from the keyboard, and she rolled back in her chair. Jackson grimaced.

"Honeywell?" Kris asked.

"It's got to be."

"Where was it taken?" Jackson's voice was all business. His eyes remained fixed on the screen.

"Alki Bakery. Jill goes there to work some nights. Free Wi-Fi."

"It's not far from your house. He knows where you live." Jackson straightened, staring at his partner.

Alex didn't respond. The implication was clear. The only way Honeywell could have known Jill's whereabouts was to follow her from the house. Somehow, Honeywell had figured out who he was. Once Honeywell had a name, it wouldn't be hard to find Alex's personal information. His phone number. His address. You name it. It was all out there.

His skin crawled as he thought of Jill walking through the darkened streets, laptop bag slung over her shoulder as she made her way to the coffee shop, oblivious to the danger that lurked.

"That means he's either in the area or has someone else doing his dirty work," Alex said, tapping the desk with his index finger. Wanting to get a closer look at the embedded image, Alex clicked on the car. The ghosted outline of a text box showed that there was something else selected.

Heart racing, Alex used the mouse to move the text box off of the red car, to another part of the screen. As he did so, a message appeared. The red text on a red image had rendered it undetectable in its original form, but now, against the white background, he could read it plain as day.

Dear Alex, Your wife is very pretty. A little old for my taste, but I have been known to make exceptions.

"Son of a bitch," Jackson said.

Alex thought back to that night in California and to the flat, blue eyes of Jerry Honeywell. Was Jill in danger? Goddamned right she was.

"I don't get it. Why play the cat-and-mouse game? Why not just kill her?" Alex's jaw tightened reflexively.

"Easy. Honeywell's a smart bastard, and he's warning you to back off. He knows you're not going to let him go. You're going to come after him. You went all the way to California to track him down. The bastard thinks if he threatens your family, maybe you'll let it be. He can stay safe. Lie low. Fly under the fucking radar."

Alex rubbed his fingers across the stubble on his chin, eyes still fixed on the photograph of his unsuspecting wife. If Honeywell wanted to up the stakes, he'd find out just how tenacious Alex could be. There was no way he would let the sadistic son of a bitch anywhere near Jill again. Next time, there would be no place for him to hide.

"Where's Jill?" Jackson asked, big arms folded across his massive chest.

"In California this week on business."

"Just as well. Buys us some time."

"As long as he's not involving his friends in the Bay Area," Alex said, thinking about Honeywell's connection with the motorcycle gang.

The chances of involving the Gunns in any kind of plot to harm Jill was a long shot, but couldn't be entirely discounted. As soon as it was feasible, Alex would place a call to Agent Jacob Wilde from the ATF. With the tight surveillance net the ATF had cast over the gang, if Jill was in some real danger, they would know about it.

Jackson rocked back on his heels as he mulled over the possibilities. Kris Thompson remained silent, awaiting instructions from Alex on what to do with this new evidence. She did not have to wait long.

"Let's put a trace on the email address. It's unlikely we'll get anything, but it's worth a shot."

"Right away," she said, rolling back to the desk.

Jackson trailed Alex to his office and leaned against the wall, his arms folded across his chest. Jackson's next words chilled Alex still further.

"Does Jill have a gun?"

"No."

"You might want to consider getting her one." Jackson pushed away from the wall and clapped a hand on Alex's shoulder. "Good thing she's a deadly shot."

CHAPTER THIRTY NINE

Jill tilted closer to the compact, making a final touchup to her red lipstick before she pulled away. She had to look the part for her rendezvous with Casanova. The woman reflected back at her from the small mirror bore a vague resemblance to the woman who ran the first foster home Jill stayed in after Sam died.

Straight blond hair framed her face, brushing the tops of her shoulders. Her full lips twisted into a pout and her eyes sparkled blue, courtesy of the colored contact lenses she wore. She could pass for Dana Evans at a first glance. Satisfied, she stowed the compact in her oversized Coach purse. She heard it jostle against the loaded gun.

The tight black dress left little to the imagination, neckline plunging dangerously low between her full breasts. The short skirt ended just above her knees, showing off her shapely legs to every advantage. The spike heels she wore made her appear even taller than her five-foot, nine-inch frame. *Dressed to kill,* she thought, and stepped from the elevator.

Looking cool and confident, Jill strode down the hallway of the Quad 55 hotel toward Casanova's suite. Within, though, she could feel her heart racing. She remembered letting herself into Peter's room. Waiting for him in the dark. Pulling the trigger and ending his miserable life. This game was different. Kenneth Cox would be a full participant in the night's festivities. And she was playing a role.

Jill stopped in front of the door and drew in a deep, steadying breath. She'd done her homework. She knew all she needed to know about Kenneth Cox—his name, address, Social Security number, his wife's name, what kind of car he drove, even how much he had paid for his house. She'd planned every detail with meticulous care, playing the scene out in her head again and again. And she was prepared to do whatever she had to do to make her problem go away. For the first time since his email landed in her in-box, Jill felt totally in control of the situation.

Kenneth Cox answered on the second knock. His unnaturally bright smile almost blinded her as he stepped back to invite her in. The videos had not done him justice. He looked better fully clothed, without the monstrously twisted expression on his face. In a situation like this, he would almost pass for normal, and she understood how the other women in the videos were lured in. But, as any good lawyer would tell you, buyers beware.

"Lilith."

His hungry look swept over her, and revulsion roiled at the pit of her stomach. She countered his greeting with a saccharine smile of her own.

"Casanova."

He'd spared no expense on the suite. Beautiful, understated elegance everywhere she looked. Furnished with comfortable contemporary pieces, the suite was designed to satisfy every creature comfort, and Casanova had taken care to set the mood just right. The overhead lights were dimmed. Soft jazz played in the background. *How romantic,* Jill thought. *Be still my cold, beating heart.* A wicked grin spread across her face.

"Call me Ken, please," he said, breathing his name in her ear as if imparting a secret. He reached for her oversized purse, but her look stopped him cold. He stepped away, hands raised in the air in a disarming gesture. The surprise on his face settled into an uneasy smile.

"Can I get you something to drink?"

"Champagne, please," she drawled in a fake southern accent. "After all, this is a special occasion."

Casanova grinned. According to his profile, he liked southern women, and so Lilith hailed from a small town in Georgia. Jill was playing to her audience. The role fit her new persona, and she felt powerful.

"Of course," he said, turning toward the window.

The ice bucket sat at the ready, a bottle of champagne already chilling. Despite her casual stance, Jill was on full alert. She tracked his every movement to make sure he didn't slip anything into her drink. After all, Peter and his date-rape drug started this whole deadly chain of events. She couldn't afford to make any mistakes, not with so much at stake.

With a subtle twist of his wrist, he uncorked the bottle with a muted pop. Golden bubbles raced to the top of the champagne flute, then receded. She kept her eyes locked on him, accepting the glass with a seductive smile. Her warm fingers grazed his. Kenneth turned and poured a glass for himself.

Jill set the heavy purse down on a nearby credenza.

"A toast?" he asked, raising his glass.

She laughed, and mirrored his pose.

"What shall we drink to?"

"To a perfect night," he said, clinking his glass against hers.

"Just so," she said, smiling darkly, and sipped the champagne.

Tonight would be a night like no other, guaranteed to end with a bang.

Kenneth stepped closer, and Jill stiffened. The fresh, citrus scent of Dolce & Gabbana cologne wafted off Cox's warm skin. He leaned in looking for a kiss, but Jill dodged away, swinging her free hand in a wide arc.

"This is some place you have here," she said, striding toward the window.

Kenneth's lips twisted in an enigmatic smile.

"I like to travel well."

He followed her to the window. Positioned close behind, his body, only inches from hers, radiated heat. His hot breath fanned her bare shoulder, prickling the hairs on her arm. She suppressed a shudder.

"So I see. It's a stunning view."

From here, Jill could make out the iconic outline of the Transamerica Pyramid jutting up into the night sky. City lights twinkled on a canvas of charcoal gray. Kenneth trailed a lazy hand along her arm. Jill squelched the urge to grab his fingers and twist them back until they snapped. She was playing a role, after all, and touching was part of the game.

He stepped even closer then, and she could feel his body press against hers—hard chest, flat belly, long legs, and something else hard, down there. Damn it. How could she be so careless? Standing in front of the window gave her nowhere to move, no easy way to pivot out of range.

Tipping her glass back, she drained the remaining champagne. Jill held the glass up over her shoulder.

"Refill?" she asked.

She felt, rather than heard, Kenneth's sigh. Obediently, he took the glass from her and set off to fetch more champagne. Jill tracked his movements in the window until he moved out of range, then trailed him to the ice bucket. Relieved to be out in the open again, she glanced around the suite.

From this angle, she glimpsed the king-sized bed piled high with pillows. The creamy comforter looked soft and cozy. Studded with earth-toned accents, the color scheme was designed to set a soft and comforting mood. A frown wrinkled her brow. What a shame it would be to spoil their pristine perfection with crimson droplets of blood.

"Something wrong?" Kenneth asked.

"Not a single thing," she drawled and took the glass he offered.

He stopped to refill his own.

"So, Kenny, do you have any friends in the city?" Jill asked, eyeing him with keen interest.

The expression on his tanned face froze for a fraction of a second. He recovered quickly, though, and smiled, flashing his perfect teeth.

"A college friend, actually. We keep in touch online."

Peter? Were they old college friends? Jill watched his face for something else—some indication of how Peter's passing affected him. Kenneth's curious gaze fixed on Jill. His expression gave nothing away.

"I think it's great you maintain your friendships. I don't have a single thing in common with my old college friends. They post pictures of their kiddies, expecting me to gush. It's amazing what passes for entertainment on the web these days, don't you think? Tell me, Kenny, what's the most outrageous thing you've posted?"

Jill thought about the sex videos. She watched. He fidgeted, looking uncomfortable. He forced a shrug and an awkward smile.

"Hey, you know the Hook Up motto: Don't Ask, Don't Tell."

It was his politically correct way of telling her to back off. Jill got it. What's more, she appreciated it. After all, she had her own secrets to keep.

"Why yes, that is true." Her soft voice was almost a purr. Stepping closer, Jill brushed her arm against his as she fixed him with a long, deliciously coy look from beneath lowered eyelashes. "What would life be like without a few secrets, right?"

Kenneth swallowed hard. She watched an internal struggle play out across his face. Caution. Doubt. Desire. Brushing past him, Jill glided to the window and pulled the drapes closed.

"Hope you don't mind." She gestured toward the windows. "I'm into a lot of things, but exhibitionism is not among them. Besides, you never know who might be watching."

His smile was narrow. Setting his glass down, he closed the distance between them. His thick hands ran up her arms. His blue eyes burned as bright as hot coals.

"Do tell, Lilith. What other sorts of things might you be into?"

"I'm afraid you'd be shocked if you knew." She tossed her hair back, dropping a shoulder to expose her bare neck, fingers touching her throat, grazing past the jagged scar without pause.

"I might surprise you. Very little shocks me," he said, grinning like an idiot. He looked more relaxed now that the conversation shifted. He gripped her shoulders and leaned close nuzzling her ear. A chill rattled down her spine.

"Nice perfume. What is it?"

"It's a custom blend. I call it Aphrodisia."

Kenneth chuckled, appreciating the irony.

"Do you do this a lot?" Jill asked.

"What's that?"

"Meet strange women in hotel rooms?"

"Do you?"

"Meet women? Rarely."

His breath caught, and she could feel his interest spike. Jill smiled, enjoying his predictability. Her eyes strayed over his shoulder toward the bedroom. Her gaze hardened, and she thought about the women he victimized. Blackmailed. How he had threatened her. The headiness of the charade evaporated and Jill focused in on her intent. She would silence Kenneth Cox. Permanently. No more sex videos. No more threats.

"Oh, I almost forgot." Kenneth stepped back, patted the pockets of his pants, his head swiveling around in search of something. "Damn," he muttered, more to himself than to her.

"What's wrong?" Her spine stiffened and her instincts pricked.

"I forgot something."

"What?"

"A lighter. I've got some candles. I don't suppose you brought one."

Sweet Jesus. Romance. She suppressed an eye roll.

Without a word she crossed the room and fished through her purse. Careful not to let him see the contents of her bag, she found what she was looking for. Her fingers closed on the matchbook, and she pulled it out of her purse and handed it to him. With a quick glance, she saw it was one that she had picked up from the restaurant in Gastown on her trip to Vancouver with Alex.

Alex. The thought of him made her heart plummet. What would Alex do if he knew the dangerous game she was playing? He couldn't find out. She was here to ensure he would not find out. It was time to move things along and finish the game before things went too far.

Kenneth busied himself with lighting the candles arranged on the mantel across from the bed while Jill studied the glowing white pillars with sharp interest, looking for the hidden camera. All too soon, he was back at her side, standing so close she could feel the heat radiate from his body.

"That's better," he murmured as his warm fingertips grazed her cheek. She barely stopped herself from flinching at the unwelcome contact. An image of her stepfather flashed through her mind, and she pushed it aside. This wasn't the same. She wasn't Kenneth's victim. Not Kenneth's, or Peter's—or her stepfather's, for that matter. She was in control.

Casanova leaned in closer and nuzzled her neck. His warm breath fanned her bare skin. She held still, revulsion at his touch awakening the hate at the pit of her stomach. Touching was part of the game, she reminded herself. Foreplay. A necessary prelude for what was to follow. Her shoulders relaxed.

He turned her so they were facing and flattened a hand against her back, pulling her closer. Jill trailed her hand across his hard chest and slowly undid the top button of his shirt. Kenneth's breath quickened. He reached for the zipper of her dress, but she stopped him with a playful look.

"Oh, I know it's good manners to let a lady go first, but in situations like this, I prefer to take my time. We've got all night."

Kenneth smiled, and Jill pulled the next button free. Well, okay. It wasn't exactly true. Kenneth Cox didn't have much time left at all. Twenty minutes. Maybe a few more. That was all.

"Your dress is gorgeous, but I'm wondering how much better it would look off of you." He slid a finger beneath the strap, easing it down, until it fell down the curve of her arm. The side swell of her beast was bare, and his gaze lingered on the newly exposed flesh.

"All in good time."

She finished unbuttoning his shirt and swept it from his shoulders. His skin was darkly tanned. He was a gym rat, she thought. A commercial real estate agent from Miami, Florida, wouldn't get that much exercise on the job. His skin was so perfectly tanned that she wondered if he augmented the natural benefits of the sun by going to a salon. Maybe there was one attached to his gym. He was a vain creature. Most exhibitionists were. He had to look good for the camera.

Jill thought about the videos and all those women, and hate slithered through her veins. Kenneth reached for her. This time she went willingly into his arms. His hands found the zipper to her dress, and it purred as he slid it down. She let the dress fall from her shoulders, down past her breasts, to pool at her feet. She kicked it away with tip of her high-heeled shoe.

"Very nice," he said, his hungry gaze admiring.

A rush of power and pleasure raced through her, and Jill felt alive. She brushed against him, like a cat looking for affection. His arm snaked out around her waist, and she was pulled against him. She felt his hard erection press into her. She planted her hands on his chest and gave a playful push. He held tight.

"Where do you think you're going?" His voice was gruff, and he kissed her exposed neck. Jill shuddered, knowing that she had to bring this act to a close fast, before the situation got out of control.

Her gaze darting toward the credenza across from the bed, she looked for a camera, and did not find one. That didn't mean that he didn't have one hidden there. Given his extracurricular activities, she would bet money that he had one stowed somewhere. There would be time to search for it later, after she'd "neutralized" him.

"I brought a little surprise for you," she said.

"What kind of surprise?"

"Well if I told you, it wouldn't be much of a surprise, now would it?"

"I suppose not." He relented, releasing his grip.

"Why don't you finish undressing, and wait for me over there?" Jill pointed toward the bed.

And like a good boy, Kenneth did as he was told. His belt buckle jingled and his slacks fell to the ground. He stripped off his boxer shorts, and Jill glanced away. Standing in her bra and panties, she waited until he was stretched out on the bed, in all his naked glory, before uttering her next command.

"Close your eyes."

"This better be good," he growled.

She laughed.

"How could it be anything but?"

Kenneth smiled, revealing his large, over-bright, hateful teeth, oblivious to Jill's cold stare.

"Tell me, Lilith, what did you bring along in your little bag of tricks?"

"Something unexpected. You like games, don't you?" The warm southern lilt ebbed from her voice. Kenneth didn't seem to notice. He stretched out on the pillows, hands propped behind his head, perfectly content to wait.

Jill's pulse raced. She crossed the room. She reached into her purse. With a quick glance over her shoulder, she pulled the gun from its hiding place. Clad only in her bra and panties, she planted her feet in a wide stance, spike heels clawing into the carpet.

"Okay, I'm ready, Sugar" she said.

Kenneth's eyes opened slowly. The smile died on his lips as he caught sight of the gun.

"What the fuck?" he gasped and scuttled across the bed like a crab. He flattened himself against the headboard. "Lilith?"

Jill stripped the blond wig from her head and tossed it onto the credenza.

She liked the fear she saw blazing in his eyes. She liked the way his mouth yawned open in slack-jawed wonder. She liked the cold feel of the gun in her hand.

"You can call me Jill," she said.

Recognition flashed across his face. He raised his hands in supplication as she took aim.

"Surprise," she said, and squeezed the trigger.

CHAPTER FOURTY

Detective Luka Petrovich stepped through the heavy glass doors into the modern lobby of the Quad 55 hotel. Guests swarmed the front desk like bees as Luka breezed by the restaurant, cutting a diagonal swath through the crowd on his way toward the elevator. His hair fell carelessly over his forehead in a dark tangle, compliments of the brisk morning breeze that swept off the harbor through San Francisco's downtown core.

"Good morning," he said to an attractive blonde passing by. She smiled.

On any other morning, he'd be tempted to stop and exchange pleasantries. But on this particular morning, there was a dead body cooling in the executive suite, so with a grin of his own, he continued on his way.

Coming to a halt in front of the bank of elevators, he pushed the button and waited for the car to arrive. Seconds before the doors opened, he pulled an almond croissant out of the bakery bag and took a big bite. Confectioner's sugar dusted his top lip as he chewed on the pastry, savoring the sweet, flaky taste.

The elevator glided to a smooth stop at the thirty-second floor, and Luka stepped out into the hallway. He could see the police officers milling around the door of the suite. Yellow tape sealed off the crime scene. Luka flashed his ID at the young sentries who stood guard in the hallway, and paused outside the open door. A uniformed officer waited by the windows, staring over at the bed, his fleshy face grim. The sloped bulk of his belly strained at the buttons of his uniformed shirt, and the straight line of bushy eyebrows lent him an old-school air echoed in the downturned caste of his thick lips.

A forensics technician was poised over the bed, clicking off photographs to document the placement and condition of the body. The flash of the camera punctuated her movements. Luka peered over, admiring the way her jeans clung to her every curve.

Wadding the remains of the croissant into his mouth, he stepped through the door and into the suite. In no particular rush now, he licked the powdered sugar from his fingers one by one.

The naked, blood-splattered body was draped across the ivory bedspread, eyes staring sightlessly at the ceiling, arms spread-eagled. Luka gauged the male to be in his mid to late thirties. Dark rust-colored spots studded the carpet and walls. As he moved closer to the bed, a sliver of almond fell from his jacket onto the luxurious carpet at his feet.

The technician stopped and glanced up from her work to peer over at Luka. Her raven hair was pulled back from her face in a long ponytail down her back, and he could see the familiar high cheekbones and large, dark eyes. Casting him a friendly smile, she shifted the angle of the camera and continued to document the placement of the body.

Luka had fond memories of Maria Lopez. Well, of her body anyway. She was long and lithe, with perfect, caramel-colored skin. Their no-strings, friends-with-privileges relationship suited them both just fine. It had been months since he'd seen Maria, and, staring at her ass in the form-fitting jeans, he tried to remember why.

"Who the hell let you in here?" An officer strode from the window to the center of the suite and confronted Luka. "Don't you know you're contaminating the crime scene?" He shook his head and pointed at the almond sliver on the carpet. "Stupid son of a bitch."

The muttered words forced the edges of Luka's lips up into a condescending grin. Maria stared over at the officer and inclined her head toward Luka.

"Come on, McLean, don't you know who this is?" Maria's voice betrayed her own amusement as she met Luka's eyes.

"If I knew who the fuck he was, Lopez, would I ask?" He spat the words out through clenched teeth, and Luka didn't miss the venomous look she shot McLean from behind the lens of her camera.

"Then allow me to make the introductions. Officer Tom McLean, meet Detective Luka Petrovich. Homicide."

Luka smiled at her, and Maria dipped the lens of the camera a fraction, long enough to wink before she turned. He was right. It had been too long since he'd seen her.

Pausing by the window, Luka pulled his notebook from his coat and noted the location and time of his arrival on the scene. He looked up from his notes and glanced outside. Through the steady haze of drizzle, the outline of the Transamerica Pyramid was partially engulfed by the dull gray fog. He could hear the whine of a streetcar, crammed with commuters on their way to work, as it sped down Union Street. Clusters of pedestrians flooded out of the BART station like ants.

Smart location, Luka thought. *Easy access.* There were so many ways the perpetrator could have gotten to and fled from the crime scene.

"I don't give a fuck who he is, he's contaminating my crime scene," McLean growled. His bushy brows creased together in a deep frown. Luka turned from the window.

"What have we got?" Luka ignored the reproof, his subtle Russian accent turning his *w*'s into *v*'s.

"Kenneth Cox, white male. Thirty-five years of age. Married. He's an out-of-town commercial-real-estate hotshot. Found dead this morning by Housekeeping." McLean's voice was strained, as if it pained him to have to impart the case facts to a lower life-form. Luka ignored the sulky resentment in his voice.

"Where's the maid?"

"She's in the room across the hall, calming down. Couldn't understand a damned word out of her mouth, she was so spooked. Hope you know Spanish." McLean shot a sidelong glance toward Maria.

"Anyone else see anything?" Luka was all business now.

"Not so far, but we're still interviewing the staff and the other guests."

"When did he check in?"

"Yesterday afternoon."

"Alone?"

McLean sighed loudly, as if Luka was wasting his precious time. Finally, he nodded.

"Any outgoing calls from the room?"

"A few. We're tracking them down now."

"Any messages?"

"One from his wife, last night about nine p.m."

Luka nodded and glanced back over at the body on the bed, wondering if Cox was already dead by that point. Nothing like a call from the wife to spoil the mood.

"Get me a full background check on our victim."

McLean walked him through the scene, tracing the path of the first officers on the scene. Luka documented the entry and exits, furniture placement—anything that could indicate there might have been a struggle.

"Where was this guy from?" Luka called over to McLean.

"Miami. He was in town on business."

"Doesn't look like there was much of a struggle." Luka noted the half-empty champagne bottle still sitting in the silver bucket. The ice had turned to water long ago.

"Glasses?" he asked McLean.

"One, half empty on the bedside table. The other is on the table. Clean. Like it's never been used."

"The guy isn't drinking champagne alone, so maybe she washed it before leaving."

Luka's use of a female pronoun was not lost on the officer, and McLean's furry eyebrows rose slowly. Female perpetrators were rare and almost always involved with the victim in some way.

"Or maybe it was some woman's husband who got here in time to break up the action," McLean offered.

"Maybe, but in that case, you'd still find two dirty glasses. There'd be more signs of a struggle."

Luka was getting a picture in his head of a romantic interlude gone wrong. A lover spurned after learning that her intended was not going to leave his wife?

"Maybe it wasn't that kind of date."

"Meaning?" Luka's voice was even as he continued to survey the room.

"Well, this is San Francisco ..."

The innuendo was clear. They'd have to pursue every angle. Perhaps Kenneth Cox was hiding more than an affair from his wife. Wouldn't be the first time.

"Did you find his wallet? Was there anything missing?"

"Cash and credit cards seemed to be intact," McLean answered.

Taking another long look around the hotel room, Luka saw nothing else that seemed oddly out of place. The crime scene looked too clean for a crime of passion. Careful. Calculated. Whoever did this took their time.

Luka stepped back toward the bed, his eyes taking in every detail of the body. It looked like one clean shot through the chest. If death wasn't instantaneous, it didn't take long for the victim to bleed out. His eyes focused in on the hand dangling off the bed, and he took a step closer.

"Have you found the guy's wedding ring?"

"What?" McLean asked.

"His wedding ring. It's missing."

"How do you know he was wearing one?"

Luka gestured toward the victim's ring finger. "Look, there's tan line where his wedding ring should have been. If he deliberately removed it, then it's probably somewhere in this room."

McLean shook his head. "No sign of it yet, but we'll keep looking."

Luka scratched his neck and took another look around the hotel room. It was going to be a long day.

CHAPTER FOURTY ONE

Jill arrived home from the airport late Friday night. The smell of the Christmas tree filled the room with a clean, piney scent. Molly did not come to greet her, and Jill looked up to see two eyes staring down at her from the top of the stairs. The dog's demeanor was problematic. Even Alex had noticed her response to Jill. He'd asked her if it was possible that Molly was going senile. Seven years old seemed a little young for that kind of behavior, but still, in Alex's mind, it was the most plausible explanation. Jill had mumbled something mildly reassuring before changing the subject.

She discarded her suitcase at the foot of the landing and continued through the house into the kitchen. The lights were low, and she could see Alex standing with his back to her, his face reflected in the windowpane as he stared out at the darkened night. A warning flare shot off in her head, and she slowed to a halt.

There was something about the rigid line of his shoulders that caused her pulse to lurch into an uneven gallop. Grasping the corner of the granite counter top, she broke the silence.

"Hi." She sounded casual, but her insides tightened like a vice. No way he knew what she'd been up to in San Francisco. She'd been careful, but still, she couldn't shake the uneasy feeling unfurling at the pit of her stomach.

"How was your flight?" He turned at last. He did not smile, and instinctively, she took a step back, toward the door.

"Uneventful." She took in a deep breath, and forced her tone to remain light. "Have you eaten?"

"Not hungry. Thanks." The tinkle of ice in his glass drew her gaze to his hands. In the dim light she could see his long fingers wrapped tightly around a tumbler. Alex was drinking alone, a sure sign that whatever he was holding back had him tied up in knots. This had become a more frequent occurrence since he had taken on the Watson case.

"How was your week?" Rummaging through the refrigerator, she extracted the fixings for a sandwich. Busying her hands was an excellent way to steady her frayed nerves. She couldn't afford to jump to conclusions. Keeping a cool head was top priority. Besides, if Alex did know her secrets, there would be plenty of time to panic. Decades, as she rotted in jail.

Silence stretched out between them, and finally Jill looked up. Alex was staring at the empty glass in his hand. Meeting her gaze, he deliberately set it on the island, where it made a soft, clinking sound.

"What's wrong?" she asked, quelling the flutter of panic in the pit of her stomach.

Alex shifted his weight and took a step toward her, his hands splayed on the granite countertop.

"Could we sit?" He gestured toward the table. Jill set the knife down before following him across the room. She sank down into the chair opposite Alex, keeping her eyes glued to his face as she searched for some indication of what was bothering him. Typically Alex didn't play games.

He opened his mouth as if to speak, then closed it again. He rubbed his hands across his face and then sat back with a sober star. Jill's anxiety grew.

"So there's been a development in the Honeywell case," he began, voice halting.

Relief flooded through Jill, the respite so strong that she felt light-headed. The breath she'd been unconsciously holding let out in a rush. This wasn't about her. This wasn't about the string of dead bodies she'd left behind in California. This was about Alex's pet case. If she wasn't so relieved, she might actually be irritated. His whole world seemed to revolve around the damned case. Abby Watson's damned case.

"What kind of development? Do you know where he is?"

"Not exactly." Alex shook his head, his mouth set in a grim line. "But we do know where he's been."

Jill cocked her head, eyebrows arching as she tried to grasp his meaning. Where he'd been. Why did it matter, unless it provided some kind of clue to his whereabouts? And why was Alex being so careful in the way he shared this information with her? This sounded like the kind of news they'd talk about over wine. Why did it warrant a family meeting?

Alex leaned forward, placing an object on the table between them. Jill hitched in a breath as she caught sight of the gun. What the hell?

"There's no good way to say this, Jill. Honeywell has been following you. Or at least, he was." Alex sat back, staring at her as she put the pieces together.

"What do you mean? Where?" She felt short of breath, and her pulse throbbed at the base of her throat.

"He sent me pictures of you at Alki Bakery. He must have followed you there."

Jill's lips parted as the image flashed into her head of the man she'd found watching her.

"Shoulder-length blonde hair, blue eyes. He had a cell phone ..." The words tumbled out in a rush.

"You saw him?"

"I caught a guy staring at me. There was something creepy about the look on his face. He didn't stay long. Once he knew I'd seen him, he dialed a number on his phone and left."

"Do you remember what time?"

"Around ten-thirty I think. Why? Is it important?"

Alex didn't answer. His eyes still rested on her, but she could see that his focus had turned inward. Maybe he was putting this information together with a set of assumptions. Whatever it was, he was not sharing.

"He's using me to get to you," she said at last.

Alex nodded, his eyes shifting to the gun. His hand reached across the table to cover hers, and she could feel the warmth of his fingers penetrate her skin. The hairs on her arm prickled. Her racing pulse slowed. She knew she should be worried about the psychopath following her, but things would have been so much worse if Alex—

The thought stopped suddenly as she caught the shift in Alex's expression. He looked perplexed. There was no other word that seemed to fit.

Jill eased back in her chair and pulled her hand out from underneath his. Crossing her arms, she waited for him to speak.

"This is serious, Jill. He's killed other women—girls."

"I know," she said quickly.

"Then why don't you look more worried?"

Hard as she tried to stifle it, she couldn't stop the crooked smile that curved her lips.

"I'm wearing my fear on the inside."

He clearly didn't appreciate the joke, so she continued, nodding toward the pistol.

"Look, I'm assuming that this is what the gun is about. You want to make sure I can protect myself. I don't actually think freaking out is going to help the situation or make you feel better. If I'm wrong, let me know, but be warned, it will take me a few minutes to work myself up into a full-blown frenzy."

He raked his hands through his hair and shook his head.

"This isn't funny, Jill. I want you to start carrying the gun with you. I can't be with you every second to make sure you're okay."

His lips flattened into a grim line. Her attempts at humor fell flat.

Jill could read the concern on his face. It was evident in the dark circles under his eyes and the tense lines etched into forehead. There was no way to put him at ease. No matter what she said, he would worry, so Jill quit trying to reassure him. Instead, she picked up the gun and examined it.

The grip fit nicely in her hand. Alex had chosen well. She checked the magazine before setting it down again.

"It's registered in my name. I've picked up ammo."

His voice trailed off, as if the surreal nature of the situation gave him pause.

"Try not to worry. I'll be careful. I promise."

"I'll also need your phone."

"What for?"

"The department is testing a new cell phone application. It works with your phone's GPS software to feed the location of the originating call into the 911 emergency system."

"Doesn't it automatically do that?"

"Well, not exactly. Even though today over half of all 911 calls are made from cell phones, in most cases the best we can do is to get a general location-based on the closest cell phone tower. We can narrow it down to an area within a several-block radius, but not an exact location. This application will provide more info on where you're located, so if you hang up, they know where you called from. I've been testing it on mine already, and it seems to work pretty well."

Alex fell silent. He ran a weary hand across his eyes before meeting her gaze.

"Look, Jill, I'm really sorry about this."

"Sorry?"

"About all of this." With a broad sweep of his hand, he gestured toward the gun. "I'm sorry my job brought this crazy son of a bitch into our lives, and now I've put you at risk. This isn't how it should work. Ever. I'm so sorry, Jill."

Pushing her chair back, she rose and rounded the table, stopping behind him. She planted a kiss on his hair, fingers kneading his knotted shoulders. She could smell the liquor on his breath, and she wondered how much he'd had to drink before she'd arrived. The smell of boozy breath conjured an image of her stepfather. Sam had been a mean drunk, but Alex was nothing like him. He was the one person she could trust.

"Not your fault. But I wouldn't complain if you decided to quit your job and become a real-estate agent, or something."

That won her a low chuckle, and at last, Jill could feel the tension in his body ease.

"Sure I can't make you a sandwich? I'm starving."

CHAPTER FOURTY TWO

Weeks after Kenneth Cox's body had been planted in the ground of a Miami cemetery, Christmas passed in a blur of brightly colored paper and twinkling lights. There were family celebrations and quiet nights at home. But after three days of sleeping in late and getting caught up on prerecorded television programs, Alex looked twitchy and decided to go into work. He told Jill that he was worried the headway he had made on his recent backlog of cases was disappearing as new ones flooded in. She knew the real reason, of course. He was still searching for Jerry Honeywell, and while the case had dipped on the overall department priority list, it was still at the top of Alex's.

Jill, on the other hand, opted to camp out at Alki Bakery and use their free Wi-Fi to check Lilith's mail. Kenneth Cox, a.k.a. Casanova, was dead. One down, but there was still one to go. She had to find the dark-haired man from the video.

Seated at a table near the back of the bakery, Jill nibbled on biscotti as she looked out the window. For once it wasn't raining, and the locals were taking advantage of the "good weather" to take a chilly stroll along Alki Beach. The bakery teemed with life as folks ducked through the door to warm up with a cup of coffee and a treat.

Jill's thoughts strayed back to the hotel in San Francisco and the encounter with Kenneth Cox. A search of the hotel room had uncovered a small hidden camera. No doubt intended to capture their tryst for upload onto his private pornographic website. Putting a stop to his covert activities felt pretty damn good, and the careful planning increased her confidence that she hadn't left a trail. She was safe. All those years of listening to Alex drone on about how they tracked their suspects hadn't been a waste of time.

"Penny for your thoughts," a man at the next table said.

Jill started visibly at the interruption. Her knee hit the table, and the coffee mug rattled against the scarred surface, slopping over the edges. She swore softly, her fingers rubbing her throbbing knee, and glanced over. The man was in his thirties, with the coloring of a Siberian husky—dark hair and freaky blue eyes. Small silver hoops twinkled from his ears.

"Trust me, they're not worth that much." Jill forced a quick grin, careful not to maintain eye contact for long. Shifting back to her laptop, she busied her fingers on the keys, hoping that he would just go away. An uneasy tingle raced down her spine. Paranoia or intuition? She didn't know which.

Regardless, Jill reached down to edge the laptop bag closer to the leg of her chair. The gun Alex had given her was safely tucked inside, close by in case she needed it.

"I doubt that. I'll bet there are all sorts of interesting things going on in that pretty head of yours," the man persisted. His smile seemed disarming enough, and reluctantly Jill looked up.

"Listen, I don't mean to be rude," she began, careful to keep her tone friendly, "but I've got a lot of work to do." Despite her efforts, an edge crept into her voice.

He raised his hands in a quick movement that had her scraping her chair back and gripping her bag. The stab of panic she felt must have flashed on her face. His palms-up gesture was designed to put her at ease.

"Okay, calm down. Just trying to make conversation."

Jill gave a brief nod and looked away, releasing the tight grip she had on her bag. Jill glanced at the cell phone she had sitting beside her computer. She could call Alex if she needed to, but that was a last resort.

With a muttered curse under his breath, the man stood and moved to a table closer to the window. A long sigh escaped her as she felt the tension drain from her body. Maybe she'd overreacted, but a girl couldn't be too careful, especially with creeps like Jerry Honeywell lurking.

Jill shook off the thought. Focusing back on her laptop, she called up her online profile. She grinned at Dana Evans's picture. While not a perfect match for Lilith's vital statistics, it had been close enough to lure in Kenneth Cox and the sixty other hits that had come in since she had last logged on.

Now it was time to go hunting for the third man involved in the sex-video ring. It didn't take long to find him. He called himself Joel Goodsen. If you pictured your ideal stockbroker or CEO type, he'd look just like this: compact build, close-cropped, dark hair, all-American face. Sharp. Focused. Ruthless.

She smirked. Surely it wasn't his real name. No one in the shark tank used their real name. Jill pressed her lips together as she considered his profile. Every detail oozed success. She wondered what drove him to the kind of twisted, thrill-seeking behavior he and his sick buddies made their hobby. Whatever it was, he'd live to regret the shitty choices he'd made. She'd make sure of it.

Opening a new browser window, she typed the name "Joel Goodsen" into the search screen and scanned the results. None of the hits seemed to match the online profile. There was, however, one reference that made her smile. Joel Goodsen was the name of the character Tom Cruise had played in *Risky Business.*

At least the asshole had a sense of humor. Risky business. Well that just about sums up life in the shark tank.

She typed Joel's name in the chat window. Half a second later, Joel pinged back. Jill's pulse began to pound, and an electric energy surged through her. Hairs pricked at the back of her neck as she shifted forward in her seat. The hook was baited; all he had to do was bite.

"How's life in the Big Apple?" Jill typed.

"Not in New York at the moment."

"Where in the world are you?"

"Nursing a merger in San Francisco."

Jill could feel her pulse throb in her ears as she read the reply. San Francisco. Dumb luck. What were the odds?

"Not quite the same as nursing a hangover, but I do feel your pain."

"LOL. Sure. Dull. Throbbing. Inescapable. Kind of like the city itself."

"Ah, I take it you don't like the financial powerhouse of the West Coast."

"Powerhouse? Hardly."

The cursor blinked at her from midscreen. Leaning back in her chair, Jill took a sip from her latte as she thought about Joel. He's definitely type-A, nothing flirty about him. He communicated in crisp, clipped sentences—probably conducted his transactions that way, too. Nothing personal, ma'am, just the facts.

"So how long are you stuck in paradise?"

"A few more weeks."

"Poor thing, living out of suitcases in a hotel is a drag."

"Corporate condo."

A high roller. If he was telling the truth, he was employed by a pretty high-powered firm. Of course, that was a big *if*. Everybody in the shark tank lies.

"Good view, I hope?"

"It's okay. Within walking distance to Chinatown."

"Authentic dim sum is a good thing."

"Got that right, but what would a girl from Georgia know about dim sum?"

There it was; that hook into the encounter. Up until now, he could have been chatting with a work colleague. He'd just swallowed the bait. Would he run with it?

"Oh, I've traveled a little."

"The Midwest doesn't count."

Jill's lips tightened as she stared at the screen, and she bristled at the insinuation. He had her pegged for a midlevel corporate hack, smart enough to work in a plodding business environment, but not sharp enough to play with the big dogs. Boy, was he in for a surprise.

"LOL. Sorry to disappoint, Sugar, but I've never been to Kansas City. New York, Seattle, San Francisco, Boston, yes, St. Paul, no."

"Shopping at Macy's doesn't count."

Jill gritted her teeth, hating him more with each word. He was a condescending chauvinist, and she was going to enjoy teaching him a lesson.

"What are you trying to say, Joel? No girls in that exclusive boys' club of yours?"

"Sure, we all have assistants. Couldn't get by without them."

"I'm sure they help organize your work life in the same way your wife manages your home life."

"You know what they say; behind every successful man is a good woman."

And I hope she's packing heat, Jill did not add as her fingers tapped the keys lightly.

"Lilith?" The cursor blinked as he waited for a response.

Jill stared at the screen. She thought of Peter, Kenneth, and Joel and their sex videos. She thought about the other women they'd hurt. Used. Jill's fingers tapped on the keys.

"You know, I was just thinking," she typed into the browser window. "It's been ages since I had good dim sum."

CHAPTER FOURTY THREE

Alex pushed back in his chair and finished the remnants of his tuna sandwich.

"Shit," he muttered as some mayonnaise dripped onto the budget spreadsheet fanned out across his desk. Captain Lewis needed a quarterly update by three o'clock, and Alex was spending his lunch hour crunching numbers. Normally he would avoid this type of task like the plague, but in this case, he was doing penance. At least, that's what Jackson called it, good lapsed Catholic that he was.

Dabbing the sheet of paper with a napkin, he managed to clean up most of the watery mess. At least it was still legible. Gaze still focused on the even columns of numbers, he crumpled the waxy sandwich paper and tossed it in the garbage, saving the garlic-laced pickle for last.

"Good news, Boss," a voice called from his doorway.

Alex swung his chair around. Kris Thompson stood with a smile on her face and a printout in her hand. She wasn't wearing her glasses, and he had an unobstructed view of her eyes. Hazel. Why had he never noticed that before?

"What's up?"

"We've got a tip on Honeywell." An incandescent smile lit her face.

"Where?" Alex's mouth suddenly felt dry.

"Yakima."

"How solid does it look?"

"Pretty solid. Retired cop says that the guy who fixed his truck looked a lot like Honeywell. The locals are on their way to confirm."

Alex winced and rubbed his forehead with his open hand. What if they bungled the arrest? If Honeywell escaped this trap, he might just beeline it across the mountains to Seattle and make good on his threats against Jill. A printout of Honeywell's chilling threat sat pinned under the lip of Alex's monitor, and he eyed it with a sense of foreboding.

"Where is he staying?"

"He's sharing a house on the west side of town with a couple of other guys."

"Shit." Alex slammed his fist on the desk. "Shit, shit, shit." The thought of not being there to bring Honeywell in was frustrating beyond words.

Jackson lumbered down the hall, eclipsing Kris in the doorway.

"Christ, you look like you're going to puke. Something wrong with the tuna fish?"

His partner leaned against the doorframe, eyes fixed on Alex, concern registering in his deep voice.

"Is it Jill?"

Alex shook his head.

"Honeywell," Kris said.

"Where?"

"Yakima."

Jackson's face broke out into a broad grin.

"You want to go get the fucker?"

* * *

Kris's lips formed a tight line as she handed the electronic tickets to Jackson and Alex. Breaking the rules wasn't in Kris's DNA, and the stress of doing so showed on her face. She was strictly a by-the-book kind of girl. But they had pressured her to use department resources for an unsanctioned trip across the mountains, capitalizing on the fact that Captain Lewis was in an all-day meeting with the mayor and had left strict orders not to be disturbed.

While all that was true, it was more in line with the letter of the law than its spirit. Authorizing his officers to engage in an arrest outside of their jurisdiction was something for which he would not only forgive an interruption; he'd damned well expect it.

While Alex chose to hide behind the excuse of not wanting to disturb the captain, the trio knew the truth. There is no way in hell that Captain Lewis would agree to the trip. Not after California. Not after the ass whipping he had taken from the ATF.

"You're going to get us fucking fired," Kris mumbled.

Alex's eyes snapped to her face, his jaw hanging slack in disbelief. He'd never heard her swear before. Not a *shit* or a *damn*. Certainly not an f-bomb. He expected nothing less from Jackson, but from Kris? He flashed a reassuring smile and lightly squeezed her shoulder. Surely she had to realize that if anyone's ass was on the line, it was his.

"Not all of us—just me. You know the golden rule: it's better to ask for forgiveness than permission." Alex checked his watch and nodded to Jackson.

"Yeah, I'll remember that when Lewis is picking his teeth with my femur. No John Wayne stuff," Kris called after them.

"Yes ma'am," Alex said.

"You know, Shannon, I like you better now that you're breaking the rules," Jackson grinned.

"Bending them. And I don't think that Kris shares your opinion."

Without so much as a backwards glance, the budget updates were abandoned, and Jackson's low chuckle reverberated down the hall.

***

The Alaska Air flight arrived at Yakima's McAllister Field five minutes ahead of schedule. Stepping out into the bright afternoon sun, Alex and Jackson made their way toward the black-and-white waiting outside the terminal. It was a cool thirty-eight degrees, but Alex barely noticed the cold wind blowing through his light jacket. Anticipation had the blood pumping fast through his veins. They were close to bringing Honeywell in. He could feel it.

Alex ducked his head into the open window of the cruiser and fastened his gaze on the officer behind the wheel.

"I'm Detective Shannon, and this is Detective Levy."

"I'm Mitchell." The young officer cocked a thumb toward the backseat. "Hop in."

The two piled into the car, and the uniformed officer accelerated smoothly away from the curb. Mitchell was a young red-headed cop with green eyes and translucent eyelashes. Glancing over, Alex gauged him to be in his mid to late twenties. An average-looking kid with a square jaw, set in a decided frown. He probably wanted to be the one to take down Honeywell, and letting two Seattle cops horn in on the action was the last thing he wanted to do.

"Hey, thanks for letting us crash your party." Alex flashed a lop-sided grin. "I wanted to be here in person to bring this bastard in."

Mitchell nodded but didn't say anything right away. When he did, he was all business.

"We've got two guys watching the house. There are at least three people in there. They got home about four p.m. and haven't moved since. Looks like they're watching television."

Alex looked out the window, watching the houses fly by without really seeing them. His thoughts turned to Natalie, piecing together her final moments. He could envision the dark interior of the hunting cabin in Winthrop, the musty smell of the threadbare couch where they had found her shoe.

According to the medical examiner, she put up a hell of a fight. But in the end, Honeywell ended her young life by wrapping his strong, grease-stained hands around her neck and squeezing until she stopped thrashing. Sometimes at night, when he closed his eyes, he still saw her bluish fingertips poking up out of the snow: frozen, gruesome spring flowers.

Now it was time for Honeywell to pay.

"It's just a few blocks from here."

Mitchell's voice brought Alex back to the present. He propped his elbow against the door frame and rested his chin against his balled fist. The neatly kept houses near the airport gave way to sagging, rundown neighborhoods. They flew by row after row of small, military-style bungalows with peeling front doors and listing front porches.

Mitchell slowed and brought the cruiser to a stop near a faded yellow house, its white shutters hung slightly askew. He pointed down the street to a brown sedan parked under a canopy of trees a block away.

"Officers Howe and Bentley are down there. See the blue bungalow?"

Alex and Jackson followed the trajectory of his outstretched finger with their eyes. Both nodded.

"That's where Honeywell and his buddies are holed up. We've got backup a few blocks away."

Alex nodded and opened the car door, his eyes directed toward the door of the blue and white house, as if waiting for someone to appear. The shirttail of his navy button-down hung loose over the waistband of his faded jeans and concealed the bulge of his weapon. Jackson said nothing as they approached the brown sedan, but tension tugged at the corners of his mouth.

"You ready for this?" Alex asked softly, stealing a glance at his partner out of the corner of his eyes.

"Son, I was born ready," Jackson replied, an unexpected smile parting his lips.

The two edged around the brown car, squatting down by the passenger window. "Shannon and Levy," Alex said quietly, showing his badge as he checked out the two cops sitting in the car.

"Suspect is in the house. As far as we can tell, there are three of them. We haven't seen guns, but we expect that they're armed."

"How do you want to run this?" Alex's pulse picked up pace as he got his head in the game.

"We've got a guy dressed like a pizza-delivery dude. He's going to knock on the door. We're going to cover him up. You two go behind the house in case anyone runs. We've got more backup standing by. They'll move in on my word."

"Got it." Alex straightened up. "Let's do it."

Alex took the lead and strolled across the street, adopting as casual an air as possible. His eyes swung left and right, taking in as many details as he could as he approached the house. Traffic was light. There were a few cars driving down the block, passing by without a glance. A couple of young boys were walking across the street, their loud voices carrying as they took turns punching a skinny kid in the arm—good-natured ribbing.

Alex turned into the neighbor's driveway. His feet crunched on the packed gravel. In a quick move, he jumped the low fence and crept along the side of the house. Crouched against the siding, he drew his weapon.

The weight of the gun felt good in his hand, like an old friend, as he inched his way toward the back corner. Despite the cold wind, sweat trickled down the back of his neck while he waited for the other officers to get in position. He heard the rustling branches of the pine trees at the back of the house and the buzz of voices in the living room.

The sharp knock on the door was closely followed by the sound of footsteps. Loud voices rang out, and Alex heard muffled shouts. Gunshots fired. The back door burst open, and Alex caught his first live glimpse of Jerry Honeywell since the darkened parking lot in California as he shot out the door at a full gallop.

Alex took off after him. Honeywell sailed over the back fence. His long limbs cleared the ragged chain-link edge with no effort at all. Alex followed suit, his stride settling into a steady rhythm. He kept his eyes fastened on Honeywell's back.

They were racing through a neighbor's backyard and down a winding alley when Honeywell darted right. Alex skidded around the corner and caught the bright flash of Honeywell's shirt as he disappeared around the side of a two-story brick house.

Alex willed himself to pick up the pace as he pumped his arms hard. No way he would lose Honeywell now. He slowed as he got behind the house, and his eyes scanned the backyard. For a moment, his heart sank as he thought he'd lost the suspect. Then he saw some movement from the corner of his eye, and he spied Honeywell running across the street toward a wooded park.

Cars skidded to a halt nearby. Alex bolted across the street and into the park. Sweat stung his eyes. A kid on a bike swung out in Alex's path, and he dodged it without missing a beat. He could see Honeywell running ahead toward a small pond.

Maybe it was wishful thinking, but Alex could swear that Honeywell was slowing down. The sound of kids playing filled Alex's head as he raced by. The edge of the park was in view, and Honeywell glanced quickly behind him. The sight of Alex gaining galvanized him, and he shot ahead.

Alex was breathing hard but still feeling strong as he continued to give chase. He was suddenly glad for all the late-night runs with Jill and Molly through the streets of West Seattle. He was sure that Jackson and the other officers would be on their trail, but kept his eyes focused on Honeywell's back. He couldn't afford to lose Honeywell. Not now. Not when he was so close.

The outskirts of Yakima were largely industrial, and they were passing into a section of town that was made up of warehouses and factories, places where they shipped their bountiful crops across the mountains. They sailed past the train tracks.

Honeywell scaled a chain-link fence and dropped into the parking lot of what looked to be an abandoned factory. He struggled over the fence and landed on the asphalt with a thump.

Alex jumped, his fingers grasping the metal links to scale the fence. He propelled himself over the top and onward. Honeywell rounded the corner of the factory, and Alex followed.

He slowed, his chest heaving with his labored breath. He peered cautiously around the corner. Honeywell had disappeared from view, and Alex raised his gun, gripping it tightly in his hand. He hugged the factory wall, sensing that Honeywell was close. He reached the back corner of the factory and swept his gaze wide.

Honeywell was trying to force open a door and enter the factory. The door was not cooperating, and Alex took aim between the suspect's broad shoulders.

"Freeze, asshole," he called out, gun pointing straight in front of him as he gripped it with both hands.

Honeywell's head swiveled, cold blue eyes vacant as he met Alex's stare. Quickly he dropped his hand to his skinny waist, and Alex thought he saw the metallic glint of a gun as Honeywell turned to face him.

"Don't move," he called out again.

"Fuck you," Honeywell yelled, raising his hand. Gun metal flashed in the sun, followed by the loud crack of a gun's rapport.

Alex swerved, but not before he felt the heat of the bullet tear into his arm, loosening the double grip on his gun. The impact knocked him off balance. He fell sideways, his free hand flailing out to steady himself against the wall. Honeywell crashed into the door with all of his force and stumbled inside, out of Alex's line of vision.

Alex's breath came in ragged gasps, and he ignored the searing pain in his arm. He edged down the wall and paused at the doorway, allowing his eyes to adjust to the low light. Honeywell raced toward a rack of metal shelves.

Alex cut down the other side, gained ground, and with a quick move, launched himself at Honeywell. They collided full force. Pain radiated through Alex's body, and he pulled in a ragged breath.

Alex managed to regain his footing first. Honeywell, knocked off balance, stumbled to the concrete floor. His gun clattered to the ground beside him.

Working on instinct, Alex kicked the gun out of reach and slammed his shoe down between Honeywell's bony shoulder blades. The barrel of his Glock pointed at the back of Honeywell's head. He shoved his foot forward to rest in the curve of Honeywell's neck. His wounded arm burned. Hurt like hell, in fact.

"Well, well, the infamous Jerry Honeywell." Alex allowed a smile to cross his lips. "Somehow I expected you to be … oh, I don't know … smarter." He had him. He finally had him. Victory was so close, Alex could almost taste it.

"I don't know what you think you've got, but I guarantee you it won't stick."

"That's what you think, motherfucker. We've got you cold. You're going to need a goddamned good lawyer to represent you, and based on your financial records, the only lawyer you can afford will be a court-appointed attorney. Good luck with that."

"I wouldn't bet my paycheck on it, cop," Honeywell muttered between clenched teeth, his strained voice ringing hollow in the vast, abandoned space.

"Whatever you say, asshole." Alex applied even more pressure with his foot, forcing Honeywell's face flat against the cold concrete floor.

"I'm not just going to nail you for murdering Natalie Watson. Lisa Cullen's hit-and-run has been reopened, too. You remember Lisa, right? Blond hair, pretty face, aborted child? Oh, and I know about Kayla Miller, the girl from Medford."

Honeywell clenched his teeth, his gaze angled up toward Alex. The hard glimmer of hate burned in his eyes.

"You better pray I never get out of jail, boy," Honeywell said. "When I do, I'm coming after your pretty wife. If you're lucky, I'll even let you watch."

Alex increased the pressure, pinning Honeywell in place. A thrill of satisfaction shot through him as a pained gasp escaped Honeywell's lips.

"I just want to know one thing. What did you feel when you killed Natalie?"

Honeywell flashed a cold smile, his eyes vacant as he strained to look up at Alex.

"I felt nothing," he said in a flat hiss.

A dizzying wave of rage surged through Alex's veins. The son of a bitch was smiling. Alex's vision narrowed as he stared down at the man on the floor. He wanted to pull the trigger. He wanted to end this miserable fuck's life.

What kind of human being killed an innocent teenage girl and felt nothing? If he was able to do something like that, what else was he capable of? Alex's jaw was clenched tight, and his fingers gripped the gun hard as he stood with a foot pressing down on Honeywell's neck.

He couldn't. Alex took a deep breath and gathered every ounce of self-control he could muster. He willed himself not to pull the trigger.

The sound of Honeywell's labored breathing echoed in the empty factory. They were all alone, without another soul in sight. Alex's mind crossed over into forbidden territory. There was a gun on the floor with Honeywell's fingerprints. The warm blood streaming down his skin at a steady pace was proof enough of a struggle. If Honeywell was dead when the others arrived, who would question how it happened? Any credible story he concocted would be taken as fact, and this case would be closed. No questions asked. He'd be considered a hero.

"Come on, Alex. Pull the trigger," Honeywell goaded as if reading his mind. "You know you want to. Do it for Natalie. Do it for your wife. It will be the only chance you get to get rid of me for good."

Alex's anger cooled into a cold, calculating certainty. His hand was rock steady as he pointed the barrel down at the base of Honeywell's skull. Far away he heard the wail of police sirens. What was there to stop him from sending a bullet through this bastard's brain? Wouldn't everyone be better off if this son of a bitch was dead? Honeywell's demise would provide closure for Abby and her parents. Jill would no longer have to look over her shoulder. Everybody stood to gain if Alex simply pulled the trigger. His hand tightened on the gun.

"Alex," Jackson called from the doorway.

Alex flinched, and the moment was gone. Swinging his head around, he caught sight of Jackson's sweaty face. Their eyes locked, and Alex knew that Jackson had understood his intent. Neither said a word as Jackson stepped forward, footsteps ringing on the concrete floor. He removed his handcuffs from his belt.

As if from a great distance, Alex watched Jackson crouch down to snap the cuffs around one bony, white wrist. Jackson glanced up, and Alex stepped off of Honeywell's neck and moved back a few paces, giving his partner room to work. Alex held his gun steady, still trained on the suspect.

"You okay?" Jackson asked, nodding toward Alex's injured arm.

"Yeah." Alex did not move his eyes away from the back of Honeywell's head.

"You have the right to remain silent, you piece of shit," Jackson said. Twisting the man's other arm roughly around his back, he secured the second wrist. "You have the right to an attorney. If you cannot afford a lawyer, we will appoint the stupidest goddamned one we can find to represent you."

As Jackson finished reading Honeywell his rights, the Yakima officers poured through the factory door, quickly taking control of the scene.

Like a fly on a wall, Alex watched the Yakima officers haul Honeywell off the floor and lead him out of the warehouse and into the frosty January day. Only then did he holster his gun and clap a hand across the wound on his arm. Jackson slowly made his way to Alex's side.

"Good work, partner." Jackson slapped Alex's shoulder.

"Jesus." Alex cringed and swore through clenched teeth. Pain seared through his arm.

"You should get that looked at."

"Thanks, but it looks worse than it is."

"Maybe so. But Jill would never forgive me if we let something as insignificant as a bullet mar that perfect body of yours." Jackson's eyes sparkled in amusement.

"Get bent," Alex said as he strode toward the door, out of the darkened factory and into the cold night. Despite the twisted cop humor, he couldn't manage a smile as he looked down at his bloody arm.

As he stepped out into the cold wind, Alex wondered what kind of cop he would have been if Jackson had stepped through the factory door thirty seconds later.

CHAPTER FOURTY FOUR

Jill smelled the roasted coffee beans from a nearby café as she made her way off 19th Avenue. The dense clouds over San Francisco formed a thick blanket that choked out the light of the moon. A faint glow from the streetlights barely penetrated the darkness. She wasn't worried about things that went bump in the night, though. With the Glock stowed safely away in her pocket, she was equipped to deal with almost any situation.

The soft soles of Jill's boots made no sound on the cold concrete path as she wound her way toward the botanical gardens, where she had arranged to meet her date. The same chilly night air that kept the crowds away from the park invigorated her. Meeting him out in the open was only slightly riskier than meeting him at a hotel. Here, there were no surveillance cameras to capture her image. And she was in the mood for something a little different, a little risky business.

Jill followed the curve of Martin Luther King Jr. Drive east. Shaking the bangs of the blond wig out of her eyes, she averted her face. A young man—black, wearing a baseball cap—passed by. She could feel his eyes linger on her, and her stomach clenched. Would he try to engage her in conversation, or worse? In a pinch, she could take care of herself. But grappling with some stranger wasn't how she intended to spend the evening.

It wasn't until the sound of his footfalls faded in the distance that she felt the tension ease in her shoulders, and she lengthened her stride. She thought about the sex videos and Joel, who liked to hurt women. She'd take care of him. She'd make sure he never hurt anyone else. While she wasn't exactly performing a public service, she preferred to think she was leaving the world a better place, like taking out the trash.

Joel Goodsen was waiting by the main entrance to the botanical gardens, dressed for the cold weather in a black wool trench coat and cashmere scarf. Though it was dark, she could still make out the sharp angles of his face underneath the sodium lights. He looked a little older in person than the picture he'd posted with his online profile. But he was blessed with sharp good looks that would get him noticed in any crowd. With dark hair and brown eyes the shade of milk chocolate, he couldn't be more different in appearance from Kenneth Cox.

"Lilith," Joel said, using her online handle from the Hook Up website. "Your name does you justice."

The smile on his face looked frigid, and with a half smile of her own, Jill noticed the dull gleam of a platinum wedding band on his left hand. She wondered what Mrs. Goodsen was up to this very moment. Was she at home with the kids? Working out with her personal trainer? Did she know what her husband was doing on the other side of the continent? Would she like being a widow with access to his money?

"Hello, Joel." She stopped in front of him. The slight southern accent added a layer of warmth to her voice, and made her feel more in character. How she liked to play games. "So glad you could meet me."

"We have reservations for eight, so we'd best get moving."

His tone was crisp, all business, the kind of voice she would expect from a man who negotiated multi-million-dollar deals. Without offering his arm, he continued down the path that mirrored the drive toward the California Academy of Sciences, still heading east.

"Don't tell me you're still on New York time. Surely you've figured out by now on the West Coast, time is more fluid. Meetings start late, reservations start later, things just take longer. So relax, we'll be fine."

Joel forced a chuckle, but she could tell from his ramrod-straight posture and stiff smile that he had no intention of relaxing. Maybe he wasn't capable of it. Control was his thing. She thought about the videos. Her eyebrows rose. Apparently he applied different risk-tolerance models to different parts of his life.

"Nothing quite like a walk in the park after a long day at the office." She glanced over at him. "Is it as big as Central Park?"

"Bigger. And darker." Joel looked uneasy. His eyes swept the path for any signs of danger.

"You're not afraid of the dark, are you?" Jill couldn't help teasing him, especially since it was obvious how much he despised it. "Don't worry, I'll protect you. I know jujitsu."

This remark made him smile. It was a condescending smile, and Jill had the distinct impression Joel placed his confidence in few women, considering them a lower life-form. She found it easy to hate him.

"Did you learn it at a women's self-defense class?"

"Our instructor was a Navy SEAL. I could kill you with my thumb." Stripping off her light glove, she held the digit up for his inspection. Actually, it was the index finger of her right hand and the gun in her pocket that would prove his undoing. But that was getting ahead of herself, she mused with a twisted grin.

"I feel better already."

The city sounds of traffic mingled with the rustling of the leaves as they wound their way deeper into the park. If Jill was nettled by his sarcasm, she didn't let it show. After their pithy exchange over instant messaging, Joel was turning out to be the flinty chauvinist she had taken him for. She was going to enjoy this.

"Where are we going?" she asked.

"The restaurant is part of the Academy of Sciences. It's called the Moss Room. Comes highly recommended."

"Sounds nice. Take many of your women there?"

His eyes narrowed, and he glanced sharply at her, as if trying to decide exactly what she had meant by the remark.

"Only the good-looking ones."

Jill let the quip pass without comment as she peered into the darkness ahead. The place she had scoped out was not much farther now. She could feel her pulse build momentum as they drew closer.

They reached the junction of Martin Luther King Jr. Drive and Middle Drive East. This was exactly where Jill wanted to be, and she led the way off of the main path into a dark little nook called Shakespeare's Garden. What better place for a romantic rendezvous? Joel's pace slowed. He stopped and turned toward Jill. Irritation flashed in his dark eyes.

"Look, not that this isn't fun, but we don't have time for a nature walk. We've got ten minutes to make it to the restaurant." He tried to reassert control.

"Look," she said, mimicking him, "you're not going to enjoy what I have in store for you if you don't try to relax a little. You're not afraid to take a few risks, are you?" Jill brushed past him, taking care to make contact and heighten his interest. It was more than just playful touching when she pressed herself against him. "Besides, it's faster to go this way."

"Are you sure? It's dark, and I don't want to get turned around."

"I know what I'm doing. You'll see," she purred in his ear as she slipped past. The traffic noise from the city streets subsided, and an eerie quiet settled between them. After a moment, she turned to glance back at him. "You are coming, aren't you?"

"Not yet," he muttered under his breath, and she chuckled at the joke. He affected a more relaxed air. Jill could tell it was an act, but at least the asshole was trying.

Jill led the way down the curvy path and paused outside the wrought-iron entrance to Shakespeare's Garden, waiting for him to catch up. The darkness closed in on them. Jill could hear the sound of their footfalls on the cobblestone path. They passed underneath a dense canopy of trees. The branches wove together, appearing like black lace against a charcoal sky. She slowed as she came to the stone sundial in the center of the path and turned to face Joel.

Without preamble he pulled her against him, his mouth descended quickly, and he kissed her hard. She froze for a second, instinctively wanting to shove him back. But she was playing a role, and Lilith gave herself up to the moment. Her hands slid up the thick fabric of his trench coat and knotted around his butter-soft scarf.

At last he raised his head, eyes barely visible in the dim light. Without a word, he pushed her back through the darkness, across the uneven lawn, until she was pinned against the trunk of a huge red-wood tree. He leaned forward, pressing his mouth against her throat. His hand snaked through her layers of clothing and unceremoniously mashed her breast.

Her breath caught and her head reeled. A wave of anger washed over her. Presumptuous bastard. This was her dance, and she was going to lead. She needed to get control of the situation. Fast. Placing her hands on his shoulders, she eased him back to give herself some breathing room.

"Why the rush? My mama always said to beware of a man in a hurry. We have all night."

Jill could see a muscle twitch in Joel's clenched jaw. He was a man who liked being in control, which made the situation more danger-ous. *More fun,* she amended. She felt the rush of anticipation sizzle along her nerve endings. But now it was time to bring the final act to a close.

"Tell me, Joel, do you like to play games?" Easing forward, Jill nib-bled on his ear, her hand dropping below his belt line until she found what she was looking for. Touching him aroused all kinds of emotions in her: contempt, loathing. Pushing those feelings aside, she focused on her goal and watched Joel's head tip back. His eyes closed; his lips parted. She had his full attention now.

Oh yes, he liked playing games all right. Joel Goodsen. Risky busi-ness. Sex with strangers. She would bet money that he not only liked to play games, he liked to win.

"What exactly did you have in mind?" His breathing was ragged, and Jill pulled back. For the first time all night, a playful smile tugged at the corner of his lips.

"How about a little hide and seek? That is, if you're not scared of the dark. Trust me, I'll make it worth your while."

The challenge was meant to be a not-so-subtle swipe at his masculinity. With a thin-lipped smile he took the bait. And while Joel tied the cashmere scarf around his eyes, Jill pulled out the gun.

"Ready or not, here I come."

CHAPTER FORTY FIVE

Alex had to admit that despite his throbbing arm, he felt pretty damned good. After months of frustration, Jerry Honeywell was finally behind bars. He delivered the news of Honeywell's arrest to Natalie's parents in person, the last stop on his way back to the station.

The decision to leave Abby a voicemail had raised his partner's eyebrows, but Alex chose not to explain. The renewed attraction he felt for Abby was complicated, and fueling it by going to see her on such an emotionally charged topic was like running around with a loaded gun in your hand. Stupid.

The unauthorized trip to Yakima was even worth the serious reprimand they had both received from Captain Lewis. The mood in the cybercrimes unit was subdued; the entire staff was walking around on eggshells. Kris Thompson had spent the last few days avoiding Alex altogether, and that was fine by him. With his arm in a sling, he was cheerfully clearing out some of the less critical cases from his backlog.

Washing two Advil down with his cold coffee, Alex picked up the phone and dialed a familiar San Francisco number.

Luka Petrovich picked up on the third ring, the tone of his voice terse, as if immersed in other matters and resenting the intrusion.

"I've got good news for you."

"Alex?"

"You got it, amigo."

"I could use some good news." Amid the lyrical Russian accent, Alex could hear the smile in Luka's voice and pictured him reclining back in his chair.

"We got Honeywell."

"Great news. I want all the details."

Alex spent a few minutes bringing Luka up to speed on their trip to Yakima, brushing off any concerns about the gunshot wound to his arm.

"Given half the chance, I'm sure that Stone would have shot you himself, not to mention me." Luka's hearty laugh filled the phone, and Alex could well imagine ATF Agent Russell Stone's feelings on the matter.

"Well, he's not the only one. Captain Lewis is not my biggest fan these days, either. But sometimes you've got to do what you think is right, even when it bends the rules a little."

"Ain't that the truth!"

They both laughed. As the sound died away, Luka grew serious.

"Did you hear about Kayla Miller?"

Alex's gut instinctively ratcheted tighter.

"No."

"What was left of her body was found by a couple of backcountry skiers on Mt. Shasta."

Alex groaned softly and rubbed his forehead where the beginning of a headache was taking shape.

"What do you mean, 'what was left'?"

"Wolves had gotten to it. They found a few pieces of her in the snow. It's unlikely we'll ever know what happened to her."

"Shit," Alex said. He was sure Honeywell was responsible for Kayla's disappearance, and now they wouldn't get a chance to prove it. Justice for Natalie would have to serve for Kayla as well. He let out a long, hissing sigh. "So, what have you been working on?"

"'Tis the season to be jolly. I don't know why the murder rate spikes during the holiday season, but we've been hammered lately."

"No kidding."

"You know, I'm working on a case that reminded me of you."

"Should I be flattered?" Alex asked with a half smile as he directed his gaze out the window at the drizzling rain. "Do tell."

"I've got two dead bodies. Both crime scenes feel like a blind date gone wrong. And I've got no clear ties between the victims."

"You've checked escort services?"

"No luck there. Also, their financial records look clean. No unusual transactions."

"What about local working girls?"

"Possible, but it's kind of coincidental that both victims were from out of town. Local girls would mean local johns and local victims."

"Interesting. What about an online dating scenario? Your victims could have been trolling any one of dozens of dating sites."

"That's an angle I'm looking into, but our computer forensics guys have a backlog of cases. I was wishing I had someone like you to help. Mine is at the back of the queue."

"If you want me to take a quick look, I can do that. Have your team upload the disk images, and I'll see what I can find."

"That would be great."

"Sure. Have your techs talk to mine and we'll get the ball rolling.

"Thanks, man. I appreciate the help.

"Sure thing."

✳✳✳

It took a couple hours and a couple of phone calls from Kris to get the disk images of the victims' computer hard drives uploaded. It took even less time for Alex to verify that both men belonged to a common online dating site. One in particular, Hook Up, specialized in married people looking for extracurricular affairs.

A slow crawl through the victims' hard drives revealed that both men had shared some connections: three women, all of whom had similar profiles. All were attractive, athletic, married women in their early thirties. Obviously these women had not used their real names on the profiles and instead used clever pseudonyms. With the help of a few of his diagnostic tools, Alex found that two of the women had been naïve enough to use their online handle in more than one social-networking site. Following the cyber trail, he was able to forge links to their actual identities. The third woman proved more of a challenge.

Browsing to the Hook Up site, he saw Lilith's smiling image staring up at him. Was the woman behind Lilith's pretty face a murderer? Maybe. Maybe not. It was hard to say without knowing more about her. But in his experience, it was typically the people who had something to hide that took such elaborate measures to cover their tracks. In this case, he wondered what dark little secrets Lilith might be hiding.

Downloading a copy of the picture to his desktop, he launched a beta version of a face-recognition utility he was working on. He would do a search through a number of other common social-networking sites to see if he could find a match. If she hadn't used her email handle elsewhere, maybe he could find her face.

Pushing back from his computer screen, Alex grabbed his coat. It was well past six o'clock, and his stomach reminded him that he had somewhere else to be.

CHAPTER FOURTY SIX

"**C**an I get you a beer?" Emma asked Alex as he relaxed back into an overstuffed leather chair in the living room. Mike placed a protective hand on Emma's shoulder.

"You sit. I'll get it," he said, not waiting for Alex's answer. "He looks like he could use one." His brother's smile was lopsided as he left the room. Mike was right. All the way over to their house, Alex was thinking about the name Lilith. There was something familiar about it, something he couldn't quite put his finger on.

"You'd think I was handicapped and not just pregnant." Emma sighed with a touch of exasperation, sinking obediently into the cushions of the couch. Her hand strayed to her gently rounding belly. She was just beginning to show, and from the glow of her skin, Alex guessed that she was feeling fine, having just passed into her second trimester.

"Enjoy it while it lasts." Alex's smile was affectionate. "Mike is not known for his chivalrous behavior. I suggest you milk it for what it's worth."

Entering the room with his long, rolling stride, Mike handed the bottle to Alex and took a seat next to Emma, his arm thrown along the back of the couch. Absently Alex started to pick at the Fat Tire label, tearing little strips of it away from the chilled bottle. Glancing up, he caught Emma's eyes on him, and he stopped fidgeting and took a sip.

"What are you working on these days?" Mike's tone sounded casual, but the calculated look that Alex saw in his eyes told another story.

"You know, exciting stuff like making tool updates and giving online safety course lectures at community events. Lewis has me chained to my desk for a while, until my arm ... "His voice trailed off, and with a twitch of his head he indicated his arm, still cradled in its sling.

"Does it hurt?" Emma asked, the skin around her lively blue eyes crinkling as she grimaced.

"I'm fine."

"At least you got the bastard. I'll bet Tom Watson is sleeping better now, knowing the guy who killed his daughter is behind bars." He cast a glance toward Emma. "I don't know what I'd do if something like that happened to our kid."

Emma patted Mike's knee absently, her eyes still appraising Alex. Part of being a reporter was having good instincts, and Alex had no doubt that right now, Emma was sensing his preoccupation.

"So, how is baby watch?" Alex asked, making an effort to push Luka's case aside for a few hours. He would go back to the office after dinner to see what else he could dig up on Lilith. Right now he would focus on Emma.

"Good. The baby started to kick." Her smile was incandescent, joy shinning in her eyes.

"That must be exciting."

"What about you and Jill? Any talk of babies yet?"

If Mike saw him flinch, he gave no indication. Just the mention of Jill's name was reminder enough of the argument they'd had about this very topic only a few months ago. She had made her feelings abundantly clear, while seeing Abby with her daughter had only sharpened his desire for kids of his own.

"Some talk. With Jill's new promotion, she's in San Jose now more than ever, so the timing isn't right."

"Might not want to wait too long, I hear potency tends to drop as you age." Mike's jibe was accompanied with a sly smile, and Alex chuckled.

"Well, if you're any indication, it seems like I have a few good years left in me."

"That's enough out of you." Emma's elbow dug into her husband's ribs. "I'm sure Alex is going to hear enough of that from your mother."

"Hopefully, having one grandchild will be enough to satisfy her familial instincts in the short term." Alex paused, sipping from his bottle. "With any luck, the kid will take after his mom and not have your ugly mug."

Mike's chuckle died away. After a beat of silence, Alex glanced up.

"Hey, Emma, mind if I run something by you? Strictly off the record, of course."

"Shoot."

"Does the name Lilith mean anything to you?"

"Lilith Fair? Sure, it's the name of an all-girl rock-and-roll tour. Sarah McLachlan was the headliner."

"Huh," Alex remarked, staring at his beer bottle. Maybe that's why he knew the name. Maybe the tour had made a stop in Seattle. Maybe Lilith was a music fan whose real name was Sarah.

"There is another famous Lilith, though."

"Feminists unite," Mike said, raising his bottle in jest. The remark earned him another jab in the ribs from Emma. After shooting him a disapproving look, she continued.

"There are those who speculate that Lilith was Adam's first wife, before Eve. Modern feminists view her as an icon for her bold struggle for independence from her mate. In most mythological references, she represents chaos and seduction."

Emma's words sent a jolt of recognition through Alex, one that made the very hairs on the back of his neck stand up. He fought to control the expression on his face while his mind transported him back to the University of Washington, and the network-security class he had taken with Jill. The domain name she had used for her network was Lilith. Over coffee, she'd explained that Lilith was a biblical and mythological figure, greatly misunderstood.

It had to be a coincidence.

Emma glanced at the clock on the mantel and stood to her feet.

"The chicken should be ready."

"I'll help," Mike said, also rising.

"No. You stay and keep Alex company. I'm perfectly capable of handling dinner."

Emma rolled her eyes at Alex, who reclined back into the plush leather chair as she trailed out of the living room and down the hall to the kitchen.

"So what's bugging you?"

The directness of the question shouldn't have surprised Alex. For the second time that night, he stifled a flinch as he gripped the beer bottle.

"What makes you think there's something bothering me?"

"You've got that tense look on your face. It's the same one you used to get right before a math test."

Alex cracked a smile.

"Yeah, well, we won't talk about you and English Literature."

"Just because I thought that *Jane Eyre* was a steaming pile of shit does not mean that English Lit stressed me out."

"Right. Whatever." After a theatric roll of Alex's eyes, Mike laughed, a sound that was close to a chortle. As the laughter died, his face grew serious again.

"Is it Jill?"

Alex was careful to keep his expression neutral as he let the question hang in the air. As much as he loved his brother, Mike was the last person he would talk to about Jill. The first thing he planned to do when he returned to the office would be to check the dates of the San Francisco murders against Jill's travel schedule. With any luck, that would rule out all possible involvement between her and this case. What kind of freaky coincidence was the Lilith connection anyway? It seemed far-fetched. So why was it still bothering him?

"Jill's fine."

"She's spending a lot of time on the road lately."

"Yeah, well, that's part of her job." Alex tried not to sound defensive, and failed. Mike did little to disguise his attitude toward Jill, and Alex tried to avoid any situation that would endanger it from dipping lower.

"Are you sure that's it?"

On the surface, Mike's question sounded innocuous, but Alex knew there was nothing casual about the insinuation. Frankly, he was surprised that Mike had the balls to lay it out there. Blunt. Feeling anger prickle at the back of his neck, he met Mike's stare head-on.

"Of course I'm sure." The note of finality in Alex's voice left little doubt that this conversation was over. Mike looked away, focusing his gaze out the living-room window where the dark night closed in.

"Sorry. Hope I didn't overstep."

"Forget it," Alex said, finishing his beer and setting the empty bottle on the table. Just then Emma appeared, announcing that dinner was served. As if sensing the tension in the room, she looked from Mike's face to Alex's and then back again. His reassuring smile did not quite reach his eyes.

"Great. I'm starving." The lie was well intentioned. While the smell of chicken and rosemary was appetizing, Alex had lost his appetite. All he wanted to do was get back to the office, where he could do some more digging into Lilith's identity.

***

Traversing the quiet hallways, Alex heaved a small sigh of relief as he noted that the light was not on in Captain Lewis's office. Explaining his after-hours presence to Lewis was something he'd rather avoid.

Pushing through the double doors, he saw several team members still working at their computers, eyes fixed to their screens. Kris Thompson had her purse slung over her shoulder, cell phone cradled to her ear, when she caught sight of him. For an instant, she looked like a kid with her hand caught in the candy jar. Then she dipped her head, acknowledging him with a quick nod, and angled the phone away from her mouth.

"I left a fax on your desk."

"Thanks." As he passed by, she avoided his gaze.

Was she hiding something? The evasive maneuver suggested deception. Or maybe she was still pissed at him, Alex thought. Wherever she was going, she had taken pains to look her best. Jackson had mentioned a boyfriend, and maybe he was right. Maybe she was the type of girl who didn't mix business with pleasure.

With a quick wave he ducked into his office.

The thick fax on his desk was from Luka and included more details on the two crimes. Thumbing through the reports, he tallied up the similarities. Both men were married, successful, in their late thirties, and from out of town. Both had been killed by gunshot wounds, same caliber of weapon fired at close range. Both crime scenes were left clean. Both men were missing their wedding rings. Apparently this killer was taking trophies.

He checked the dates of the murders against Jill's travel schedule and felt a sinking sensation spiral at the pit of his stomach. Jill's business trips spanned the dates when the murders took place.

The database search on Lilith's photo was still progressing and would likely continue well into the night. In the meantime, he tried to learn more about Lilith in a way that would not raise any flags on his system. An hour later he was no further ahead. Lilith had carefully covered her tracks, and without opening an official investigation, he couldn't do much more to drill in on her real identity. And he couldn't do that until he was reasonably sure that Jill was in no way involved.

How could it be Jill, though? What possible motivation could she have for luring and murdering complete strangers? None of it made any sense. He knew he had no choice but to keep digging.

There were two things he needed to do, and quickly. Alex needed to find out Lilith's identity, and he needed to rule out any possibility of Jill's involvement in the San Francisco deaths. But how could he do that? Alex pushed back in his chair, angling his eyes toward the ceiling as he searched for possibilities.

It wouldn't be hard to design a piece of spyware to place on Jill's computer, the type of thing that would report on what websites she was visiting, who she sent emails to, her instant messaging activity. The difficult part would be getting it installed on her machine.

Maybe he could design it as a script and embed it in an apparently benign attachment. If he did it right, she could open the attachment without ever realizing that it had triggered the script. He'd also need to implement it in such a way that it would not load when she was inside the ZyraNet domain. Their firewall might set off an alert. It would be tricky, but doable.

Alex tented his long fingers beneath his chin. The thought of bugging Jill's machine did not sit well with him. It was worse than snooping in her purse, and he felt squeamish at the very thought of invading her privacy. Still, what choice did he have? How else could he truly rule her out as a possible suspect?

As he brushed his fingers lightly against his lips, the solution to his second problem came to him. There was one sure way to learn more about Lilith.

Alex took his time reading the online profiles of both of the victims, looking for commonalities. What had it been about these two guys that had attracted Lilith? On the surface they were very different men.

Casanova was a plaster-it-on-thick sensitive type, his hook to lure in women. Joel Goodsen was different, a no-nonsense get-down-to-it kind of guy. He was attractive in a corporate kind of way that exuded intelligence and power. Not many women would be drawn to both. Finding no obvious connection, he decided to change his approach. He would create a profile that incorporated characteristics of both men.

After all, sometimes catching a predator meant using the right bait.

CHAPTER FORTY SEVEN

"You're on fire," Rachel Meyers said. She hung back, letting the crowd filter out of the meeting room. Jill shot Rachel a sly look.

"I'm sure I have no idea what you mean."

"Sure, and that slick little maneuver you used to sidestep Barry's pet project and have it land in Dana's lap was purely coincidental." Rachel's sideways glance was shrewd. "Don't get me wrong. I admire a deft political play as much as anyone. But I do have to admit that I felt a little sorry for her. She's way out of her league."

"Maybe she'll welcome the challenge."

"Sure. Or maybe she's in way over her head, and you just threw her an anchor."

"You're such a pessimist," Jill scoffed. A dry laugh escaped her lips.

Jill had arranged lunch with Rachel but needed to swing by her office in order to grab her purse before they left. Rachel cocked an eyebrow.

Jill flashed an enigmatic smile as she ducked inside the office door. With one hand she set her laptop down on her desk, and with the other she scooped up her oversized purse. "You know what this place is like. You've either got to sink or swim, so you could interpret delegating the project to Dana as a valuable lesson. It's an excellent way to get more visibility."

"Would that make you her mentor?" The edge in Rachel's voice was unmistakable.

The flippant response she had formulated died on her lips as she caught sight of a ladder set up in the middle of the hallway just down from Dana's office. A maintenance worker stood at the bottom looking up. His coworker stood on the third rung from the top. The breath caught in Jill's throat, and she was unable to prevent her eyes from straying to the corner of Dana's office, to the ceiling.

"What are they doing?" Jill asked, her voice tight.

"Don't know. Replacing lights. Why?"

"No reason. I thought they tended to do that stuff after hours."

The lie was a clumsy one, and she avoided meeting Rachel's eye. If they went crawling around in Dana's ceiling, they would find the gun that she had stashed there, the gun that Jill had used to kill two men in the Bay Area in as many months. It was neatly wrapped in a T-shirt that she had taken from Dana's very own gym bag.

Trying hard not to dwell on the possible consequences of the maintenance work around Dana's office, she trailed Rachel to the elevators. The afternoon was uncharacteristically cold as they left the ZyraNet offices, and they wasted no time in getting to the Bistro.

Jill's throat was dry, and she declined the offer of wine, deciding to stick with water. As Rachel perused the menu, Jill picked at her cuticles. She tried to wipe the image of the maintenance workers out of her mind. It was probably nothing, and she'd circle back around Dana's office when they returned to the building. Maybe they would be gone by then. Maybe she should find another hiding place for the weapon.

"So what are you having?" Rachel asked.

"Oh, a seafood Cobb salad."

"Always watching your figure." Rachel clucked her tongue while examining the menu. "Well, I'm going to splurge and have the grilled salmon ciabatta."

Jill smiled at Rachel, taking a long look at her companion. There was something different about Rachel. She looked younger somehow. It wasn't her hair. It wasn't her clothes or her makeup, both of which were perfectly in synch with her contemporary style. It was something about the look in her eyes. She looked happy.

"Are you celebrating something?" Jill asked, her spider sense tingling.

"As the matter of fact, yes." Rachel's Cheshire-cat smile heightened Jill's curiosity.

"Well then, out with it. What are we drinking to?"

"To my divorce. It's final."

"Congratulations." Jill raised her water glass, clinking it against Rachel's.

Rachel took a sip of the pale golden Chardonnay, her lipstick leaving a pink crescent on the rim of the glass.

"Thank you. I can't believe you're the first person I've told."

"It's good to see you happy for a change."

"If I'd known I was going to feel this good after the divorce, I would have done it years ago."

Jill sipped her water. The salty smell of seafood in the air made her feel a little queasy. The waitress set a basket of fresh bread on the table, and Jill took a piece, nibbling on the edge in hopes that it would settle her stomach.

"No kidding. I've got to say, I'm surprised that it's put you in such a good mood. Last time we talked about the ex, you were pretty angry."

"True."

"Did Barbie dump him?" Jill used Rachel's pet name for her ex-husband's girlfriend, the twenty-something he had met online.

"Better, actually. I've met someone."

"Well, look who's playing her cards close to her chest. Details, please."

"He's in computer software, of course. Forty-nine, divorced with grown kids."

"And I'll bet he has a name."

"Ben."

"How long have you known him?"

"A few weeks."

"Well, good for you. That's terrific news. Can he cook?"

"He can make a pretty mean pancake."

"Are you sleeping over?"

"Are you my mother? Besides, I'm not the type to kiss and tell." Rachel's smile was coy.

"Since when? Seriously, good for you."

Rachel straightened as the waitress approached with their food. She set the plates down on the table and asked if they needed anything else. Both declined. Rachel picked up the sandwich and took a dainty bite.

Jill's stomach rolled as she looked at the seafood salad. With a trembling hand, she pushed the plate back, her fingers straying momentarily to her lips. Rachel paused, looking across at the table at Jill, concern etched in the lines around her eyes.

"You okay?"

✳✳✳

Much to her dismay, Rachel hovered by Jill's elbow as they made their way back to the office. Jill took the long way, passing by Dana's open door. She was relieved to see that the maintenance workers were gone. The gun was safe.

"You're sure you're okay?"

"Yes, Mom, I'm fine. I've probably got a flu bug. Sorry for ruining your celebratory lunch. Next time, I promise not to vomit. I'll even spring for champagne."

"Big spender. In that case, it's a date," Rachel said. She took a step toward the door. Then, pausing, she threw a concerned glance back at Jill. "You're sure you're not knocked up?"

Jill's mouth dropped open and she stared at Rachel.

"I can't believe you even asked that."

"So, I take it that's a no," Rachel asked with a smile.

"That's a hell no."

"Okay, okay. I thought it was worth asking. You never know." With a brief shrug, Rachel left the office. Unfortunately, the briny smell of the grilled salmon ciabatta did not.

CHAPTER FORTY EIGHT

Setting up his online profile for the Hook Up website had been easy. Wading through the list of women pinging him was much harder, Alex mused. Mark Wilson was a producer for a new reality television series, and apparently there were a lot of women who loved show business. In two short days, his in-box overflowed with messages.

Methodically he examined each, searching for any sign of Lilith before hitting the Delete key. He tried hard not to adopt a cynical attitude about the general state of the human condition. But at times like this, it was a little harder than it should be.

Alex sat alone at a scarred table in the Diva coffee shop, just off Greenwood Avenue, waiting for Abby. She had called earlier in the morning to arrange a meeting. He figured she needed to see him to discuss Honeywell's arrest. Additional details might make the end of the nightmare seem more real. He could have made an excuse. He could have called to cancel. But in truth, he wanted to see her.

Arriving early, Alex used the opportunity to see if Lilith had taken the bait. So far, it didn't look promising. He ran his fingers across his chin as he read the next message.

"That's not a happy face," Abby said, standing beside his chair.

He smiled reflexively. She looked lovely. The dark circles under her eyes had faded, and a faint pink glow warmed her cheeks. He stood to give her a quick but awkward hug. The sling around his arm made him twist around her.

"How are you doing?" Abby nodded toward his arm. Her eyes brimmed with worry.

"You know, I'm fine. Can I get you a coffee?"

"Actually, I was wondering if we could take a walk." Her blue eyes strayed to the window before moving back to his.

"Sure, just give me a sec."

It took him a few minutes to empty his coffee and pack up his computer. It wouldn't be much longer, only a few more days, before he could ditch the sling. It couldn't come fast enough for Alex. Aside from the general inconvenience of having to master the one-handed task, he was tired of answering the constant stream of questions. People meant well, but sometimes he wished they could just mind their own damned business.

"Got everything?"

The sky overhead was a patchwork of dappled gray. Although no rain had fallen yet, it didn't look far off. A gentle wind ruffled Abby's hair around her pretty face, and she kept her eyes down, as if studying the sidewalk intently. Alex waited for her to speak. They'd walked two blocks before she said the first word.

"I can't believe that Natalie's gone. I still expect to see her whenever I go to Mom and Dad's place." She raised her chin but kept her eyes trained ahead. "I don't know how long it takes to accept the truth."

"How are your parents doing?"

"They're okay. Better now that Honeywell is in custody." She peeked up at him from the corner of her eye. "We have you to thank for that."

Alex's stomach lurched as their eyes met. He quickly looked away. Although it was true that they had finally apprehended Honeywell, there was a part of him that wondered if they could have done more to save Natalie. For him, this would never feel like a victory.

"Glad we tracked him down. At least he won't be free to hurt anyone else."

Abby nodded, and Alex could see the tears filling her eyes. He stopped and enveloped her in another awkward hug. She clung to him, arms wrapped around his waist. She looked up, and their eyes caught. And this time, he didn't look away.

The feel of her in his arms was so achingly familiar. So right. And, as if it was the most natural thing in the world, she rose up on her toes and their lips met.

It was not the peck on the cheek that passed between friends. There was no mistaking the intention of the kiss, and Alex stood rooted to the spot, the taste of her lips familiar. Achingly familiar. And Alex responded, leaning forward to deepen the kiss. Her soft lips parted beneath his, and everything else fell away. There was only her.

After roughly three seconds of head-spinning insanity, reason prevailed. As much as part of him wanted to suspend reality, he knew what giving into his impulses would mean. There would be consequences. For him. And for Abby.

It wasn't fair. He couldn't let his doubts about Jill cloud his judgment.

With his good hand, Alex gripped her shoulder before gently pulling away. Her blue eyes pierced his with a searching look before the blood rushed into her cheeks, staining them red. She looked down quickly. He could read the embarrassment on her face as she took a hasty step backward.

"I'm sorry." Her voice was barely audible over the sound of the cars passing by. "I didn't think …"

"It's okay, Abby. But you've got to know that this can't happen. Not now. Neither of us could live with the consequences." Alex kept a steady grip on her shoulder until she met his eyes again. He couldn't stop his finger from touching her soft cheek. With a small nod, she pulled out of his grasp, folding her arms into a tight knot against her chest.

"I know. It's just that everything is so screwed up. I guess I've always kind of wondered. You know—if there was something left between us. I'm sorry."

She looked mortified.

He had wondered that, too. But telling her how he felt wouldn't help either of them. If anything, it would only complicate the situation more. And she deserved better.

Cupping the back of her head with his hand, he pressed his lips to her fragrant hair. For a brief moment, he closed his eyes and savored the sweet smell of peaches before he released his grip on her.

"It's going to be okay, you know? It may not seem like it now, but you'll find a way through this."

Unshed tears shimmered in her eyes. She cleared her throat, and her head nodded in jerky movements. She blinked.

"I should get going," she said at last.

Alex watched her walk away. He hated himself for hurting her again. Why couldn't he stay away and let the past go? It was the best thing for both of them. He knew it. But part of him wanted to go after her.

Leaning into the damp wind, he doubled back onto Greenwood, toward his parked Jeep. The ring of his cell phone interrupted his thoughts.

"Shannon here," he said, picking up on the first ring.

"Alex, Jackson's been shot."

CHAPTER FOURTY NINE

Alex pushed past the knot of people clustered around the waiting-room door at Harborview Medical Center toward the familiar face of Captain Brad Lewis. Lewis stood, removing his hand from the shoulder of Michelle Levy, Jackson's estranged wife.

"How is he?"

"He's in surgery."

Michelle looked up, her tear-stained face saying everything that Captain Lewis had not. Alex stepped forward, taking both of her hands in his good one. For a brief moment he held her gaze, until he could no longer stand the pain pooled in her dark eyes.

"He's going to be okay." Alex's words were soft, and he wasn't sure who he was trying to convince, Michelle or himself. "He's strong."

Michelle nodded, hitching in a deep breath.

"Thanks for coming."

Alex nodded and released her trembling fingers. He watched as she clutched the sodden tissue she had balled in her lap. Catching Alex's eye, Captain Lewis inclined his head to the side. Alex stood and followed him down the hall.

Out of the corner of his eye, he caught sight of a familiar face. Kris Thompson was seated near a cluster of cops, her drawn face turned toward him as they passed. He was surprised to see her. Although she was part of the fabric that bound the unit together, Jackson was on the fringes of their circle. Her worry for his well-being was apparent, a fear that Alex himself channeled into action.

"What the hell happened?"

Mindful of the family's proximity, he kept his voice low.

"Honeywell was released. The judge threw out the search warrant from Winthrop."

"What? On what grounds?"

Lewis shook his head and shot Alex a sharp look. Michelle had glanced up. Several other faces swiveled in their direction, including that of an older black woman who was seated beside her.

"The judge ruled that the scope of the search warrant was too broad," Lewis said, leading Alex a little farther away from the crowded waiting room.

"That's bullshit. Why didn't we catch this in the jail release report so we could have …"

"Could have what, Alex? Could have been more careful? Come on."

Alex blew out a long breath, angling his eyes toward the ceiling as he fought to regain control of his anger. It goddamned well did matter. Not knowing Honeywell was back on the streets had put them all in danger. Lewis was right about one thing, though. It was too late to second-guess now.

"Where did it happen?"

"On Eightieth, near Aurora Avenue."

Alex cringed. Jackson was attacked mere blocks away from where he had met Abby.

"Anyone see anything?"

"We have an eyewitness. The man she saw fleeing the scene doesn't fit Honeywell's description. She said he's tall with dark hair, leather jacket, earrings. She's working with a police sketch artist now."

Alex stopped, his face twisted into a painful grimace. While the description didn't fit Honeywell, he did know one other person who it might. The only thing that concerned him now was how quickly he could get himself hooked into the manhunt.

"Who do you have on this?"

"Everyone."

Lewis's gaze was steady as Alex's mind thrashed. Honeywell knew Jill's habits. Could he also have targeted Jackson?

"What can I do? Where do you want me?"

"I want you here." Lewis's voice was firm, his face dead serious.

"You're fucking kidding me. You can't really expect me to sit on my hands while Honeywell is out there. I should be looking for him. I know him better than anyone."

Lewis's hand gripped Alex's forearm.

"She needs you." Lewis nodded back toward Michelle's bent form.

"Fuck that." Alex yanked his arm away and took a reeling step backward. "What good can I possibly do here?"

"Listen to me, Shannon." The use of his surname, along with the James Earl Jones tone of voice, told Alex that he was not going to budge. "If this was Honeywell, you're a potential target. The last thing I need is to be down two officers. Besides, this is where Jackson would want you to be—taking care of his family. That's an order."

Alex clenched his jaw, teeth grinding together, hating everything about the hospital, from the sound of the beeping monitors to the antiseptic smell of the corridors. He knew he had no choice in the matter, though. Michelle had the support of her family, and Jackson would understand. Being trapped in the hospital was torturous when he wanted to be out hunting for Honeywell. After all, Honeywell was hunting those closest to him.

Alex acknowledged the order with a curt nod. There was no point in arguing. Lewis would not be swayed, and he couldn't afford to flagrantly disobey orders. Instead, he stalked down the hallway in search of some coffee. Michelle could probably use some, too. It was going to be a long night.

Striding down the corridor, he pulled the cell phone out of his pocket. Thumbing through the list of numbers, he found a California area code and pushed Dial.

"Detective Shannon. To what do I owe the pleasure?" Agent Jacob Wilde of the ATF answered on the third ring.

"Where is Duke?" Alex asked.

***

The eyewitness had picked Duke out of the photo array by the time Alex arrived home. Jackson had survived surgery, but the doctors were tight-lipped about his prognosis. If the number of tubes going in and out of Jackson's body was any indication, the next few days would be critical. Michelle had sent Alex home to get some rest, promising to do the same, as Jackson's mother held vigil in the ICU waiting room.

Rest was the last thing Alex wanted. Fresh from the shower, he wandered the house room by room before sitting down at the kitchen table, placing a wicker basket in front of him. Bills and other pieces of assorted mail overflowed its sides. Jill usually took care of paying the bills, but typically it wasn't until the basket overflowed onto the counter before they resorted to shredding and filing. Grabbing a fist full of papers, he sorted them into piles.

As he went through the hefty stack of documents one by one, cable, cell phone, and Puget Sound Energy statements piled up. It took half an hour to sort through it all. In the end he had relegated Jill's credit-card statements into a smaller pile.

Thumbing through them, he fished out the statements for the past few months. Head bowed, he examined each one line by line, fingers brushing through his short hair. He stiffened as he came to mid-November.

There was a line item for airfare, which coincided with a last-minute business trip. There were two things that bothered him about the charge. First, Jill's company typically paid for airfare directly. The destination was the second. Jill had said she was flying to San Jose. The ticket that she had charged to her credit card showed a flight to Reno. ZyraNet had no office in Reno, but it was close to Lake Tahoe.

There was also a charge from Avis. She had rented a car. Where had she gone? Alex made a note to call Avis and check the mileage for the rental period. He frowned as he scanned the list of charges, all the while aware of the connection: Jamie King had died in his cabin at Lake Tahoe.

Lower in the list, he found a fifteen-dollar charge from an Internet lookup site, the type of service you would use to do a reverse lookup on an email address. Who was Jill looking for? With a warrant, he could get details on the transaction. Without it, all he could do was wonder.

Nothing else jumped out at him as he scanned the financial records. There were a few cash withdrawals from California ATMs, but nothing that was inconsistent with a shopping trip or typical business expenses.

Alex took a deep breath as placed his laptop on the table in front of him. He logged into his personal email account, and he clicked on a notification from the spyware application he had installed on Jill's computer. It referenced a variety of websites she had visited, online shopping portals, weather forecasts, news sites. There were no hits on Hook Up.

Before he could breathe a sigh of relief at not seeing any hits to the site he was particularly interested in, his stomach clenched as he viewed the results of her Google searches. Jill was looking for news stories on Kenneth Cox and Peter Young. Kenneth Cox was the victim in one of the San Francisco murder cases. The name Peter Young didn't ring any bells, but he made a note to do some research.

With a growing sense of dread, he turned back to his laptop's screen and located the results of the face-recognition search. They were a couple of days old. But with everything that had happened, he hadn't had a chance to look at them yet.

Alex clicked on the link in the email. It led to a well-known professional networking site. The photo was a match for Dana Evans. His brow creased in a deep frown as he stared at the woman's profile. Dana Evans was the director of Product Management for ZyraNet, the company that Jill worked for.

Why did her name sound so damned familiar? Alex searched his memory. It was possible that Jill had spoken of her during one of their many conversations about work. He suddenly remembered where he had heard the name. Jill had talked about Dana Evans the night they went out to dinner in Vancouver.

Jill had said that Dana Evans was having an affair with Jamie King, and now Jamie King was dead. There were two possibilities. Dana Evans was Lilith, or Jill was setting up Dana Evans.

Why would she do that?

Alex's pencil scratched against the page of his notebook, and Jill's face began to quickly take shape. Only it wasn't a smiling Jill that stared up at him. He almost didn't recognize this Jill. Her expression was darker, as if she was guarding monstrous secrets. Was Jill having an affair with Jamie? Had she been involved in his death?

With a sinking feeling, Alex slumped back in his chair. He wished he could call up one of the guys from the movie *Men in Black* to use that flashy tool to erase the last few days from his memory. The trail of evidence was building. He couldn't rule out the possibility that Jill was somehow involved in the San Francisco murders.

As much as he wanted to ignore Luka's case, he couldn't turn a blind eye to what was staring him in the face. He had to find out as much as he could about Jill's whereabouts. What if someone else stumbled on the connection to Jill? What if he could find the one piece of evidence that exonerated her?

He had no choice but to keep digging.

CHAPTER FIFTY

"**W**hat are you doing home?" Jill said as she spied Alex. He was seated at the kitchen table, a stack of bills beside his open laptop.

"I could ask you the same question." His voice was flat, and she could see the thick matt of stubble on his cheeks. He looked like he hadn't slept in days. "You're back early."

Jill set her purse down on the countertop. The smell of fresh coffee filled the kitchen, and she poured herself a cup. Molly sprawled on the kitchen floor beside Alex's chair. She did not rise to greet Jill. Instead, she shifted, positioning herself between them. The subtle rise in Alex's eyebrows told her he caught the shift in Molly's protective stance.

"Yeah, I wrapped up my meetings and decided to catch an earlier flight. I'm wiped."

"You okay?" Alex asked, not taking his eyes off of her face. There was something about the way he was looking at her that set her on edge. He looked wary.

"I think I've got a bug, and I've really been dragging the past few days." She sat down across from Alex, glancing at the stack of bills distributed on the table. "What's all this?"

"I had some time, so I thought I'd sort through the mail. I don't think you could cram another piece of paper into the basket."

Dropping his gaze to the pile of papers in front of him, he began to methodically stack them.

"Is that all?" Jill tried to keep her tone light, but anxiety knotted in her stomach. Alex was probably just paying the bills. But why did she have a feeling there was more to it than that?

Alex snapped the lid of his laptop closed and set the bills on top of it.

"Actually, no." He ran his hands roughly over his face, fingers pressing against his closed eyelids, before looking back at her.

"Jackson was shot yesterday."

"What?" She felt a jolt of shock electrify her. She stared at Alex.

"They think it may have been related to the Honeywell case."

"But you caught him. He's in custody."

"He was released."

"Why?" she asked, trying hard to let her head catch up with what Alex was saying.

"The judge presiding over the case threw out the Winthrop search warrant."

Jill didn't have to ask Alex how he felt; anger and contempt were clearly evident on his face.

"How's Jackson?"

"He's out of surgery, but it's still too soon to say."

Jill's fingers pressed against her lips as she thought of Jackson. He had to pull through. She said as much to Alex, whose flat stare offered little comfort.

"Do you think Jackson was his main target?"

There was more to her question. They both knew it, but she couldn't bring herself to ask it directly.

Alex's halfhearted shrug did little to inspire confidence, and his gaze stretched out toward the picture window. Jill stole a quick glance outside. From where she stood, the churning gray waters of Puget Sound were peaked with stiff whitecaps. A long time seemed to pass before Alex looked back at her.

"Who knows? I'm going to head back to the hospital soon. What are your plans?"

"I've got a couple of errands to run. Then I might take a nap."

"Want a ride?" The request was undoubtedly spurred by Honeywell's threat. But with the gun Alex had supplied stowed in her hand bag, she felt safe enough.

"You should get some rest. How's Michelle?"

"She's hanging in there. You know how tough she is."

Jill nodded. Whether they were together or separated, Michelle was living every cop's wife's nightmare. Part of her thought that she should go to the hospital with Alex, but there were other things she needed to take care of first. She still hadn't deleted Lilith's profile. Maybe she would head over to Alki Bakery and do just that.

"Give her a hug from me."

"Sure." He drew in an audible breath as he looked at her. "I guess it goes without saying, but with Honeywell out there somewhere, you need to be extra careful. If you see anything suspicious, call 911 immediately."

"Of course," she said as her eyes drifted toward the drawer where she had stowed her gun.

Alex didn't touch Jill as he passed by. In fact, he didn't so much as cast a backward glance as he stepped through the doorway.

A chill raced up her spine as he left the room.

***

Jill browsed to the Hook Up website and opened her profile page. *Time to say good-bye to Lilith,* she thought as she glanced through her overflowing in-box.

Lilith had served her purpose. Now it was time for her to go away.

"Would you like a refill?" Joey asked, hovering over her with a full pot of coffee.

"No thanks," she said, starting a little at the interruption. Turning back toward her screen, she saw the pop-up window. There was someone wanting to chat. Was she free?

Why not? Jill smiled, glancing around. This was, after all, her swan song. Come hell or high water, she was determined to bid a fond farewell to Lilith, once and for all.

"Well, look who's online. Lilith—at last."

"At last?" she wrote back in the chat window. She took a moment to browse to Mark Wilson's profile and saw that he was an attractive married man based in the Los Angeles area.

"I emailed you a few days back, figured you were blowing me off."

"Now why would I do something like that?" she typed, enjoying the anonymity of these encounters. There was freedom in playing a role.

"Better offers?"

"Sure. They're lined up around the block just waiting for their chance."

"And I've managed to jump the line. Sweet."

Jill found herself smiling as she read his words. There was something light and flirty about him that she liked.

"What are you doing online in the middle of the afternoon? Shouldn't you be working?"

"Well, I could ask the same about you," he wrote. "Just taking a few minutes to relax, blow off some steam. I've been working double time on a project. You know what they say: 'All work and no play makes Mark a dull boy.'"

The words struck a familiar chord in her, and Jill's mind flashed to Jamie King. She had once said something very similar to him. Was it only a few months ago that he had died? It seemed that a lifetime had passed since he'd fallen into his snowy grave.

"So they say." Jill's fingers clicked on the keyboard, and she pushed the image of Jamie away. Some things were better forgotten.

"What kind of project?"

"Casting for a new reality television show."

"Reality show? That sounds exciting."

"I guess. Can be a little painful. Despite what you may think, not all Americans have talent. How about you? Where do you find yourself these days?"

"Seattle."

"Business or pleasure?"

Jill hesitated before answering. Why had she told him her whereabouts?

"A bit of both," she answered. "You?" Best to deflect the conversation. The damage was done.

"Would you believe Portland?"

"Ah, the Rose City. Nice."

"I'll be in Seattle next."

Jill's throat constricted at the words. The invitation in Mark's message was implied, but his intentions were clear. She could tell him that she'd be gone by then. She could ignore him. She could respond in so many ways.

"Know much about the city?" he asked, prompting her.

"A little."

"Any places you could recommend?"

"What are you looking for?" Her heart was beating fast as she stared at the blinking cursor. The ball was in his court.

"Drinks, dinner, nothing too heavy."

Mark was outside of the norm. There was nothing pushy about him, nothing crass. The conversation was light, entertaining.

"You might want to check out Purple. It's a place on Fourth. Trendy. Good food. Good wine."

"Sounds great. Want to join me for a drink?"

Jill could hear the beat of her own heart as she stared at her screen. It was that simple. She could say yes and set up another encounter, or exit this world once and for all. She knew what she *should* do.

"Maybe, but just a quick drink." She stared at the screen. It was as if someone else had written the entry. Was she crazy?

"You free tomorrow night? Say seven o'clock. I'll be the guy in a black shirt with a cosmopolitan."

"Cosmopolitan? You're joking, right?"

"Can't a man be secure enough in himself to enjoy a fruity pink drink?"

"LOL. I suppose it's possible," she wrote, not sure she believed it.

"Well then, come and see for yourself."

"I'll be there," she promised.

"Peace," he typed. Then the chat window closed.

This was madness. What in God's name had possessed her to set up the date? Her work with Lilith was done. It was time to cover her tracks. Meeting Mark on home territory was out of the question, regardless of how tempting the offer.

Jill took a few minutes to delete her profile, reading no more of the messages that were queued up in her in-box. Minutes later, Lilith was a cyber ghost. *And not a moment too soon,* Jill thought.

It was too easy to be sucked into the lure of the online world. It was as if Lilith had a mind of her own.

CHAPTER FIFTY ONE

Jill knew she was breaking the rules. She knew she should go home and forget about him. Forget about Lilith. Forget about everything. But the voicemail from Alex saying that he'd be home late had her pointing the car downtown as her curiosity got the better of her.

Was it curiosity or compulsion? Jill tried hard not to dwell on the answer as she entered the crowded restaurant, hands thrust deep into her pockets. Not waiting for the hostess, she made her way to the stairs near the back of the room that lead to the loft-styled lounge.

The air was alive with the buzz of chatter—coworkers meeting for drinks after a long day at the office, young women working hard to carry on engaging conversations with their dates.

Jill drifted through the room like an iceberg, weaving in between the tables, her eyes surveying the crowded room, searching for a man fitting Mark's description. In their last exchange, he said that he would be drinking a fruity cosmopolitan, the metaphorical equivalent of carrying a red rose. The whimsical visual it provided appealed to her.

Not coming tonight would have been the smart thing to do. Taking any further risks by associating herself with Lilith was crazy, no doubt about it.

But still something drew her here, a desire to play the game one last time before saying good-bye to Lilith forever. Maybe she wouldn't even identify herself. Without the blond wig, she bore only a passing resemblance to the photograph posted with her online profile. Maybe he wouldn't even be here.

But she didn't believe that.

Her heart beat as fast as a hummingbird's wings, the thrill of the hunt rising, as she approached the bar. Her shoulders straightened and her gait was long and fluid as she crossed the room. She felt the tingle of anticipation sizzle across her skin as she fell into a character, like an actor assuming a role.

Jill's eyes fixed on a man sitting at a table alone near the bar. He was wearing a black shirt, a cosmopolitan sat on the table before him, and a knowing smile parted her lips as she approached.

A quick-witted greeting died on her lips and the blood froze in her veins as the man turned his head and his profile came into view. Recognition flooded through Jill, triggering an instinctive reaction to run. Before she could act on it, the man turned and a familiar pair of brown eyes met hers. A clean escape was no longer an option.

Alex. How could it be Alex? She stood rooted to the spot, her thoughts coming in a jumble. It had to be a coincidence. But how could it be?

He rose to his feet, looking uncertain, which Alex never was. With great effort, she pinned a smile to her lips and walked toward him.

"Hey, what are you doing here?" she asked, infusing her voice with a lightness she did not feel. "I thought you were working late on a case."

"Taking a break. Mike called, wanting to grab a drink," he said, matching her smile. "What about you? Got a date?"

Alex's words were pregnant with meaning, and Jill's throat constricted. Looking up into his face, she forced a warm smile.

"I didn't feel like going home to an empty house, so I called a friend." The lie sounded clunky. Suppressing a cringe, she eased into the seat across from him.

"What friend?"

Jill dodged the question by asking one of her own.

"What brings you here? This isn't your usual kind of place." The tone Jill used was deceptively light, but there was nothing casual about the way she studied him, looking for any signal that he was on to her. "And since when do you drink cosmopolitans?"

"I'm evolving," he said, easing back down into his chair. Jill's mind whirled. There was no way Mike would suggest this place. He was a hard-core Pyramid Brewery kind of guy. Meeting Alex here was no accident. She was certain of it. He was on the job, all right, and she had a big problem.

"Do you mind if I ..." she left the words hanging as she gestured toward his drink.

"Of course," he said, his eyes not wavering from hers. She read caution in his relentless gaze.

Jill's hand shook as she reached for the glass. She sipped the drink slowly, the icy liquid burning a path down her throat, as she tried to slow her racing pulse, and gather her thoughts.

How much did he know? How could he possibly have found out her secrets? She had been so careful to cover her tracks. But as she stared into his cold brown eyes, it occurred to her that the one emotion she had not read on his face was surprise.

"Are you okay?" he asked. "You look pale."

"I'm just tired." She used a smile to try and mask her mounting sense of trepidation. Her brain worked quickly, processing this new revelation. This changed everything. The stakes of the game were suddenly very high. If Alex knew her secrets, what was her next move?

"Who did you say you were you planning to meet?" Alex picked up his drink and took a sip.

"Megan. She should have been here already," Jill noted without checking her watch. "In fact, maybe I should give her a call. She may have been held up at the office." Jill stood to leave.

"You could stay for a drink." His eyes never left hers, and she was sure that he was gauging her every reaction. "We haven't had a chance to get caught up."

"Well, like I said, I'm kind of tired. I'll probably just bail. Give my best to Mike. See you at home." Jill clutched the strap to her purse as she stood.

Alex nodded, his expression flat, and Jill stared at the dark circles under his eyes. How long had he known?

A memory flashed in her head. She was back in her college networking class with Alex, and he had just circumvented her network security system. He'd sent her a text message asking her out for coffee. In fact, Alex was the only one able to hack through her defenses. Had she underestimated him?

With a slow nod she turned to go, forcing herself to walk slowly when all she wanted to do was run.

CHAPTER FIFTY TWO

Alex gripped the handles of the cardboard box tightly. The sharp edges bit into his fingers. The harsh overhead light cast dark shadows between the haphazard piles of boxes that littered the garage floor. Working his way toward the back of the stacks, he jammed his box in the corner, depositing others on top of it, and threw a tarp across the stack, just for good measure.

Confident that his box would escape detection amid all of the other junk in the garage, he stepped back. Mike and Emma were pack rats. The evidence of this behavior was all around in the accumulation of tools and household items that were as good as abandoned within the walls of this dusty tomb. A search warrant wouldn't include the buildings outside his own house, so it would be safe here, for an indefinite period.

The silence of the garage was at fierce odds with the buzzing in his head. It seemed as if the crowd noise from the restaurant had followed him here. Only it wasn't the laughing voices of strangers that filled his head now. It was the clamor of his own thoughts, and he desperately wanted to shut them out.

There was now no doubt in his mind that Jill was Lilith Fair and that Lilith Fair was linked to the two San Francisco murders. Lilith was stalking men online and setting up dates. He'd traced her identity to Jill. How much longer would it take Luka, or someone else?

Granted, Jill had been careful. She'd covered her tracks after she'd pulled down Lilith's online profile, and he'd made a few leaps in logic to connect Jill to the crimes. But there were still loose ends that could be used to trace her identity.

Some of those loose ends were packed away in the box he'd just finished stowing in this garage and would remain buried until he figured out just what he was going to do with this new information. The files he'd received from Luka, the credit-card bills, his notes—he'd cleared it all out of his office, just in case someone came looking. And someone would. Eventually.

That left the question of what to do about Jill. Alex ran his hand across his burning eyes. It wasn't just his dust allergies kicking in. The weight of the situation coupled with the lack of sleep made it difficult for him to think. He felt numb.

The choices were limited, really. He could turn Jill in, hire a good lawyer, and hope for the best. He could let her go. But one thing was for damned sure: life would never go back to the way it was. There was another option, one that remained barely acknowledged. He had a gun. He wouldn't be the first officer to use his firearm to make his problems go away.

His hands clenched as anger burned through his veins like battery acid. How could he have not seen what Jill had become? Molly had seen it. Molly had shied away from her weeks ago, and he had given it little credence. How could he have been so blind? How could he have missed the dark transformation that she had undergone? None of it made sense. Why would Jill do this?

As if working on their own volition, his eyes strayed to the corner where he'd stashed the box. If he was planning to turn her in, why had he bothered to stow the box at all? After all, he had sworn to uphold the law. It was the right thing. But it wasn't quite that simple when it came to Jill.

Alex flinched at the sound of a slamming car door. He needed to get out of here before Mike made it home. The last thing he wanted to do was explain to his brother why he was here. Was it only a few days ago that Mike tried talk to him about Jill? How many times had he defended her?

Casting a last glance over his shoulder, Alex extinguished the lights and headed for the door. A quick glimpse of the street outside the house told him that Mike's car was nowhere to be found. Relief flooded through him, and, hunching his shoulders against the fierce wind, he headed back toward his Jeep.

"Alex?"

His heart stalled at the sound of her voice. The strong wind swirled her blond hair around her delicate face, her wide eyes inquisitive. He stifled a curse. He was tired of lies, but it seemed like there was at least one more he'd need to tell.

"Emma, I didn't know you were home." His lips twisted into a lopsided grin, and he took a step toward her. The circle of light from the streetlight penetrated the darkness and cast a pale glow on her ethereal face.

"I thought I saw your car. Why don't you come inside? Mike's not home from work yet. I was going to order Chinese, if you'd like to stay. To be honest, you'd be doing me a favor. Storms always sort of freak me out, and they say it's going to be a good one. I'd love the company."

Her self-deprecating smile made his heart twist painfully as he looked at her. Closing the distance between them, he took her cold hands in his. His eyes drifted down, catching sight of their intertwined fingers before he let his hands fall to his sides.

"Sorry, I can't stay, and you should get inside."

"Are you okay, Alex? You look—"

"Tired?" he finished for her.

Alex could read the concern on her face as she looked up at him, and he could only imagine what she saw there. Those keen reporter instincts wouldn't allow him to hide for long, which was yet another reason he needed to get out of here. Fast.

"It's been a rough week." He forced a smile.

"That's the understatement of the year."

"Yeah." Alex cleared his throat and looked over toward the garage. "Hope you don't mind, but I was poking around to see if I could find my drill. I've got a couple projects I've been putting on hold while my arm healed and well ... I thought I'd lent it to Mike, but I didn't see it in there."

"Maybe it's in the house. Why don't you come take a look?"

"It's okay, another time." He hoped that Emma didn't catch the note of finality in his voice. Turning his eyes back toward her, he gripped her elbow, gently spinning her around.

"You should get inside though. The rain's going to start soon, and there is no point in getting wet."

"Not you, too," she grumbled. "I'm getting enough smothering from Mike. I don't know if I could take it if you started to hound me."

"That's what brothers do."

Emma's laugh was muted, as if she still sensed there was more to his visit than he was letting on.

"Tell Mike I'll give him a call this weekend."

"You sure you don't want to stay?"

Alex paused, staring long at Emma before he was able to answer.

"Jill will be home soon. I've got to run."

Emma nodded, and without another word he headed to his Jeep. Climbing behind the wheel, he took one last look at the house. Emma stood with her arms folded, hair flying in the wind. She didn't take her eyes off him as he waved and pulled out into the street just as the first hard pellets of sleet began to fall.

CHAPTER FIFTY THREE

Jill stepped through the back door into the kitchen. The heels of her boots echoed on the hardwood floor. The room was in shadow, the stove's light casting a faint, eerie glow.

Jill scanned the room. This place where she had spent so much time felt different somehow. The granite countertops shone hard and slick. Not a dish out of place. This room where she had laughed with Alex was now silent, impenetrable.

She closed the door behind her, shoulders hunched, feeling the weight of her decision pulling her inward. Her gaze drifted across the room to the glossy surface of the refrigerator—the stainless steel doors smooth and without a smudge. Her mind flashed years ahead in an instant. Noisy kids running through the kitchen, sticky fingerprints on the refrigerator door handles, artwork pinned to the surface with small, colorful magnets. *All the things that might have been.*

She pressed her hands on the cold surface of the countertop, steadying herself. Drawing in a deep, sobering breath, she could smell the ripe apples sitting in a ceramic bowl on the island, their ruby-red skin lending a cheerful splash of color to the room. Beside her hand, a stack of mail was placed near the counter's edge—a mix of junk mail, bills, and catalogs. Evidence of their everyday life together.

Jill had no time to waste. She had already been to the bank, pulling out as much cash as she dared. Some of it she had used to purchase a train ticket. Alex would be home soon, and she needed to be well on her way before he walked through the door.

She straightened, shifting her weight between her feet. Tension bowed her shoulders, a dull ache winding its way down to her lower back. Her right hand rested on the drawer where she had stashed her gun. She'd need to take that with her. Pushing away from the island, she started, her heart slamming into her rib cage as her eyes caught sight of him.

Alex sat silently in a chair at the kitchen table, watching her intently, his eyes almost black in the darkness. She studied him for a long moment, his expression blank, revealing no clues. She saw the liquor bottle sitting in front of him beside the empty tumbler. The coppery tang of fear filled her mouth, and she remembered her step-father's stony silence. Dread knotted her stomach, and she felt like she was caught in the eye of the storm.

"When did you get home?" she asked, fighting to keep her voice neutral.

"A while ago." He leaned back in the chair, his arms hanging slack at his sides. "Where have you been?" His tone was demanding.

She averted her gaze and forced a light smile. "I met Megan for a drink. She got hung up at work, so we met at the Red Door instead."

He turned his head to the side, rolling his eyes in exasperation.

"Come on Jill, we both know that you didn't meet Megan tonight." His eyes shredded her as he continued to study her face. She felt chilled by his gaze, once loving, now cold, as if he was looking into the face of a stranger.

There was a hard edge to his voice as he continued.

"We both know why you were at the bar. Enough games. Enough lies already. Where have you been?" His open hand struck the surface of the table with a loud smack. The glass rattled.

Jill took a step backward and leaned against the island for a moment, grasping for a response. She sensed the fury coiled beneath his icy exterior as she continued.

"I took a drive to clear my head."

Alex shook his head, his hard eyes still boring into hers.

"I know, Jill. I fucking know what you've been doing. Stop lying to me."

He picked up the glass and flung it across the room. It shattered against the door frame in an explosion of glittering shards. She jumped at the violent outburst. He turned his head and peered out the window, his sharp profile etched in the glass behind him.

"I know what you've been doing, Jill. I wish to God I didn't."

She surveyed his hands clenched tightly into fists, the long, tapering fingers that could bring images to life on paper now squeezed so tight that his knuckles turned white. Hands that had gently stroked her hair and touched every inch of her body. These were Alex's hands, strong and powerful, yet capable of such tenderness, balled into fists of rage because of her.

Her throat tightened, making it hard for her to breathe. He knew her dark secrets, she reminded herself. Her worst fears had been confirmed. A ragged breath filled her lungs, and she stifled the urge to scream. If she knew Alex, he was already two steps ahead.

Jill's heart pounded. Sweat dampened her palms. She had to act now. With each passing second, control was slipping away. It took all of her self-discipline not to give into her fear and go for the gun.

She knew Alex was waiting, and he'd already planned his next move. She had to hold back until she understood what game he was playing. There were no second chances.

"Okay, so you know," she prodded him. "How did you find out?"

His smile was bitter in the darkened room. He leaned forward, resting elbows on the table.

"You're not as smart as you think you are. I've been tracking your online movements. I know what sites you've been visiting, who you've been messaging. By the way, Mark sends his regards."

"Fuck."

She shook her head. One stupid mistake had cost her everything.

"Who have you been working with?" Her voice was rock steady as she worked out the logistics of her plan. "How did you get involved in the case?"

"Luka Petrovich, the San Francisco detective I was working with on the Honeywell case, asked me to look into the online-dating angle of his two open homicides." Alex paused and held her gaze. "Imagine my surprise."

"Small world," she said, mocking him.

He jumped to his feet. The chair clattered against the window behind him.

"So that's all you have to say for yourself? Who the fuck are you?"

He shook his head as he rounded the table and stalked toward her. She shrank from the fury she saw burning in his eyes.

"You know me," she said finding her voice at last. "I'm your wife, the same woman you sleep beside every night."

Alex shook his head as he stopped in front of her, flexing his hands as if he was trying desperately to control the urge to hit her. He placed one hand on either side of her, deliberately trapping her against the island as he leaned in. She could smell the whiskey on his hot breath. The loathing in his eyes was hauntingly familiar. She'd seen the look before, in her stepfather's eyes.

"You're not the woman I married. You may look like her. But the woman I know would never have done the things that you've done. I don't know you, Jill. I wonder if I ever did."

"Don't be so naïve, Alex." Her voice gained strength as she stood straight, refusing to shrink from him, her own anger building. "You can't imagine anyone taking matters into their own hands?"

"Take matters into your own hands? As in self-defense?" He choked out a dry laugh. "I may seem stupid. God knows, you've had me fooled for a long time. What you did to those men sure looks like cold-blooded murder from where I'm standing. What gave you the right?"

Jill's eyes narrowed and her hand snaked up, ready to slap him hard. He reacted quickly and caught her arm before she was able to strike, holding her wrist aloft as his eyes bore into hers. Her lips curled into a sneer.

"What do you know about it? What do you know about any of it?"

"I know you had an affair with Jamie King. I know you went to Lake Tahoe the day that he died. I know there were two men found dead in San Francisco. They had the bad luck to meet a woman called Lilith. Sound familiar? Those men had families. And I know you're framing Dana Evans for your crimes."

"Don't worry about Dana Evans. She'll be fine as long as no one finds the gun, and let me tell you something about Jamie King. He was going to squeeze me out of my position and make my work life a living hell. What right did he have to jeopardize my career? What happened to Jamie was an accident, but I can't honestly say that I was sorry to see him die.

"And Kenneth Cox, well, he was a piece of work. He and his buddy Joel recorded their exploits with married women and posted them to a website." Her face distorted with the hatred that poured out of her, and her blood was on fire as she yelled at Alex. It felt good to finally let go of the secrets she had so carefully guarded. She squared her shoulders, took a deep breath, and felt a weight being lifted from her. Whoever said that the truth could set you free might have been onto something.

"And just how did you end up in Cox's hotel room, Jill?" Alex's voice was dangerously quiet. He dropped her wrist but didn't budge an inch, standing so close to her that she could feel the heat from his body.

"He threatened me. I couldn't let him get away with what he was doing. I had to act."

He cocked his head and fixed her with a contemptuous stare.

"Sorry, I'm not quite following. You picked him up on an online dating site and somehow you're the victim?"

"He was an arrogant prick who got what he deserved. Someone had to teach the poor fuck a lesson." Her breath came in ragged gasps. She didn't want to tell him about the rape captured on video and posted for the whole world to see. That was her own private humiliation.

"What lesson was that exactly?"

Jill lifted her chin, the angle defiant.

"He can't do the things he was doing and just get away with them." She was breathing heavy as she stared at Alex. "How many other women had he exploited? Would you have preferred I let him get away with it?"

Alex looked away, as if he couldn't stand to hear the words.

"Stupid," he muttered under his breath.

The word exploded in her head, and she narrowed her eyes.

"Who are you to judge me? Do you know what it's like to have someone treat you like a commodity? He got what he deserved."

"Let's say that Kenneth Cox was a lowlife, preying on women. Let's say I buy your line of bullshit about saving other women from him. What about the other guy? What did he do to you? Poor bastard thought he was going to get a romp in the hay and had no idea what he was in for."

His sarcasm ripped through her hard shell, and she tried not to wince at the jagged shards of ice in his voice as they found their mark.

Jill struggled to contain her emotions, and she took a couple of deep breaths to calm herself. Her voice was suffused with chilly control when, at last, she answered.

"He was part of Cox's sick game, too. He liked to tie his women up and hurt them. That's the sort of thing he did for kicks. What was I supposed to do? Let him?"

His eyes rounded in astonishment, and he shook his head slowly from side to side.

"Jesus, Jill. Do you even hear yourself? They're at fault for fucking around on their wives? And what about you? You're some kind of hero? A vigilante? Bullshit. You're a married woman luring victims into your deadly web, pretending to be someone else. When did you fall in love with the game, Jill? Did it make you feel powerful? What exactly did you feel as you looked into their eyes and pulled the trigger? Did you feel anything? Mirror, mirror on the wall, who's the deadliest bitch of all?"

She clenched her jaw shut and snapped her head away from him. "Come on, answer me," he goaded. "What exactly did you get out of this? Was it worth it?"

"Fuck you."

"Yeah, you did a pretty good job of that, too, didn't you?" His smile was bitter.

"Oh, poor Alex," she scoffed. "Did you just wake up to find that life wasn't as simple as you planned? Not everyone is good or evil. We all have many sides, even you. You can't tell me that, in that moment when you held your gun to Honeywell's head, with no one else in sight, you didn't want to pull the trigger and put an end to his miserable life. Come on, Detective Shannon, admit it. You're just as human as I am. Don't pretend you've got it all figured out. If it was that simple, you'd just slap the cuffs on me now and bring me in, no questions asked."

Alex clenched his jaw. His expression suddenly shifted, as if a switch had gone off inside him. With one hand, he cleared the end of the island, sending the apples and mail flying, the ceramic bowl crashing to the floor behind her. With the other, he grabbed Jill's shoulder and expertly spun her around, slamming her into the countertop as if she weighed no more than a rag doll. He pinned her with one hand, her face pressed flat against the cold granite, as he kicked her feet apart.

"You know, maybe you're right," he said, his voice drained of all emotion. "Maybe it is that simple, and to think I've been making it more complicated."

"Alex," she said, her voice strangled as she realized she had just pushed him too far. Her anger, her pride had sent her over the edge, and now she had lost control of the situation. She had to stop him. She had to get through to him before it was too late.

"You have the right to remain silent."

"Alex, let go."

"You have the right to consult an attorney. If you can't afford an attorney, one will be appointed to you by the court." She barely recognized his voice. It was as if he was a complete stranger.

He kept her pinned against the countertop. Jill struggled, but from this angle, she had no leverage. She felt anger in his every movement, anger in the heat wafting off of his body, just inches from hers.

"Alex, you're hurting me."

Jill pleaded with him as he twisted an arm behind her back, holding her prone. She imagined him reaching for his handcuffs. If he cuffed her, there was no way she could reach the gun. The gun was her only leverage. Second by second, Jill felt the situation slipping out of control, her options narrowing.

"Do you understand your rights?" he asked.

"Alex, there's something you don't know." Panic flooded her voice.

The pressure he was exerting on her arm abated ever so slightly. Alex's laugh was chillingly dry.

"I'm sure there's a lot I don't know, Jill, even more that I don't understand and maybe never will. I guess I'm going to have to find a way to live with that."

"I was raped." She blurted out the words in a desperate cry. As much as the admission pained her, she had to find some way to get through to him.

Alex exhaled violently, as if he had just been sucker-punched in the gut. He released his hold on her and took a step back. She straightened and turned to face him, reaching for him with a trembling hand.

His expression was as cold and hard as stone, but she could see confusion surface in his eyes. When he made no move to touch her, Jill pulled her hand back and rubbed her shoulder as she continued to hold his gaze.

"What did you say?" he asked, eyeing her with wary skepticism.

"I was drugged and raped by a man named Peter Young."

He rubbed his hands across his face.

"Jesus, Jill. What did you do? Did you execute him, too?"

Jill winced. Execute? It was a brutal characterization. If Alex saw it that way, so would a judge and jury. She shuddered at the implications and gathered her thoughts. Instinctively she reached for his hand, wanting him to understand. And this time he didn't pull away.

"He lied to me. He said he wanted to interview me for his magazine. But after he got me back to the hotel, he drugged me. After I realized what had happened ..." Jill trailed off, looking out the window. Thinking about what he'd done, and her hate. "You know better than anyone what would have happened if I'd reported it to the police. Date rape is hard to prove. Maybe he would have been convicted. Maybe not. Either way, my private life would be on public display. Either way, it would never be right. I couldn't let him get away with it, Alex. I couldn't."

Alex recoiled. Spinning away, he fixed his horrified gaze out the window and stared off into the stormy night. The thunder rumbled outside, and he spread his hands wide on the countertop, his head hanging low between his shoulder blades. Jill continued in a shaky voice.

"Peter Young recorded the encounter and shared it with his sick buddy Kenneth Cox. They traded sex videos like playing cards."

"He blackmailed you?"

"Cox threatened to expose me if I said a word. What was I supposed to do? Let him ruin my career, our marriage?"

Alex didn't respond as she edged silently around the island to the drawer. Settling herself, she planted her feet in a wide stance.

"I couldn't let anyone take away what I have, what I've earned. Not Jamie. Not Peter Young or Kenneth Cox. And not you."

Silently, Jill eased the drawer open and her hand closed on the gun. Their cards had all been played. Alex couldn't live with what she'd done. She couldn't go to jail. There were no choices left.

Wrenching the pistol from its hiding place, she aimed it at his head, leaving no time for second thoughts or regrets. At that same moment Alex raised his head, and she caught his reflection in the window, long enough to register the look of shock and fear on his face before her fingers tightened around the pistol grip.

CHAPTER FIFTY FOUR

Jill gritted her teeth, trying hard to stop the barrel of the gun from shaking. Tears formed in her eyes. She blinked them away. What was wrong with her? She knew what she had to do. The moment she saw Alex at the bar, she knew that there was only one way out of the trap. Alex had to die. She knew she was right. She knew it was the only solution, so why couldn't she pull the fucking trigger?

The gun clattered softly against the countertop. Hands still shaking, she stepped back.

"What now?" Jill asked. All the fight drained out of her, and she stared at the gun placed between them on the granite surface. Without breaking eye contact, Alex reached out. His long fingers wrapped around the pistol's grip, and he tucked it safely into his belt.

"Now we talk about options."

Fear fluttered inside Jill's chest as she stared at his resolute expression. Options. She could think of few options Alex would find palatable.

Would he let her run?

The hum of the refrigerator and the ticking of the mantel clock were the only sounds to punctuate the silence between them. It was too quiet in here, and for the first time, she realized that Molly was nowhere in sight. Molly, who hadn't left his side for a week, wasn't there to protect her master. So where the hell was she?

Alex let out a long breath and raked his hands through his hair.

"I know a few lawyers, Jill. Good ones."

Her gut clenched as she considered that particular option. What good would a lawyer do? She was guilty. A good lawyer might mean the difference between a death sentence and life in prison. Either way, her life was over.

"You can't really expect me to turn myself in." Her voice was barely more than a whisper.

"Someone else is bound to put the pieces together, Jill. Secrets like this don't remain hidden forever."

She rounded the island quickly, closing the distance between them. She reached out toward Alex. He took an instinctive step away, hands held up, as if warding her off.

The expression on his face spoke volumes. Despite everything they had shared over the past five years, she was a stranger to him now. A monster.

Jill's hands dropped, hanging useless at her sides. She could see the next steps unfold before her as clearly as if she were turning the pages of a book. There would be a trial. Prison.

Alex turned away from her and pulled a cell phone from his pocket. The illuminated screen cast a greenish glow on his fingers as he dialed, and Jill's head started to spin. The police? A lawyer? She didn't know.

The sound of her thudding pulse filled her ears, and she closed her eyes, trying desperately to find some other angle, some way out of the trap.

All at once she felt cold, hard, metal press against her throat. Her breath caught, lips parted in a choked gasp. Before she could react, an arm clamped around her waist like an iron bar, and she was pinned against a strong, compact body.

Alex turned. Astonishment and fear registered in his eyes. He dropped the cell phone on the table. The color drained from his face, and he looked like he had seen a ghost. He didn't have to tell her who it was. She knew by the stricken look on his face. The tip of the gun burrowed into the soft flesh of her neck.

"Well, well, now, Alex. I didn't know your girl liked to color outside the lines." Warm breath ticked her ear. The hairs on the back of her neck prickled.

His voice was soft, intelligent—not at all what she had expected.

The cool barrel of the gun drifted along her throat, soft as a caress, and she shuddered as her eyes locked on Alex's face. She could see no fear there now. His expression was cold and stony as he stared at Jerry Honeywell.

"You sound like my kind of girl, Jill. What do you say we have a little fun? I told Alex here I'd let him watch."

An eerie calm settled over Jill. She knew this game. Honeywell wanted her scared. He wanted her to beg. He was the same kind of sick bastard her stepfather had been, and she steeled herself for whatever would come next. Experience taught her to survive. She wouldn't break. She wouldn't give him what he wanted. She would fight.

"Not as long as I'm breathing, you sick fuck."

Jerry Honeywell's soft chuckle filled her ears, and she could hear the muted tsk-tsk cluck of his tongue as his arm dug painfully into her midriff.

"Well, that's not usually my kind of thing, but I've been known to make exceptions before." His tongue flicked out and licked her ear. Jill flinched. The gun pressed harder into her neck. Hate surged through her. Hate made her strong.

"It's not her you want," Alex said, interrupting Honeywell's foreplay, studying his adversary through narrowed eyes.

"Well, ain't that sweet?" Honeywell drawled. "Detective Alex Shannon to the rescue. But let's be honest, Alex. Your girl here has done some very bad things. I might actually be doing you a favor by getting rid of her."

Honeywell's weight shifted behind Jill as he repositioned the gun. The tip now pressed squarely into the soft flesh underneath her jaw. Her breath caught. She pushed the sparks of fear back and focused on her hate. She scanned the countertop looking for something she could use as a weapon, something she could use to distract Honeywell.

Where the hell was Molly?

"How did you get in here?" Jill asked through gritted teeth. "The house is being watched."

Jill thought about the squad car Captain Lewis had posted outside their house after Jackson's attack. She'd cut through the backyard to avoid being seen.

"Oh, you mean the police officers your husband was kind enough to dismiss when he got home? Made my job a hell of a lot easier, I have to say. Duke was planning to take care of them. But turns out, Alex saved us the trouble. I suppose he didn't want any witnesses for your little showdown. Am I right, Alex?"

"Where's Duke now?" Alex asked.

"I'm right here."

Duke materialized from the shadow of the darkened doorway. The silver hoops in his ears glinted in the dim light. His flat blue eyes met hers and Jill pulled in a sharp breath.

"Duke here took care of your dog. She was kicking up quite a fuss. Wouldn't do to disturb the neighbors."

Alex flinched, and Jill saw a flicker of pain spasm across his face. In an instant, it was gone.

"How's your partner?" Duke asked. His lips spread wide in a junkyard-dog grin. "He wasn't looking so good last time I saw him."

Alex's jaw clenched tight as his gaze shifted toward Duke. The same hate she felt was reflected in Alex's cold stare. Jill lunged, pushing off Honeywell, hoping to catch him off guard. But he was too strong. He held her pinned tight against him. The gun dug painfully into her flesh.

"Jill." Alex shook his head. A warning.

"Try it again, bitch. I'm fucking begging you," Honeywell breathed into her ear.

Jill heard a rumble coming from the table. Alex's cell phone shimmied across the surface. The ringer was off, and it was set to vibrate.

Did she hear sirens? Impossible. Wishful thinking on her part. But then she caught Honeywell's reflection in the window. His attention shifted to the cell phone. His grip loosened a fraction, and Jill knew this was her only chance. She slammed the heel of her foot down hard on Honeywell's instep.

Honeywell gasped and she pushed off hard, sinking an elbow solidly into his gut. Leaping forward, she broke free of his grasp and stumbled toward Alex. In one fluid motion, Alex grabbed her shirt and shoved her back behind him. She fell, hurtling toward the backdoor. He reached for the gun he had tucked behind his back. Her gun.

The crack of gunfire rang in Jill's ears as Alex crumpled to the floor, inches from where she lay on her side. She smelled the acrid stench of cordite and blood. Looking up, Jill saw a red stain bloom on the front of Honeywell's shirt as he fell.

Honeywell's gun clanged to the floor, and without hesitation Jill grabbed it and leveled it at Duke. She pulled the trigger and emptied the clip into Duke's broad chest. Duke's head hit the floor with a sickening crack. The swelling pool of blood assured Jill he was dead.

She heard the sirens draw closer. Jill scrambled toward Alex, palms firmly planted over the wound in his chest. She tried desperately to stem the flow of blood. She moved one hand to Alex's throat. She felt a pulse, weak, but there. Blood seeped from beneath his body, soaking her bent knees as she crouched over him.

"Stay with me, Alex. Help is almost here," she whispered in the darkened room. "Stay with me."

CHAPTER FIFTY FIVE

S unlight warmed Jill's back as she stretched a long strip of packing tape across the flaps of the cardboard box, sealing it closed. Gently placing the tape gun at her feet, she picked the box up and set it on top of the shortest stack lining the garage wall.

Molly groaned softly. She lay, half propped against line of boxes, head resting on the asphalt. The fur around the wound in her shoulder had mostly grown back. Jill could still see the four-inch crescent shaped scar where Duke's bullet had wounded the dog. Molly didn't run anymore, but she got around reasonably well.

Cool wind ruffled Jill's hair, bringing with it the floral scent of the fruit trees now in bloom. She would miss this, these rare Seattle days in early spring when the rains had passed and the air carried the freshness of the season.

The crunch of footsteps on gravel perked Molly's ears. Jill turned. Jackson lumbered down the driveway toward her. The smile that settled across his wide lips was subdued. His gait was slow, each step proof enough that there were still some lingering effects from the shooting.

"You're looking a little the worse for wear," she said, raising a hand to shield her eyes from the sun.

Jill smiled. She would miss the deep, velvety warmth of his voice. Jackson reached for her, enveloping her in the gentlest of bear hugs. She closed her eyes. Good-byes weren't her strong suit, and she'd said too many of them already. The lump in her throat dissipated, and she stepped out of the protective circle of his arms.

"You look like you're making good progress." Jackson nodded toward the boxes littering a third of the open space. Molly struggled to her feet and ambled toward Jackson. Her tail wagged low around her hindquarters. Jackson bent to scratch her behind the ears. Molly's tail swung in lazy arcs.

"Getting close."

"Sure I can't help you with this?"

She appreciated Jackson's loyalty. In the months since Alex's funeral, he had dropped in to check on her regularly, while everyone else had silently dropped away. Molly plunked down on the concrete beside Jackson, her bulk wedged against his leg.

"I don't think your doctor would approve."

"What he doesn't know won't fucking hurt him."

"Superman. Right. I forgot." Jill wagged her head. Having survived a vicious attack, here he was older and wiser, but still larger than life.

As the laughter settled between them, Jill's eyes strayed to the interior of the garage, beyond the neatly stacked boxes, beyond the piles of items she had set aside for Goodwill, to a series of canvases she had propped in a clearing, for safekeeping.

She must have packed away dozens of Alex's sketch pads, full of drawings and caricatures—some of faces she knew, others that she didn't. Over the past few years, there hadn't been much time for more serious projects. It wasn't talent he lacked, but maybe time, or inspiration. There were at least a dozen canvases showing his skill with oil paints. He'd finished this one just before football season started.

"I found something Alex would have wanted you to have."

The corners of Jackson's mouth tightened, and she could see him pull in a deep, steadying breath. Jill pivoted and headed inside the garage. Bending down, she flipped through the canvases until she found what she wanted.

"He was planning to give this one to you for your birthday. He titled it *The big 4-0.*"

She turned the canvas toward Jackson as she approached. His lips parted, large hands reaching for it as she handed it to him. Surprise, admiration, and pain all flashed across his face in quick succession before his eyes met Jill's.

Alex had completed the portrait from memory. A smiling Jackson filled the canvas and was looking down, away from the artist. Somehow Alex had captured the essence of his friend in a way that showed the world what he saw when he looked at Jackson. The canvas reflected back a face that combined intelligence and wit.

"I knew he was good, but I didn't know he could do this." Jackson voice was thick with emotion as he shifted his gaze from Jill back to the painting.

"In the five years we were married, this was the only painting he completed. You were very important to him."

Jackson moved his lips wordlessly before angling the painting in toward his chest, as if he was unable to look at it any longer. Jill stepped forward, wrapping her arms loosely around his waist.

"You've meant a lot to both of us."

They stood silently, leaning against each other for a long moment before Jackson cleared his throat. Jill stepped away.

"Are you sure you want to do this?" He gestured toward the boxes again. "You're sure you're ready to leave?"

Her smile was tight and she angled her eyes toward the garage floor. A thick lock of dark hair fell across her forehead, and she tucked it back behind her ear. Did she want to leave? Oh yes. It was only through a sheer force of will that she had stayed this long. Besides, she would begin to show soon. The home pregnancy test confirmed what she began to suspect not long after the funeral. This was news she had no intention of sharing.

Over the past few months, Jill had methodically searched the house for Alex's notes on the Lilith investigation. If there were notes to be found, they certainly were not within these walls, nor were they in his office. If they had been, someone would have found them by now. So whatever evidence Alex had amassed was safely buried. With any luck, it would never see the light of day.

"It's time to move on," Jill said. "I couldn't stay here, even if I wanted to. Not after everything."

Jackson's nod was one of mute understanding. Everyone had expected her to move out of the house after the funeral. Instead, she stayed, insisting she was fine. Fine was an overstatement, of course. She hated the kitchen. She couldn't go in there after dark. Too many ghosts.

"You've got support here—me, Alex's family."

"I'll be fine. I'm the independent sort."

Her hand grazed the slight pooch of her belly, and she thought about the life that grew there, inside her. She wouldn't be alone. Not really. There was one part of Alex that she would carry with her.

"So what's the temperature like in Phoenix this time of year?"

"Somewhere in the nineties, I think."

"Shit." Jackson blew out a long whistle between clenched teeth. "No thanks."

"I'll take the heat any day. It's going to take decades before I miss the rain."

"You're not going to become a Cardinals fan, are you?"

Jill's smile was wry. Jackson was every bit the Seahawks fan that Alex was.

"Not a chance," she assured him.

Silence stretched out between them. There was nothing left to be said. Jill felt her throat constrict. She was never one for long send-offs, and Jackson's eyes were soft on her face.

"I need you to take Molly. The move would be hard on her."

"Just two old dogs in recovery, eh, girl?"

Molly wagged her tail.

"I'm not going to say good-bye," he said at last.

"Good. I hear they're overrated." Her smile was a painful twist.

Tucking the canvas under his arm, he bent and buzzed her cheek with his lips. She squeezed his arm, then let go.

"Take care of yourself," she said. "No more putting your superpowers to the test by taking on bullets."

"Yes, ma'am." He flipped her a mock salute. "Let me know when you get settled."

Jill's nod was noncommittal. She cinched the leash to Molly's collar and handed it to Jackson. Arms folded across her chest, she watched him lumber down the driveway, Molly sticking close to his side. Jackson paused, taking a long look at the canvas before placing it carefully into the trunk. Molly jumped into the backseat. Her head dipped behind the headrest. With a final wave, he climbed into his car and pulled smoothly away from the curb.

Jill drew in a deep breath and felt the tight band compressing her chest ease. There wasn't much left to be done now. A few more boxes to pack. The remaining items would be sold off at auction. She wanted few reminders of the life she was leaving behind.

Her thoughts turned away from the past, moving beyond Alex to a new life, a new beginning. Closing the garage door behind her, Jill stepped out of the shadows and into the sunlight.

ACKNOWLEDGMENTS

Although I've never been one for long-winded acknowledge-ments, I did want to thank the many people who shared their time and expertise with me as I wrote *Deadly Lies.*

First, to the experts I consulted during the course of writing the manuscript. Captain Neil Low of the Seattle Police Department and Constable Leigh Drinkwater from the RCMP consulted on what must have seemed a countless number of procedural aspects of the story. Former FBI agent Faye Greenlee shared her unique perspective on psychopaths and helped me understand the complex motivations that drive Jill. Michael Lee, security expert, advised on a number of computer security scenarios. Despite all the experts who shared their knowledge, I knowingly bent and in some cases broke a few of the rules around law enforcement and computer security in the writing of the book; such are the benefits of writing fiction. If you find gaps and errors in the story, please remember that my fictitious mind can be far more forgiving of some of the finer details of reality; and the weather is always sunny and the people friendly, too!

Second, thanks to the readers who provided feedback on numerous drafts and helped improve the story along the way. Gordon Patchell, Stella Du, Kevin Rice, Pam Oyanagi, and Ginna Bladassarre; without you, I probably wouldn't have finished the book. In the middle of the fourth draft, I had the pleasure of meeting an exceptional author, Erica Bauermeister, who offered excellent insights on the story, and on writing in general. To Patty, Megan, and Angie, who threatened an intervention if I didn't publish the damned book. And to Mally, who was gracious enough to take time out of her busy schedule to show me the sights of San Francisco; I likely wouldn't have been able to find my way out of the airport, not to mention making it to Shakespeare's Garden, without you.

Finally, thanks to Geoff Robison, who designed the cover; Don Skirvin and Carl Walesa, who edited the final draft; and Lloyd Bondy, who provided his photographic expertise.

Made in the USA
San Bernardino, CA
11 April 2014